THE SEA OF CLOUDS

Sheila Jenné

ALNITAK PRESS

PROLOGUE

LUCY

I arrived at Phobos, after a months-long journey from Liberty Station, carrying nothing but a small duffle full of second-hand kit. It hadn't been an enjoyable trip. More like the subtle version of being transported home in irons. The ship, unlike most, was equipped with a long-distance radio antenna, through which the details of my late adventures had flashed their way to Phobos ahead of me. By the time I arrived, the Admiralty knew as much about the loss of Liberty Station as anyone in the Navy.

Anyone, that is, but me. Fitting my testimony into the exact shape of what they knew had taken up most of my time on the voyage. I would have to explain to the Admiralty how I had managed to lose the Empire's most valuable economic and strategic resource, without letting slip any of the truth, which was that I'd done it on purpose.

The easy thing, after turning coat and betraying Mars to the rebels, would have been to stay on the station, let them write me down as a deserter. Next easiest would be to pretend it had never happened and try to be a loyal officer from there on out.

But I had chosen neither of those courses. I was here to spy on the Martian Imperial Navy, to do it so brazenly no one guessed, and to do it effectively enough that it gave the rebels some kind of advantage.

The first thing any spy needs is a private communications channel, so I followed the sign that read *Radio Office*, trailing my duffel behind me. The faint gravity brushed at my inner ear, no good for pinning anybody's feet to the floor, but enough to tell me which way was down.

I handed myself along the wall, dodging clumsy landsmen who didn't know how to handle the microgravity. Last time I'd been here, I'd been one of those lubbers, barely able to handle my own duffle. It was quiet here today; no riots or graffiti. I wondered if that meant the unrest on Mars had simmered down too.

The radio office was staffed with a number of clerks, none of whom appeared to be the man I was looking for. I parked myself in the food court across the concourse and waited. If they were on three shifts, sooner or later I'd get a look at all of them.

The crowds passing through Phobos looked the same as ever: enlisted spacers in white, officers in dark blue, civilians in every color. The military sailors were more numerous, but there was plenty of civilian shipping still passing through, even despite the embargo from Earth.

Somewhere down the concourse a chime rang. Eight bells. The clerks across the way went inside their office and new clerks came out. Including one who matched the description I'd been given: short, slim, dark, three rings in the right ear, tattoo running from his jaw down to his neck.

I waited a few minutes before slowly rising and dragging my duffel onto my shoulder. Looked up the concourse, looked down, checked my pocket watch. Didn't want to look too purposeful.

The man with the three earrings hovered behind the counter

in a close approximation of standing. "Good evening, sir, may I help you?"

That marked him as a Navy man, at least by background, though he wasn't in uniform. A civilian would have said *ma'am*. I put one elbow on the counter, as if to lean, though I had no weight to lean with. "I need to send a message," I said. "I need you to tell the Tall Jockey that Lafayette arrived."

1

MOIRA

The pirate king of Liberty Station was in a mood. You could tell by the way the Martian deserters forgot themselves and knuckled their foreheads and called him sir, imagining they could soothe his temper with careful discipline, like they had for their old Navy captains. You could tell by the way some of the Earther pirates stomped around as if they were under one g, looking like prancing ponies when they shot up much higher than they meant to in the Mars-normal gravity.

But mainly you could tell by the shouting. I could hear it from clear out on the concourse. "If you *can't be arsed* to *clean the bloody water tubes* like I *fucking told you*, then I don't know why we're *wasting station air* on a *fucking mudeater!*"

The door of the office slammed open and Coelho came out. The commandant, they would have called him on a Martian station. Coelho didn't have an official title, but we called him the pirate king and meant it. He had the flashy style of one, and the temper to boot. His dark curls glistened with hair oil, and his red velvet coat went down to his knees.

Behind him stumbled one of the Earth pirates, dragged by one arm. She was a younger spacer, eyes wide with fear, gabbling, "I'll do it, I swear, I just got behind—"

He crossed the concourse to the nearest airlock, cranked it open, and flung her in. She cowered on the far side, too afraid of him to make a break for it.

I pushed away from the wall. Not interfering, yet, but ready to.

Coelho cranked the lock shut and stood, arms folded, fuming, for a long minute. At last he cranked it back open and let the girl out. "Just don't let it happen again," he said at last, while she hiccuped and rubbed at her streaming eyes. She bolted for the water reclamation system, and he stalked back to his office.

Only when the door was shut did I lean back against the wall. "I thought I was done seeing airlockings when I left the Navy," I muttered to Marron, who sat in his wheelchair next to me.

He let out a short bark of laughter. "I can tell you didn't serve long with Coelho," he said. "They're his favorite. And he doesn't always let them out."

I frowned. "He'd better not try it on any of *my* men."

"He'd have a mutiny on his hands," Marron agreed. "Speaking of…"

I looked over at him. His graying head, as he sat in his chair, came only to my elbow. It was strange to have him there—in space, he was always at eye level if he wanted to be. The gravity here on Liberty was too much for his space-wasted legs, and he needed the chair if he didn't want to risk breaking the brittle bones. "I don't follow."

"Some of the men don't care for Coelho. Our old crew especially. And if you wanted the job for yourself…I'm just saying, you wouldn't get much opposition."

My chin jerked up. "I came here to get away from the Navy, and because once I'd done that, I needed somewhere to be. I didn't have any illusions about what it was going to be like. I know pirates aren't idealists."

"Some of us are," he said. "Lucy really got me steamed up, talking about Mars. She got this station for you. Because she wanted to build something that was better than where both of you came from. At this point I'd be heading back to Mars myself, to overthrow the whole classist mess, if my legs worked." He gave them a sharp slap.

I folded my arms across my chest. "If you came from Mars, you wouldn't talk like that. Don't you think if the Emprex could be knocked off their throne, just like that, we would have done it by now? After a while, you stop daydreaming of making it better and settle for at least getting away from it. Which I did."

He craned his neck to look up at me. Embarrassed, I slid down the wall into a crouch. Not fair to tower over him like that. He jabbed a finger down at his armrest. "Why'd you let Lucy go off like that then? I thought she was going to be fixing Mars from there, and you'd work on fixing it from here!"

I looked away. "She needed a reason to go."

"What's that supposed to mean? You lied to her?"

"I told her she could keep an eye on it for us. That's all. I just—I couldn't stand the idea that she could go home and would choose not to."

"She would have stayed for you!"

"But she didn't want to," I argued. "It was obvious. Or would have been, if she'd thought about it for two seconds. She sacrificed so much for her family. If she'd stayed with me, if the word had gotten out she'd deserted, her family would have lost everything. She might have said it was fine at the time, but I knew she'd resent me forever. The only person she loves more than me is her brother."

"I think she loves you more," said Marron quietly.

I gave my head a tight, sour shake. "Evidence says no. Because I gave her the choice and she chose to leave."

He glared at me, his black eyes shining out from a sea of deep brown wrinkles. "Chose? Bullshit. You sent her away and she left because she thought she could help you that way, and you're not doing shit with her sacrifice."

I snapped back to my feet. "If I could free Mars for her, I would, okay? But I can't. We can't even make this fucking station run right."

It was true. The dream had been to recruit pirate ships to run the mining routes and sell the gasses back to Mars. But we had gotten few ships to sign on. There was more profit in piracy.

Interrupting my thoughts, Coelho's door swung open again and his curly head popped out. "Moira, in."

I pushed off the wall and sauntered over, not too quickly. I'd dealt with more vicious commanders than him. But I could feel Marron's eyes on my back as I walked away.

Coelho threw himself back into the large chair behind the desk and put his boots up on the table. "Lost another ship today. Martian ship *Utopian Sunrise*, on its way here loaded with everything we wanted. Close enough to hear the distress call, too far to help."

I nodded. I'd assumed his temper tantrum had stemmed from something of the kind. "Been a while since one has made it through." I sat down in the chair across from him, without having been invited to. My little way of not deferring to him like everyone else did.

He didn't seem to notice. "We're self-sufficient enough to manage for a while, but we're losing money every day we're out here. This isn't what I expected."

I shrugged. "Well, it's not like Earth was paying you much either."

"Better than this!" He pulled one foot off the desk and leaned forward over the other. "I've got half a mind to ditch the whole thing. Go back to piracy. Knauss would forgive me if I gave her the station."

My heart raced. I looked languidly away—an automatic reaction to tension, becoming even more casual. If Lucy couldn't get me to betray my feelings, Coelho certainly couldn't. "You could probably do that," I said.

"What would you do, if I did?"

"Dunno. Knock around the system. See what work my crew and I could find."

He frowned. Probably disappointed at not getting a bigger reaction. He tried a more blatant approach. "Are you loyal to me, Moira?"

I blinked at him. "You gave me my ship. Of course I couldn't forget that."

"There's talk, around the station. Maybe you've heard it."

"Some things. All bullshit. I've seen your job; I don't want it."

"Well, then. So long as I can trust you. I have a job for you." He took his other leg off the table and sat up straight. "We've got to drive those pirates off the route between here and Mars. I know how they're thinking. It's cost-benefit. Without the Martian Navy hanging around, it's easy pickings to get the merchant ships passing back and forth. I need you to take the *Mariposa* and take the upstream route. Take or destroy as many pirate ships as you can. Make it too risky to be a good bargain."

The undercurrent of his words was easy to detect: *I don't trust you, I need you away from the station, and your crew too.*

But what could I do? It was do as he said or mutiny like Marron wanted. And I had had my fill of that already. Coelho wasn't my choice of leader, but he was keeping Liberty going and that was all I really wanted. If we could get it functional, it would help Mars as much as the pirates—erasing the harm we'd done to Mars's war effort against Earth, and keeping the terraforming project supplied.

But I couldn't set my goals any higher than that. Lucy was different. Lucy had *ideals*, always had. Disillusion her about the Empire, and it only made her want to take it down and replace it with something better. She would never believe that a certain amount of horribleness was always going to be there. Any more than she'd believe that here, on her precious Liberty Station, people were still getting thrown into airlocks for screwing up.

"I'll give it a shot," I said, rising to my feet and throwing him a mock salute.

On the way to the *Mariposa*'s launch, I was ambushed by Marron, Nguyen, and Yao, three of my closest crew. "Are you going to do it?" demanded Nguyen, the slight young man with the goatee.

"I told Marron I wouldn't, and he's obviously talked to you," I answered shortly. "What do you think would have changed?"

"He called you into his office for something," said Yao. She was too young to be a sailor, not that that ever stopped Mars from recruiting children. "Might have been looking to pick a fight."

"He suspects me because somebody's talking treason around the station. Hope it wasn't any of you." I led the way into the airlock, where the empty gray tube of our launch was docked.

Yao cranked the door shut, and Nguyen manned the outer lock. Marron kept his eyes on me. "What did he say?"

"He's getting rid of us," I said. "Sending us to trawl the trade route."

Yao's eyes lit up. "Action."

"Hopefully."

"You don't have to do it," argued Marron. "What's he going to do if you refuse?"

"There will be fighting," I said. "I don't feel like watching anyone else get thrown out an airlock. *Especially* not any of you."

"I didn't get this old without learning how to take a calculated risk," he said. "The odds—"

"Are in our favor either way. He's not planning to abandon the station. Sure, he doesn't run it how I would. But he's doing what he can, with the ships he has. If we can clear the route, he can make money. As long as he's making money, he'll keep Liberty as it is."

I manned the helm. Behind me, everyone was in their places. "Cast off," I ordered, and Yao shut off the magnet that kept the launch in place. The centrifugal force of the station flung the launch away at the speed of an express train, and for a moment we had all we could do to adjust the launch's trajectory back toward the *Mariposa*. Marron included. As soon as we had cast off, he rose out of his chair and manned a rear thruster with his powerful arms.

Once the launch was aimed to match speeds with the ship, Marron made his way back up to the bows. "I can't help but think, our trip will bring us close to Lucy."

That detail had not been lost on me. We hadn't even sailed yet and already my knees felt weak. Of course there wasn't the slightest chance we'd cross paths; even if by some miracle Lucy was stationed to a ship heading toward Liberty, I wouldn't be able to say a word for fear of breaking her cover.

But somehow the thought of even crossing orbits put butterflies in my stomach.

"I know it," I said, and started the deceleration.

2

LUCY

I tucked Moira's note into the bosom of my gown. It was that sort of gown, the kind that pushes up the breasts until you can barely see over them, and can stuff any number of small objects down. Not my usual knee-breeches and frock coats, but I had the feeling this was the sort of event where even half the men would be wearing gowns. Trousers don't have enough room for the amount of lace and jewels you want to wear to an Imperial ball.

The hired carriage pulled up outside the palace and the footman opened the door. Taking a deep breath, I alighted on the plush carpet runner and pulled my shoulders back. My bosom canted forward even more alarmingly, but no matter. I knew I looked perfect, or as perfect as my budget had allowed. The cornflower blue gown had been made over several times, but the lace on it was new, and my mother had helped me alter it so it fit the more relaxed silhouette of the current fashion. But over a corset, still—nature hadn't given me the waifish figure that the style had been made for. Hair was still ostentatiously formal these days, so my indifferently-colored locks defied gravity in a powdered assortment of braids and pin-curls.

I entered the immense, baroque ballroom to the sound of my name: Miss Lucy Prescott-Chin of Hellas, Midshipman, Imperial Martian Navy. I approached the Emprex, where they sat in an ornate armchair, surrounded by their family, and made a deep reverence.

"Your Imperial Majesty," I breathed, inclining my head as low as I could without throwing off my hair's center of gravity. "It is an honor to be present here tonight."

The Emprex beamed. How can I describe them? In a room full of ornate hair and ostentatious gowns, theirs outshone them all. They wore red damask, studded with gemstones, and a snowy jabot of lace at their throat. Their hair—almost none of which could possibly be real—arced almost a foot high. Nestled within the powdered locks was—I almost laughed—a model ship. Not to scale. The body of the ship was the size of a spool of thread, and shimmering sails of silver foil stood out a foot in either direction.

"Another officer to grace my party," the Emprex said, turning to the Princess Consort.

The Consort smiled at me. "You see, this ball was our little thought for how we could help the war effort. Invite the flower of Mars' youth and also as many officers as we could find at home, in the hopes that more would be inspired into commissioning."

I had gathered as much from the invitation. "I certainly hope they may, Your Highness."

Beneath its thick white makeup, the Emprex's face grew

somber. "The ancestors know we need them. The shipyards are turning out all the ships they can, and we've impressed thousands of men, but officers are harder to find. I'm surprised you're still a midshipman, with how fast they're promoting officers."

"This is my first time home since I was commissioned, Your Majesty," I answered, trying not to sound defensive. "I'm supposed to stand the lieutenant's exam next month."

"Ah." They gestured to the side, where their two children were sitting. Princess Sofia Maria, the elder, was older than I and married. She would be our next Empress, the ancestors willing not for many years yet. But the gesture was for the younger son, Prince George Konstantin, who sprang obediently to his feet.

"Kostya, you must ask her to dance," the Emprex continued. "My son has a space voyage in his future himself, you see. Perhaps he can ask you about it."

I let the prince lead me away, relieved to at least have the most intimidating part of the evening over. The Emprex was, to my mind, more of a symbol than a person: a symbol of the entire Empire, its stability, its power. To meet them in the flesh seemed almost too much. Especially when I'd broken my oath to serve Mars and Emprex. At the time I had been abandoning my allegiance to an idea. Facing the person I had betrayed felt different.

The Emprex's son was a less daunting prospect. He would not have stood out in a crowd: large dark eyes, a thin face, sleek black hair halfway down his back. But he was arrayed almost as gorgeously as his imperial parent, in a royal blue tailcoat embroidered in gold.

"So," the prince began, bowing and taking my right hand to begin the dance, "you're almost a lieutenant."

"After less than a Martian year of service," I answered, embarrassed. "I hope I'm ready."

"I'm sure you are." His dark eyes gazed down on me intently, as if there were no one in the room but us two. "You certainly seem intelligent."

I faltered a step of the dance and quickly recovered. Barefaced flattery. I hate it when men flirt with me; it shows an appalling lack of research. My romantic affiliation is a matter of public record. If you can't be bothered to look it up, you're not sincerely interested. It's such an obviously manipulative ploy.

"You dance well," he murmured huskily, pouring about a gallon of sex appeal into those three little words. God, if I could master that trick, I would have had women eating out of my hand. There was a time that had been all I wanted.

I decided to spare him further embarrassment. "It's taking all my focus to do it," I said. "I usually lead."

It took him a second to follow my hint. Then he threw back his head and laughed heartily, the bedroom eyes immediately abandoned. "My apologies, Miss Prescott," he said in a more normal voice. "I should have asked." He dropped my right hand, picked up my left, and began to dance backward. "Luckily I'm just as good at following."

That was right; his own romantic affiliation was indifferent. When his coming-out hit the social papers, my father had shaken his head. Was he sincerely interested equally in men and women, or was he only trying to widen the pool of available spouses? Not many young people were that mercenary, but then not many young people were princes. He might never have made an uncalculated move in his life.

I led the prince in a slow turn, which he executed flawlessly. "So, your highness," I began. "You have an upcoming voyage. Are you commissioning as an officer?"

"Ah, no," he said. "My parent didn't want me to take that risk. I am being sent to Venus on a diplomatic mission. But it means I'll have to go to space for the first time. I've never been further than Phobos before. Any advice?"

I tipped my head to the side, thinking it over. "Bring cologne," I said at last.

He laughed. "Cologne?"

"I'm serious. You'll be breathing the same air for months, and the men don't bathe. Bring cologne, twice as much as you think you'll want." I swirled him out into a faster spin, which made his long hair and knee-length coat flare out dramatically. Surely there were plenty on the floor who would appreciate that sight, even if I didn't.

"Good to know, Miss Prescott," he said with a wry smile when he landed back in my arms. "Ever been to Venus itself?"

"Nobody ever has," I said. "Well, hardly anybody. I suppose the Venusians have."

"Desperate times call for desperate measures," he said. "And they've approved our visit, which means they're at least willing to entertain the possibility of a treaty. We've been asking since the war started. I don't know what changed their mind."

"Possibly that we lost Ares Station to the pirates."

He blinked. "You would think that would make us a less desirable ally. We'll have less to offer them now than we would have had."

"They don't want allies," I said. "They like being a neutral party in a divided solar system. If they're thinking of taking sides, it might mean they're worried the status quo might be threatened."

His graceful steps faltered for the first time. "You think they think we're losing the war?"

I shrugged. "I think they're considering the possibility. And, if they're willing to put themselves out to prevent it, that might make a great deal of difference."

The music came to a crescendo, and I gave the prince a gentle dip. He was too much heavier than me to try anything more dramatic.

He bowed over my hand before taking my arm and leading

me across the floor. "I have to spread myself around more tonight, but I know who you should talk to. Miss Yekaterina Liu-Johnson will hang on every word of this political talk. She always does when I bring up the subject."

I allowed myself to be introduced to the lady: tall, somewhat dark of complexion, with a natural curl in the waves of hair that were allowed to hang free from her coif. I made my curtsey. "Miss Liu."

She folded her fan, revealing deep red lipstick—an excellent choice, on a face like hers. "Miss Prescott. I see the prince is moving on to greener pastures. Struck out with you, did he? He ought to research the guest list. I know I did."

My cheeks warmed as she took my hand. The next dance was a country set, where we couldn't speak much. I whirled her up and down the lines of partners, separating to step around another couple and clasping her hands again after. A terrible dance for talking, yes, but an excellent one for flirting. Every time we reunited, her eyes sparkled with another smile. I matched hers, unsure if it was because it was the right, political thing to do or because I couldn't help it. She was playing the same game as the prince, I could tell, but this time it was working on me. Whatever would Moira think?

The dance ended at last, and we sank, panting, onto a settee. "Well, you're energetic, aren't you?" she asked with a curl of her red lips. "Some of these Navy people, they come home and can barely make it down the set."

"They're neglecting their exercise, then. It really shouldn't take above a few days to adjust back to Mars gravity." A man in black and white offered me a drink on a tray, which I accepted.

Miss Liu took one also. "Ah, you're a very dedicated officer, then. Just what the Navy needs right now."

I took a careful sip from the sparkling glass. It wouldn't do to drink too much, not here, where I had come to be Moira's eyes and ears and not give too much away. "I doubt the Admiralty would agree with you there," I said. "They think of me as well-meaning but dense. I'll be allowed to take the lieutenant's exam before my next posting, but I expect it will be a long time before I have even a temporary command. I've botched too many important jobs."

"Oh, they misjudge you, then. Kostya introduced you to me as 'interesting.' Dense people are never interesting."

I deflected the compliment. "He told me you like talking politics."

"Not quite true. I like *listening* politics; I have none of my own. Here at court you can make far too many enemies if you have strong political opinions."

"It's the same in the Navy. Certainly I've had an opinion from time to time, but I don't share them with the chain of command. What if I lost out on a chance at preferment because someone was offended by my views?"

She smiled, dark eyes sparkling. "So you do have opinions. Tell me one."

Damn. "Well…" I should have figured this out ahead of time. I had been a fervent populist, a Russet, back in the day, but that was too radical, too close to what I thought now. "I think," I said at last, "that the political discourse has become far too polarized. The Greens hate the Blues, and everyone hates the Russets and the Grays. It's far too easy to accidentally give offense, simply by seeming to support one party or the other. When I feel we all, perhaps, agree a great deal more than the politicians and journalists would make us believe."

A lukewarm speech, borrowed from my mother's political beliefs, which could be summarized by, "Can't we all be friends?" My father, a loyal Green, would storm, "Not with the Blues, I can't!"

Miss Liu's smile broadened. "You sound delightful. Perhaps the real radicalism is admitting that nine-tenths of what we squabble over, we believe only to have something to talk about."

She wasn't wrong, given that these four parties only represented the tiny minority of Martians who had a vote. Parliament spent its time arguing about which of the noble interests it ought to represent, while representing very few of the interests of the majority of Martians.

"It's better than the weather, at least," I agreed.

"You'll find the higher you go in society, the less people care," she said. "Look at the whist players there. Who do you see?"

I cast them a glance over my wineglass. "Is that … the Prime Minister and the opposition leader?"

"The very same. A Green and a Blue, but at every high-level event, they're thick as thieves."

As we watched, a third joined the party: Vasily Chin-Hawking, a distant cousin of mine and the People's Tribune. His role was to represent the common people in Parliament: one single voice for the vast majority of the population. And here he was, playing whist with the people oppressing his constituents.

I looked away to hide my anger. "My father would be furious. He hates the Blues. We're a country family, after all. The end of farm subsidies made him so angry he cut off all his Blue friends. Not that he had had many to begin with." I put a little disapproval into my tone.

"The voters care so much more than Parliament does. I swear it's no more to them than whist."

"When really," I ventured boldly, "there's not a finger's difference between the two parties. Not compared to the Russets."

"The Russets are just radicals," she said. "Encouraging these colonist riots. We had one in Cassini just yesterday. Several police were injured."

I gave a shocked little blink, though I'd read about it in the papers. "Things are different from when I went to space last fall. I don't understand why it's happening."

She shrugged. "There are always malcontents. And this Khan

impersonator, handing around all those leaflets swearing he's still alive, doesn't help."

"Oh, *those*," I said. The social reformer was alive, I'd shaken his hand, but I couldn't possibly betray any hint of that. "My father thinks it's the Russet party leader who writes them."

"If it is, he should be drummed out of Parliament," said Miss Liu indignantly. "Founders ought to stick together."

I took another sip of wine, feeling a little sick with all this lying. Just because I was better at it now didn't mean I *liked* it. "Certainly we have a great deal more in common with each other than any colonist."

Miss Liu offered me a ride home in her carriage, which I accepted. I would have had to order one, a tremendous expense. But one can hardly ride the hydrobus home from the Imperial Palace. It doesn't even stop there.

"It's strange I've never heard of you," I said, as the carriage headed toward Parliament Square. "Are you often in Landing?"

"I have a house here, by the waterfront," she said. I immediately revised upward my assessment of her wealth. "My family's seat is in Cassini, but I'm the third child."

Puzzling. Where did a third child get money for waterfront houses and private carriages? Cassini didn't even boast any peers. Was she like I had been, poor but driving herself deep into debt to trawl for a wealthy spouse?

If so, her interest in me couldn't be serious. She said she'd researched the guest list, and two minutes of research would have made our poverty explicit, now we'd given up the town house and most of the estate. "I'm hardly ever in the city," I admitted. "My family are all inveterate country people."

"Hellas is a lovely area. I can't blame you."

The carriage suddenly jolted to a halt, and I pulled up the shade to look out. There was a crowd blocking the way. I could see winking stars of torchlight and dim rectangles that were the signs, unreadable in the darkness. "Some kind of protest," I said.

Miss Liu put her head out the window to talk to the coachman. "Can we turn around?"

The horses stepped awkwardly, trying to bring the carriage around, but behind us the way was already blocked. A row of police marched up the avenue, elbow-to-elbow in their black uniforms and gold buttons. They carried riot shields and nightsticks.

A chill crept down my back. I wasn't afraid of protests, and my class had little to fear from police, but the two together could get volatile fast. I'd read enough in the papers to know that.

"Quickly!" snapped Miss Liu, in a very different voice. "Get as far to the side of the street as you can. Up on the sidewalk, if you can get the wheels up."

The carriage jolted as the driver tried to obey. "Should we get out and try to walk?" I asked. I'd avoided any number of conflicts by looking casual.

"Dressed as we are?" Miss Liu demanded. "They'd tear us to pieces."

I put my hand to the sleek bamboo silk. I'd been so proud of this dress, its cheapness and its expensive appearance. This crowd would be as taken in by the illusion as the party guests had been. It bespoke nobility, and who knew how careful they'd be about sorting out their enemies any more specifically than that.

"We'll get out of the carriage and duck behind it, once it's close to the buildings," she said. "If the police manage to get past us, we can get out behind their line."

We were not so lucky. By the time we struggled out of the carriage, the mob had pushed past us and pressed up against the line of police. Through the carriage windows, I could see only chaos. The police captain, on horseback behind the line, called through a bullhorn, "By order of the Emprex, this illegal gathering must disperse!"

But the shouting of the crowd drowned out anything more he had to say. The police line staggered as the crowd threw themselves against the shields, pushing and shoving. "Why don't they go the other way?" I asked in Miss Liu's ear.

She pointed. "Another police line over there. They're penned in."

That shocked me, like nothing else yet had, and I began to tremble. The police weren't trying to disperse the crowd. They were trying to punish it for protesting in the first place. Every time I thought I had been disillusioned enough about the Empire, it shattered another illusion I hadn't realized I still had.

The far side window of the carriage shattered and I ducked involuntarily. "We can't stay here," I said. "If we can reach the police, won't they let us through?"

I tried to move that way, but the carriage horses were there, feet skittishly dancing on the cobblestones. They were far too frightened to pass that closely, and too close to the wall to give a wide berth.

There was a whoosh, and flames started to lick at the carriage. Someone had thrown a torch in the window. The horses reared, terrified. The coachman, standing at the horses' heads to calm them, lost hold of the reins. They bolted, dragging the flaming carriage behind them.

I shrank back against the wall as the crowd surged up close to us. It didn't seem anyone noticed or cared about us at the moment, not with the police a few yards up ahead. Someone a few feet away from me was pulling up loose cobblestones from the road and hurling them forward at the police line. Good red Martian stone, for braining red-blooded Martians. Did they realize the police themselves were commoners too? Or did that only make the crowd angrier, knowing the cops were class traitors as well as oppressors?

There was a shattering sound and the street started to fill with smoke. "Put your handkerchief over your nose," Miss Liu shouted in my ear. "It's gas."

How did she know so much? Was this a thing the Landing nobles were used to? I reached for my handkerchief, but it was in my handbag, which I'd left in the carriage. Reluctantly I tore a piece of blue silk out of my skirt and held it to my face. It had been such a pretty gown.

Miss Liu linked her arm into mine and began pushing forward. With the gas spilling out a few yards away, the crowd was beginning to thin here. People were shoving up against the riot shields, but further back, people pressed backward, hoping for another way out.

I was too close to the line now to see the police at all. Just a dark scrum of people. But over their heads, I could see the police captain, wheeling on his white horse. Raising up my arm, I waved frantically at him. Would he even recognize us as nobles, in a place like this, in the dark? But he was looking behind him, crying an order to someone further back that I couldn't see.

There was a sudden snap of gunfire, at least a dozen shots almost at once. Beside me, a man crumpled to the ground, and the woman beside him bent over him screaming.

He'll be trampled, I thought. But instead the pack of people scattered, trying to flee the gunfire. The police line shoved forward, reaching us at last. The cop nearest us lowered his riot shield. "You two ladies don't look like you belong here," he bellowed over the chaos.

Miss Liu, steadfast until that moment, began to cry. "Please, officer. We just want to get out of here."

The policeman, a dark, thin young man, pulled out of the line, letting his comrades fill in the place where he'd been. Behind the line, I could see the company of Imperial Guard who had been firing on the crowd, in their spotless russet coats.

Taking my arm, our policeman led us over to the commander. "Sir, I have some women here who weren't part of the riot."

"Everyone here counts as part of the riot," the officer snapped, before looking down and seeing us. Abruptly he swung down from his horse. "Founders?"

"Yes," Miss Liu sobbed. "We were trying to make it home from the Imperial palace—we didn't know about any of this."

He patted her shoulder awkwardly. "See them home, Jenkins. Be back as soon as you can. We're loading everyone we can catch into vans on Constitution Street."

Jenkins led us down the street, past the company of troops and into the bare avenue beyond. Cold yellow lamplight spilled onto the cobblestones. "You ought to get a new coachman," he said. "A good one keeps track of where things like this are happening."

"I may have to," Miss Liu said. "And a new coach." A laugh broke through her tears.

"What are your addresses? I need to get you home."

Miss Liu named an upscale street at the waterfront. I gave the address of the friend I was staying with. "You could come home with me instead," she suggested. "After what we've been through, I could use a cup of tea and a talk."

I paused a moment. It wasn't that I didn't want to get to know her better. She might be influential; I could hardly afford to turn down contacts who could put a word in the right ear.

But on the other hand, she was an attractive woman who wanted to take me home with her. Propriety forbade her from making her offer in more explicit terms, but I suspected more than tea might be on order. "I must get home," I said after a moment. "My nerves are frayed. I'm going straight to bed."

Once I was alone in my own cab, I checked in my bosom

for Moira's letter. To my surprise, another letter was tucked in on top of it. Who had been so deft as to tuck a note down my dress without my noticing? I racked my mind for all the people I had danced with, all the people I had touched, even the footman who had fastened my cape around my shoulders at the end of the evening.

I shrugged and opened it up. Whoever it was, they were playing at some kind of politics, and I needed to know what side.

Khan wants to see you, it read.

3

MOIRA

I lifted my glass to my eye. Now that wasn't a common sight. Given the vastness of space, two ships passing within firing distance was rare enough. The odds of a third ship coming in sight of a battle in progress were even lower. Yet there, ahead of the *Mariposa* and a few points south, two ships were firing on each other. Each had taken in sail, and tiny flashes of torpedoes sparkled along their sides.

Yao, our youngest spacer, hung eagerly next to me. "It's a battle, right? Something we could help with?"

"Yes," I said, "that's definitely a Martian ship, a merchant I think, and likely a pirate attacking. Good eye."

"Can I try out my new flechette pistol?"

I sighed. Yao had an obsession with making new gadgets. It had been her clever idea with grapples that had let us take the *Mariposa* last year. With the way the strategies of battle had stagnated for a century, a creative mind could surely give us an advantage.

On the other hand, her gadgets were maybe fifty-fifty on actually working. "Fine," I said at last, "but bring a cutlass too."

Handing back the glass, I pushed off aft. "Marron, beat to quarters," I called as I came down the sail deck. "Nguyen, prepare to take in sail. Borisov, are my engines ready?"

I alighted on the quarterdeck and stood at attention at the rail. With a deep breath, I squared my shoulders and flicked an imaginary speck of dust off my trousers. This part I always loved. Couldn't help but love it. The ballet of a ship going into battle, every soul aboard coordinating in perfect harmony, and me at the center of it, conducting the dance.

The men chanted as they worked the levers that tucked the sails away. Through the aft window, I watched until the last shimmering silver fold had smoothed down against the hull outside. Then the careful about-face with thrusters, putting the stern toward the enemy so a rocket thrust would slow us down. Ass first, and fart to slow down. That's how Maxwell, rest his dirty mouth, had taught me to remember it. The stars slid across the window, and at last the two ships hove into view.

"Emergency burn on my mark…mark!" I hit my stopwatch. Down below, Borisov fired the engines.

Unlike the delicate thrust imparted by the sails, the emergency engines packed a punch you could actually feel. I held onto the rail with one hand to avoid drifting, while the other held my watch. Twenty seconds should about do it. "Cut engines," I ordered, and a crewman repeated my order down the hatch.

The burn came late enough that we were nearly on top of the fighting ships before the engines cut out. We had almost matched speed with the other vessels, crawling nearer at a snail's pace.

From the forecastle, Yao shouted, "They're not disengaging!"

I smiled. The men hated it when they got all worked up but never got a chance to fire the guns. Blue cannons, I call it. This time the enemy had chosen to stick around. Perhaps they weren't sure which side the *Mariposa* was on.

"Tickle 'em with the stern chaser," I ordered. "Then come about for a broadside."

Their first broadside cost us a broken arm among the crew. Nguyen was caught hanging onto his gun instead of bracing properly, and the sudden impact had been more than a single arm could take. The second made Ntumba yelp, as she was making her way down to help him. But nobody was hurled against the bulkheads to their death, which was lucky for a cannon battle. I hoped the pirates weren't having our good luck.

"They should be softened up by now," I said, as we drew close to the pirates. I signaled heave to and surrender, which they naturally ignored. If they hadn't been hungry for a fight, they'd have burned emergency fuel and gotten away. "Starboard gun crew, to the airlock!"

We didn't try any fancy tricks with the pirates, just a standard boarding party at the fore airlock. A ship this size wouldn't have a large complement, and they'd be well rattled by now.

When the lock breached, Yao tried her flechette. It went off all right, with a small bang of gunpowder, but the man she hit looked more puzzled than killed.

I lunged forward with my sword and took care of him. "See, this is why I stick with the classics."

She pocketed the flechette and drew her own cutlass. "I just need to get the velocity higher."

With a kick to one pirate, I slashed at another. "You get it too high, you'll hole my ship."

Rolling her eyes, she got another pirate in the gut. "I know what I'm doing."

She probably did. At fifteen she was already one of my handiest sailors. Given the constraints of no electricity, no holes in the hull, and no dangerous ricochet, she would eventually come up with something that revolutionized space warfare, I had no doubt.

The blur of combat was interrupted by a shout of surrender.

Looking around, I saw that another launch had docked across from ours—the merchants stirring themselves to their own defense at last.

I met the merchant ship's captain on the deck of the pirate ship. He was a noble, though surely not a wealthy one if he was out here shipping cargoes himself. "Thanks for the assist," he said, saluting with his sword. "I'd have struck my colors in another minute."

"It's nothing," I said. "We're patrolling this lane for Liberty Station."

"I have to admit, once you turned broadside and we saw your name, I wasn't sure which side you were going to support! I don't think the pirates knew either."

"You've heard of us?"

"At Phobos they talk of little else. The Admiralty is said to be furious."

I grinned. A Navy warship and most of her crew, slipped through their fingers and working for the enemy. I'd be mad too. "So, you want this ship?"

"We're really not crewed to be taking prizes," he demurred. "I'll give a few men if it helps you manage it, in exchange for a share of the cargo."

The only useful cargo turned out to be seeds and cases of dehydrated milk, both presumably captured from another Liberty-bound merchant. I handed them over with my compliments, since he was headed that way. In exchange he gave us four sailors.

Those four, plus six of my crew, were enough to take the ship back to Liberty. But just before we were ready to part ways, one of the new sailors approached me. She was a petite, mousy-looking woman with a bashful manner. "Excuse me, sir, could I speak with you? My name is Harrington."

I touched my forehead to her, a reflex from my Navy days.

She was no noble though, by her speech. A commoner like myself, I thought. "What is it?"

"If it's all the same to you, sir, I'd like to come aboard your ship instead."

I tilted my head. "Why?"

"I don't get along with that man, there." She pointed inconspicuously at one of the other merchanter sailors.

"Should I not have accepted him?"

She shook her head quickly. "No, he's a fine sailor, we just … we have a history, and I was hoping to switch ships when we got to Liberty. If I could do it now … Well, only if you have a convenient berth for me. I'm a hard worker. I'm qualified in EVA."

"Rated Able?"

A quick headshake. "I'm new to sailing, not to space—I was a stationer, before this. This is my first voyage. But I'm learning fast." She met my eye for the first time. Her eyes were a pale, foggy blue—startling after the colorlessness of the rest of her.

I chewed my lip. I wasn't out here to do charity work, bring people where they'd be happiest. I was here to pilot a ship. But if she could take the position of EVA master for me, it would free up Goldstein to go with the prize, and he might like that. Get back to Liberty sooner, and the prize crew would have a little more experience along. "Let me see what I can do."

4

LUCY

Outside the train window, Olympus Mons steadily filled more of the horizon. From here, all I could see were the red cliffs of its edge, and beyond, a little hazy purple-and-white hump. But that was deceiving—the mountain was fifteen miles high, only so broad that from the edge, the peak was already disappearing below the planet's curve.

This was where the mysterious note had brought me. If it could be trusted, I would finally meet the great social reform leader again. Of course I had no way of verifying it. If I'd had contacts with Khan's organization, the Russet Brotherhood, he wouldn't have had to deliver the note that way—I'd have asked to see him already through those channels. And Moira wouldn't know either. If she'd tried reaching out to Khan since we'd parted on an Earth ship, she hadn't mentioned it.

But I could hardly ignore it. Khan was, in my estimation, possibly the greatest man of our generation. The one who had survived seven years in Deimos Prison after all of Mars thought him dead. And who had, despite his broken body, returned to Mars to continue pushing forward the cause of freedom. If anyone could give me ideas how to use my cover as a Navy officer to help take down everything that was oppressive about the Empire, it would be him.

The conductor passed up and down the aisle, announcing our next stop in Armstrong City. All at once, narrow, red-brick row houses sprang up on either side of the tracks. I peered out at them with interest. My entire life, I had moved only in the higher circles of Martian society; it had never occurred to me to take much personal interest in how the other half lived. Moira had changed all that. So I took in the broken windows swathed in cardboard, raggedy children playing in the street, tired women sitting out on the stoops. What would it be like to live like that? I couldn't fathom. I had been poor, in the sense of never having money to spend, but it wasn't the same.

The train plunged into a cutting, lined with brick, which reflected and magnified the faint rattle of the wheels. I was about to look away when I saw the graffiti. Six-foot-high, white letters read, GOD FUCK THE EMPREX.

Beneath, a row of workers in gray coveralls wielded long brushes to scrub the letters away. Chains led from each man's ankle to the next. Prison labor.

The chain gang fell away behind, and the train pulled slowly into the station. I shrugged my old greatcoat over my shoulders and shoved on my battered hat. The neighborhood I was here to visit didn't look kindly on well-heeled strangers.

Armstrong City was a newer settlement, since the time of the Singularity. Before, factories had been built anywhere, powered by solar or nuclear power. Now that electricity was banned for almost all uses, the only sensible place to build a factory was along a river. The city was a long corridor of factories along the swift Armstrong River, which poured glaciermelt off Olympus Mons.

I made my way along Front Street, where one factory after

another sprawled, each clanking and thumping with activity, even late in the evening as it was. The water wheels could turn all day, so the assembly lines had to do the same. Men carrying dinner pails trudged in, and dirty men with empty pails trudged out. Shift change.

I found the side street I needed and headed into a warren of alleys. The evening light didn't penetrate here, and deep shadows hung everywhere. More and more windows were boarded up. Sometimes the row would have a gap, like a missing tooth, where a house had collapsed. The bricks and fittings had been scavenged, but random trash piled in the gaps. The street itself was the same—cracked, pitted, and growing weeds in places.

The house I needed was number 45. Though the brass marker was gone, I could still read the number on the door, where the paint was a little less faded. After one last glance around, I knocked on the door.

There was no answer. I frowned and checked the note. It was the right address. What if something had happened to Khan since I'd gotten it?

Gingerly I tried the knob and pushed the door open. The front room was empty, and looked like it had been for some time. Dust and trash lay in the corners, though the middle of the floor was clear.

I took a deep breath and shut the door behind me. It wouldn't be strange for Khan to hide in a back room, though it was certainly odd that no one was guarding the door. Probably Khan had had to change hideouts at the last moment, and my entire visit was a waste of time. But I wanted at least to check the rest of the house to be sure.

The room led straight back into another. This one was clean and swept, and held a table, two chairs, and a man. He wore a tattered coat, dirty scarf, and a flat cap—the standard Armstrong City uniform. On the table before him was a game of solitaire.

He paused and looked up, with a card still held in one hand. "What is Mars?" he asked, in a rough Armstrong accent.

I hesitated. If it was meant as a password, I knew the answer. Khan had always said Mars was the planet and people; he would expect me to know that. But something wasn't right.

"I'm sorry," I said, in my most officious Founder tone. "Is Soledad Khan here? I've had a note from her. At least, I think it must be." I pulled out the note and inspected it, as if unsure if I'd missed something.

I'd planned this response, if I came up against anyone but the reformist leader. Soledad Khan was a Landing prostitute; only too plausible that a Founder might have dealings with one. And the note had only given a last name. Mars had thousands of Khans.

The man laughed, and said in a completely different accent, "Jolly good, Lieutenant Prescott. We had to be sure about you."

My shoulders relaxed. I had made my guess based on the man's hands, which were smooth, uncalloused, and clean. No real factory worker has soft hands, and it's hard to ever get them perfectly clean. "What, like a test? Are you with the Admiralty?"

"Not precisely. I work for the Privy Ministry. Have you heard of us?"

"No, sir."

"You're not meant to." He took off the hat and scarf and laid them on the table. "The Admiralty, of course, has vetted you thoroughly. But since you'd been out of contact so long, we needed to make our own investigation."

"Satisfied?" I asked. My heart was pounding, but I kept my voice casual.

He shrugged. "So far. There are some terrible elements in the system these days. Even within the empire. I understand you survived a near-mutiny, before you were even attacked by the pirates."

"Your source is faulty," I huffed. "I foiled a near mutiny."

The man smiled. "Of course. What's your opinion on that, by the way? What caused that mutiny—or any mutiny, for that matter?"

I frowned for a moment, as if considering the question for the first time. It gave me a moment to think what part of the truth, if any, to say. "Discipline," I said. "A condemnable want of discipline. It does no good to discipline the men if the officers lack self-control themselves."

"Are you disciplined, Lieutenant?"

"I try to be."

"I hope you will exercise that discipline over your own tongue. This meeting of ours never happened, do you understand me? The Ministry prefers to operate more subtly than the usual chain of command, but I assure you—we shall speak to the Admiralty about you if we have any complaint."

I turned as if to go, and then turned back and frowned. "What is this Ministry?" I asked. "Who do you answer to?"

"To the Empire." He smiled thinly. "As do you."

On the train home, I pulled my hat over my eyes and pretended to sleep. I was disappointed I hadn't seen Alexei Khan—he was, after our meeting last year, a friend as well as an idol. The man had single-handedly started the equal-rights movement on Mars. He would have had some idea of how I could help Moira from here. She hadn't given me any direction herself, and I wasn't willing to simply wait out the war.

The one idea worth investigating was Khan's disappearance. I knew he had been arrested, and there had never been a public record. I had hoped he could give me some hint as to who in the government was responsible: the Emprex, Parliament, the Admiralty, the Landing Police? It could have been anyone with clearance to dock at Deimos Prison.

I hadn't gotten the interview I wanted, but I did have a lead: this Ministry the man had mentioned. If he knew Khan's passwords, that meant his Ministry had investigated the Russet Brotherhood closely. Perhaps they had been the ones to kidnap him the first time, and if so, they were surely interested in catching up to him again.

Which would explain why I hadn't heard from Khan. With someone actively hunting him down, he could hardly afford to trouble himself with Navy officers already under close scrutiny.

I sighed and huddled a little deeper into the uncomfortable train seat. No help from that quarter, and no hint from Moira in her letters either. I was simply going to have to find a mission on my own.

That mission, I decided, was to track down this Privy Ministry. I would find out who they worked for, whether they had kidnapped Khan, and what goal they were trying to achieve.

That last one, I thought I could guess: the quiet smothering of any infant liberty movement that might break out among the common man. Which made them my enemy.

5

Lucy

The lieutenant's exam, like my university exams, was oral. Just me and the examiner, in a small room in the Admiralty building. He was an old captain, white hair immaculately tied back in its queue, back a little stooped. Too old to go back into space, most likely—if he wanted any chance at coming down again.

I had spent much of my leave studying the naval handbook, the star chart, and all my astronavigation notes, so most of the exam went by easily. I fired answers back at the examiner as fast as I could.

"Forty knots."

"Two hundred leagues out, forty-nine degrees downstream of Regulus, sixteen kilometers south."

"Article four, subsection two."

"Ten lashes, five if the spacer is a minor."

"Fasten the tether, then hand over hand along the rail."

The examiner paused. "And what should you do if you learn of disloyal or seditious thoughts in a fellow officer?"

I blinked. That hadn't been in any of the material I had been told to study. "Report it?" I ventured.

"Tell me, Mister Prescott, and be honest. What do you think of traitors?"

I felt a calm like water washing over me. This was my life now. To coat the outside of myself with all the certainty I had once felt. "I hate them, sir."

"How much do you hate them?"

"I would run them through with my own sword, sir. Worse than pirates."

He shut his exam book. "I have to apologize for the extra questions," he said, waving me to sit at last. "They were just added. You know we lost the *Mariposa* to pirates in the past year."

"I do know, sir. She was my ship." No point in trying to hide that, it was on my record.

"And you know your crewmates deserted to the pirates?"

"Yes, sir. Except for the captain, the lieutenants, and my fellow midshipman, who was killed."

"But one officer deserted."

"Yes, sir."

"We've all been racking our brains here, wondering how it happened. What inducements the pirates offered. Perhaps there was too much familiarity between the captives and their captors. Perhaps sailors don't have firmly enough in their minds what their duty is. All we can do is test the loyalty of the men we trust with command. And we've made a change to the regs; you'll need a new copy. It is no longer permitted for a captured sailor, whether officer or spacer, to give parole. They must refuse all familiarity with their captors."

"Understandable, sir."

"I know you've been sworn to Their Majesty's service already, but you'll need to make an additional oath now. We've added some things."

"So I passed, sir?"

"With flying colors, Mister Prescott. I must say, your record didn't leave me expecting you would be so adept. But I did see a recommendation that navigation is a strong suit of yours, so perhaps I shouldn't have been surprised. Just remember that, as a lieutenant, judgment is just as important as trigonometry. The kinds of careless mistakes that could be overlooked in a midshipman won't pass muster now."

"I understand, sir."

I stood and made the oath, skin prickling. I knew, I felt perfectly easy in my conscience, that it was the right thing to do. That I was loyal in my way, because I was loyal to the people of Mars, because I was loyal to Moira. But hearing my tongue lie and lie and lie still hurt. I wondered if it would ever stop hurting. And whether I wanted it to.

The captain handed me an envelope. "Your new orders."

I sat back down and opened the packet. I was being assigned to the *IMS Adamant*, Catherine Vasiliev-Scott commanding. Lieutenant Vasiliev, in command of a ship already? It was a cheering thought; I had liked Vasiliev when I served under her on the *Mariposa*.

Then I read the mission. Travel to Venus as escort to His Highness, Prince George Konstantin. I blinked and read it again. That was a *much* more prestigious position than I had expected, especially with my deliberately-cultivated reputation of ineptitude. Had I made enough of an impression on the Prince that he had requested me specifically? I reviewed our conversation—I had said, at best, one intelligent thing. It didn't seem likely.

Perhaps officers were so short there had been no choice. In any event, I couldn't imagine a better mission, if I hoped to have any chance of influencing things for Moira. I refolded the paper and slid it back into the envelope.

"You'll have two weeks before shipping out," said the captain, rising to shake my hand. "I recommend as much physical training as you can fit in, and a medical exam."

"I always train hard, sir," I answered. "Thank you, sir." I snapped a sharp salute and left the room.

I spent the rest of my leave exercising. The lack of gravity aboard ship wastes away the body, and I had known I would only have two months to spend gaining back muscle and bone mass before having to do it again. Now I redoubled my efforts. Most likely, I'd never descend to Venus myself, but if I had the chance, I needed to be ready. Venus's gravity was triple ours, almost as high as Earth's. Normal fitness wouldn't be enough.

My makeshift gym was in the old habitat beneath Hellas Manor, where my ancestors had first settled. In those days, it wasn't enough to wall in a pocket of atmosphere; the radiation was so severe they had to tunnel underground. Every old house on Mars has what amounts to a fallout shelter underneath.

Ours was cheerless, with concrete floor and walls. Blank gaps in the ceiling had once held electric lights. Now fiber optic cables led down from the surface, bringing in light from outside.

My mother came in one morning while I was buckling myself into my weighted vest. "Lucy, have a look at—what is the vest for? We're not invading Earth, are we?"

I strapped lead cuffs around my wrists. There was even a little weighted headband. Apparently, Earth babies spend their first several months learning to keep their enormous heads up under triple gravity. I had to play catch-up with them now. "Just trying to build back my muscles as fast as I can, Mother. I've only got two weeks, and then months in the black."

"I think I still have your old heavy vest somewhere..."

"It wouldn't fit me now." Founder children were commonly weight-trained—leaded vests and shoes, from when we first learned to walk. A strategy to make it possible for us to visit Earth if we ever chose to, by making us develop the bone and muscle an Earth child would have. Starting in adulthood would be too late.

"I remember you hated having to wear that vest. You'd be bouncing off the *walls*, till I managed to catch you and put it on. It wasn't even about the weight training—I needed something to slow you down!"

"I was mad because William didn't have to."

"We learned to pick our battles with him. And, well—it didn't seem he'd ever be likely to travel."

My brother has what Martians call the noble condition, though more than just nobles get it. On Earth they call it autism. When he was younger, even getting him to wear clothes had been difficult. Everything was too itchy, too confining. A lead vest would have been much worse.

"It was pretty much the only thing I was ever jealous of him over," I reassured her. "I wasn't much older than that when I began to understand why things were different for him."

The weights dragged me back toward the floor—an oddly familiar sensation, despite the years it had been since I'd felt it. I picked up my sword—a blunt replica—and began my drills.

"Does being in the Navy really require so much violence?"

"We *are* at war."

She sighed. "I worried about you the whole time you were gone before. Even before you went missing. And now that you're back ..." She sat on a crate to watch me. "It's going to be hard to let you go. William was always the one I worried about. You, I assumed, would be fine. Go to school, get married, do the conventional things ..."

I lowered the sword, panting. "I wanted that life. It just ... didn't turn out that way."

"It's my fault, I suppose."

It was—she and my father had squandered years digging themselves more deeply into debt, until there was no way to get out of it but my joining the service—but I knew better than to get into it. "It turned out for the best," I said, raising my sword again. "I like the Navy more than I thought I would."

"But if something happens to you—"

I gave up the idea that I was going to get any exercise done, and hung the practice sword back on the wall. "I've left a letter for you. In case anything does." If I died, or if my cover was blown, they deserved the truth. There was also an emergency plan for them, if they couldn't manage without me. So far their attempts to make their own income to survive on hadn't gotten very far.

"What comfort will a *letter* be if—"

"It's more of a comfort to me," I said, shifting my shoulders uncomfortably. One hundred fifty pounds, real gravitational weight, was no joke. "Last time, when I was captured and couldn't get word to you, I worried about you constantly. This way, at least I'll know I've made a plan."

"What plan?"

I sighed. It was really better the less they knew. If they knew there was money in the letter, I couldn't trust them not to open it. "Plan A is for you to keep the house, if at all possible. I know you're still trying to pay off the mortgage. Plan B is for you to stay in the area. Ideally, you could get work at another noble house."

"As *servants*?"

"You've seen the work done often enough," I pointed out. "But you'll want to stay here. William can't live in the city."

"Naturally not," she said. "He never could abide the noise. But perhaps one of those hospitals—"

"No!" I said, more forcefully than I meant to. "I checked one out, while I was in the city."

My mother frowned. "And? Was it a good place?"

"It was a horrible place. I can't bear thinking about it. That anyone should have to go there. You shouldn't have to be born lucky to get the care William does." I shut my mouth to stop a rant that wanted to bubble up.

Martian society was broken, in more ways than just asylums for the disabled. I could talk about the cracking streets in Armstrong City and the gilt in the Emprex's palace and what it all meant about the neofeudal system, the deep divide between Founders and colonists. But—

"It's hard enough for me to worry about my own family, without having to get worked up about every other person on the planet," said my mother. And there it was. She wasn't actively classist; she just couldn't bring herself to care very much about anyone but us. "Anyway, I don't think we have to worry about any plans past A. Your father is harvesting grapes now. If he can turn his wine hobby into a career, we could pay our expenses just on that."

"Is that what that is?" I gestured to her hands, where she'd been twisting the same green stem the whole time we'd been talking.

"Mm. Yes, it's my one worry." She held it out to me.

I inspected the leaves. They were curled on the edges and slightly yellow. Nestled inside the curl were a few tiny yellow-green insects. "I haven't seen these before."

"Neither has your father. He has a book of all the pests that have made it to Mars. This isn't any of them."

Mars was a perfect place to avoid pests, since no plant got here without extensive inspections and a long voyage. No living thing was here but the ones we'd chosen—and a few which had, over the centuries, snuck in. We had meal moths, and cockroaches, and a few other very hardy enemies, but few could weather our long winters.

"You should take that to a botanist," I said. "At the university, they're sure to have books that could identify it."

Feet clattered down the stairs. We both turned to see William, his light brown hair mussed and his shirt open at the neck. In his hands was a book, which he shoved into my hands.

My mother, drawn by inexorable habit, reached up to smooth William's hair. "*Sailing for the Absolute Beginner?* What do you think Lucy could want with that book?"

"It's his way of reminding me I promised to read it so I could go sailing with him," I explained. I handed the book back and started taking off my weights. "I did read it all, William. Can't promise I will actually be any good at it, but I'm willing to try."

Eyes still fixed on the book, William smiled broadly, his body unconsciously dancing a little with excitement. He'd been after me to learn to sail my entire leave. One of the few things that hadn't been sold was his little catboat.

"Are you sure that's safe?" my mother asked. "What happens if you capsize?"

"We can both swim, Mother," I said, touching her cheek with a light kiss.

"Don't get any seawater in your mouth!" she cried after us. "It's full of perchlorates!"

I squeezed William's elbow as we went up the stairs together. "Thank you for bringing me. I've always wanted to learn."

Sailing with my brother wasn't exactly training hard. But given I would soon be gone, it seemed right. I had been gone so long. And I did want to let him teach me.

Or rather, to read some manuals and then go out on the water with him and hope I figured it out. He doesn't speak, so I couldn't expect much formal instruction.

He certainly was happy to have me, though. He shoved ropes into my hands and took the wheel, grinning broadly. "I've never done this before," I warned him. "I've sailed in space, but that's not the same thing."

We took the boat out, and by keeping a close eye on what he was doing I managed to follow his lead well enough. It was a fine, hot day, and we had both stripped down to shirtsleeves and knee-breeches without shoes or stockings. The water shone a deep blue, too disturbed by waves to reflect the puffy clouds overhead, and the red cliffs of the basin edge looked pinkish in the haze. A perfect day, as hot as Mars ever gets.

"I get a week at home," I said. "The *Adamant* sails on the 24th of Leo. That'll leave me a few days to get there by train and elevator."

He turned the helm over without warning, and I scrambled to pull the sheet over to the other side. "You're supposed to say 'helm's alee,'" I told him, as I finished tying it down fast. "That's what the book says."

He only laughed at me, staring out at the water.

"It's really not much like solar sailing," I said. "The sun always comes from the same direction. None of this scrambling around."

He faced into the wind, his brown hair blown off his face and his eyes laughing. I took a deep breath, trying to capture the mental picture. Besides Moira, he was the person I loved most in the world. The reason I had done almost everything I did since I had joined the Navy. And, deep down, the reason I had come back to Mars instead of staying on Liberty Station with Moira.

As long as the Navy thought I was loyal, I could still pay William's way. His care wasn't cheap; he had a fulltime caregiver and relied heavily on his routine. Part of that routine included staying here, at the seaside, at Hellas Manor. My family's fortune was gone now, all spent and sold away to settle debts. It was only my earnings that allowed them to keep the house.

I couldn't deny this presented a temptation to me. I might reach a point where I had to choose: my reputation with the Navy or the right thing to do. It might happen that doing the right thing led to my dismissal from the service, or, if they found out I'd been passing intelligence to Moira, my execution. That was an abstract worry. More visceral was the fear of what might happen after: poverty for my family. The loss of the house and everything that made William's life happy.

As I'd told my mother, I'd explored other options. Not everyone with William's condition was noble, which implied there had to be some way poor people managed. And indeed there was: a neat white building near the edge of town, a place called Mercy House. I had had a nurse take me around.

Sterile hallways, with little windowless rooms. No razors, no shoelaces, nothing with a sharp edge. Because, "you know," the nurse had said with a meaning look. I did not know, at first. William had never wanted to hurt himself.

In a classroom, a little boy was being made to look at a bright letter A. He didn't want to look at the letter. He wanted to flap his hands. But every time he flapped them, a little switch flicked out from the teacher's hand.

"A little harsh, don't you think?" I had asked the nurse.

"They don't have the luxury of doing what they want all day," she answered. "Sooner or later they must learn to be useful. To earn their keep. If they do well, they will be allowed out each day to work. But to find that work, they'll have to learn to be appropriate."

I had fled from that terrible place. William could never, ever be sent there. Not while there was breath in my body. And not after, if there was anything I could do beforehand.

Even spelling it out like that made me feel selfish. What business did I have spying for Moira if it put William at risk? But then, perhaps it was just as selfish to protect my own brother so passionately when that other boy, the one who wanted to flap his hands instead of look at a letter, was still there. Our whole empire was broken, deeply sick, and it affected more people than just my family.

It felt hopeless that anything could ever change. That somehow Moira and Khan and I could break the class system, transform the Empire, end the cruelty we had once taken for granted. But what could I do but dare to try?

The sail suddenly rippled with a loud flapping sound, and I jerked to attention. William had turned the tiller again, and I'd been too lost in thought to switch the boom over. I hurried to untie the sail from the cleat, but when I got it loose it only swung wildly. It slammed into my gut and swept me overboard.

I came up spitting bitter water. William was still on deck, capturing the swinging boom and tying it down. Only then did he reach over to pull me out.

I flopped onto the deck, dripping. "There's got to be some kind of signal you could do," I said, holding back a smile. "It's not like you don't know how to shout when you've a mind."

Then I started to laugh, and he threw back his head and laughed with me.

"You *let* me fall in, didn't you?" I accused. "That's why you let me come at all, for the thrills of watching me get wet. I'm onto you."

I lay across the bows to dry off. It wasn't like I really minded a dunking, not in this heat. "I want to know you'll be all right when I'm gone," I said. "My pay will be disbursed to the solicitor, but if it stops, you'll have to rely on yourselves for a while. I've talked to Mama and Papa about thrift and I *think* they get it. And there's their little wine venture."

I didn't know how to tell him what was really going on. Or if I should. He was better at keeping a secret than most, but was it right to leave it weighing on his mind? Would he understand, when we'd carefully explained the importance of obeying the law, why I was breaking it?

"There's a lot of complicated things going on," I said at last. "I can't tell you all of it. But I want you to know, if you get bad news about me, that everything's under control. I have a plan to keep myself safe, and a plan for you also. It …" I swallowed hard. "It's possible I won't be able to come back. For a long time." I didn't want to say *ever*. "If that happens, I'll try to write. We'll see what I'm able to do."

We reached the end of the tack, and this time I caught his motion in time to bring the boom over. "Just remember, whatever happens," I said, once the sail was secure again. "Remember that I love you, and am doing everything I can for you, even when I'm far away."

He didn't like that, I guess, because he threw the tiller over. This time we both fell in the water.

"Message received, skipper," I said, grabbing hold of the side of the boat. "Enough of my drivel."

6

MOIRA

J ust think," I said, lounging sideways in the air above the quarterdeck, "how close we'll be."

Marron's arms were folded across his chest. "No."

"It would be criminal not to stop in on her when we're right here."

"It literally is criminal for you to do it. You're a deserter, a wanted woman. They'll kill you if you try to pass through Phobos."

"Only if they recognize me," I argued. "I bet someone somewhere is making fake papers I can get. Khan got some."

"And if you bump into someone that knows you, you die."

"I'll die if I don't see her," I said sulkily.

We were a few weeks out from Mars. The plan was to use the planet to kill speed, then start heading back downstream, toward Liberty again. The trade route between the two was getting longer all the time, this time of year, and more space meant more room for pirates to work.

"I don't think Lucy would want you risking your life like that," Marron continued.

"She *left* me. She doesn't get a say."

"If you're so mad at her, why do you want to see her anyway?"

"Because of her glorious breasts, what else? Have you *seen* them?" I grabbed the rail, spun myself around, and shot off toward the aft window to look out at the small pink disc of Mars. "I'm in love with her, stupid, I don't care how horrible she's being."

Marron started cranking up the radio. The *Mariposa*'s radio had a limited range, but we were starting to get near enough to have a hope of picking up something. "Part of why you keep me on as first mate is because I can tell you when you're being a fucking idiot," he said to my back. "This is one of those times."

I sighed. I missed Lucy so bad it hurt. And Mars. What I wouldn't give to be bending low over a horse's neck right now, galloping through the wild grasses while rusty mountains sliced into the sky alongside. The recycled air here smelled like men's sweat and farts and algae. I pressed my hands against the window, wishing I could open it and catch a breeze. No breeze for thousands of klicks.

"I know," I said at last. "Maybe when the war's over. She promised she'd come back then. Get a civilian job."

When the war's over. What an optimistic thing to say. War broke out between Mars and Earth like the common cold—over and over, granting no immunity from the next one. This war would end when Earth got tired of spending money on it, and Earth had deep, deep pockets. And even then, would Lucy really leave her family for me? Not for good. Maybe for a torrid visit every six months or so. Some relationship.

Marron stopped cranking and the radio crackled to life. That would happen regardless of where we were—the sun blasts out radio waves in all directions, a scream on every frequency that waxes and wanes but never stops. But among the fuzzy static was an intermittent beep. "We're in range," said Marron.

I cocked my head and listened to the beeping. It sounded like a manifest list—somebody making an offer of goods they wanted to ship to Liberty. If businessmen still thought it a worthwhile bargain, perhaps the pirates were leaving the trade route alone now.

"I'll want to transmit in a moment," I said, dashing off a few lines in spacer union code. It was a simple cipher, but enough to keep anyone from accidentally overhearing.

Trey, I'm in the area. Any messages for me?

Trey was my contact on Phobos, an old friend who worked radios. He'd assigned Lucy and me radio numbers, and slipped our messages past Naval Intelligence.

It took a few hours for him to come on shift, and then the radio chattered to life.

Only about a hundred. Tell your girlfriend I'm going to start charging by the word.

I grabbed a pen and dutifully jotted down the letters as they beeped through. The code Lucy and I had decided on was too complex to translate on the fly. It relied on hiding the letters of the message inside a longer letter, so the text itself was a wandering mess of comments about the weather and people's health.

My tongue sticking out of the corner of my mouth, I started decoding. Why did it have to involve so much fucking math?

The first began,

Your letter was waiting for me when I arrived at Phobos. I cannot express the joy it gave me to hear (so to speak) your voice again. I have it tucked in my bodice; it seemed to me you would like that.

"You bet your tits I would," I muttered aloud. That was a mental picture all right. And, despite Lucy's ladylike prudishness, absolutely intentional. The closest she was capable of coming to an innuendo.

The first letter had no surprises. Lucy had survived her court-martial, as expected. Her family was well. All little nothings, but reading her words seemed to bring her presence into the room. I could almost smell her bergamot cologne. I licked my lips. I'd do more than smell her, if I could get near enough.

The second letter had more news. Lucy was going to parties; there had been some kind of riot. There was a confusing mention of "forces on Mars opposed to what we're doing," but not to be worried because she felt she was "holding up my cover adequately."

"I can't figure out what she's up to," I said. "Is she playing some kind of spy game?"

"Probably," said Marron. "You might have sent her away to keep her out of trouble, but she was never going to do that."

I kept reading. "Holy shit, she's going to Venus!"

"What's holy shit about that?" he asked. "Mars trades with Venus all the time."

"She's not going to trade. She's going on a diplomatic mission. Even in code, she doesn't want to say who with, but it seems to be somebody important. I wonder if Venus is planning to take sides in the war after all."

Marron snorted. "Them? Never. Straight democracies never go to war. It's only when the people making the decision aren't the ones who pay for it."

I decoded another sentence. "Even if I could get near Phobos, I'd just miss her. She'll be gone before we cross Mars orbit." Just saying it made me ache. To come so close…

"It would have been worse if she were still there," Marron pointed out. "You still couldn't go. Better this way."

After the last letter there was a postscript by our Phobos contact.

I've also got a letter here for you from a Bill Singh. Message begins. Don't know when this will reach you, sweetie. I have bad news. Papa was thrown from a horse and is badly hurt. Hard to say yet how serious it will be yet. I've gone in debt to the doctor; our credit is good so don't worry on that count, but if you want to send anything it'll be appreciated. Message ends.

I reread my dad's message three times. Badly hurt how? Hell, how'd he get thrown from a horse at all? Ramesh loved horses; he understood them. In thirty years training them, he'd rarely been hurt at all.

Marron left the radio buzzing to itself and came over to the window. "What is it?" His voice had lost its casual tone and was deep with sympathy.

I put my hand to my face. It was damp, and the top page of my notebook was crumpled in my hand. I smoothed it out. "It's one of my dads, he's ... I've got to get home, do you understand me? I've got to."

7

LUCY

I arrived in orbit a day early, because I remembered the amount of chaos there usually was ahead of launching. And because I wanted to talk to my contact.

Phobos Station was the only way on or off Mars. Once a free-orbiting moon, it was moved into a stationary orbit to serve as the counterbalance for the space elevator up from Landing. It was mainly a military installation, so you would think the Empire would be able to control everything coming in or out.

But that wasn't strictly the case. A certain amount of smuggling came through every day, through the civilian shipping sector. Customs stamped the outside of every crate, but it wasn't practical to open every one and see what was inside. Silks, coffee, dried tropical fruits—anything Mars was too cool to grow, you could buy from Earth for a price. The governments of both planets notwithstanding.

It might be a good income stream for Moira, I thought as I passed the radio counter. With trade legal between here and

Liberty, and between Liberty and Earth, it could be a hub for the smuggling of all kinds of contraband.

I saw Trey at work, but didn't pause. His colleagues might remember me. Better to meet in a different place next time. I moved slowly, to give him a fair chance of seeing me, and headed up through a round portal to the observation deck.

This was a transparent bubble at the top of the station, housing a food court with a view of the stars. It was busy, but I bought a foil pouch of tea and found a table. I hooked my toes under the bottom rung of the chair to keep myself in place, in Phobos' barely-existent gravity, and tried my tea. It was lukewarm and bland thanks to being brewed below boiling. Phobos was kept at half an atmosphere's pressure, to save on nitrogen, and that meant water boiled before it was hot enough to brew. And then they always cooled it further, because scalding liquids weren't a nice thing to have loose in microgravity. I sighed. It would be months before I could get a decent cup of tea again.

But above my head, the view reminded me of all the reasons I had missed being out here. Space is a miserable place, by many measures: bad food, no baths, lingering smells, unspeakable lavatory facilities…and yet thousands of people keep throwing themselves out in it, again and again, because once they've seen the stars, the stars as they really are outside an atmosphere, they can't go back. My old friends beamed at me steadily: Regulus, Denebola, Castor, Pollux. Without a sextant I couldn't take a proper reading, but the back of my mind was already working on an estimate.

To my right, the arc of Mars curved away. It was night, now, in Landing, but a crescent of light shone across Elysium and the Aeolian coast. Hellas was out of sight from here. I wondered if William was on the water right now, or not.

Someone sat down across from me, and I turned back toward the table. Not Trey. But my disappointment only lasted a second.

"Sir!" I said, pushing myself smoothly to my feet. "Congratulations on your promotion!"

"I'm not really promoted." Vasiliev angled her right shoulder toward me, so I could see she only wore one epaulet. "Only captain for the voyage, I'm afraid. But it's my first command and I'm still pleased."

"Of course," I said, resuming my seat and craning my neck back toward the window. "Which one is she?"

Outside, to the left, a number of ships hung motionless. Or, as Vasiliev herself had taught me, *relatively* motionless. Squat cargo ships, long passenger ships, cigar-shaped warships with rows of gunports down each side, below the folded sails. And one, close by, completely unlike the others. She was sleek and slim like a silver needle, at least a hundred feet long. Yet she was no more than thirty feet in the beam, her folded sails making an appreciable lump.

I glanced back to Vasiliev, who smiled. "I can see you've found her. The IMS *Adamant*. Brand new, extra light. She can make twice the acceleration the *Mariposa* did."

"But she's got to be cramped inside, at that size." I thought of the *Mariposa*'s narrow decks, and all that had had to fit between them.

"Less than you'd think. She has no cargo. No engines at all, and no fuel. You can imagine the mass that saves."

No emergency fuel meant no decelerating to engage the enemy. I sighed. "Of course. I didn't really put it together till now. We won't be seeing combat, not with passengers."

Vasiliev nodded. "So no prize money to hope for. We have a few guns to warn off attackers, but our main strategy will be outrunning the enemy."

"It'll take some clever sailing, though, to be sure not to need any fuel."

"No leeway for error. Yes. Especially given the sort of passengers we'll be carrying."

Neither of us said *the prince*. Not here in a public food court. But we both were thinking the same thing, I suspected: this might be the most important mission either of us had ever flown. There would be no margin for error in the sailing, yes, but even more so, there would be no margin for error politically. We'd have the prince and his entourage breathing down our necks the whole time.

"How did you—" she began, at the same time as I started to say "I wonder why—" She grinned. "You first."

"I just find I'm—surprised," I said. "That they would select a lieutenant commander for this mission when there are full captains available. You have plenty of experience, but this doesn't seem the kind of ship anyone would give someone for their first command."

"Funny," she said. "I was going to ask you the same. Why they would pick a green captain and a green second mate for this mission. My first mate, at least, is seasoned. Michael Shen-Armstrong, you probably don't know him. But people say he must not be that bright, or he'd surely have made captain at his age. He'd been a lieutenant ten years already when the war started."

"*I* have a reputation for being not that bright," I said, somewhat sourly. "Which will probably follow me my whole career, at this rate."

"That's what I was going to ask you about. The Admiralty thinks you're stupid because of how you lost the station."

"I hardly lost it single-handed," I protested. "Nobody else was able to save it either."

She held up an apologetic hand. "I know that. But it still confuses me. I know you're not stupid. You're the best midshipman I ever taught."

"At navigation," I said quietly. "It was suggested at my exam that I should remember raw intelligence isn't enough to succeed in the Navy. That judgment is an entirely separate thing, and I need to work on it."

She regarded me a moment. Suspicious? It was true that the story I'd told the Admiralty didn't paint me in the best light. It relied on me simply forgetting to show up where I was supposed to be, not once but twice. If I hadn't helped negotiate the peaceful handover, those errors probably wouldn't have been forgiven.

Vasiliev knew me as more responsible than that. On the *Mariposa* I had never been late to duty, not once. But we had only served together a few months. I watched her consider the facts she had and make a decision. "There is no teacher like experience," she said at last. "I'm sure you'll improve." Was that her choosing to accept my story, or filing away her doubts for another time?

"I certainly will try," I said.

She pushed up from the table. I made as if to follow. "Are you going over to the ship now?"

"Not yet," she answered, waving me back down. "I have a few errands to run first. Meet me by airlock 1A in twenty minutes."

1A. Yet another sign of this mission's priority. I'd be under a much brighter spotlight than I had hoped, when it came to maintaining my cover. But on the other hand, a much higher chance of finding out something important.

At last I caught a glimpse of Trey approaching—casually, as if he had no particular seat he was looking for. He sat sideways in the chair across from me, as if to signal he was here to watch the stars, not make conversation, and dropped a slip of paper into the air between us.

I let it drift until it was in front of me before snagging it out of the air. A message from Moira. The facing message was long and rambling, leaping from romantic nothings to comments on minutiae. It was hard to compose these things and get in all the letters necessary for the real message.

The real message was this:

I'm furious I'll miss you by so little. And no chance to write while you're on your way either. Write me when you get there.

Be careful, this is way more attention than I wanted you to have. God I miss you. If you were here I'd…

My cheeks heated and I folded the note. That part, I would read alone. "I'm going to Venus," I said quietly. "You'll need to hold all my messages till I signal you from there."

"I will," he said at the same volume. He pushed up from the table and whisked away through the air. I sat a moment longer with my message and my tea. Moira was irrepressible as ever. Even with the letters of her words split and scattered, so I had to pick them out and reassemble them, the tone of her voice came through: half mocking, half passionate. That little hint that said, *I know this makes you uncomfortable, officer, and that's why I'm doing it. Because let's be real, we both get off on making you uncomfortable.*

I tucked the paper into the inside pocket of my coat and made for airlock A1. She wasn't wrong.

❧

When Vasiliev and I boarded the ship, the first mate was standing on the quarterdeck, supervising an almost empty sail deck. Michael Shen-Armstrong, that would be. He was rangy, all big bones with nothing much on them. Wisps of straw-colored hair, working loose from his queue, floated above vague blue eyes. He saluted. "Captain."

"Mister Shen," she acknowledged. "May I introduce our second mate, Lieutenant Lucy Prescott-Chin."

I saluted. "Sir."

"There's hardly anyone here yet," Vasiliev said, turning away from the quarterdeck. "Care to join me on a tour? You'll need it; this ship is different from most."

She led me and my opposite number forward along the sail deck, a large space the length and width of the ship, though only ten feet high. "You see that this much of the ship is the same," she said. "The sail controls need room to operate."

"Are they bigger than the sails on other ships, sir?" Shen asked, as we passed the massive wooden levers that would extend and fold the masts.

"A little," said Vasiliev. "There's a limit on how big we can make them and still be able to fold them up again as needed. You could see from outside that they're bulky, even furled. But most of the extra speed we get from the lower mass."

"Naturally," said Shen. "F equals ma; if you lower the mass, you increase the acceleration linearly."

I cast him a glance. It was a rather obvious statement—that equation was part of what we did every day; he might assume Vasiliev and I would know it too. But if I was looking for confirmation that he wasn't too bright, I hadn't seen it yet.

The captain led us to the upper decks—or rather, the upper deck. "To keep the sails in the middle, the housekeeping deck is below the sail deck instead of above," she explained. "Up here there is only the algae deck."

It was a long, low-ceilinged room running the length of the ship. I inhaled the familiar scent of yeast and algae—like a brewery next to a pond. Sun streamed in from the window overhead. Or, I might better say, the window in this room was pointed toward the sun. That was close enough to feel like "up," to a human mind that expected one.

"You can see we've put the water processing system here as well," Vasiliev continued. "To keep it near the water tanks, and to save space below. Which—well, you'll see."

Passing back down through the sail deck and below, I soon saw what she meant. The lower decks were close, even closer than the *Mariposa*'s. There, I could barely fit upright between ceiling and floor. Here, the only choice was to curl up my legs or hang at an angle. The compressed wood of the decks and bulkheads was still fresh and light-colored, but that didn't do much to make it look spacious. Nothing could.

"Is this the gun deck, sir?" I asked, half incredulous. There were a few five-pounders and that was it.

"I told you, they don't plan on us needing to engage the enemy. If a ship comes from behind us, it'll never be able to catch us, and if it's coming from the opposite direction, it'll have time for one broadside at maximum before we're well out of range."

I fell silent. One broadside could do damage enough, and what if an enemy's speed happened to be close to ours? Earth ships, trawling their orbit, went thirty knots even without using sails or fuel. Could this ship reliably go faster than that?

The gun deck seemed oddly short, and as we moved aft I saw what the trouble was. Giant berths, stretching down through the storage deck, each with a full-sized door. Vasiliev smiled at my incredulous stare. "I know, it's like a traveling hotel. It was felt there was only so much we could expect civilians to tolerate."

She let us peek inside one. A full bed, with russet and gold coverlet and straps to keep the sleeper inside. Velvet hangings. A lightweight plastic dresser, painted black. The ceiling was at least eight feet high. "Empty space doesn't increase the weight," she said, a little defensively. "Anyway, if we can transport the passengers with a minimum of complaints, it'll be that much easier on us."

"Best not to let the men get a look inside, though, sir," I said. "If they're sleeping on that tiny gun deck..."

"We'll only have a complement of twenty," she said. "No need to fill up a gun crew or boarding parties. Of course that will change all of the usual work rosters."

I nodded slowly. One of the challenges on a Navy ship was to make work for the number of spacers we needed to get through the battles. When we weren't in battle, we couldn't just let them sit around. Forty spacers can think of a world of trouble when their hands are idle. Twenty would give us the opposite problem; they'd be run off their feet.

The rest of the tour showed us the environmental control room, the exercise room, and the storage—mostly food and spare sail and mast material. No need for much ammunition, or any fuel. The oxygen tanks, at least, were the usual number.

"I need to get back to the station and start putting together my crew," said Vasiliev, having led us back to the sail deck.

"Do we need to organize a press gang, sir?" asked Shen.

A slight frown appeared between her eyebrows. "I've been told not to," she said. "After what happened with the *Mariposa*, the Admiralty is suspicious of pressed spacers. It's one thing on a normal mission, but on one this sensitive…" She trailed off. "I'll have to speak with the other captains here in port. I'm allowed to requisition whatever men I need, but I don't want to make enemies either. It may take the rest of the day. You two, use the men I have so far and get the ship looking its best. The passengers arrive first thing in the morning."

Captain Vasiliev shuttled the prince and his entourage over herself. The rest of us, Shen and I and all the men, were turned out in our finest, at attention on the sail deck. The men craned their necks to see the prince as he came through the airlock to the sound bosun's pipe. He cut a fine figure in a long dark coat edged in gold braid, with his sleek black hair floating free in a starburst around his head.

"Allow me to introduce my officers, my prince," said

Vasiliev. "Lieutenant Michael Shen-Armstrong, my first mate; Lieutenant—"

"I've met Miss Prescott," said the prince, meeting my eye with a delighted smile. "Sorry—Lieutenant Prescott. What a surprise to see you here."

I bowed, touching my hat. "Your Highness." That was a puzzle. If he hadn't requested me for this mission, who had? Could it really be a coincidence?

Vasiliev introduced our three midshipmen, fresh-faced in blue coats. They made their awkward salutes. Then the captain straightened and addressed the men from the quarterdeck rail. "You were selected for this mission because of your demonstrated loyalty and valor. And while it may gall your spirits to miss out on combat for the next few months, be assured that this mission may do more for the war effort than any other you've yet served." Then it was the Navy hymn, "Rule Imperium," and the men leapt to their stations.

"I can show you your cabin now, my prince," the captain offered, "unless you'd rather see the sails deployed."

"I couldn't miss it," he answered.

As he passed by me with his entourage, I recognized another face in the group. "Why, Miss Liu!" I cried. "I didn't expect to see you here!"

She was neatly outfitted in close-fitting breeches and a short red coat. Her dark hair crisscrossed her head in neat braids. "Ah, Lieutenant—Prescott, was it?" she asked coolly. "What a surprise." Then she passed on to press against the stern window with the others. I was left blinking after her. All that overpowering attention at the Emprex's party, and now she barely remembered me?

"She's the new assistant foreign minister," said Vasiliev quietly. "You know her?"

"Met her at a party, sir. She didn't strike me as the political type." Except insofar as aspiring to marry rich was political. But what about all that talk about politics and how little it mattered? Foreign minister was an imperial appointment, and thus theoretically nonpartisan, but it still didn't match the impression I'd gotten of her as a careless young woman playing the marriage market. I clearly wasn't as good at reading people as I'd thought.

"All hands, prepare to make sail," Vasiliev called in a louder voice. "Mister Alves, if you would?"

The bosun, a small, dark man with muscular shoulders and a shaved head, shouted, "Mainmast aloft!" The men hauling at the mainmast levers began the chant to synchronize their motions, but I had stopped listening.

"Sir," I said quietly to Vasiliev, "was that an Earth accent?"

She nodded. "Alves defected from Earth. He has experience in this kind of courier ship."

"Do we know we can trust him, sir?" I asked mainly because I felt that was what a loyal lieutenant ought to ask. But I also had my own doubts. If this ship was piloted by an Earther, would we even arrive at Venus? I had no desire to spend the rest of the war in a Luna prison.

"He came over with rafts of intelligence," she said. "Things I don't think Earth wanted us to know. The Admiralty trusts him."

That's no evidence, I wanted to say. The Admiralty trusts *me*. But I held my peace. The men finished unfolding the mainmast and moved on to the foremast. The huge levers took three men each to move. The men hooked their feet into floor straps and pulled down. Outside, the slim, light masts unfurled, fold upon fold, for miles.

"Align at two hundred nineteen point six degrees," the captain said, and the bosun cranked the wheel around and locked it down. Then, at last, it was time to unfold the sails themselves. The men cranked at a hydraulic pump, while behind me the prince and his entourage gasped. I knew the sight: shimmering fabric, mirroring the stars, unfurling as the spars opened. It cut the vast spangled darkness in half, turning it into something the mind could process: a night sky over a still lake, perhaps, alien only by its strange angle.

"Sails open, intact, and aligned," reported Shen from the stern window.

"Signal Phobos that we are ready for launch."

With a pocket mirror, Shen sent the flash message. A moment later he announced, "The laser has fired, sir."

The acceleration imparted by the laser, even on this light ship, was too faint to detect. It would take days before we picked up much relative speed. But, over the weeks it took to get to Venus, we'd soon be plowing sunward at a good clip.

Vasiliev went aft to the prince's entourage. "Your Highness, sir, madam. Shall I show you to your cabins? They are just below. The servants may berth with the men."

"My valet will sleep in my room," said the prince firmly. "I need them at all hours."

The valet was a small, dark, unobtrusive person in all black. "Let me fetch you a hammock, then," I offered. They gave a deferential nod.

Outside the passenger cabins, the prince, the foreign minister, and Miss Liu milled around, exclaiming at the cramped quarters (ha!) and having their luggage brought in. I passed them, the valet behind me, in search of a hammock.

"You'll be more comfortable in the prince's cabin anyway," I commented, as I opened the locker where they should be. "The men aren't quiet, here on the gun deck." No, nothing but oxygen bottles and masks. Damn.

"I just need to be settled by the time the prince's anti-emetics wear off," they said. "He was sick as soon as the elevator got near the top. The doctor says at some point he needs to get off of them or he'll never adjust to space."

"That's a fact," I said, and opened the next locker. Success!

I handed them a hammock and moved to the next locker. "Here. This should have—yes." I took out a thick stack of folded paper bags. "For—well, you can guess. And tie his hair back. Loose hair doesn't play well in space."

They smiled. "Very thoughtful. Thank you, Lieutenant—"

"Prescott," I filled in.

"Sagan," they replied. Taking the spacesickness bags and the hammock, Sagan picked their way aft again to rejoin the others.

8

MOIRA

The *Mariposa* didn't so much hit orbit as get hit by it. Her upstream course put her almost in a collision course with Mars, and she couldn't rely on a braking laser to stop her. Instead she came in low with her sails furled, burned off some velocity in the upper atmosphere, and slung into an eccentric orbit far from the crowded areas around Phobos.

Trey had come through with a promise of false papers, though it took more than half my available cash to pay for them. Marron scowled his protest, but he knew better than to keep arguing when my mind was made up. "Take someone with you. I'd go, if—"

I glanced pointedly at his legs. "I don't need anyone with me."

"Nguyen would," he suggested. "Or Ntumba."

"They're both deserters too. All the Martian crew is, and I don't have money for a second set of papers."

"An Earther then. Foulet?"

I glanced at the petite woman polishing a sail lever below. Her scrawny appearance was deceptive; she was a martial arts master and utterly without remorse when it came to taking lives.

"Foulet scares me," I said under my breath. "Anyway, traveling with an Earther will make me *much* more conspicuous. There's a war on; she'd be held up for hours in customs. That's if they let her go down the elevator at all. No Earthers."

"No Martians and no Earthers…" Marron trailed off. "Wait. Harrington's not a deserter. Take her."

The quiet, mousy woman had been unobtrusively helpful since she'd come aboard. After the merchant captain had left her behind, I'd assumed she must be useless as a sailor. But, while she wasn't experienced, she worked hard and had learned most of the ropes by now. By the time we got back to Liberty, I meant to rate her Able.

"Fine," I said, rolling my eyes. "If it makes you happy. But it's highly possible she pulls a runner when she gets down to the surface. She already ditched one crew. Maybe she just doesn't like space that much."

⌀

Trey met us at the airlock with the passport. "Things are jumpy here," he said. "Lie low and don't attract attention. There was another impressment riot yesterday."

"Another?" I tucked the booklet into my jacket. "Is that a thing now?"

"More and more," said Trey. "It's not an organized thing, but when it happens, all the spacers' union guys join in."

"Including you?"

"Me? No. I can't afford to lose my job. I'd be no use to you if I did, would I?"

"Just checking. Did Lucy leave?" My heart raced, even though I knew of course she had.

"Yeah, I saw her on her way out. She looked fine."

I groaned. "'Fine.' You're killing me, Trey." Turning behind me, I nodded to Nguyen, who was piloting the launch. "Stay in orbit for a week if you can. If I don't call you back, just go. Or if they spot you. I'm not having you risk anything for me."

"Isn't that Marron's call?" asked Nguyen. "I don't think he'll—"

"You hogtie him and man the wheel yourself if you have to. I'm not having it." I turned to Harrington. "You got your papers?"

Harrington patted her pocket. "Right here."

I grabbed my bag with one hand and the wall with the other, propelling myself down the narrow concourse. The private-shipping airlocks at Phobos were grungy, the walls dim with grime. After passing several airlocks and weaving through the usual streams of people, we arrived at the crossing of several concourses and a customs post.

The uniformed stationer glanced through my passport. "What ship did you come in on?"

"*Labyrinthus Venture*," I answered promptly.

It was in orbit outside; a reasonable answer.

"Staying on the station or going downstairs?"

"Downstairs. Staying with family."

The man stamped my passport and let me through. I silently let out a breath. I'd been through here dozens of times, it was always a quick formality, but this time I was a wanted criminal.

Then he turned around and said, "Wait."

I froze. Did he recognize me? I didn't recognize him. But then, I had been knocking around this station between trips for years. People knew me. Most of them would know enough to keep their mouths shut, but would he?

"You almost went off without your girlfriend," the man said with a grin, gesturing to Harrington.

Right. I laughed. "So I did. Sorry, babe." I cast Harrington an apologetic look.

Harrington took her passport back from the stationer and came through to grab my hand. "Ready, honey?" She looked shyly up at me. A better actress than I might have thought.

The elevator itself was only a little beyond. "I wonder why he thought we were gay," Harrington said idly, as we settled into our third-class seats.

"Probably because I am," I said. "Not you?"

Harrington shook her head, pink blooming into her pale face. "Sorry, I guess I assumed about you."

"No worries." I stowed my small bag into the pocket on the ceiling. It weighed nothing now, but over the course of the flight it would try to tumble toward the back of the car. "I have a girl-friend, so it's not like I'm going to hit on you."

"Oh—who is it?"

"No one you know." I winked. "She goes to a different school."

Harrington did not do a runner in Landing, though I careful-ly left her chances to do it. I had no time to babysit, and I'd only brought her because Marron made me. But instead, Harrington made herself useful finding a train schedule and buying two tick-ets to Nepenthe, with transfer slips for Gagaringrad. From there we'd have to look for a hydrobus to Schaeberle, where my parents lived now.

After Lord Chin-Prescott, Lucy's father, had sold his horses, my father had been out of a job. He'd opted to stay with the horses, which meant he was stablemaster now for a lesser but wealthier lord on the other side of Hellas basin.

"Where are you from, anyway?" I asked as we boarded the first train.

"From here," she said. "Landing. All my life."

"City slicker, eh? Hope this trip doesn't disappoint you. There's not much to do in the countryside."

"It's not like I've never left the city at all," she objected. "I went to Elysium on a school trip once."

I chuckled. "It's nothing like Elysium, that's for sure. Picture fewer beach umbrellas, more cows."

The train ran westward, along the shore, for the first several hours. Mars is divided largely into ocean in the north and cold desert to the south, making the coast in the middle the most populous region. We passed harbors, factory towns, and miles of farms.

We had just curved away from the shore to bypass Mt. Apollinaris when a low, urgent *thump* came from the front of the train, followed by a deafening screech. The first sound triggered my reflexes enough that I automatically braced myself against the seat in front of me, so when the train car lurched I wasn't hurt.

Harrington, though, was flung forward against the seat and then started to slide sideways. The train car was beginning to tip.

I flung out an arm and grabbed Harrington around the waist before she could slide into the aisle. Then, as if drifting through water, the car slowly overbalanced and fell onto the bank.

There was a tremendous, tearing crash as the side of the car hit the rocky ground and rapidly decelerated. Not that I was paying much attention; the impact was too much for the handholds I had, and for a moment I knew nothing but chaos as I tumbled across the aisle and down toward the ground.

When everything was still again, I took stock of myself. Legs, both bruised but moveable. Arms, functional. Head, bumped but not concussed, I didn't think.

I lay on top of a pile of luggage. Everything had tipped out of the rack; my attempt to brace myself had slowed my fall enough that I'd landed on it, not under it. Curled up next to me, Harrington stirred.

"You all right, sailor?" I asked.

Harrington sat up blearily. A cut on her forehead dripped blood into her eyes. "I ...*think* so?"

"Come on then," I said, starting to dig through the carpetbags and duffles. "Thank god we're in third class. Gentlemen love those hard-sided suitcases."

"I think our bags are probably a loss."

I gave her a withering glance. Well, maybe she'd had a knock on the head. "I'm digging for survivors, if you care to help."

The next suitcase I moved revealed a bloody arm, not moving. The bag after that exposed the rest of the body. Quite obviously dead. I had been afraid of this. I turned away, moved on to look for someone who could be helped.

The train had fortunately not been going its top speed, thanks to the curve of the track, so things were better than they might have been. Most of the people who had been sitting next to the windows on the lefthand side were dead, either cut by glass or killed by hitting the rocky ground at such speed. But those who had been on the right side were almost all alive, and those on the aisle mostly were. I focused my efforts there, and at last Harrington came to help me, taking suitcases from me and flinging them in a pile.

Vaguely, I realized she might be dealing with panic. The explosion had triggered all my Navy reflexes: a cold, almost clinical detachment; quick triage; the instant skip of my eyes away from someone as soon as I found they could not be saved. But these weren't sailors, so I forced myself to mutter what reassurances I could. "You'll be all right. Here, lean on him. Hold that arm close to your chest."

I kicked out the back door of the car, which was stuck, and started helping people out. "Get out as fast as you can," I called to those behind me. "I haven't heard the engine go, which means it still might."

"I heard a bang," said an old woman. "Wasn't that it?"

"Didn't sound like an engine explosion to me," I said. "Sounded like a bomb."

We clambered out from between the cars and headed up the

bank. From there, I could see the damage. The bomb had gone off under one of the passenger cars, which was totally destroyed. But it was a blessing in disguise. A few seconds sooner, and it would have gone off under the engine and turned it into a flaming ball of hydrogen.

Hydrogen isn't, of course, the safest fuel for trains. But with no fossil fuels anywhere on the planet, and electricity illegal, hydrogen was the most efficient option. Just inconveniently explosive.

The engine sat on the tracks half a mile ahead, having been cut loose by the bomb. Men were walking back to assess the damage.

"It's a bomb all right," confirmed the engineer, when he'd had a look. "More of those anarchists or republicans or whatever they call themselves. I hope they're happy, killing dozens of people and most of them common too. How the hell they can expect any sympathy from the rest of us with stunts like this, I couldn't tell you."

"How are we going to get to Nepenthe?" asked the old woman.

"We've radioed up the line for a new train. Shouldn't be more than a couple hours."

Harrington pulled me aside, across the grass to the wooden fence separating the railway from the neighboring farm. "What do you think about all this?"

"About what, the delay? I'm not excited about it."

"About radicals! Bombing trains! Is that our sort of line, since we're," she dropped her voice, though we were far from the others, "pirates?"

"No, it fucking isn't," I said. "I never heard of such a thing."

"It happens all the time now," said Harrington seriously. "Bombs on trains, bombs in factories and government buildings. They say it's Khan's movement."

I frowned. Khan had never written a thing about bombing trains. "I'll believe that when I see it," I said at last.

9

Lucy

The first few days of the voyage were a rush of activity, as everyone tried to figure out what they were supposed to be doing at any given time, how to get the wood of the decks scrubbed and the water treated and the laundry washed with so few people. My tasks as a lieutenant weren't that different from what I had done as a midshipman, but now I had the midshipmen to watch over as well.

The senior midshipman, Ivanov, had years of experience under her belt, so she was a big help. She had already shown the other two their berth and taught them how to clip up their hammocks, run a fan, and tell time by the ship's bells. But the second, Hartnell, was on his first mission despite being seventeen or so. He was surly all the time—never blatantly disrespectful, just slow to answer and sour in his tone. He didn't have to say he didn't want to be here with us, because he made it obvious every moment he was awake.

My watch was assigned the third, Zhang. He was twelve, cheerful, eager to please though rather poor on follow-through. I could have done worse. He was too young for the men to haze; instead they kept an eye out for him when he was off duty and kept him out of trouble.

The first two days out from orbit, Alves the bosun barely slept. He was too busy carefully adjusting the sails so they presented the exact same angle to the launching laser, even as we slid sunward from Mars. Then, as Phobos passed out of alignment, we were carried by the orbital laser at Mars' Lagrange point. It was important to catch every photon of that laser we could, since it was many times more powerful than the sun. Once we passed out of its range, nothing else could give us so much acceleration until we were close to Venus.

The second day out, I was on watch when the blinding light from aft finally winked out. A moment later Zhang vaulted the quarterdeck rail—he'd spent all watch coming and going, carrying messages from the forecastle, the sail deck, and anywhere else. "Sir, the passengers say their head is backed up."

I rubbed my forehead. It was one thing after another with these passengers. The prince was still completely incapacitated with space sickness, but the other two seemed to live to annoy the crew. Was it possible to get a bath? Why did the crank fans make so much noise? Were there any more pillows anywhere? I did not answer—though I wanted to—what the hell do you need a pillow for? Is your neck tired of holding your head up in no gravity or what? Do you think we cut two thirds of the guns out of the ship to fill up the saved mass with pillows and little mints to put on them?

"Have Torres look at it," I told him. "And inform the captain we are ready to reverse the sails."

Vasiliev appeared on deck in short order, twitchy with repressed excitement. "Shall we see how these new sails handle? Mister Alves, prepare to reverse sail."

Alves shouted orders, and the men began to work. It seemed

the larger sails were so unwieldy they had to be partly furled before they could be pivoted about to their new bearing. The mainsail was taken in, then the foresail, and at last Alves turned, one at a time, the great wheel controlling each.

The first pivoted smoothly about. But when the foresail had come halfway about, one of the reefing levers abruptly crashed from the floor to the ceiling. The men hung in the air, stricken—none hurt, but all acutely aware that they could have been.

"What the hell happened?" cried Alves. "What was that lever even doing down? I told you to put it up!"

"You said make a reef, sir," stammered the bos'n's mate. "I made one, you didn't say two."

"One reef means two levers, you nitwit. On a sail this size it takes two levers to make one full reef."

By now I was halfway up the sail deck. A glance from Vasiliev had directed me up to the forecastle, to take a look out the window and see what was amiss.

It was exactly as I might have imagined. The foresail, insufficiently furled, had crashed into the mainsail and gotten fouled with it. A cloud of sparkling fog around the broken spar showed a hydraulic line had been breached. At least one.

By the time I returned to give my report, both Alves and his mate hung at attention before Vasiliev. "I am sorry, sir," Alves was saying. "I failed to account for the inexperience of the crew."

"Inexperience my ass," the mate spat. "Begging your pardon, sir. I've been working sails ten years. I know what he said and that's exactly what I did."

"Perhaps in Earth Force that's how they speak," said Vasiliev. "But it was your job to verify all sails were properly furled before you inverted them, Mister Alves. I do hold you responsible for this accident."

"Accident," muttered the mate under her breath.

"What was that, Mister Bergeron?"

"Nothing, sir."

I gave my report on the sail, and Vasiliev nodded gravely. The sail should be fixable, but the men's mistrust of Alves couldn't be so easily glossed over. "Mister Alves, you will do the repair," she said at last. "You know these sails and it's only right to fix what you broke. I'm sending Lieutenant Prescott with you. Please defer to her judgment as required." A glance to the bosun's mate telegraphed, *See, I'm sending someone I trust out with him, he can't get up to anything.*

I turned to Alves. "I'll show you where the EVA suits are."

❧

Two hours later, we were creeping along the foremast, trying to find the source of the hydraulic leak. The fog had dissipated too much to pin it down, so the only thing for it was to inspect every inch. Our tethers snaked away behind us, down the long expanse of the mast to the tiny ship, small as a toy from here.

"Not too fast," I warned Alves. "The masts here are thin, they can't brake you if you're moving fast."

"I know that," Alves snapped sourly. "Sir."

I let it go. The man had broken a delicate piece of equipment, on which our lives relied completely, and it wasn't exclusively his fault.

"So go ahead," said Alves. "Ask the question."

"Excuse me?"

"The question everyone asks. I know you're thinking it. Sir."

For a moment I was baffled. What's Earth like? Why did you come here? And then I realized what it must be. "You mean, how do we know we can trust you?"

He gently grasped the mast, slender here as a radio antenna, and brought himself to a stop. "That's the one." He inspected the hydraulic line, found it undamaged, and carefully set himself in motion again.

"You just want me to ask it, or were you planning to answer?"

He gave a soft grunt. "You can trust me because I hate Earth more than any of you do. That's the reason."

"You hate your own planet?"

"It's a cesspool," he said. "Oh sure, there are nice parts, but nobody can ever afford to live there. Anything that's worth a profit is farmed in tidy little lines, and anything that's not is bulldozed for the shit that is. Almost two hundred separate countries, with their separate little governments, and somehow a dozen men run everything. Because if you've got enough money you can make a nation dance your tune, and those men are richer than God."

"Two hundred countries?" I asked, baffled. "If there are that many governments, then who runs Earth Force? Is there a planetary government?"

He laughed. "Earth Force isn't a navy, not like you think of a navy. It's a corp like all the others. The other corps that operate off-planet pay Earth Force to protect their interests. And to keep trying to take you over, whenever they feel it's a profitable wager."

"And you worked for them?"

"I did." He braked again to inspect another segment. "I thought, this planet's a crock of shit; maybe I can get out into the stars where there isn't so much trash everywhere. Stretch myself out. There was good money in it, too. First time in my life I made enough to spot my family a loan when they needed it. Even health insurance. I got my mama a new hip." The leak wasn't there, and he moved on.

"It wasn't what you'd hoped?"

"Oh, it was at first. Then I got downsized. Laid off. You see, Earth Force realized, like every damn corp on the planet has realized, that full-time employees with benefits don't make sense. You can turn a much bigger profit if you turn to private contractors. So more and more, that's what they do."

"Pirates," I said. "We've been facing a lot more of those than Earth Force, these days."

"That's the idea," he said. "And it just burns me up. They make it so you can't make a living on Earth or in space, and once you're pushed into the one job left, you're disposable. They'll throw you at jobs too big for you, and if you wind up dead, they've saved their money. My girlfriend tried that route. I told her no, but she said hey, got to make money somehow. And her ship was lost not a month later. Earth didn't care."

"I'm sorry," I said, not least because presumably it had been the Martian Navy that had killed her. But also because I knew he was completely right. That had been exactly the treatment Moira had gotten as an Earth contractor.

He pulled himself gently to a stop. "Gotcha, you little bastard." He unslung the repair kit from his shoulder and opened it up. "Sorry, sir. I forget about the sirs. Earth isn't big on reminding people we're not all a big, happy family. It's harder to see what's going on when your CO says 'Hey, Frank, you working hard or hardly working? We're all on the same team, gotta pull together!' Big slap on the shoulder, you get to thinking he's your dad, not the guy who makes triple what you ever will."

"Is it just a simple tear or are we going to have to take the whole tube out?"

"Little bitty guy. Patch should do." He rifled through the kit carefully, sausage fingers inside pressurized gloves making the simple operation much harder.

"How long have you been on Mars?"

"Oh—hardly any time, really. I was down for two months, getting debriefed, and then when they started building this old girl here, they shipped me up to Phobos to advise. Earth has ships like this, you see. Not in Earth Force, but to get themselves around.

The bigwigs don't like spending months eating Spam and pissing in a vacuum cleaner."

He had forgotten, again, who I was and how he was supposed to talk, but I didn't care. He reminded me of Moira's first mate, Marron, though they looked nothing alike. Marron was a human mountain. But the Earther irreverence was the same.

"Well, how do you know Mars is any better than Earth?" I ventured. "You can't just join up with us because you don't like Earth."

"I know one thing, you don't have any fucking corps. There's shit you do that's utterly ridiculous, it's like a godawful period piece, but if the fairytale works, who am I to judge? That boy indoors thinks he's a prince, and you know what? That makes him one. Because he believes it and he's got you all believing it, and it's a spell that's forcing Earth to believe it. The corps own Earth, they own space, they own every single fucking thing in the system—except you. Because you pushed them back. You made them respect you. So hell yeah I can join you because I hate Earth. You're the anti-Earth."

I was just enough of a pedant to point out, "Well, there's Venus too."

"Ha," he said. "Venus. Now there's a joke. They got out and locked the fire exit behind them. How's that gotta look to the rest of us? What's the point of getting free of Earth if you won't let anybody else do the same?" He finally got the patch off its backing and smoothed it onto the hydraulic tube.

"You're not wrong," I said. "I'm hoping this mission will stir them up a little."

"I have my doubts."

I flipped the switch alongside my helmet to call back to the ship. "Run some fluid in that line. We think we've got it."

We waited while the mast gently stiffened itself out below us. The tube tensed as it passed us, but nothing spilled out. I kept looking till the ripple had run its way to the end of the mast. No more leaks.

"Thank you for your work, Mister Alves," I said, to restore the formality we'd let drop over the spacewalk. "I see no reason to doubt you, after this conversation."

" 'Preciate it," he said. "Sir."

After unsuiting and making my report to the captain, I went down to the tiny berth I shared with Shen to change my clothes. Vasiliev had agreed to take the rest of my watch in exchange for me taking some of hers, so I had a few hours. The sweaty jumpsuit I'd worn under my spacesuit went in the laundry bag, and I treated myself to a clean shirt. I left my tricorn hat off—here onboard ship, where there was no indoors or outdoors, hats were worn only when we were on duty.

What I really wanted, especially with a new watch ahead of me, was a cup of tea. Weak shipboard tea was at least something, so I made my way up to the galley. Tucked away in one corner of the sun deck, it was nothing but a few pressure cookers, a magnetic plate to secure them, a small rack of spices and utensils, and a large Fresnel lens.

Cooking in space is a challenge. Fire consumes oxygen, which makes it absolutely out of the question. An electric coil would work, but it would require adding a whole electric circuit to that part of the ship. The *Adamant* had electricity in only two places: the radio and the space suits. Getting legal approval to add another would rely on there being no other solution, but there was another source of heat on the ship: the sun. The lens focused the heat enough to boil water in a few minutes.

Normally tea on a ship is weak, because the air pressure is

lower than on Mars and the water boils away before it ever gets truly hot. But I had a craving and nothing better to do, so I spent a truly unreasonable amount of time cobbling together a miniature pressure cooker for my tea with a foil packet and a clamp.

After exactly four minutes of steeping, I took off the clamp, fastened a straw onto the opening, and tasted it. Perfect. It would be better with milk, but the aroma of good tea was really enough. It was hot enough here in the diffuse sunshine to make me sweat, but I sat right there in the air and sipped my tea.

Alves probably wasn't wrong about Earth. That upset me—had always been the thing that upset me most about my betrayal. That the war was always framed as a binary, Mars or Earth, and if I opposed Mars, I was bound to tip the scales toward Earth. I had taken from Mars the space station that had meant so much to the war effort. Leaving it in the hands of pirates hadn't been as bad as Earth getting it, but it was bad enough that now Venus was (if I guessed their motives correctly) worried we'd lose the war.

If Alves had spent more time on Mars, he'd have noticed we weren't his perfect fairytale. He'd have been handled with kid gloves by the Admiralty, treating him to the best Mars had to offer while milking him for all the information they could. Would his loyalty last past the first flogging he witnessed?

If it didn't, I felt confident he wouldn't break for Earth at least. If he could somehow be put in touch with Moira, he might go her way. She could probably use a man like him. But I wasn't sure how I could influence him at all without destroying my own cover.

My tea-inspired reverie was interrupted by someone coming up the hatch: Sagan, picking their way from object to object, as people do when they haven't yet got the hang of space. "Oh—hello, Lieutenant. Do you know where the cook is? The prince thinks he can stand a little tea and crackers."

I grinned, feeling generous. "You don't need the cook," I said.

"I have just revolutionized shipboard tea brewing and I feel the need to share. Let me show you."

I walked Sagan through my new tea ritual. "Tea in space usually isn't brewed right," I explained, as we waited for the water to heat.

"I know," they said sourly. "We had some at Phobos."

"I still don't have milk. You *could* have milk in space, but given the weight limits—"

"I quite understand. Luckily the prince prefers his black in any event. But are there crackers?"

"There's a little packet. They won't last, but it's useful to have them on hand for the first days out. Some cooks manage to bake a kind of substitute, but I can't recommend them. Honestly, I can't recommend much of anything the galley makes. Especially not the algae. It's very wholesome and keeps away the scurvy, but it tastes like pond scum, because it is."

The thermometer hit one hundred degrees, and I covered the lens again. "Now all you need is to wait four minutes for it to steep. Or a little less, since we started with the bag in. I'm still perfecting my technique."

"Of course." They accepted a hot mitt to hold the tea pouch, took the tea, and turned to go. I took the crackers and followed them down through the ship to the prince's cabin.

At the door, Sagan turned. "Wait here a moment. I need to ask something."

When they reappeared, it was to straighten formally and announce, "The prince requests the pleasure of your company at tea."

I followed them inside, a little embarrassed. I hadn't expected that.

The room was still pin-tidy, almost unchanged from before he had arrived. The prince sat wrapped in a blanket, still looking a little green. "Ah, Lieutenant Prescott! Sagan was telling me of your help. Much appreciated."

"I didn't mean to curry favor, Your Highness." I bowed in the air, still flustered. "I'm only very particular about tea."

"That's why I appreciate it so much," he said. "I notice when people are kind to my valet. Everyone's considerate of *me*, to the point that it means nothing. To be kind to a servant shows admirable condescension."

"To be returned by admirable condescension from you to me, sir?"

"Hardly. Isn't your father a marquis? Or is that a different Prescott-Chin?"

"The same. But that's nothing to you, sir. You could walk to breakfast on a row of marquises and nobody would object."

He laughed out loud, then winced. The sharp head movement had surely triggered another wave of nausea. "Come, sit. I don't mean to spend the voyage talking only to my own delegation."

I took the other chair in the room, wrapping my ankles around the legs to keep myself in place. Sagan stayed afloat, hanging behind the prince's chair like a guardian angel. And perhaps that was what they were. If a prince brought exactly one servant with him, it seemed unlikely that servant wasn't also a bodyguard.

I gestured to a book hanging in the air near the prince. "What are you reading, sir?"

"Oh, all about Venus. They're quite open for an entirely closed society, if you know what I mean. You can't go there, but they'll tell you all about it."

"I found it so on Aphrodite Station, sir."

"So you know they have a completely egalitarian society? Or they claim to. I suppose they can say what they like." He sipped his tea and munched a cracker. "All I can think is, I would have been captivated by the idea when I was young and radical."

"*You*, sir, had a radical phase?"

"Oh, yes, didn't you? You seem about the age to have hit the time when you rethink everything you've taken for granted, right as Alexei Khan started writing. I think all of our generation were secretly Russets."

I felt stripped naked. Was it really that obvious? That common? "I suppose it's normal, sir," I said cautiously.

"Oh, I cried like a child when he died. I thought, for a few years there, that we were on the cusp of an inevitable change. Injustice was like a tension, which sooner or later must break, collapse, resolve. If it was that bad, surely it could not last. After he died—or after we thought he died—I realized that perhaps injustice is the natural thing, and equality is the unstable one. Look at us, and at Earth. Our ancestors broke away from Earth to escape the tyranny of a few, and the very first thing they did was create their own elite. Perhaps there *is* no other way to manage a society. Some will always have a head start, and they will always use that head start to lord it over the others."

He risked nothing talking like this. He was the Emprex's son; he could say what he wanted and no one could touch him. I risked everything if I agreed with it. For all I knew, he was baiting me into some kind of damaging confession. I couldn't take that chance, not when I'd already told Liu I was apolitical. But I couldn't miss the chance to ask questions of my own. I couldn't just perch on my chair, too intimidated to find out what only he could tell me.

"After we thought he died, sir?" I asked. "You think it's true then, that Khan is still alive?"

He gave me a conspiratorial grin. "It sure sounds like him, in the pamphlets. I don't know anyone else who writes like that."

I couldn't help smiling back. "It is his style, sir."

"If it is him, though, it's a problem," he said, smile vanishing. He tapped his lips with a finger. "Because someone faked his death. Not himself, I don't think—he never would have left the cause right when it was reaching a climax. But not the Emprex, either. I know them. They *liked* Khan. Just on a personal level—the man was a living saint; you had to admire him no matter what you thought of his cause."

"A person can admire someone and still want to silence them, sir." A flush rose to my cheeks. I was accusing the Emprex of kidnapping, to their own son, no less.

"No. Not them. No. My parent doesn't even *believe* the whole thing. They think the Khan letters are being written by Falwell."

I nodded. It wasn't proof the Emprex wasn't responsible, but it was as close as I was likely to get. "Do you think something will change this time, sir?"

"No," he said sadly, "I don't. The noise in the streets is louder than ever, but it doesn't matter in the end. Things don't reach a breaking point. People just discover they can bear more than they thought. One must hope that Parliament will do better, that they will listen to the Tribune, that small changes happen and make things better. But I'm not even sanguine about *that*. Ten years ago, there were twenty Russets in Parliament. Now there are five. Five voices for equal rights will never be heard over ninety-five for Founder privilege." He sighed and picked his book back out of the air. "If Venus is really something different, it will shock me."

He fell silent, returning to his book. It was my cue to take my leave. I bowed to the prince, exchanged an unreadable glance with Sagan, and went out.

10

MOIRA

My dads had settled at an estate grander than Lucy's. Not bigger, but fancier: bushes sculpted into animals, mosaic paths, a lodge that looked like a noble's town house all by itself.

The people there, however, weren't as friendly. A sour-faced gardener pointed us toward the stables with the muttered comment, "And mind you don't trample the grass."

At last the stables came into sight: a cluster of yellow pine buildings, circling a courtyard of dirt. A boy was lunging a young horse outside.

The stablemaster's apartment was on the second floor of the largest stable. My father Bill opened the door to my knock and stared at me like he'd seen a ghost. "Moira?"

"Hi, Dad. I got your message about Papa. Came as fast as I could."

Bill kept standing in the doorway, staring, for half a minute. I drank him in with my eyes: tall, rangy, skin brown and glossy like good leather. Exactly the same, only the gray had crept a little further out from his temples. After a moment he recovered him-self. "You'd better come in. Is this young lady a friend of yours?"

"Harrington's on my crew." I followed Bill into the little sit-ting room—just like the one we'd had growing up, smelling of hay and leather, decorated with mismatched furniture. Perhaps a bit smaller, or maybe I was bigger.

Bill shut the door and went to the woodstove in the corner to put the kettle on. "You should have told me you were coming."

"Why, so you could talk me out of it?"

"Yes! This is crazy, Moira. We've been managing. It's not worth your life."

"If anything happened to Papa, and I wasn't—I had to, Dad. In case."

Bill took a deep breath and let it out. "Well. That was unnec-essary, as it happens. The doctor says he's out of danger of dying."

I felt dizzy. Only now could I admit, even to myself, I'd been afraid he was dead already. But it was an odd way to put it, "out of danger of dying," rather than just "out of danger." "What *is* he in danger of?" I asked softly.

My father chewed the inside of his cheek. "It's not…for sure, yet." He poured out two cups of tea and handed one to Harrington. The other, he set on the sideboard. "If you'll excuse us, Miss Har-rington."

I followed him into the bedroom, which was almost com-pletely dark. Blankets had been pinned up over the curtains, to block more of the light.

"Ramesh," Bill whispered. "You awake, love?"

"I heard visitors," said Ramesh from the darkness. I couldn't see him, but his voice was as strong as ever.

Bill sat down beside the bed, in his usual fireside chair which had been pulled in here. I knelt down on the other side. As my eyes adjusted, I could make out Ramesh's head and his dark eyebrows. Nothing else.

"Papa, it's Moira," I said, groping on the blanket for his hand.

His hand grasped mine, and I squeezed tightly. "What are you doing here, kid?"

"Came to see you. You all right? Concussed?" It would explain the dark curtains.

He waved his free hand dismissively. "Almost over that part. At least doctor thinks so. Bill, did you tell her she shouldn't be here?"

"I did, for all she listened. She never did before, why should she start now?"

"Dad won't tell me what's the matter with you," I burst in. "I need to know."

Ramesh rubbed his face with his free hand. "I'd forgotten how pushy she is."

With every sentence he said, I started to feel a little better. He might be in bed, but he sounded his old self. His brain was surely all right, and that was the main thing. Everything. "So?"

He looked away and sighed. "It's only that I can't feel my legs, is all."

My belly went cold. "You hurt your spine?"

"Mm. Doctor says the nerves might reconnect, but they might not. Spines are funny things."

I sat back on my heels, stunned. For another man it would be a challenge. Life-changing, for sure: a new job, new life skills. But for him? A man who lived and breathed horses and nothing else in the world?

Bill put in, "We're allowed to stay here for a couple months, to wait and see. The squire doesn't want to lose him if there's a hope he'll be useful again."

"Useful?" I hissed. "He has more knowledge in his head than anyone else in the business put together! If he had the *least* sense—"

Ramesh patted my hand. "Please don't shout, kid."

I put my head down on the side of the bed and cried. Selfish of me to come here only to shine a spotlight on what they had to deal with. Selfish to cry when both of them had their brave faces on. But I had never been like Lucy, able to stand there with a face like marble no matter what happened. That was Founder nonsense, I'd always said, and here for the first time, I wished I had it.

Ramesh murmured to his husband, "Did you tell her *why* she shouldn't be here though? She's not acting like you told her."

I lifted my head from the bed, scrubbed at my eyes with my arm, and hiccupped. "What?"

"The crown knows you were involved with what happened at Liberty," Bill said quietly. "They came by here months ago, asking after you. There's a big reward out for anyone who finds you, on or off Mars. Alive by preference, dead acceptable."

I sniffed hard, trying to turn off the tears like a faucet. The shock was helping. "But I don't know anyone here," I said. "They won't know me."

"If you hang around us, they'll put two and two together. You have to go, the sooner the better."

Stricken, I looked from one of my parents to the other. "But I just got here."

"I'm sorry," said Ramesh. "I would have liked you to stay longer too."

The faces of everyone I'd seen or talked to flashed through my mind. The gatekeeper at the lodge, the sour-faced gardener, the boy exercising a colt. Had I told anyone my business? Or did I just ask the way to the stables?

"You're right," I said, jumping to my feet. "I'm not sorry I came, but I'll get out of your hair before I can bring any trouble."

"Baby girl—" Bill stood up.

"It's okay," I said, rounding the bed to give him a quick, inadequate squeeze. God, I needed a hundred of these, after all this time. "Have you asked the old squire for a place to stay? I know he would." Lucy's father would do anything for mine; the two had bonded over horses for decades.

"I couldn't, not when he's in so much trouble himself," said Ramesh. "He'd never have let me go in the first place if he could have afforded to keep me. We're thinking of going to the city, somewhere Bill could get a job."

"I'll look around, when we're there," I said, stooping to kiss his forehead. I pulled a wad of cash out of my pocket—what was left after all the expenses of getting here—and set it on the bedside table.

Back in the sitting room outside, Harrington waited placidly on the couch, hands wrapped around her teacup. "Sorry, sailor, time to go," I said. "I'd meant to stay the night here, but it looks like we have to head back to Schaeberle village. I'd like to get as far as Gagaringrad tonight if possible."

"The next hydrobus is at four." Harrington stood up and put her bag on her shoulder. "And another at five-thirty, if we can't walk the whole way by four."

I looked out the window. The land here rolled a little, in memory of ancient dunes, and the road dipped in and out of hollows before reaching the faraway lodge.

And along that road, not far from the gate, was a black van. Hardly anyone in the country drove powered vehicles except deliverymen and hydrobus drivers; they were expensive to fuel and ugly to look at. Peasants walked and nobles rode. But a black van like that? Nobody drove those but police.

"We're going to have to," I said. "I'm pretty sure five-thirty will be too late."

We hurried down the rough wooden stairs, through the stable, and outside. The boy who had been working in the yard was gone. Harrington started toward the road.

"No," I said. "There's a better way."

In the pasture behind the stable were all the best horses,

beasts I knew from back at Hellas Manor along with unfamiliar ones they must have bought more recently. My favorite was still Orbit, properly Orbital Resonance, champion of the Aescraeus Stakes and the Hesperia Classic. I'd helped train him since he was foaled. Now he was out to pasture, his racing career over, but still valuable enough as a stud that the squire here had thought him worth buying off the Prescott-Chins.

It took a while to find him in the pasture, sneak up on him, and bribe him with grain. For Harrington, I got Belle, mainly because she was gentle enough to be easy to catch. "You ride?" I asked.

"A couple times at fairs? I told you, I'm Landing born and bred." She tilted her head back to stare at Orbit with big eyes.

"You don't have to come with me," I said. "The police aren't looking for you. You can walk to the village and meet me in Gagaringrad tonight."

"I promised Marron I'd look after you," said Harrington firmly. "I'm sure I can ride a horse."

Grimacing dubiously, I made a stirrup to boost her up. Madness, expecting her to ride bareback, even as far as the village. At least Belle wouldn't dream of bucking her off. If she slid off, well, the gravity was low and the grass was soft.

But Harrington settled into a surprisingly good seat, and I gave her an approving glance before leaping onto Orbit's back. "We've wasted too much time," I said. "We'll have to cut across the park."

It was hard to worry much about the police behind us when I was on a horse's back again. The leggy Martian thoroughbreds fairly flew across the ground without half trying. Orbit was eager to go faster, but I signaled him to hold back. Wouldn't want to leave Belle in the dust with Harrington.

Beside me, Harrington's eyes were wide, but she kept her

seat. Luckily Belle needed no direction; she wanted to do whatever Orbit was doing.

We left the carefully-manicured park and traveled for a while through rougher territory: the wild grass that had been introduced to spread all over Mars, early in the terraforming game. A few trees and shrubs dotted the dunes.

At last the village came in sight, and I jumped down. I turned to help Harrington, but she had already tumbled off. "Phew," she said. "That isn't as easy as it looks!"

I sent the horses toward home with a slap and headed to the bus stop. By my watch, the bus would be here—oh, there it was, lumbering along the main street. We rushed to catch up and swung aboard as it paused for us.

As the bus rolled out of the village, hissing with steam, I looked out the window. Two police stood at the crossing where the road from the manor joined the village road, staring toward the park.

"Not a moment too soon," I murmured in Harrington's ear.

11

✳

LUCY

Being a lieutenant came with one perk: a berth shared with only Shen instead of two people and one cannon. But also one disadvantage: I was no longer expected to take most of my meals belowdecks with the crew, but had to take them all in the officers' mess.

The food was better—reconstituted meat and vegetables from foil packets instead of beans, rice, yeast, and algae—and the conversation was not, all things considered, so bad. I was allowed to speak at the table now, as midshipmen were not. But after my time with the pirates, the separation between officer and spacer felt artificial and awkward.

And, of course, there were the passengers to deal with.

"I don't understand," the Foreign Minister, Blackwell, was saying. "I was given the impression that this voyage would be somehow more luxurious than standard. That this was some kind of special ship just for diplomatic missions. But I've been uncomfortable literally every moment since we boarded." He picked at the stew glued onto his lightweight plastic plate with its own gravy.

"No Navy ship is comfortable," said Vasiliev dryly. "The extra luxury consists in you not having to stay on it nearly as long. It may be hard to believe, but Their Majesty's hardworking sailors are this uncomfortable for a year or more. And in smaller berths, too."

The prince, now recovered enough to join us at meals, turned his dark eyes to Vasiliev. "For my part, I'm nothing but thankful. I can't help but notice the constant efforts your crew make for our comfort."

Miss Liu, jealous of his attention, spoke up. "You ought to say for *your* comfort, my prince. I haven't noticed anybody's been put out for Blackwell and me at all."

That was a blatant lie, but the prince turned the floodlight of his gaze back on her. "Of course," he said soothingly, "I should remember that. If there is anything you lack, come to my berth; I'm sure we have it there."

It turned my stomach, watching him flirt back and forth like that. If indeed it was flirting. It seemed his way, to want to throw himself intensely at anyone who was nearby, show them how important they were to him by treating them like the only person in the room. Being at table with five other people was challenging that ability.

I excused myself as soon as I politely could. It was my watch soon, which made as good an excuse as anything. This time of evening, everyone who wasn't on watch was gathered on the gun deck, messing in little three-dimensional clusters. I approached one, half-consciously drawn to make conversation, but the talk stilled and they saluted instead.

It gave me a pang. As a midshipman I'd been welcome anywhere. And on Moira's ship, class didn't exist. I might have freed my mind from class requirements, but the rest of Martian society continued as it had. Nowhere in the Empire was any table where Moira and I could eat together.

Sighing, I went back up to the sail deck. It didn't matter how much I fought for commoners' rights; I still wasn't one and that was always going to matter more. Especially as I couldn't tell them any of it.

"Sir," said one of the men—Hendricks, the arms master's mate. "I saw something strange and I need you to come and look at it, sir."

"Of course." He led me to the port aft airlock, the one where the launch was docked. Beside that was the weapons locker, an upright cabinet that was always kept locked.

Only it was not locked.

"This was shut last night, when I had my watch," he said. "I could swear to it. And tonight it's open. I come straight to you so you would know it weren't me that opened it."

"Do you know who did, Mr. Hendricks?"

He screwed up his mouth, like he wanted to spit but didn't want to deal with the flying glob afterward. "A judas, sir."

"Excuse me?"

"They show up sometimes, sir, in a crew. Always wanting to start something. Always suggesting that maybe we could mutiny or cause some other trouble. But they aren't real. If you go along with them, they rat you out and everyone who was a part of it gets airlocked. Word goes around. If someone's always trying to start trouble, you steer clear."

I stared at him, wondering if this was paranoia speaking, or something else. "Any guesses who?"

He shook his head. "Nobody's said anything, sir. I felt like we were a real crew that could trust each other. Except for …" He trailed off.

"Alves?"

He gave a short, almost invisible nod.

"I don't think he'd have access to this locker," I said. "I will ask the captain. It could be she unlocked it for an inspection and forgot to lock it again."

I got the key from the captain, who had *not* unlocked it. "I keep the keyring in my pocket almost always," she said, brow furrowing. "Unless the officer of the watch needs it. Shen had it yesterday to open the stores, but he brought it straight back. Left it by my place at dinner."

I took the key back to the locker. A brief inspection showed nothing missing, no signs of tampering. Twenty-six cutlasses in rows, stuck on a strip of magnet. I shut it, locked it, and carried the key back to the captain.

Shen could have unlocked it. I had no reason to mistrust Shen, but the same could be said of anyone. Even Vasiliev could have, if she'd wanted to test the men, but I didn't see a reason for not telling me if so.

The other possibility was that someone had abstracted the keyring at dinner. Which broadened the list of suspects considerably. The prince, Blackwell, or Liu could have done it. Or whoever had been serving that meal—the second watch midshipman, Hartnell, and the prince's valet, Sagan.

None of them were common spacers; none of them had any real reason to do such a thing. But neither did anyone. Say Hendricks's claim was true, and spies regularly infiltrated Navy crews to stir up trouble. Who would be behind that?

It was a leap, but my mind couldn't let go of the possibility that it was the Privy Ministry again. It was the same as they'd done to me—dangle in front of me a chance to betray the Empire, in the hopes of catching me in the act.

Why wouldn't they do something like this? Especially after the loss of the *Mariposa*. They would want, first of all, to flush out any possible mutineers. But as an added bonus, if word got out, men would turn suspicious of any crewmate who proposed a mutiny.

I pushed back and forth across the quarterdeck, the null-gravity version of pacing. If I were a secret government ministry, the very first place I'd put an operative was on this ship. I had already suspected someone's very careful hand in the selection of the officers: a commander with no experience, a lieutenant who had managed to dodge promotion for fifteen years, and the failure who had lost Ares Station. That wasn't a careful selection for loyalty. That was a careful selection for *incompetence*.

Did someone want this mission to fail? Easier ways, if that was all it was. Unlocking the weapons was nothing, unlikely to actually threaten the ship, while it was fairly easy to prop a gun hatch open and let the air all leak out if someone wanted to. Hell, I could think of half a dozen ways to disable the ship or kill the crew, if one had a mind to do it and didn't care about surviving. I had been in such a mood before myself.

No, there was a more complicated plan at work, and I wasn't yet sure what it might be. The most important thing now was to keep them from flushing *me* out. If I could find them before we got to Venus, so much the better.

The incident was a reminder to be more careful. Here I was, chosen by a person or persons unknown, specifically for my incompetence, I suspected. But instead of trying to keep that cover, I'd been trying to be a perfect officer. Partly because I was trying to mimic the person I'd been before. Partly because I liked Vasiliev and didn't want to let her down.

It was time to screw up. Since my main crime in the loss of Ares Station had been falling asleep and failing to show up when expected, I should oversleep once in a while. That was more difficult than I predicted. I was attuned to the ship's schedule; when I heard seven bells, my eyes popped open whether I wanted them to or not. And when I closed my eyes and pretended to oversleep, Shen came and woke me.

I wondered if Shen was the judas. He had a reputation for incompetence as well, but I'd seen no sign of it. Maybe he instead had deliberately avoided promotion in order to . . . fulfill some scheme of the Ministry's? If the Ministry had made contact with me, it could just as easily have gotten to him.

When we were awake at the same time, I tried to get his story out of him. Perhaps somewhere in there would be a clue.

"What led you to join the Navy?" I asked one morning, plying him with tea fixed by my special recipe. We were on the sail deck, where most of the crew gathered when they were off watch and awake, as the gun deck was too cramped for skylarking.

"Parents wanted it," he said shortly. "There isn't much property in the family to manage, and it'll be years before it comes to me in any event. I needed something to do with my time. Get me out from underfoot." There was a note of sourness in his voice.

"You don't like it?"

He shrugged. "No complaints, really. It was hard at first, but now I know what I'm doing it's easy to do my duty."

Easy wasn't how people usually described the Navy, but I could understand that. There was hard work, and discomfort, but it wasn't confusing. I knew what to do and how. "You're a good lieutenant," I ventured. "Do you ever resent you were never promoted?" And wouldn't that be a great way to manipulate a man, promise him the promotion he felt he deserved?

But Shen shook his head emphatically, making the loose wisps of his hair trail behind him. "I never wanted command. I've had it, you know. Prizes. But I didn't care for it. Taking orders is uncomplicated; there's never any confusion. Hardly anything is yours to decide. But in command, you're making decisions every moment. And the crew … you don't only have to set the sails, you know. You have to manage the human factor. If you aren't strict enough, they take liberties. So you try being stricter and they all hate you. I chose a man they disliked as bosun's mate, and I swear they were near mutiny by the time we reached Phobos. How was I to tell who to choose? You're not supposed to let the men rule themselves."

I nodded. I could say that it would have served him much better to ask the men whom they thought was most able. But perhaps that was the sort of revolutionary thought the judas was here to root out. I barely dared to say anything, with that suspicion afoot.

"It sounds difficult," I said at last. "I have never been in command. Not of more than a launch."

"You will, if the war goes on much longer. You should ask Vasiliev to train you in that. You won't learn it from watching me." He looked glum. Maybe that was all it was keeping him from promotion. If he'd done badly every time he'd commanded a prize, they'd never give him a ship of his own.

On the other side of the sail deck, men were drinking their rum ration and singing. I'd been listening to the songs with half an ear, mostly about drinking and fighting and their sweethearts back home or in every port. But the tune had changed to a plaintive one, something new.

> *There once was a butterfly of blue, red, and green,*
> *A bonnier critter has never been seen,*
> *But cruel birds had lashed her to pull a great wheel*
> *Which crushed Martian soil to make Martian steel.*

My eyes darted to Shen's face. Was he hearing this? Did it mean anything to him? But he was only fiddling with his empty tea pouch, rolling it up and then smoothing it flat. The singers went on.

She pulled from the traces, she threw o'er the wheel,
She flew free and sang out her true heart's appeal,
Then she painted her wings in red and in black,
And both bird and beast she did boldly attack.

It was the *Mariposa*, rather transparently. The name meant "butterfly," some shipbuilder's fancy. Nguyen had made any number of songs about her. This one I didn't know, but it sounded like his work. Nothing fancy, but easy to hum.

The birds and the beasts tried to take her to heel,
But then she captured a mightier wheel.
She named her wheel liberty, it spins in the black,
And all creatures are safe there, and nothing shall lack.

The men moved directly on to a different song, and Shen continued to take no notice. I sat with my thoughts racing. There I'd assumed only the Admiralty knew what had happened on Liberty Station. Instead, the news was likely all over the system by now, carried by songs. Did everyone know what the songs meant? Hendricks, the ship's self-appointed bearer of tales? Alves?

Anyone on the ship with revolutionary sympathies would have to be very careful about explaining the songs. But without an explanation, I supposed they could sing them anywhere. Even in front of us officers. And if we called them on it, they could simply plead ignorance. Just a song they'd heard at Phobos, or anywhere.

I'd committed to help Moira preserve Liberty's independence. I wasn't trying for a whole revolution. I'd assumed it wasn't time. Khan's rhetoric, last I'd read of it, was still of mild, step by step reform. The people wouldn't be ready for more than that. The *Mariposa* was an outlier, pushed into mutiny by the wrong circumstances.

What if, instead, the people were much closer to revolution than I thought? What if the common people weren't a sleeping giant? What if they were only shamming, like I had been trying to do?

If so, we wouldn't have much warning when the whole revolution started.

I longed to talk to Moira. I didn't know what her views were on a revolution. What side she would want Liberty to take. What I could do to help. I knew the Martian system was unjust, but what were the steps between this and anything better? Khan would know. Moira would know. But I? I was still an outsider. Always would be.

All I could do was try to be ready for anything.

12

MOIRA

Landing was as bustling and noisy as ever. The hiss of buses, the shout of navvies, pedestrians rushing by. I had never cared for it, though in the years I sailed on a merchant ship I'd come here often. As good a place as any to take your gravity leave, if you couldn't go home.

I went straight to the Spacer's Rest, a grimy little inn close to the elevator. Harrington tagged after skeptically. "Don't we want to get elevator tickets first?"

"Nope. I told Marron to hang back a week and I want to enjoy my full week."

"But what about the," she glanced around her nervously, "well, anybody seeing you?"

"Landing's a big city. Trying to find anyone here is a needle in a haystack. And I feel confident there are no snitches here."

We went inside. It was smokey and dim, with wood shavings underfoot and dark, weathered wood tables. It was only medium full, too early in the evening to be loud, with a few tables of drinkers and a darts game in progress at the back. "Nor health inspectors," Harrington muttered, eyeing the stains on the tables and floor.

I got a room and managed to scrape off Harrington with the errand of visiting the telegraph office to check for messages from Marron.

Not that the woman wasn't nice; there was nothing about her one could point to as annoying, but she was just always *there.* Sometimes you wanted *not* to have a person perpetually at your elbow. I was beginning to suspect Marron had promised her a healthy bonus if she kept me safe. Or a slit gut if she didn't. Marron was familiar with both carrot and stick.

The bartender was the same one from the old days. "I don't remember your name, but I remember you're a beer drinker," he said.

"My passport says Martha, so let's go with that." I took the mug.

He registered the hint. "Ah, I thought it had been a while since I'd seen you. Lying low?"

"For the next couple days, and then I'm gone," I said. "Maybe you can help me while I'm here. My parents are looking to move to the city. I'd like to hook them up with a job and a place, or at least a person they can talk to for one. Any of the union boys still running that line?"

"You're a brother yourself?" I nodded. He lowered one eyelid in a half-wink. "Yeah, you talk to Pedro. 'Ey, Pedro!"

A man came over from the darts game, one dart still in his hand. He tucked it over his ear. "Union business again?"

"Not that kind of business," said the bartender quickly. "The jobs stuff."

I raised an eyebrow. "I did hear the union was busy these days." I wrapped both hands around my mug and leaned forward on my stool. Talking treason with the union boys, now that was like old times. How to dodge the press gangs, how to avoid paying duties on your imports, where to find the mid-space rendezvous where you could get banned Earth goods. Nobody actually wanted to hurt the Empire, but sting the tax collectors and the officers while making a little for yourself on the side? Nothing wrong with that.

"The Navy is what's busy," said Pedro. "They've stepped up impressment, and it's not like we don't know why. They're losing so many, they have to keep getting more. Sorry if we don't care to die for their war."

"Enough of us have already." I raised my mug a fraction.

"Right. And there's not a bloody lot we can do, not if they're doing it on the station every couple of days. One thing to make yourself scarce when you know a ship is heading out, but they're always heading out."

"Hence the riots."

"Yes. Which at least make a point."

"We need to do more than make a point."

"You got a better idea?"

I glanced around. Even in a place like this, you couldn't be completely careless. "Well, there's Liberty."

Pedro scoffed. "Now there's a joke."

I tried not to look offended. Unsuccessfully. "What's the matter with it?"

"We don't want to stop being Martians! We want to be free Martians. Shipping out of Liberty means never getting to come back."

"Till Mars changes."

"It'll never change if the best keep leaving."

I grimaced. "Fair."

The man left me his card, with a list of contacts for my dads when they came to the city. When he went back to his darts, someone else climbed onto the stool beside me. At first I didn't even look up. I'd gotten done what I came for. May as well go upstairs tomorrow; there was nothing left to do here and I'd feel better with the customs check behind me.

"It looks like leaving for Liberty doesn't mean you *never* come back," said the woman who had sat down next to me.

I looked up sharply. "Doesn't it?"

"I won't say your name, since it's obvious they want you if they can get you. But I recognize you, from the old days, and I know where you've been since then."

I looked her up and down. She rang no bells: a stout woman, in her forties, with the indiscriminate ethnicity that was so common in Landing. Two earrings in one ear and tattoos on her arms suggested a spacer, but most everyone was here. No doubt we'd drunk together in this bar before. "What do you want?"

"A friend of mine wants to talk to you. He hasn't seen you since you did him that favor on Deimos."

Khan. My stomach sank. I wasn't here to get involved in revolutionary politics. I was here to lie low and help my parents, for all the good I'd done at either goal. "And what does *he* want? I don't have much to offer, from where I am."

"I think he has people for you. Don't you lot want people?"

"We want ships more." I finished my beer and pushed the mug away. "But we'll take anyone."

"He's in the city now. I can take you to him."

"Better idea. You have him send his people to me. I have a ride coming in a few days." That was as close as I cared to get to the great man. Five minutes in his presence, and I'd be setting myself on fire in the public square or something. He was too intense to be around if you didn't want to get in revolution up to your neck.

Just then, we were interrupted by Harrington. "There was a message for you."

"Did you read it?"

Her blue eyes were innocent. "It's in code."

I smirked and took the folded paper. "You have to learn union code in the business. It's always good to know. I'll teach you when you get back to the ship." I unfolded it and cast my eyes down the page.

Navy got too close for comfort. We're moving downstream a tetch. Gonna check the downstream Trojans for pirate traps. Should be back in three weeks. Lie low, be safe, remind Harrington she's algae food if she doesn't keep an eye on you.

I sighed and shoved it into my pocket. "Never mind," I said to the sailor beside me. "I *don't* have a ride."

"You can still come, if you want to. I know he wanted to see you. Not just for business. He didn't get to see your girlfriend when she was here and he wanted to hear how she's doing."

"Fine." I got up off the stool. "Is it far?"

The woman looked hard at Harrington. Harrington gazed back steadily. At last I had to say, "Harrington, go upstairs. That's an order."

Harrington's face fell, and she turned around and started climbing the stairs. I followed the woman out of the bar.

We took many turns, dove into a crowd only to dive back out on the same side, ducked down alleyways. "There a tail on you?" I panted.

"I'm assuming there's a tail on *you*," said the woman. "Your crew's defection was big news, and if you haven't been arrested yet, my guess is they want to use you to reel in a bigger fish."

"I haven't been arrested yet because I've been careful," I shot back. "Who's 'they'?"

"Ever noticed the police always seem to know things they couldn't know if they were following procedures? How important revolutionaries just disappear in the night or die of 'natural causes' right before something big was going to happen?"

"Like *he* did." I didn't say Khan's name, since she'd been careful not to.

"Exactly. They call themselves the Privy Ministry, allegedly, which is as good a name as any. After what happened last time, we aren't taking any chances with who we admit close to him."

We finally ducked into a house, were admitted into a back room by a guard, and took a long stairway down.

All old Martian houses have deep basements, and Landing is the oldest city on Mars. When the terraforming was complete, people simply built up from their underground habitats. In many of the houses, the old habitats had been filled in, but some kept them for storage.

Khan was not in the basement of the house we entered. Instead, we had to walk along a long, mold-scented hallway carrying chemical lights. "This was the road, in the old times," whispered my guide.

"Hope you know your way around," I whispered back, as we took a turning in the dark.

"I just hope the Ministry doesn't. Most of the maps were lost; we had to make our own when we came down here."

We entered, at last, another habitat. It was the standard cheerless red-brown concrete, but the inside was filled with warm yellow light from several oil lamps. A man in the outer room greeted us with, "Ah, good. He wants to see her."

"And you think I'd be bringing her here if I didn't know that?" my guide fired back.

I was waved into the back bedroom alone. The great man sat at a desk, in a wheelchair, scratching a pen across a page. He looked up, and his seamed brown face was wreathed in smiles. "Moira!" he cried. "I'd heard you were on Mars."

"If I'd known it would get around that much, I'd have gotten a haircut or something." I sat down on his narrow bed, the only other seat in the room.

"Trey keeps me informed. Hopefully the Ministry doesn't know about you yet."

"They probably do. My family says they came around looking for me a while back. Of course I didn't know that before I showed up at their house."

Khan frowned. "You shouldn't stay here too long then."

"I don't mean to. When my ship circles back around in a few weeks, I'm on it." I pushed away regret. That moment, riding horses in an open field, was everything I'd missed, but you can't always be having fun.

This moment, in a musty bunker, was more of what Mars would be for me from now on. My sentence as a deserter wasn't just something to dodge at the border. It would follow me everywhere.

"Can you bring a few people out, when you do go? I have some people whose names and faces are too known; I'd like to get them and their families out so they don't have to stay down here with me forever. They might be useful to you."

"Plenty of work to do on Liberty, of every kind," I said. "As soon as I know when we'll be leaving, I'll pass word to you."

"Thank you." He rested his head on the back of his chair. "How is Lucy? I wanted to see her when she was here, but she was far too closely watched. The Admiralty was looking for any sign she might be disloyal."

"She was well last I heard from her." Honestly, she'd sounded blissful. Fancy parties, sailing with her brother, a new prestigious assignment ... *she* hadn't had to give up a thing. She'd given lip service to missing me, but that hardly seemed credible with all the fun she was having. "She's on her way to Venus now. Some diplomatic mission."

"Ah, very good."

I tapped my fingers on my knees, feeling vaguely disappointed. Here I'd feared Khan would fire me up to join the revolution, and instead we were making small talk. "Look," I said. "I want you to understand that Liberty wishes you nothing but the best. But we're kind of struggling right now. So if you brought me here to suggest some kind of alliance, anything beyond taking your people out of harm's way, I can't do it. It's all we can do to keep the station functional at all."

Khan nodded. "I quite understand. I thought you'd say something of the kind."

"Why, because I'm not the type to join a revolution?"

He blinked. "No, because I know your situation. You have very few ships and a mining industry to replace on your own. You're exactly the type of person who *does* join a revolution. But you've done so already, haven't you? The claiming of Liberty."

"I wasn't doing it to be revolutionary," I said. Even in my own ears, my voice sounded sullen. "I just needed a place to stand. And Lucy did most of it anyway."

"It made more of a difference than you think. It's giving people hope."

I bristled. "That's the last thing I was trying to do. Hope is toxic. Hope kills people."

His eyes softened. "Who taught you that?"

"My parents. They always told me to stay out of any of that mess. Under this system, if you keep your head down, you can build a life. It'll be hard, and you won't get everything you dream of, but you can get something. But if you try to fight back, you'll end up killed. They didn't want that for me." I swallowed hard, thinking of Ramesh in that darkened room. Neither he nor Bill had said one word in criticism of my desertion. But if I hadn't done it, I could have been there for them, couldn't I?

"I *have* to have hope," said Khan. "Without hope, I'm a man with bones like chalk, living in a hole."

I pressed my lips together. Who was I to lecture him, really? "Maybe you're right. Maybe there will be change someday. But me? All I want is the war to end so Lucy and I can be together. Make a little home for ourselves out in space. Best we can do, under the circumstances."

"Don't you want more than that?"

"Of course I do! But ..." I couldn't put into words what I felt. The hope I'd had when I was younger. The rage and despair that had driven me out into space. The long years working my way from one end of the system to the other, trying to swallow the insults of the officers so I didn't get spaced. How was a desire for better supposed to survive all that? "I'm tired," I said at last.

"There's a stage beyond tiredness," Khan said. "When your back is against the wall so you *must* act."

"Is that what's causing all the bombings?" I asked. "And the riots?"

He lifted a finger. "Violence has been part of the system for generations. What riots do is make that violence visible to you. To everyone. People are shocked by hearing three officers on a press gang have died, when they never cared that hundreds were forced into service every year. But." He spread his hand flat. "I should tell you that neither the riots nor the bombings have anything to do with me. The Brotherhood has organized several demonstrations, *peaceful* demonstrations. Of course they didn't stay peaceful. The police see to that. But I try my best to make sure we speak out in the most peaceful ways we can."

I frowned. Somehow I had assumed the revolution was all one thing, with Khan at its head now. "So the press riots aren't you?"

"No. That's your friends, the spacer's union." He shuffled papers around on his desk. "This here is them asking me to write a pamphlet telling spacers to take Phobos. This one is the Russet Workers asking me to come out in favor of industrial sabotage. This whole stack is the Common Suffrage Movement—bunch of

Founders who think they're going to help—telling me to tone down my message or they'll never get more members in their group."

"They're treating you like a figurehead."

"Worse. Like a messiah. Like I was supposed to swoop down from heaven and solve their problems for them. Bah." He turned his chair away from the desk and back to me. "I'm balancing so many competing interests. They'd all like to unite, they would happily do it under me, but they don't all want the same things."

"So your Brotherhood is just—"

"That small group of people who are actually doing things my way. Of course to get anywhere we'll eventually have to work together with everyone. But that's my project, not yours. Liberty is at least doing no harm, which is more than I can say for a few of these radical groups."

I relaxed at last. Khan intimidated me; he was more Lucy's type than mine. The type to kill themselves trying to change the world. But at least he wasn't going to drag me into it.

Of course that was all a feint to put me off my guard, because he followed it with, "Here's what you can do for me, if you care to. Or Lucy, if you're still in touch with her."

"I told you—"

He raised a hand. "Just, if you can. If you're in a position to find anything out. I need to find out who's setting the bombs. I know the impressment riots are the work of the spacer's union; we've talked about it, and I don't agree but I understand they are doing what they can. But the bombs are a strange thing. Not one, so far, has killed anyone of note. It doesn't feel like a populist project, to me. Nobody I've talked to will claim credit. Of course everyone assumes it's us—even you did. They call us violent anarchists. But I suspect something else."

"This Privy Ministry?"

"Possibly. If you found proof, we could take some kind of action."

I sighed. There wasn't really any point in saying no. It was something I could do with my head down, so I wasn't going to be the asshole who brushed him off. "I'll keep an ear out."

13

LUCY

We made unbelievable time sliding sunward as we barreled downstream. I found myself wondering why all ships couldn't be like this. But, of course, if most ships needed to be combat-ready, they'd need both engines and guns.

Vasiliev took the time to teach me sailing. I was an expert in navigation by now, but had never learned how to angle the sails. They had to be adjusted daily. It was critical to present the same face to the sun at all times, so that the angle of the sunlight against the sails didn't change as we moved along our orbit. But, thanks to the slight variations in solar output from day to day, our attitude shifted.

Just after crossing the line of Earth's orbit, the solar output started building. Not that we could tell with the naked eye. Instead, the radiograph trended upward and the masts strained.

Vasiliev fussed at the sails nervously. "I want to use every photon of this we can get," she explained, "to make the best possible time. But there's only so strong they can make a mast. If this builds to a real storm, we could lose one."

She cranked up the radio and listened to the static, like a rain blast on a tin roof. "The sun isn't just for basking in," she commented as it ran out of power and died down. "It's screaming, all the time, on every frequency. Light and heat and radio. We forget, sometimes, that it's just as happy to kill us as keep us warm."

"How do we know when a storm is coming, sir?" I asked.

She shook her head. "We don't. It comes from the sun to us at the speed of light, and nothing can go any faster than that." Turning to lean over the rail, she called, "Alves! I've decided. We're taking a reef. Torres, go tell the passengers to remain in their cabins until further notice. They're a little better shielded." She descended to the captain's mess to redo her trajectory, and the men fell to work reefing.

"How come the brass get special shielding?" Alves asked his mate nervously, as they locked the levers into place. "Isn't the inside of the ship shielded too?"

"It's shielded good enough for you and me," replied Bergeron. "If you get too cooked with radiation, there's pills for that. But the prince might have the next Emprex in his balls right now. There's nothing that important in yours."

"Haven't got any," Alves replied. "I get my manliness from a bottle."

"Just as well," she said. "Too long in space will scramble 'em. That's what comes of carrying something that important on the outside."

I repressed a smile and pretended I didn't hear, happy to see the two could have a conversation now that wasn't hostile. But they broke off anyway when Vasiliev returned and sent Bergeron to watch the radiograph. "The second that needle comes down, I want that reef let out."

She was interrupted by Ivanov, who had been peering out the stern window with a glass. "Captain, I believe I have sighted the enemy."

Vasiliev and I both went to look. It was true, an Earth ship was behind us, with sails spread. She was heading leeward as we angled sunward, so she would cross within a few kilometers behind us.

The captain sighed. "Damn it. She'd be a perfect target too."

"Can we even avoid engaging, sir?" I asked. "She'll pass so close. A little fuel burn and she'd be on top of us."

"Not at the rate we're going," she answered. "If they want to stay close for more than one volley, they'd have to kill their leeward acceleration *and* speed up by several knots. They can't do it, not with twice the fuel our ships ever carry. And they'd miss this fine weather too."

"Will you tell the men, sir?"

"I can hardly help it. She'll be passing close enough to see without a glass. They won't be happy we aren't engaging."

That was an understatement. After weeks of boredom, everyone was ready for a fight. It was the highlight of any voyage; a chance to let out any bad feelings that had settled onto the ship, and an opportunity for valor. Besides, after a battle, they would get a double ration of rum and the promise of prize money later. Expecting the men to run from a fight would make them feel like cowards.

She made the announcement, and the mood of the ship immediately soured. No one dared to grumble openly, but they cast her villainous glances when they thought no officer was looking.

"Isn't there work enough to keep you busy?" I demanded of Alves, who was pushing himself furiously back and forth across the sail deck. "The captain wants the last reef of the mainsail let out."

He gathered a few men and, snarling, gave the orders necessary. They set to work with grim faces—after all, they were just as frustrated as he was. Or almost. Alves had the added burden of having never seen combat against Earth at all. He'd been waiting an Earth year for a chance to strike against his old homeland. He'd have to wait longer.

I returned to the quarterdeck to keep an eye on the enemy ship. She had adjusted her sails to a steeper angle, to push downstream instead of leeward, but in the time we had, that wouldn't make much difference. She was holding her emergency fuel. She'd made the same calculation we had, then.

She crossed our orbit an hour later, slowly passing across the middle of the aft window. We could just see the ship itself from here, a tiny dark speck nestled in the circular, Earth-style sails.

Suddenly I heard a faint *shunk* from below my feet. A soft sound, but utterly unmistakable to any sailor.

"Someone's fired off a weapon, sir!" I cried. "One of us, I mean."

Vasiliev shouted, "Get to the aft gunroom and bring that man here!" Spacers scrambled to obey. Outside the window, the rocket lit and streaked away.

That it might hit the sail was a given; the sails were kilometers wide, and even close-hauled as they were, they still presented a huge target. But a torpedo punching a tiny hole in a sail was nothing much to be proud of. That could be repaired in an hour's spacewalk and hardly any material cost.

Instead, the whole starboard foresail started collapsing. Folding in on itself. I hung at the window, dumbstruck, as the foremast tore half away from the sail membrane and floated like a broken limb. "Sir!" I reported. "It hit dead in the starboard foremast. They've lost the whole sail."

"Irrelevant," she said flatly. "We were ordered not to enter combat on this voyage. I need the man that did this."

They dragged him up by the quarterdeck railing, where he hung in the air, if not at attention, at least not showing any obvious resistance.

Alves.

"Did you hear my order to take no action against the enemy, Mr. Alves?" A flush in Vasiliev's cheeks belied her forced calm.

The Earther nodded. "It was a good shot though, right?"

The captain's fingers twitched against her sides, as if they itched to flog him right now. "Do you make the decisions aboard this vessel, Mr. Alves? Or do I?"

A look of embarrassment passed over his face. "You do, ma'am. Sir. Captain. I just got excited." He looked up at her hopefully, as if he thought this would be enough.

She turned away. "Take him below and throw him in irons."

Alves had time to register a look of shock before the men holding his arms spun him around and led him down the hatch to the gun deck. Once he was gone, the staring crew remembered themselves and turned back to their work.

I came over from the window and braked myself at the rail, beside the captain. "The enemy vessel is well out of range, sir."

She was quiet for a long moment. Then, "He thinks getting clapped in irons *is* the punishment."

"Very likely, sir. He must have read the regulations, but..."

"Clearly it didn't sink in." She drummed her fingers on the rail. "If it were any other man I'd flog him."

"But?"

"Well—" She spread her hands. "He's an Earther. He isn't used to our ways. He seems to think he was just a little overenthusiastic. Maybe on an Earth ship that sort of thing is acceptable. But, dammit, I can't let that sort of insubordination stand! We're all alone out here in the black, and if I can't trust him to follow orders, I can't have him on my ship."

"I'm not sure you can have him on the ship if you *do* flog him, sir," I said softly.

"I don't follow."

"He's with us now because he hates Earth. Not because he loves Mars, particularly. You flog a Martian, he hates it, but he loves Mars enough not to hold a grudge. But him? What if a flogging makes him change his mind? He turned on one planet, he could turn on us as well."

"Where's he going to go?" she demanded. "He won't go running back to Earth, not with how much he hates it."

I shut my mouth. I had been honest up to now—I thought flogging him was a real concern—but I couldn't be honest with my next thought. He could go running to Moira. There was a third option now and there were so many people with grudges against both who could flourish there. But he had no way to get there, and I had no way to tell him about it without risking he'd betray me.

At last I said, "He won't desert. The question is whether you can *trust* him, between here and Venus."

She took a long, slow breath in and out. "I'll be in my cabin."

The punishment she finally announced was, in theory, a mild one. The cold box. All it meant was to leave a man in irons in one of the airlocks throughout the night. It was cold in there, till you warmed it up with your breath, and then it would get humid and stale. Not a pleasant time.

But you weren't supervised. And the emergency vent lever was easy for anyone to reach. If any man in the crew felt uncomfortable with having you on board, he had only to drift by, twist the lever, and drift off again. No one had to know who had done it, and there would be no consequences.

It was a punishment usually given for a man who had put his shipmates severely at risk. The captain would leave his fate in the crew's hands. That way, they could choose to forgive him or choose to get even. Every man on the ship had to agree for the man to live.

It was not, perhaps, the right punishment for insubordination. But I saw the wisdom of it. Did the crew think Alves was truly one of them? Or did they still harbor doubts because he was an Earther?

I barely breathed the entire night watch, carefully avoiding the region of the airlock to give the men their chance at him. I had *liked* the man, and the choice of this over a flogging had been my own fault. Vasiliev would have talked herself into flogging him if I hadn't spoken up.

But in the morning, when the captain came on duty and went to the airlock to have him released, the outer hatch was still shut. Alves was within, bald head shiny with sweat, but alive.

The crew remained solemn as long as the captain was there. She gave a little speech about obeying orders, and Alves bobbed his head and apologized. But when Vasiliev had headed back toward the quarterdeck, the crew gathered around Alves, slapping his back. "It *was* a good shot, though," said one.

There was no other way he could have proven his loyalty to the crew more clearly. He had actually fired on an Earth ship. He was one of them now.

14

MOIRA

With weeks to go before Marron was due back, and funds running short, I started taking shifts at the inn bartending. Wages weren't great, but the sailors tipped, especially if they'd just come home. Navy men were always the best tippers and the most reliable customers: first, because they got paid better than civilians, and second, because they were so miserable by the time they got home.

The war, I learned, was not going well. Several ships had been lost in recent months, whether destroyed or captured it was too soon to say. If Earth had taken them, the men who had crewed them would eventually filter back home, as they found ships to take them.

The Martian sailor is a predictable soul. If he's winning, he'll put up with all kinds of shit from the higher ups. But if he's losing, if he'd been forced to flee a battle or had lost too many friends, suddenly he starts to notice how bad they treat him. The men in the Spacer's Rest were angry, and that's why they had come. They wanted to talk treason, and they didn't think impressment riots were enough.

I listened nervously to the talk. I didn't think Khan would approve of it, but it wasn't like he was the only game in town, if revolution was what people were after. Not everyone revered him or had even read his writing. All they knew was that they wanted to act, and act now, not when the war was over.

"I'm tired of the patriotic duty to put everything off till the war is over," a woman was shouting one evening. "The war is never over. Even when it's over, it's not really over. You all know it."

"But as long as we're at war, everything we do to the Empire helps Earth," said a man. "Fuck the Emprex, right? But Earth is worse."

"Do we even know they're worse?" the woman answered.

It was the perennial question, wasn't it? The devil you knew, or the one you didn't. I was familiar with both devils; one beat you and the other just screwed you over financially. It was like asking if you preferred a punch in the nose or a punch in the stomach.

But Earth, historically, didn't care at all if we had a breathable atmosphere. Back in the days when Mars had been an Earth territory, they had stymied every attempt at terraforming because it didn't make a product they could ship home. If they won the war, pleasures like riding a horse under the open sky might become a thing of the past.

At a table near the other end of the bar, somebody was waving a paper around. "I got my ballot in the mail," he said.

"What'cha gonna do with that?" a brawny man asked. "Light your stove? Mulch your garden? Wipe your ass?"

The young man folded it carefully and put it in his breast pocket. "I always vote," he said. "Sure the candidates are bastards, but usually there's a better and worse bastard."

The only person we commoners were allowed to vote for was the Tribune. Although the post had to be held by a noble, his job was to defend the rights of commoners in Parliament. Of course none of them ever actually did that, which is why hardly any of us bothered to vote.

"Not this year," said the brawny man. "The only thing worse than each of them is the other one."

"Did you hear what we're doing with those?" a woman asked, lowering her voice and leaning in. I drifted a little closer. "Write-in campaign."

"Write in who?"

"Alexei Khan."

The table erupted with laughter. "He's not eligible," said the young man earnestly. "Of *course* if he could…"

"Of course he's not going to win," said the woman. "But it makes a point. It shows you're not satisfied with how things are going, that you refuse to pick either one of them. Why vote for a Tribune who doesn't actually believe we should have rights?"

I found myself too involved in their conversation, involved enough I got excited. I stepped around the bar and put a beer in front of the young woman. "Better than that," I said. "They always announce the numbers, don't they?"

The young man frowned. "I suppose…"

"Aren't we always trying to figure out how to coordinate a decent protest? How to get everyone to commit at the same time so it's not just an isolated uprising? If everyone writes in the same name, we'll see what the numbers are. People truly committed to change. If the number is large enough, then who knows?" I shrugged. It was coming back to me how long a shot it was, how unlikely that enough people really wanted change, and how unlikely they were to succeed even if they did have the numbers. "At any rate you'll know how many you are."

"You?" asked the woman whose idea it had been. "You're not going to do it?"

I frowned. "If my ballot ever arrives, I will," I said. "It must have been lost in the mail."

The group laughed again. I was far from the only felon in the Spacer's Rest.

15

✳

MOIRA

A letter for you!" chirped Harrington as she came into our tiny room.

I took the note and glanced at it. Just an update from Marron; still no chance for a pickup soon. They had indeed found a nest of pirates in the Trojan asteroids and it was taking some time to clear out.

"They're planning a strike at the workshop," Harrington went on.

Her colorless hair was tied back neatly and she wore a plain, pale blue dress: her uniform. She worked as a seamstress now, assembling garments with a foot-powered sewing machine. It didn't sound like bad work, but the shift was midnight to noon. That was too long to sit in the same position even if you weren't bending over a sewing machine.

"I suppose you'll need a new job, then." I rolled off my bed and took my apron from the back of a chair.

Harrington looked offended. "What, you don't think I want to do it?"

"You don't seem to be brimming with revolutionary spirit."

"What would that even look like?" Harrington demanded.

"Simmering anger, mostly." I slung my apron over one arm and put my hand on the doorknob. "Look, it's obvious the Empire's been good to you."

Hurt turned the corners of her mouth down. "Why would you say that?"

I shrugged. "You sure don't speak up when the rest of us are venting in the bar. We've all got stories, but you? I guess you've just had a nice life as a stationer, minding your business."

She sat down abruptly on the bed. "If I don't talk about it, it's because it's hard to talk about it. Not because there isn't anything."

My conscience stung me. I tossed my apron back on the chair and sat down across from Harrington. "If you wanted to talk about it, I can listen."

There was a moment of silence, while different emotions chased themselves across Harrington's usually mild face. At last she said, "There was…a gap, between when I was a stationer and when I shipped on the *Nepenthe Breeze*. I fell for a Founder. He was always up on the station, checking on his investments, and… I assumed he was in love with me. We lived together for a while. When I got pregnant, I thought he would want to marry me."

I could hardly judge her for hoping. I had certainly shot my own shot, back in the day, even though I knew from the start a marriage like that almost never happened. If you were lucky you could maybe be a side piece.

"Of course he didn't," said Harrington, eyes filling with tears. "He didn't want to see me again. I had to leave my job; you can't be pregnant in space. Managed it for a while by taking in other people's babies, but it got to be too much. Even with five babies I was watching all day, I couldn't make rent and food. So I …" She buried her face in her hands.

I dug around for a handkerchief and handed it to her, a little worried. There were a few ways this story could end, few of them good.

"As soon as he was old enough, I put him to work. Just easy things, sorting and packing, for a few pence a day. It made a difference in my being able to buy good food for him, and I thought, well, at least it's not dangerous work, like a cloth mill or chimney sweeping or anything. And without him to watch I could get a better job myself and finally make a decent living.

"They offered to have him run packages around town for a little more a day, and I said he could take it. Just running around all day, nothing more healthy. But these hydrobuses charge around the way they do, they don't stop for errand boys who don't pay attention." She buried her face in my handkerchief and sobbed.

"I'm sorry," I said, because I had to say something.

"After that I tried to get back to work on the station, but they didn't have any openings, so I decided to go for a spacer. It wasn't…what I expected. With you, it's been better. I could focus on your problems instead of mine for a change. And not—be alone. It's been so lonely, not having anybody that belonged to me."

I sighed. "You can't let loneliness tempt you into doing something dangerous. Bad things happen at these strikes and protests. People get shot."

"You think I don't know that? You just *assumed* I didn't care about the revolution. Whenever you go out with Soares, you never even ask if I want to come."

"I go see friends that can't go out in public," I said flatly. "That's all I do. I'm not in the revolution. I stay the fuck out of it and you should too."

Harrington glared at me, mouth tight. "You shouldn't sit it out. The Empire hurts all of us. Look at what happened to your dad! You think that would have happened if people like us had the vote?"

My eyes narrowed. "I've got enough to worry about trying to

send them money and find them a place to live. I can't build them a whole better world. I do what I can." I went out, slamming the door behind me.

It took me all my walk to work to calm down. First, because Harrington's story was so upsetting. It was the kind of thing that went into the revolutionary pamphlets, tragic stories proving the Empire wasn't working for everyone. Easy to find material for those; that kind of thing happened every day. You tried not to think about it.

And then Harrington herself. She wasn't angry like the other revolutionaries, she was just sad. Sadness wasn't much of a fuel for labor organizing. Most likely, her loneliness had driven her to join in with whatever her work friends were doing. She'd probably cut and run when the cops showed up.

I'd moved on from the Spacer's Rest and was now serving coffee at a classy speakeasy for university students. On the one hand, it paid better, and I needed the cash if I was going to keep sending money home. On the other, it struck me as a likely place to look for revolutionaries setting bombs. Coffee was technically illegal, due to the embargo, so it brought the rebellious types. Young nobles seemed exactly the sort to get a tiny bit of revolutionary spirit and immediately go about ignorantly making things worse.

The banner over the shop read *Curiosity Private Lending Library*, but once within, a few turns around the bookshelves brought you to a pleasant café, yellow with lamplight, pungent with the smell of roasting coffee.

The students looked up when I came in the room. "Ah, Martha, my grand passion!" cried one young man. "This place isn't the same when you're not here!"

"You do know I have to sleep sometime." I took his cup away and carried it off to the counter. The man brewing the coffee grinned at me, as if to say, *Isn't it a delight, dealing with these people?*

"But it isn't with *me*, and that's the tragedy of my life," said the boy.

"Go along with you," I said. "If I wanted to share a bed with an infant, I'd have gone for a nurse instead of serving coffee."

It was enough of the game to satisfy him, until next time. These college boys always thought they were hilarious, and they couldn't even justify it with being drunk.

The serious woman at the head of the table seemed glad the interruption was over. "What I don't understand," she said, "is why the common people don't rise up. Their situation is worse than ever. What with this plague of aphids, and the grain price going up, and the war tax higher every month, how can they bear it?"

"The worse it is, the less they can rise up," said a red-haired boy. "Think about it. They're far too worried about where their next meal is coming from to read the Declaration on the Rights of Man, or whatever."

"They can read Alexei Khan," said the flirtatious boy.

"An appeaser," said the serious woman. "All he does is preach pacifism, and talk about someday—what good has that ever done? If he'd been serious about changing things, he'd have done it before they killed him the first time. They'll kill him for good while he's still planning that general strike of his."

"So, what's he supposed to do?" demanded the red-haired boy. "Take on the Imperial Army himself?"

"What are *you* proposing?" said the serious woman.

"I say we take it on ourselves," said the redhead. "We can't expect the common people to defend their own interests, because they're too busy trying to stay alive. That makes it our job, doesn't it? We've got to do what they can't. Have a revolution. *Force* the Emprex to listen."

I'd been standing there with the coffee pot, listening to their bullshit, but I finally lost my patience. I set the pot down firmly on the table. "No."

"Martha!" The owner had a warning tone in his voice.

I ignored him. "Don't you *dare* start a revolution for us that doesn't include us. Don't you dare."

"Martha, leave now," said the owner. "You're fired."

I took off my apron and tossed it back at him without looking. "You kids mean well. If any of you *really* want to change things for us, come talk to me. Corner of 76th and Opportunity Street, I'll be there all afternoon."

I stood at the corner for over an hour, leaning on a lamppost. Probably no point in staying longer, but on the other hand I had nowhere to go but the tiny dim room in the Spacer's Rest. Harrington would be asleep.

"Martha?"

I jumped. It was the flirty boy from the café. "I didn't expect you." Unless he was just here to find out where I lived.

"Timothy Popov-Johnson," he said, sticking out his hand. "Sorry it took so long. I was trying to convince the others to come, but they didn't trust you."

I stared at his hand till he awkwardly dropped it. "I'm not getting paid to be flirted with anymore," I said. "If that's what you're here for, don't bother."

His face fell. He had a white, sharp-looking face and light brown hair that fell into his eyes. "I'm not! I just—I guess I thought it was a fun game you and I were playing."

"Maybe keep that game for people who have a choice about playing with you." I was being too hard on him. He looked barely eighteen. But his parents clearly hadn't told him, and somebody had to.

He looked at his feet. "I'm sorry. I guess I didn't think."

I pushed off the lamppost and clapped his shoulder. "Fair enough. Come on." I set off down the street at a brisk walk, my hands in my pockets and my long legs eating up the ground. Walking in the city, you had to look like you had someplace to be.

Timothy hurried to keep up. "You said you knew ways we could actually help."

"The first way is to stop trying to do this without us. There's a lot of violence afoot right now, if you didn't notice."

"Of course there is," he said. "I'm not scared of it."

"I just don't want you contributing to it," I said. "It discredits us. And if you're not coordinating with the *actual* revolution, you're working against us."

"The others say we have to start it, and once we get it going, the people will join in."

"Pretty confident, aren't you? I know how that'll go: you start something, nobody joins you, you all get shot, nobody wants to start another revolution for a generation."

"But you don't have the advantages we have," he protested. "I read all the Khan stuff. I can see that you're just trying to get by. But then I look at my life, at the things I have and the privileges I inherited, and it's like—don't I have a duty to use this? Are you honestly telling me to go back to class and forget that I live in a— an apartheid state?"

"No," I said. "We'll need people like you, at some point. But before I can even bring you in, I have to know it isn't about ego. I do *not* have time for people who want to use this as their coming of age or a great fucking epic where you get to be the hero."

Timothy gave me a startled sideways look. "You think that's what we're about?"

"You tell me, Tim. You see more of your coffeeshop crowd than I do. But I've been working there two weeks and I feel like every single afternoon there's some jerk-off fantasy of Being the Savior of the Working Man."

He considered that, while we dodged past a row of beggars with scrawled signs explaining the tragedies that had brought them there. Five yards down the sidewalk was a food cart, selling hand pies.

I stopped. "Got any money?"

Timothy stood befuddled for a minute. "A little? The old man keeps me on a short allowance."

I pointed to the food truck and then back at the beggars. "You can't give me that speech about privilege and then not notice what's right in front of you. You only have the advantages you have, and I think those friends of yours think their advantage is intelligence and wisdom when really, what's actually possible for them to do is simpler and a lot less fun."

He rifled in his coat for a few shillings and went up to the food truck. He might be ignorant, but he was quick to learn. Not like Lucy, whose math brain went the speed of light and whose common-sense brain went the speed of molasses in January.

Once he'd distributed the hand pies to the beggars, he came back and we started walking again.

"Isn't that just temporary, feel-good stuff?" he said. "You're not changing the system. Those people will be hungry again to-morrow."

"But they're not hungry *now*," I said. "Your would-be revolutionaries love to shit on everything that isn't shooting guns in the street. Because that feels like *doing* something and this doesn't. But if they can't do this, I'm not trusting them with a gun. If it's really about helping people, they'd start here, and they don't."

"So you won't let me help? Because I didn't pick up on that myself?"

"You can follow directions," I said. "That's the important thing."

I didn't take him to Khan, not least because I still didn't know my own way into his warren. Instead, I brought him to the lodgings where Soares lived. On the way I quizzed him more about his friends.

"You say they want to be doing something exciting," I said. "Are you sure they haven't? Terrorism, bombings, that shit?"

He shook his head. "No, I've never heard of anybody doing that kind of thing. We only get together to talk philosophy. That club is pretty much the only place you can get away with saying those things."

"Don't be too proud of yourself," I said. "You probably could get away with it anywhere, if you wanted to. What are they going to do, throw you in jail? That's for us, not you."

"Well, we could lose preferment," he said. "Our whole careers could rely on that."

"Oh, well then," I said. "I fully understand. It's not like I just got fired from my job purely to give you a chance to do something better than rant in a coffee shop."

Timothy looked stricken until I laughed, and then he joined me.

We went up a rickety staircase and down a dim hall. Soares opened her door to my knock. "Who's the toff?"

"He wants to help," I told her. "Isn't there anything we need Founders for?"

Soares let us in and cleared a pile of newspapers off the single chair and paper plates off the folding futon. "How committed is he?" she asked. "Is he still afraid to break the law?"

"I don't care about that," said Timothy stoutly. "The Empire is illegitimate."

Soares chuckled. "Who's waking up the Founder kids?"

"Coffee shops," I said. "They break one law and the next thing you know, they want to overthrow the state."

"Well, there's one thing." For the first time, Soares addressed Timothy. "It's legal for Founders to buy guns."

He blinked and looked over at me. "What was all that talk back there about not starting a revolution?"

"I said *you* shouldn't." But I looked at Soares. This interest in weapons was new.

"I hope we'll never need them," said Soares. "But Khan is saying it's time to start accumulating a few. Because we might want peace, but with how fast the situation is devolving, we might not have a choice."

"I have dueling pistols," Timothy offered.

"Good. We'll set up a drop each week. We give you money, you use it on guns. Go to a different shop each time and buy just one at each shop."

"Can I get my friends involved?"

I fixed him with a stare. "Do you think your friends can handle it?"

He flushed. "Not the ones you saw today. But I have others. I don't have to tell them any details."

"Use your judgment," said Soares.

I parted with Timothy at Opportunity Street and made my way back to the Spacer's Rest. I might not be deep in the revolution myself, but I'd done them some good. Maybe. The idea of guns made me nervous, even though I made my living with cannons. Was that what it was going to devolve into, fighting in the streets? A few commoners with dueling pistols were hardly any match for the Imperial Guard.

Khan wouldn't take that step if he didn't have to. Would he? He knew as well as I did how easy it would be to make things worse. Still, if he was hiding in a tunnel from the Emprex's men, he might as well have a gun as not.

Maybe it was stupid for me to have helped at all. Khan didn't seem to grasp what his disappearance had done to my generation. How much hope we'd had, and how nothing had ever come of it. All my life things had only ever gotten worse. Why should we— how could we—believe it was ever going to change?

I may have torn Timothy a new one, but he encouraged me a little. Like Lucy did. She was probably why I'd bothered at all. As much as I hated naive Founder babies and their newly discovered sympathetic outrage, they could probably do more for liberation than I could. If they were like her, and not like the redhead at the cafe who only looked for glory.

But not many people were like her. Not many people spent months to be really sure they were doing the right thing, and would cheerfully give up their lives for it when they found it. Especially not many Founders.

I crept back into our room, where the blind was drawn and Harrington was a snoring lump in her bed. With the suddenness of cannon fire, I wanted Lucy to be waiting in mine.

16

Lucy

Aphrodite Station was a dizzying scene of neon lights and noise. I hadn't been enamored of it last time, and my impression this time was no different. Still, there was something to be said for getting to stand upright against gravity again.

The delegation was already ensconced at the Martian Embassy. The ambassador had met us at the dock and swept the prince and his hangers-on into her protection immediately. As well she should: Earthers frequented this station just as much as we did, as well as pirates of all stripes. The Venusians couldn't care less, provided you followed their draconian rules about violence of any description. Which were all very well, but wouldn't stop a dedicated assassin till afterward.

I, however, didn't need any such protection, and was at liberty to do as I pleased. What I pleased was to head to the radio office and get my hands on Moira's messages as fast as I possibly could.

Which was not helped by Lieutenant Shen tagging along. I tried hints. "It's been a long voyage. Don't you feel like cutting loose a bit? Getting away from the same old faces?"

"Not especially."

"What do you feel like doing while we're in port?"

"Don't know. Thought I'd tag along with you and see what you came up with. You seem to have someplace in mind."

Internally I groaned. The man was smart enough when it came to math—I'd seen his navigation; it was flawless—but hopeless at taking a hint. "I do, as it happens," I said, "but it's something I want to do *alone*. Something…private."

"But we're in public."

"I want to *get* in private," I said, gritting my teeth against embarrassment that I was even hinting at what I was. One of the first rules of Founder etiquette is, we don't have sex. Or rather, we all agree socially that none of us are having it. "There are places that hire out rooms where I can be in private. Do you understand?"

"Ah," he said understandingly, "you want to take a bath. We passed a place a little back."

"Shen," I said at last, stopping so I could face him. "Please go away for a little while. Maybe *you* go take a bath, if you like. I'll meet you back here in an hour if you will just leave me alone."

He blinked. I would have paid money to get my words back in my mouth. I'd been unspeakably rude, and if he stormed off in a huff, I'd deserve it. But instead he hung his head. "I'm sorry," he said. "I've been too pushy, haven't I? I was supposed to have noticed you wanted me to go away."

I sighed. I was finally realizing what was up with Shen, and embarrassed with myself for having taken so long to figure it out. Me, after growing up alongside my brother! But, to be fair, my brother was very different. "Don't worry about it," I said. "I should have started out being more direct. Would you like to meet up in an hour and see the sights? There's a museum near here, we could go and see it."

He grinned. "I would like that, Prescott. I will be back that way. Having a bath."

Messages were waiting for me, as I had hoped, tagged with my routing number. The first was from Moira.

You'll be at Venus by the time you get this. I've seen my dads. Ramesh had to give up his job; I'll be moving them both to Landing.

One of my sailors is with me, Harrington, you don't know her. But you don't need to be jealous; she has basically no boobs and I fall asleep every night thinking of yours.

I smiled. Count on her to find a way to slip that in.
The next was from my mother.

I do hope you've made it to Venus safely, and without getting hacked with any cutlasses. I worry.

Your father's grapes did very badly. Little green bugs all over. My scientist friend says they are aphids and must have gotten here from Earth. Which means smugglers. Why people don't make the patriotic choice and buy Martian goods only, I can't understand. Anyway we did make a tiny bit of wine, but only made about two hundred pounds on the lot. Your father is talking about trying something different next time. Feel free to write any ideas you have. Not so many jobs for a man of sixty with no experience.

Any nice girls on the ship I should know about? When your voyage is over, I'll invite anybody to tea you like. You can trust me to put on a good show for almost nothing.

My smile this time was exasperated. Why did she care so much if I got married now, given I had chosen a career over a lucrative connection? Of course she wanted someone to leave the house to, now that we'd saved it, but what would any child of mine do with that manor and no money to keep it up?

I wished I could bring Moira to that tea. My mother would be flabbergasted, but she knew Moira, and that would help. Still. It wasn't usual for a Founder to marry a commoner, and half the time they got disowned for it. I had no idea whether my parents would do the same. It wasn't something we'd ever discussed.

When Shen and I returned to the embassy, the others were gathered around a table, talking earnestly. Vasiliev waved us over.

"Venus, you need to understand," the ambassador was saying, "isn't a nation at all. It's a confederation. So you can't meet with the Venusian government. There isn't one. The request was made through this embassy by the conglomerate that manages this station. They say a certain number of the cloud cities have agreed you may come. The one that's hosting you is the oldest, Galileo. But even if you win them over, that doesn't necessarily commit all of Venus to an agreement. There has to be a majority agreement of cities on any terraforming-related action, and selling gasses to us qualifies. At least if we buy any oxygen or water."

The prince nodded. "I understand that. Allowing us to come at all is historic. I don't expect to have everything settled at once."

"We have approval for five people to travel down into the atmosphere," she continued. "Do you have that many people coming?"

"The three of us and two servants, yes?" Miss Liu put in.

A man I didn't know in a doctor's black coat piped up. "Not the servants, unless they were weight-trained as children. Most commoner children aren't. The gravity on Venus is almost Earth-normal; it would be miserable and possibly dangerous for them."

The prince's chin went up. "I go nowhere without my valet."

"I will *examine* your valet, your highness," the doctor conceded. "But I strongly recommend a Founder for the other seat. Surely one of the officers who traveled with you can go and assist you just as well."

"I can't," Vasiliev put in immediately. "The sails' reflectivity is down significantly from micrometeorite strikes; I need to supervise a full replacement of the film."

Shen and I looked at each other. "I am perfectly willing," I said quickly. "I was weight-trained, and my physical fitness is excellent."

Shen conceded with good grace. It had been rude of me to be so forward instead of offering him the chance, but I badly wanted the spot and couldn't count on him taking a hint.

The ambassador nodded. "I only wish I could join you," she said. "The chance of a lifetime, but my duty is here. But I can warn you. Venusians' ways are *nothing* like ours. Less even than Earthers'."

"I know they have no anti-electric laws," the prince put in.

Miss Liu gave a little gasp of horror. "Isn't that terribly dangerous? Will we get sick?"

"Electricity doesn't really make you sick," I said. "We use it in spacesuits when we have to. We only limit it to avoid another Singularity."

Miss Liu gave me a sharp look. I bit my tongue. Nobody likes a pedant.

"That is correct," said the doctor. "Those old wives' tales do some good, if they keep people from breaking the law, but I think everyone *here* knows to follow it regardless."

"When in Rome," said the ambassador. "You'll have to adapt to seeing it around. I'm not sure they can manage their cloud cities without it. And that's not the only thing that will disturb you. The Venusians are completely egalitarian. They have no experience with nobility and they won't treat you with any respect. It's *vital* that you don't take offense at this."

"Of course," said the prince soothingly. "I did read up on the way here."

"With respect, Your Highness, you've never dealt with their style before. It's—abrupt. I find it difficult, myself. And they're open about personal details we find ... impolite. Just—keep it in mind."

"We can't let them set the entire tone," objected the foreign minister. "We need them to understand that we are used to a certain respect. In all negotiations, it's important to let them know we aren't going to bend over backward for everything they want."

"Well, no ..." said the ambassador. "But—I know you know this, Mr. Blackwell, but the others may not—we will not be negotiating with individuals at all. In the end, major decisions will be put to a vote, both within the city and among cities. This isn't like sitting down to a deal at a table like this one. It's like running for office. You'll need to make a good showing with *everyone* you meet on Venus."

"Sounds like chaos," muttered Miss Liu. "I can't think how they manage anything under such a system."

Privately, I at least half agreed with her. Egalitarianism was one thing, but even Moira's pirate ship had a captain. I wasn't sure how any political body could manage without one.

17

※

MOIRA

Landing Central Station was a madhouse on the best of days. Lately, it had been worse than ever, as people crowded into the city from the country around. With the aphid infestation, whole harvests had been lost and farmers left penniless. I heard snatches of Yiddish, Vietnamese, and what might be Romani.

I spotted Bill towering over the crowd and headed over. I get my height from him—well, from his side of the family. Biologically, I was his sister's baby. But to me, there was no difference in how much he was my dad compared to Ramesh. Ramesh had woken up with me at night and put me on my first pony. Bill had taught me to patch a coat and throw a punch.

Ramesh was in a wheelchair, which their letter had told me to expect, but it still took me aback. When would I get used to him outside of a stable? How was I supposed to have a real conversation with him if he didn't have a hoof in his lap so neither of us had to make eye contact? I took a deep breath and smiled too brightly. "Did you have a good trip?"

"As good as could be expected," said Ramesh sourly.

"Very crowded," said Bill. "Especially from Aeolus on. I wouldn't have dreamed people would try to commute that far."

"And no chance of sleeping on the train," Ramesh added. "Not with people talking and laughing and snoring."

"We'll go straight to the place I have for you then," I said. "You can settle in and get some sleep."

I had rented them a place near the elevator, because my spacers' union friend had found Bill a job as a longshoreman. Every spare moment I wasn't working, I had spent looking at places, and so many had been no good. Stairs, of course, were out. It had to be affordable on what Bill could make by himself. And, ideally, furnished. They didn't want to move all their things halfway across the planet.

"You see," I said, as I held the door for them, "it's just a few steps from the main entrance. Across the hall is a retired sailor, very nice woman. You shouldn't be lonely."

Inside was a tight little studio, hardly bigger than my cabin on the *Mariposa*, done up in floral patterns. "How cozy," said Bill with the same sort of brightness I could hear in my own voice.

"Heat is included, and there's hot and cold running water," I said, trying not to sound defensive. "The curtains . . ." I tried to open them, only to see the window looked directly into the window across the alley, six feet away. I shut them again. "We can always get new ones if you don't like them."

Ramesh sighed and backed his chair into the corner. "It'll do fine, Moira," he said. "If we don't like it, we'll get something else once we're used to the city."

It was a long way from the estate I grew up on, where I had miles of prairie to roam and a warm set of rooms over the stable. There, our windows had looked out on the pasture. But that life had always been at the behest of people more important than us. Their lives had changed, so ours had had to as well. And no thought was given to Ramesh, once he had stopped being useful.

"Will you be staying with us?" asked Bill.

I looked around the tiny room. "No—no, I couldn't. I have a room for the present. It's only a week till I have to leave anyway."

On the way back to the Spacers' Rest, I stopped at the telegraph office. Lucy was on Venus at last, which meant finally getting letters from her again. But this one left me unsatisfied. A single sentence of *I miss you intensely; your letter gave me some comfort* and then on to business. Lucy was going down to the surface with her diplomatic mission, and she was utterly fixated on the work she could do there.

If they'll talk with Mars, they'll talk with us too, I think. If Liberty wants to be an actual player, we need diplomatic relations with everyone. I would just march up to the person in charge, but they are said to have none. Do you know anyone here I could talk to?

I knew any number of Venusians, though most of them would still be on Aphrodite. But it was common for them to cycle on and off the station, because they preferred to stay in their cloud cities. Surely, if I spent some time messaging old friends, I would find someone on Galileo stat.

It was pointless, though. Venus couldn't do much for Liberty even if they wanted to, and that itself was unlikely. They showed every sign of waiting out the war which (I could admit privately to myself, if not aloud) meant waiting for Earth troopships to land in Gale Crater. And cheerfully selling Earth the carbon cloth sails to get there.

Harrington wasn't in our tiny room when I got back to the

Rest. I slipped my notebook out from under my pillow and started encoding some letters.

There was one person I was almost certain I knew on Galileo. But to put him in touch with Lucy…I grimaced. I had given Marcus an earful last time we'd spoken. I had known he was about to rotate back to his stat, which had made it easy to burn my bridges. Hadn't thought I'd be calling on him asking for favors.

On top of that, I didn't want to help Lucy get deeper into the spy stuff. She could get hurt, when a big part of the point of sending her away was to keep that from happening. But Lucy would always resist any efforts to keep her safe.

She didn't want to be safe. She wanted to help the revolution.

Maybe—probably—it would do no good. But I owed it to her to try. It was that or let Lucy figure out her entire "spy" mission was a pretext. History suggested she wouldn't forgive me for that.

Dear Marcus, I wrote.

This isn't to take back anything I said in my last letter, but I need a favor. You did say I could still call you if I needed anything, despite ~~how I~~ *everything.*

18

LUCY

Are you sure you don't need an anti-emetic?" asked the pilot a second time.

So far, we were only falling toward the surface; that is to say, floating. Free fall doesn't end till you try to slow down.

"A stomach of iron is almost a requirement in the Imperial Navy," I said. "I've been through worse than a shuttle landing."

Brave words, considering I'd never landed by shuttle. Words I was regretting a few minutes later.

The first sign we were slowing down was a golden-red haze streaking by the forward window—the thin upper atmosphere, heated by our approach. Weight returned to my body, lightly at first—less than on Luna. That slowly increased, and then it started to get bumpy. It felt like riding a bicycle down a steep, rocky slope—careening downward, then one shock after another.

Beside me, the others looked pale. Sick, or only frightened? I still felt fine. Well, a little light-headed. But I had felt worse.

But that was before the S-turns. The pilot slowly eased the shuttle left and right, killing a little speed on each curve. She was flying almost completely blind now, with the red haze streaking by thicker every moment. Her eyes were on her instruments, a series of dials and a screen that showed us as a green dot on a fuzzy field.

I swallowed hard. This was like the train across Tharsis, a steep, sickeningly twisty stretch of track. Only worse, because there you could look out the window and get your bearings on the pine trees that marched along the cliff faces. Here, the only thing I could look at was the pilot, jolting against her harness as badly as I was, or the other passengers. To my right, Sagan clung to the armrests, making small gasps when a bump of turbulence hit. To my left, Liu rode impassively, her face like marble. Beyond her, Blackwell was throwing up in a paper bag. I jerked my eyes away lest I be tempted to join him.

Cold sweat prickled my forehead. How many more of these damned curves were there going to be? We seemed to be going slow enough now. I wanted to ask the pilot, but I was too busy clamping my jaw shut against a sour taste that rose in the back of my throat. The outer hull of the shuttle creaked and groaned as wind buffeted us to one side or the other.

This was madness, I thought. There had to be a better way to get from orbit to the habitat than this. Unless things were usually much smoother than this, and a storm was preparing to split the shuttle like an egg and scatter the pilot, the prince, and me to the clouds of acid. I eyed the pilot, her relaxed shoulders against the harness, her gentle touches to the yoke and the pedals. No. I could swear she was used to this. Easy as walking downstairs for her, I supposed.

"You think everything's all right?" asked the prince faintly. I glanced at his face: pale, but not green or clammy. I wished I'd had the pills he'd gotten.

I was still trying to soothe my stomach enough to answer

him when the pilot said, "Oh, this is normal. Venus is windy, I told you."

Her tone wasn't annoyed, but I cringed internally. Venusians were casual to a fault, I knew that, but if she couldn't manage 'Your Highness,' it wasn't that hard to say 'sir.'

But that curve seemed to have been the last. We steadied out into a straight line, or as straight as could be managed with the buffeting of the wind. The bile in my throat eased its pressure and consented to go back where it belonged. I took a shuddering breath and looked out the window. The red-gold streaks were gone, and I could see just below us the tops of the clouds, spread out like a solid landscape in lumps and swirls of poisonous yellow.

Then suddenly that landscape was just beneath us. It seemed we would land on the tops of the clouds, but instead the shuttle plunged down into them. My breath caught in my throat, as if my lungs had decided we were diving into the sea. The yellow-gold light was all around us now. How were we ever going to find the floating habitat in all this?

But a new dot had appeared on the pilot's little screen, and she steered us toward it. We were almost upon the habitat when it appeared through the yellow mist: two huge round masses of the balloons, joined by a flat landing platform. I caught only a glimpse before the balloons were on either side, and the landing gear gave a terrible roar while my body was thrown against the harness. We were slowing down, and quickly too. In front of us, I saw the runway suddenly end: a row of lights, a net, and then nothing but diffuse cloud. We were going too fast. We would overshoot—

No. The straps relaxed on my chest as my back touched the seat behind me again. Ahead, the steep dropoff stopped approaching, and we pulled to a stop twenty feet short of it. The pilot gave a satisfied sigh and began flipping switches. "I'll tell you one thing, you're the quietest new passengers I've ever brought down. Guess not much fazes Martians. People usually scream the whole way."

I locked eyes with the prince, and saw a quiver in his cheek. I bit my lip to keep from laughing out loud. Not much fazes us? Ha. No. Not much forces a sound out of us, it's true. You don't get through Founder boarding school if you cry out when you're not hit. Or when you are.

Unfastening my harness with shaking fingers, I hauled myself to my feet. This, at least, I had been expecting, had in fact trained myself for. A heavy weight had settled on me, like the lead vest I'd been forced to wear as a child. Only instead of centering on my shoulders, it was like every cell of my body had a lead vest of its own, pulling downward.

I turned to assist the prince, but he was already pushing himself upright. For a moment he drooped slightly, but he squared his shoulders and lifted his chin. Turning, he helped Sagan out of their seat. They struggled to get their balance, the metal braces on their torso and legs rattling faintly. As soon as they could, Sagan shook off the prince's hand and stood upright. Perhaps they, like I, sensed something amiss in the valet leaning on the prince and not the other way around.

The pilot helped us into coveralls, more like rain gear than anything else, with a hood and face mask. "Don't be fussy about it, just make sure your skin is covered or you might get a rash," said the pilot, as I carefully fastened the clasps up the front.

We all trooped in a row down a narrow metal stairway and stood on the broad landing platform. Most of the habitat was within the two balloons, but this flat space between them held a fog fence to catch condensation, tanks full of sulfuric acid, and several small, squat airplanes.

A faint, variable breeze tugged on my suit, bringing heat I could feel through the cloth. Not hot enough to burn, but hotter than comfortable. Blackwell could feel it too. "Funny, that little wind. I always thought the wind on Venus was something fierce."

The pilot turned around. "Oh, it is. It's just we're traveling with it. We're going two hundred kph at the moment. Fast as a hurricane on Earth."

"We don't have hurricanes on Mars," said the prince. "The ocean isn't warm enough."

"Want to look over the edge before you go in?" she asked. "You won't get a view this good from inside."

I wanted to demur, but the prince stepped forward, so we all went to the edge and looked down. There wasn't much to see, only yellow light scattering off the clouds in every direction, dazzling the eyes.

"There!" cried the prince. "Is that a break in the clouds?"

The pilot leaned on the net to look out. My knees felt weak just watching her do it. Perhaps that was the goal. Perhaps, like a Navy crew does to a new midshipman, the Venusians were going to take some time to find out what we were made of. Or else we were supposed to see what they were made of: brusqueness, egalitarianism, and absolutely no fear.

"Just more clouds," said the pilot. "See, you get breaks down to the next layer, which is moving slower than this layer, but you don't often get a look at the surface."

The prince craned his neck, and my arms tensed with readiness to grab him if he somehow managed to fall through the netting. "We'd die if we fell from here, right?"

She laughed, her voice a little muffled by her mask. "Not of the fall you wouldn't. The pressure would kill you first. Unless the wind tore your mask off and you suffocated on carbon dioxide. Or if you're in a cloud, the sulfuric acid would burn your lungs."

He took a step back from the edge. "How does it feel, living in a place that wants to kill you?"

"You tell me," said the pilot, heading toward the airlock. "Space wants to kill you just as bad."

The airlock blew air over us, pushing out the toxic atmosphere and misting us lightly with something to neutralize the acidic dew. We huddled in a tight knot, forced a little closer than any of us was strictly comfortable.

"Is anyone meeting us?" Blackwell asked, a note of trepidation in his voice. It seemed possible, from what we knew, that we would be simply left to wander.

"Talia is meeting you," the pilot said. "Current head of StatOps team."

"So you do have a leader."

"No." An edge entered her voice for the first time. "We have a number of coequal teams and she is currently managing StatOps. Sort of like the miscellaneous team. Everything not covered by any other team."

"What is her title?"

A blank look. "You call her Talia."

The airlock seal released with a hiss, and we spilled out, eager to put an end to the awkward moment. A tall woman with deep red hair waited, as promised, just outside. She was big in all dimensions: tall, broad-shouldered, broad-hipped. The kind of woman who could sling you over her shoulder, but padded enough it would be a comfortable ride.

Not the sort of thoughts I should be thinking at this exact moment. "You must be the prince," she said, sticking out her hand to shake his. "Do I call you George, or—"

He rose to the occasion manfully, accepting the handshake as if this were entirely normal for him. "Whatever makes you comfortable, Miss Talia."

"Oh, please." She released his hand and waved hers dismissively. "Just Talia."

Liu gave me a shocked little sideways glance. "Are we just going to *let* them call him that?" she whispered.

Oh, so you've decided we're friends again? I did not say. "No polite way to stop them," I said instead.

The airlock led out into what appeared to be a park. Curving paths, made of something smooth and white, wound among patches of cassava and peanuts. Here and there were palm trees. All tropical fruit, which made sense. It was warm in here, with a green sort of dampness in the air from all the plants.

"We don't have most of these plants on Mars," the prince was explaining. "We used to import small amounts from Earth, before the embargoes, but now any tropical fruit that makes it to Mars is smuggled. Mars just isn't warm enough for it."

"It's easier for us to just keep the climate warm in here and plant things that don't mind it," Talia answered. "Heat rises, so if we cool it down too much we can't stay at the altitude we want."

"What altitude do you want?"

"Depends," she said. "We're riding low at the moment because the wind is steady here. If it gets too stormy, we go higher."

That reminded me that we were still riding on the wind, miles up in the air, and I had a momentary rush of vertigo. The ground felt steady—almost. If I paid attention, I could feel faint changes in direction now and again. But it wasn't the sort of bumpy ride I might have imagined.

We began walking along the paths, Talia in the lead. "No sort of public transit, I'm afraid. Some of the stats have it, but we chose to stick with shank's pony. Better for our health if we walk as much as we can. And everywhere in the stat is walking distance if you leave yourself enough time."

As we moved away from the side of the habitat, the shape of the dome overhead became more clear. It was a long oval, stretching backward from where we had entered. The skin was transparent, barred with opaque stripes. "What are those, do you think?" I asked Blackwell, walking beside me.

"Solar panels, if I had to guess," he said. "Wouldn't you put them up there?"

Talia heard us and turned around, continuing to walk backwards as she went. "Yep, solar panels. There's some on the bottom as well, because the clouds reflect so good. But we leave gaps between to get light in here for the plants."

Beside me, Liu sniffed. "I still think it can't possibly be safe to have that much electricity around," she said. "A ship radio is one thing, but nobody's ever tested what it'll do to have *that* much electricity around."

It soon became clear that the garden extended almost everywhere. Paths wound here and there, not seeming to go anywhere. A few platforms rose above the level of the plants, extending spraying arms that misted the greenery. It was perplexing. Aphrodite Station was a glitzy chaos of lights and noise, and this was—downright bucolic. I saw some people, but nothing that looked like a building.

Until the path ended abruptly at a stairwell leading down. "The garden level's the nicest to walk on," Talia said, "but we're almost to the place where you'll be staying."

"Are all the living spaces on lower levels?" asked the prince.

"Of course," she said. "Plants need all the light they can get, so this level is all for them. Next few levels are living spaces, and after that is industry—chemical plants, manufacturing, that kind of thing. Put the ugly stuff in the basement, right?"

Sagan hesitated at the top of the stairs. There was no handrail here at the top, and they were already flagging behind as it was. I doubled back and extended an arm. "Sorry, I didn't think."

"Thank you, Lieutenant," Sagan said quietly and leaned on my arm. "I didn't mean to slow anyone down."

The stairs led into a wide, brightly-lit hallway of the same white plastic that made up the paths above. On the walls were large, abstract paintings. The aesthetic was pleasant, but I would have preferred some signs. Without Talia, I wasn't sure I could find my way in these halls without them.

We took a few turns before reaching a single door. "As promised," she said, pushing open the door. "Lodgings for five. I had no idea if you'd eaten, or if you'd puked your guts on the way down, or how you'd feel, so I just left a basket of snacks on the table."

It was a suite of connected rooms—or, perhaps, a single-family home that wasn't occupied. The main room was a living area with a kitchenette along the back wall, with four doors leading off to the sides. I checked them all while the others collapsed on the semicircular sofa in the main room. There were two double rooms, a single room, and a bath. The thought must have been that the prince would get his own, but of course he would insist Sagan stay with him. That meant Blackwell would be on his own, and Liu with me, most likely.

"They seem very friendly," the prince was saying when I returned. Talia had taken her leave.

"We have spoken to only two of them," Blackwell reminded. "I hope we won't be kept cooped up the entire time."

"The door isn't locked," Liu commented, trying the knob.

"With your permission, my prince, I'd like to go look around," I said. Here on Venus, I was his servant and guard, part of his household. He was *my* prince now, no longer a generic Highness. "We'll have much more freedom if we know our way around the city."

"Take Blackwell with you."

Blackwell and I went back into the hall. It was empty of people at the moment—had they given us a quiet hallway, or cleared everyone else out?

"We'll have to pay careful attention if we want to find our way back," I said, standing back to get a mental picture of the paintings on either side of the door. One was blue and swirly, the other red and splattery. I thought I could remember that.

"We came from that way," said Blackwell, pointing. "Let's try the other."

We walked for several minutes, choosing the wider hallway at each turning. It seemed everything was in a tidy branching arrangement, so the larger halls should lead us somewhere more populated.

Sure enough, the hall spilled us out onto a wide arcade. Sunlit stairways led up to the garden level, and the wide plastic street was lined with shops.

"It's strange," Blackwell said. "The decor isn't anything like Aphrodite."

Aphrodite was dim, to give the flashing neon lights a chance to stand out. Big signs tempted sailors inside the various establishments. This was bright, clean, understated. Everything was cast out of the same white plastic, and none of the shops had any signs. Probably not necessary, considering they never had any visitors. There were plenty of decorations, though: plastic sculptures of various colors, textile wall hangings, potted plants, more paintings.

Plenty of people were milling about in the arcade, carrying shopping baskets or strolling hand-in-hand. Several rode in wheelchairs as well, which meant there must be ramps or elevators somewhere. I made a mental note to locate them for Sagan.

Their clothes were in the style I recognized from the station above—jumpsuits mostly, either baggy and comfortable or tight and shiny. Some wore cropped shirts with the midriff exposed. That was a fashion Moira liked. I spared a moment's wistful thought for the ruby in her navel, which she'd gotten at Aphrodite.

Strangest to Martian eyes, though, were the body modifications. Even the roughest Martian sailor stuck to a few tattoos or piercings. The Venusians liked to dye their entire skin, either solid or in patterns, and their ears were so decorated with metal they weren't always ear-shaped at all anymore.

We must have stood there gawping long enough to be noticed, because a purple-skinned woman came straight up to us. "You must be some of the visitors," she said. "We've all been so excited. I'm Alix."

We shook hands, and I said, "We thought we'd have a look around. It's really nothing like Aphrodite."

"Is it?" she said. "I've never been. But then, it would be different. Aphrodite's a big source of income. They glitz it up to rake in the money. Here, we're among friends so there really isn't any need."

"But without signs, you can't tell what the shops are!"

"Oh, everyone knows. I guess that makes it hard for you. But you'll get the hang of it. We get people from other stats sometimes, and they find their way. People are always willing to point you around."

"What's worth seeing?"

"Hm." She played with a stud just below her bottom lip. "Every time I come here, I get a pineapple ice. You should have one."

We allowed her to lead us to the stall. "Oh—" I said suddenly, feeling the change in my pocket and realizing the problem. "I don't suppose they want Martian pounds."

"On Venus we only deal in hours," she said. "That's okay. I have plenty of hours. My treat." She peeled off several slips of plastic film and passed them to the proprietor.

"Hours?" asked Blackwell. "That's what you call your currency?"

"Yeah, because we all make the same. One an hour. We used to not do money at all, but it was a problem."

"I can imagine," I said, accepting my pineapple ice from the man behind the counter. "People wouldn't work."

"Oh no," she said. "They all worked. But the people who worked long hours got mad at the people who worked less, because they felt like they were pulling all the weight and the others were being lazy. And then people felt like they had to prove something, so they were taking more hours and the job-dist team was having to make up work just to keep everyone busy." We arrived a plastic table, and she gestured us to sit. "But that's dumb. We don't live to work. There's a lot that has to be done in a place like this, but you have to have some time that's off the clock. It's everybody's judgment call how much is best for them. So, hours."

"What about the people who can't work?" I asked, thinking of William. This work-focused world didn't seem to leave much space for him.

"Everyone can contribute," she said firmly. "Old people and children get theirs by spending time entertaining each other. Sick people get it if they listen to the doctor and rest like they should. And people whose skills aren't strictly useful, survival-wise . . ." She made a gesture at some of the art. "Everyone can do *something*."

I took a bite of my ice to conceal the sudden surge of emotion. She wasn't wrong. A part of me rebelled against the idea that coloring pictures could be equal in value to operating the oxygen plant or something. But didn't both people need to eat about the same amount? I imagined a life where my brother William could pay his way with his paintings. He wouldn't have had to depend on my precarious career for support.

"What about him, though?" asked Blackwell, gesturing with his plastic spoon at the ice man. "He just took several hours from you in five minutes."

"Well, you see five minutes of his labor," she said. "But there's making the ice, and there's the labor of the people that grew the pineapple, and the people down in Refrigeration. The price of the ice is set based on that. But he doesn't keep it. He gives it to Job-Dist and gets one hour for every hour he's open or making the ice. It's just more fair that way. Especially because, here on a stat, we're all using things all the time that we don't pay for, like the air and the lights."

"And what do you do?"

"I work a shift in the gardens . . ." she began, but at that moment I lost the thread of what she was saying. I'd been idly observing the flamboyant hair styles and colors on the people in the plaza when I saw a passerby who wasn't flamboyant at all. She had a blunt bob of blond hair and a sensible tailored suit. A sensible *Earth-style* suit.

Not that I needed the suit to jog my memory. I knew this woman. Ms. Knauss, Earth Force representative. The woman who had shortchanged Moira and given her a job she couldn't possibly complete. All with a smile on her face the whole time.

" . . . and if I need extra hours, I just do a little sex work on the side," Alix continued. "Which is kind of awesome because I'm pretty much—"

She broke off. Blackwell had swallowed a large bite of his pineapple ice at once and was coughing. I covered both his embarrassment and my shock by slapping him firmly on the back.

"That's all fascinating," I said, though I'd suddenly lost all interest in the topic. "So the economy that functions on Aphrodite is a separate thing?"

"Yeah, we operate Aphrodite collectively, and the profits go into the terraforming project and other whole-planet needs. I don't really know how all that stuff works; I mean, I know how I voted last time but if you asked me to break down the money and where it goes, I probably couldn't."

All I wanted was to hurry to the prince and tell him, *Earth is here too.* But he would want to know how I knew, and in the story I had told the Admiralty, I had never met any Earth agents. There was no plausible way for me ever to have sat across a table from an Earther woman that powerful. I could mention her suit, I supposed, but Venusians weren't conservative in their fashions. They might wear almost anything.

But if there was an Earther here, that meant Venus had invited them along with us, and neglected to mention it to us. Was there anything else we didn't know?

"Look," said Blackwell. "There's our guide."

Sure enough, Talia was approaching our table, perhaps after

having gotten Ms. Knauss settled. An awkward thought: were they trying to keep the two groups apart? Should we not be here? But she leaned on the table casually and smiled. "You all get settled? That prince of yours comfy?"

"Everything perfectly comfortable, ma'am," said Blackwell. "We've just been exploring a little."

"You can go wherever you want," said Talia. "But if you roam the lowest levels, stay out of the factory sections unless there's someone with you. There are plenty of workers around to give you a tour if you want."

"All I need at the moment is a radio," said Blackwell. "I was told we would have access …?"

"Of course. Come on, I'll show ya. Thanks for entertaining the company, Alix." She squeezed the purple girl's shoulder with a large hand.

At the far end of the arcade was a radio office, not too different from those on Aphrodite or Phobos: a long counter, with a number of clerks. You could pass your written message to the clerks, and they would pass it to the operators within. The barely-audible chattering of Morse code behind the doors gave it a comfortable sense of familiarity.

"Please, send as many messages as you need, at any time," said Talia. "They've been told to help you out." She gave us a small stack of cards, one for each member of the delegation, reading, *Diplomatic Staff. Unlimited Credit.*

Blackwell had a message already written out to transmit. I went to the other end of the counter and gave my transit numbers—both the official one and the private one I used to speak with Moira. That meant a brief wait, while the operators retrieved my messages, which had been forwarded as I had requested.

From my mother, this:

My goodness, going to Venus itself! That'll be something to boast about when you get back. Not a lot of people can say that. I can't say much because these villains are charging me by the word.

William is well. I know he sends his love because he saw me writing and brought me a drawing. I wish I could radio it to you. It's some circles and lines, I am not good at describing things. Reminded me of clouds.

I didn't write back to that one. After all, if she was being charged by the word to keep up this correspondence, she would probably bankrupt herself writing back.

From Moira, this:

God it's good to hear from you. I reached out to a contact on Galileo who's going to set up something with you. He'll call you by your code name and tell you I sent him. I've been promised he won't out you to the other Martians, though I have no idea how the forum is supposed to go down if they're keeping you secret.

Kisses and one good squeeze on the ass from me!

Forum? I wasn't sure what she was talking about there. Perhaps we would find out soon. It was clear the Venusians hadn't been entirely open about what our visit would look like.

I took a paper from the counter and sat down at a nearby table to compose a reply. What with the code, it took ages just to write *message received* but I wanted to say something else. Some kind of a reply to her shameless flirtation. But it was so hard to think what to say. I wasn't comfortable being as open as she was.

Finally I managed,

One squeeze? I think I can see my way to allowing more than one. If you're polite about it. These Venusians barely wear anything and it reminds me of you somehow. Can't think why.

Blackwell's shadow fell across my page. "Are you done writing your sweetheart yet? I want to report back."

I put my hand over the page, even though it was only the drivel my code was concealed in. "Almost finished." I knew I was blushing and smiling to myself, but that was actually a better cover than otherwise. "Lieutenant can't stop giggling over writing to her girlfriend" was a perfectly explicable and forgettable event. And it gave me plenty of excuse to use the radio often.

Once I had addressed the message to Moira's number, I turned it in and followed Blackwell.

"Our baggage arrived," said Liu when we got back. "And a newspaper. It's pretty awful."

Sagan was laboriously at work unpacking in the prince's room, carefully bending over to remove one item at a time. I sprang to help. It was insanity to bring them when Shen had been available. He could have functioned at this gravity better. Sagan was more a liability than anything. Even if they were the prince's bodyguard, that meant very little here where the gravity was triple what Sagan was used to.

"Thank you," Sagan said, as I knelt by the prince's suitcase to hand up items for them to put away. "I've been told to be careful lifting anything, but it's taking forever. Do you think the doctor was overcautious?"

"Not at all," I said. "It isn't just about your muscles. If you aren't careful, you could break a bone or slip a disc in your back." *And even if you are, you could have a heart attack or stroke,* I didn't add. Surely they'd been apprised of the risks. "I wonder at him making you come down here."

"I insisted," they said quietly. "I wanted to do my duty, and the doctor cleared me, so why shouldn't I come? I've been exercising with the prince since we found out about this mission. I would have thought I'd be handling the gravity better, after all that."

"If your bones don't get the right stresses on them in childhood, they just don't grow the same." I handed up a pile of handkerchiefs. There was something a little uncomfortable in bringing up the difference between us. That I had been carefully raised to be able to visit Earth if I ever needed to, and they had not. Because at no point in any of their upbringing did anyone consider the possibility of expensive off-planet travel.

"A Founder upbringing is a wonderful thing, Lieutenant," Sagan said, with the faintest edge to their voice.

So Sagan sensed what I did, that this was about more than gravity. I flailed for an adequate response. *Sorry? So you know, I voted Russet last time?*

But I still wasn't sure Sagan was what they seemed. What if their insistence on coming down was because they were some sort of spy, the suspected judas? There was so much that was strange about their attachment to the prince, less like a valet than like a limb. Either Sagan was far more loyal than normal, or they had an agenda entirely their own.

So I kept any expressions of sympathy to myself. "I can't deny it's been an advantage," I said at last, handing up the last stack of clothing and straightening up. "Though it still isn't adequate preparation, really. I feel like I've been in the gym all day."

"How exhausting." Sagan's voice was calm and their gaze blank, but the sarcasm somehow came through loud and clear. I picked up the suitcase and brought it back out into the living room.

"I'll put your things in this bedroom, shall I?" I asked Liu, taking up her suitcase. It felt like it was loaded with cannonballs.

"I suppose we'll be sharing," she said with a slight smile. "Blackwell claimed the other."

"I wouldn't feel right, leaving the main door unguarded," I said. "There's no lock and I don't think Sagan's going to be able to protect the prince if anyone breaks in. I thought I would sleep out here, on the couch."

She looked at the couch she was sitting on, perplexed. "You won't be comfortable."

"No." *But less uncomfortable than sharing a room with you would make me.* "I was sent with you as a servant and bodyguard, because you couldn't bring your usual servants or a company of marines. But I am a military officer and I intend to do my job."

"Suit yourself."

After everyone had finally gone to bed—ten pm by the electric clock on the wall, three am by my pocketwatch—I sat a while, reading the paper. It was printed on a rough, cheap kind of paper, probably made of plant scraps.

Most of the news was Venus specific, and dealt with items of interest from other stats. A new automated mining post was operational now on the surface, increasing the amount of minerals produced by twenty percent. A concert had been held on New Brasilia and records would eventually be made available. The inventor of a new, more efficient chemical process was interviewed.

But page six was dedicated to news from Mars. Doubtless somewhat inaccurate, but given the frequency of broadcasts and travel between Phobos and Aphrodite, it would at any rate be more up to date than anything I knew.

MARS PLANS ELECTIONS; POPULACE DOUBTS CHANGE

The Martian Empire is holding elections for the seat of Tribune, who ostensibly represents the non-landowning class in Parliament, on Decimus 28 (Leo 11 in the Martian calendar). The current tribune, Vasily Chin-Hawking, has done nothing to improve commoner rights during his tenure, but the voters have little choice. Only the Founder class is permitted to hold office at all. Even if a tribune did care to protect the rights of his constituents, he'd have little luck with one hundred votes in Parliament to oppose him.

In the recent parliamentary election, in which only the Founder class may vote, the populist Russet party lost two seats, which were both picked up by the pro-technology Gray party. Could we be seeing another planet move away from antiquated anti-electricity laws? We wouldn't count on it.

I lowered the paper to my lap. No wonder Liu hadn't liked it. But I hoped the prince had read it. It was vital, for any diplomatic efforts with them, to realize just how poorly they rated us as a nation.

As well they might. I'd been told before that Venus had a serious problem with excessive numbers of Martian sailors attempting to desert and seek asylum there. They knew Mars was barbarically unequal, from their own radically egalitarian perspective. Even though they might prefer us as an ally, from a self-interested point of view, they didn't like us personally. Many of the voters would vote against any sort of deal with us purely on principle.

Was that the idea in bringing Earth here as well? Give both of us a chance to speak our piece, so the voters could decide who was the less-awful ally or damn us both?

If so, Liberty Station was in a perfect position to shine by comparison. If they didn't want to deal with a classist empire, and they didn't want to deal with a conglomerate of mega-corps, they might leap on the idea of supporting a new, so far classless, independent colony.

If I could only find a way to present everything they needed to know without giving away my identity. Their democratic ways had seemed utopian in the abstract, but practically speaking, I had a desperate need for this deal to be worked out in a smoky back room.

19

MOIRA

Excuse me," I asked the librarian, "which way to the periodicals?"

The woman stared up at me over the wide counter of polished wood. "Do you have a card?"

"The sign says 'open to the public.'"

"You can't take books away without a card," said the librarian with a suspicious look up and down my drab jacket and trousers. The look said: *Our usual clientele is Founders, or at least the better-off sort of commoner. Not you.*

"I'm not looking to take anything away," I said, spreading my hands innocently, to show I wasn't carrying a bag. "I just want to see the newspapers from the past few months."

The woman sighed and got to her feet, heels tap-tapping on the tile floor. I glared at her primly twitching ass. Uppity commoners, the worst sort. Thought looking down on other colonists made them the next thing to Founders. But you'd never see a Founder in a million years notice the difference, so why bother?

It took me some time to collect all the newspapers that mentioned bombings. Some of the bombings had been major news events, especially the early ones. Others were back-page stories, if few had died or they were far out in the country.

I set the start date of the rash of bombings at six months ago. That was when they had started happening regularly, rather than one in a few years. Since then, they had happened about twice a month, a bit more in the last month or two. Not with any exact regularity, but not clustering either. No two had ever happened in the same week, or in the same town. Even Landing had only been hit once, on a suburban tram line.

It couldn't be just random, the act of fed-up individuals. Individuals smashed storefronts, they stabbed strangers, occasionally they set themselves on fire. Bombs were something you had to have access to.

More important, individuals wouldn't space themselves out so carefully. They'd happen, purely by accident, to do something the same week as someone else. Or perhaps one would set off a string of imitators. This was not that.

There was one other odd detail. None of the bombings had killed only Founders. They seemed random; on a train track, but not hitting the first class carriage; in an open-air market; in a courthouse, but killing only commoners except for one magistrate. Why would a revolutionary group not specifically target Founders, or even particularly bad Founders? The newspapers universally blamed "anarchists" or "republicans" and editorialized about how the revolutionaries were only hurting their own cause by killing so many of their own people. But the actual perpetrators never seemed to be named or caught. It could have been anyone.

I jotted down a list of places and dates and put the newspapers away. This was interesting, but none of it even came close to a lead. I needed to know what the bombs had been made of, where the ingredients had been sourced, and whether the perpetrators had been caught in the blast or escaped. Of course none of the papers had reported on that, if even the police knew.

I went through the ritual of opening my jacket and turning around, to prove to the librarian I hadn't been pilfering, and went out onto the street. Today Harrington had her strike. I still didn't really approve, but I decided to pass by the workshop. Perhaps there was something I could do to support the strikers—bring water or something.

When I arrived, the scene was peaceful. A line of neatly-dressed workers, mostly women, sat on the sidewalk in front of the building, arms linked. The line bent at the corner and went down the alley beside the building, presumably to encircle it altogether. Inside the windows, more workers sat at the machines, hands in their laps.

They had no signs, because they didn't need signs. Everyone knew what the Martian commoners wanted: equality in all things, starting with the vote.

But in case of any confusion, the workers were singing a revolutionary song. Their voices sounded rough and tired, and the tempo dragged. They'd clearly been at it for a while.

I walked along the sidewalk till I came to where Harrington was sitting, princess style, in her narrow skirt. "So you really did it."

"Of course I did," said Harrington. "I believe in the cause."

"Guess I shouldn't have doubted. You want some water or something?"

"We have people bringing us some. This is all supported by the Russet Workers. If you really want to help you could join the line." She made as if to pull one arm out of the arm of the woman next to her.

"I couldn't," I said. "I can't draw the attention of the police, you know that."

"Better get out of here, then," said Harrington. "The owner just left to get them, when we wouldn't let his new workers in."

I glanced up. Sure enough, a covered truck was creeping up the street, with helmeted men hanging onto the side. I turned away and sauntered up the street, a little faster than before.

Across the alley from the workshop was a café. I ducked inside and joined a little crowd watching from the windows.

Outside, the police truck pulled up. Others followed, with men in shiny helmets leaping down and arranging into neat ranks. Someone gave an order to disperse through a bullhorn, but nobody moved. The singing got louder, blending with the bullhorn in a grating cacophony.

"I hate to watch," said a woman at my elbow, "but I can't look away."

"Why do they bother when it always ends the same?" asked someone else.

A firetruck had arrived, and the police were hooking up the hose. Water slammed out, looking more like a solid white weapon than a spray. Women tumbled over as the water hit them, but some kept hanging on. Harrington's part of the line was chained to the door, so even when the water choked and toppled them, they stayed in place, hanging by their arms.

When the firehose shut off, the singing had stopped. The street was quiet again. Dripping women clung to each other and tried to get back to their feet. The police approached to drag the strikers toward the trucks. Harrington stayed in place until a policeman with a pair of bolt cutters cut the chain. Then she was dragged off with the others.

The whole ordeal had taken less than twenty minutes.

As Harrington hung limply in the arms of two officers, making herself as heavy and difficult to carry as she could, she turned her head toward me. Her eyes stayed fixed directly at my cafe window as long as she was in view.

Once Harrington passed out of sight behind the paddy wagon, I looked away. Something in the look on her face had said, *See, I told you I was serious.*

20

LUCY

I was awakened by the sound of the door softly clicking open. I threw off the blanket and leaped to my feet. Someone was outlined in the light shining from the hallway outside. Someone big.

In better gravity, I'd have vaulted over the couch and had the person in a headlock before they saw me coming. Instead I stomped around it with my fists up.

"Oh dear," said a nervous voice, and the light flicked on.

I lowered my fists. "Talia. You gave me a fright."

"I didn't realize anyone would be sleeping out here. I thought I could just sneak in with a little breakfast casserole to start your day off right." She held it in front of her like a peace offering.

"You're too kind." I took the dish from her. "The others are still sleeping."

"Well, I'll get out of your hair then. Tell them we'll have a little meeting at ten a.m. Just to brief them about what we have in mind."

She ducked out, and I was left blinking. It was six-thirty in the morning, earlier than I would have liked to get up but too late to go back to sleep. An intense craving for a decent cup of tea hit me like a broadside. And if I wanted one, the prince would soon be up wanting one too.

The kitchen held only dishes, no food beyond salt and a bottle of vinegar. I scratched a note on a scrap of newspaper and went out.

The arcade was reasonably busy. Most likely the Venusians distributed their shifts evenly, like on a ship, since there was no night and day here. Or rather, there were two days on the light side before the stat made its way over to the night side of the planet. When the sun shone, the garden crews would be hard at work, and the rest of the machinery would need to be operated at any time.

I strolled down one side of the plaza, peering under archways for anything resembling a tea shop. No luck. I crossed over and started searching the other.

A man with red swirling tattoos on his arms and face came toward me, across the open middle of the square. He fell in step beside me. "Looking for something?"

"Tea," I said. "I don't even know if you drink it here."

"You're in the Martian delegation." It was half a question.

"Yes."

"The one they call Lafayette?"

My heart suddenly sped up. I wasn't sure I needed the tea anymore. "Sometimes. Who's asking?"

"A friend of Moira's."

This was my contact. I looked him up and down. Apart from the tattoos, he was nondescript: brunet, white, late thirties. Somehow I'd thought Moira would be in touch with Talia, on the grounds that she'd work from the top down. But there wasn't a top here at all, was there? And it had never been her way in the first place.

"I can't talk now," I said. "I have to get back with some tea for the others."

"Unfortunately, we don't drink it here," he said. "We drink coffee. I hope that will do."

"I'm willing to experiment." I'd never had it. Yet another Earth product that hadn't been seen on Mars since the embargo. Or not in the drawing rooms I cared to frequent.

My contact directed me to a shop with a long line in front. A pungent, slightly burned aroma wafted out. As he turned to go, I asked, "Is there a way to contact you?"

"Ask at the chemical plant, next level to the bottom," he said. "Name of Marcus."

When I returned to our rooms, bearing a large, steaming pot, Blackwell and Liu were already up.

"I hope that's tea," said Liu, yawning.

"Best I could do was coffee." I pulled cups from the cupboard and started filling them.

"Not so much," said Blackwell. "Coffee is much stronger than tea. You'll give us all the jitters."

"Oh, so you're a coffee drinker, Mr. Blackwell?" said Liu. "For shame."

"Showing your youth, aren't you, Miss Liu? When I was your age, coffee was a legal import."

The prince's bedroom door was still shut, so I filled a cup to take to him. As I raised my hand to knock, I heard voices. "Here are your studs—ow." That was Sagan.

"You should have let me get those," said the prince. "Or better yet, I shouldn't have let you come."

"You couldn't have stopped me," the valet fired back.

I knocked, setting off a little commotion within. What kind of valet talked to a prince like that? I wondered if they meant it.

What kind of influence could Sagan be holding over the prince? Blackmail, perhaps?

Sagan opened the door, metal braces rattling a little as they moved. "Coffee for the prince," I said, holding it out.

"Thank you, Lieutenant," said the prince, standing by his bed and adjusting his cuffs. "We will all need it."

"The meeting with the Venusians is at ten, sir."

"Very good."

I shut the door and went at last to get my own cup of coffee. It was harsh and bitter, nothing like tea at all. Ah well. At least this place had a decent shower, though my turn at it would come second to last.

Once the diplomatic staff was at their meeting, I went out again in search of Marcus. The stairs to the lower levels were easy enough to find—there were some at either end of the plaza. But getting from there to the chemical plant took many wrong turns. Talia had warned us about that, and recommended a guide if we ventured down that far. In the end I had to ask for directions twice, which concerned me. I didn't want to leave a trail of people who would remember I'd been down here. But then, I was in a Martian Imperial Navy uniform. Knee breeches, white stockings, dark blue coat down to the knees. I could hardly blend in whatever I did.

The chemical plant was at the end of a long, wide hallway, which terminated in a set of open double doors. Workers in comfortable jumpsuits passed in and out now and again. I stopped one. "Does Marcus work here?"

For a moment I worried they'd want a last name, which I didn't have. But in a place this size, he must have been the only Marcus. The worker went in and came back out with my contact.

Marcus pulled a card out of his pocket, stuck it in a machine in the wall till it beeped, and put it back in his pocket. "There, I'm clocked out," he said. "All yours."

"Is that a problem for your work?"

"No, we're a little overstaffed at the moment anyway. Everyone tries to put in some time here, get to learn the processes."

He led me down the hall and down one last set of stairs. This last level wasn't exactly a floor. It was a catwalk, with railings, hanging over the curved bottom of the balloon. My knees went a little wobbly just standing there, with nothing below but the faint shine of the balloon's surface and the parallel stripes of the solar panels. Beyond that, a dark roil of cloud. We were on the night side now, with no light beyond the balloon but the occasional flash of lightning.

"So," he said, leaning on the railing. "What is it you need from me?"

I jerked my gaze away from the clouds. "What did Moira tell you?"

"She said there's a short, blond girl with the Mars delegation, code name Lafayette, tell her Moira sent me. Help her out with her project. Cryptic, but it's not like Moira and I have a code. I assume the rest of the story was too secret to radio."

"It is." I swallowed. I had hoped—what? That someone else would take charge? I wouldn't have liked *that* option much either. "How do you know Moira?"

"We used to date," he said.

I stopped breathing and looked down to hide my expression in shadow. I focused hard on the clouds below us. He could be lying, of course. My knuckles whitened on the rail. Why didn't I believe he was lying? Why did it matter so much?

"Or, well," he added, "they say spacers have a lover in every port. I don't flatter myself I was more important to her than that. But I liked her a lot. That was back when I worked at Immigration. Every few months, she would show up again, we'd spend a week together, and that would be it.

"Last time I saw her, she was … different." That would be when she'd deserted, while the *Mariposa* lay at orbit there. "I mean she's always a little bitter. You know her personally?"

I swallowed. The first time I tried to speak, no sound came out. I tried again. "I do."

"Well, what I mean is angrier than usual. Actively raging instead of cynical. Also a little drunk. She *demanded* I get her a visa. She had left her ship and couldn't go back—I only got bits of the story, but she was very insistent that going back to her ship wasn't an option. But of course Martian Navy spacers can't desert and ever go home again. I've heard that from enough of them over the years at Immigration. They're always begging us to take them. Rule of the job is always to say no, unless they have some kind of special skills or a relative here."

I pursed my lips. That was the dark side of Venus. Nice enough if you were lucky enough to live here, cared nothing for anyone who wasn't.

"I explained how hard it is to make a new stat while you're flying along at two hundred kph and fifty klicks in the air. I told her all about the trust you have to have with the people you're on it with, how our entire system relies on every single person pulling their weight and never leaving a job half-assed. We all voted on the requirements for entry and we made it tight because we know the whole thing falls apart if a few bad apples get in. It'll be different when the terraforming is done. We'll have all the room on the planet, then, and it'll be a haven for democracy—I mean that!"

He had turned earnest because of the skepticism on my face. "I believe you," I said. Or at least, I believed he did. By the time the planet was terraformed, Marcus and all his generation would be dead and gone. Would their descendants care about being a haven for democracy?

"Well, she laid into me," he went on. "Said Venus was just a bunch of hypocrites and if we really believed in the equality of everyone, that should count just as much for refugees. That they didn't need the help in centuries, they needed it now. She told me all about how terrible it is on Mars—really made me feel it. She said she never wanted to see me again.

"It really hit me where I live. It hurt. And I said, look. I'm not giving you a visa because I can't; I'm not authorized to unless you fit this list we all voted on. But I owe you something, and if you ever need anything I can provide, something that really helps the cause of your people, I'll do it.

"Then I pointed her to where some Earth contractors were hiring—they always hang around the immigration office, because they have their eyes open—and that was the last I saw of her. She hasn't even radioed till now, though I can hardly blame her for that."

I nodded, staring down at the dark clouds. My soul felt dark and hollow. What could Moira have possibly meant, sending this man to me? The Moira I remembered had never been interested in a man. I remembered all her fancies well; had listened so intently, envying them all.

Who was this new Moira? How had she spent those years we'd been apart? Did she have a lover in every port, like Marcus said? I'd been eating my heart out in Hellas and she'd been sleeping with half the system. Maybe all that time, my own heart was the only one that had been broken.

Some secret operative I was, distracted by my private heartbreak. I inhaled sharply and turned to face him. "I have a lot to lose if I trust you," I said quietly. "But I don't have anyone else I can ask. Can I count on you to keep everything I say secret? Not just from the other Martians, from everyone?"

He ran his eyes over my face. "Will it harm the stat, or Venus?"

"No," I said quickly. "I'd never ask you to compromise your loyalty."

"All right then. Shoot."

I took a deep breath. "You know about Liberty Station?"

"Earth pirates and Martian deserters, camped out in a Martian mining station. Set up their own independent republic, or so they claim."

"That's who Moira is working for now. She found her own place to get away from the Empire. As far as Mars is concerned, I'm the officer sent to protect and serve their delegation. But in reality…I'm here on Moira's behalf."

"Diplomatically?"

"Yes. Liberty Station wants to make a deal with Venus as well. We've never had diplomatic relations before, and neither Mars nor Earth will recognize us at all. But it seems Venus might."

He leaned his chin on his fist. "Why would we? Moira isn't wrong, we're isolationist as hell."

"I read a newspaper last night. You people judge Mars pretty harshly."

"Of course we do. Your human rights record is appalling. Worse than Earth's, if you ask me."

I resisted the urge to argue that point. "But you don't love Earth either."

"Nope. Capitalist hellscape."

"Liberty is neither of those. So far, there's no class structure and no big corps. I don't know if they can keep it that way, but I do know they intend to. You can't take in every stray, but Moira hopes to. Build more stations, if they need to."

"If they don't already need to, they're not much of a republic," Marcus pointed out. "It's smaller than Aphrodite."

"The whole population of Venus was once a single stat," I argued. "I think you have a lot more in common with Liberty than you do with either of the big powers."

"It's true," he said. "And maybe other people would agree. Depending on what you brought to the table—we only deal at *all* with outsiders to get what we need here. If you're just extracting gases—"

"We extract metals, too. Minerals. Some of it useful for your terraforming project."

"Okay. Well, let's say I'm on board here. I like what you're saying, but I'm just one guy. It may take some doing to get you a chance to say your piece. The forum is next week!"

I held up a hand. "Wait. Forum?"

"That was the plan, bringing everyone down here. We're hosting a live forum where the Martian delegation and one from Earth can speak their piece and see who wants to form closer ties with one or the other. Then we vote."

I buried my head in my hands. Of course, *that* was why Knauss was here. She was hoping to make a deal with Venus, just like the prince was. The Venusians had neglected to tell us about each other, probably to keep us from bringing weapons or causing trouble.

"A *public* forum?" I asked in a small voice. "Up in front of everyone?"

"Well, nat—oh. You're worried about blowing your cover."

I took a deep breath and let it out. "I will give up my cover, if I have to. When I have to. If there's something vital I can gain from it. And if this could give Liberty a good chance, I ..." I trailed off. I wasn't at all sure it would be worth it. Wouldn't Venus think first of its own self-interest, and avoid angering the two larger powers? I didn't want to blow my cover for nothing.

I didn't want to blow my cover for *anything*. If Mars came to know of my double-dealing, I could never go back again. Never see my parents, or William. Never see the sun on the Hellas Sea or the red ridge of the basin or the wild grasses that grow beside the water.

My family would lose their only source of income, of course, and be permanently shamed. Not that they had much of either money or public respect to lose. But for William it might make all the difference. He needed stability.

I'd told Moira I was ready to leave Mars forever for her. And I had been. I certainly had set out on this mission with every intent to cut bait and leave the Navy the second it was helpful to Liberty for me to do so. Because once I did that, I had no reason to be apart from Moira ever again.

But that was under the assumption that she was eager to have me back. Suddenly I thought of the night we'd said goodbye. My departure from Liberty had been her idea. Had she been giving me a chance to take care of my family, or trying to get rid of me? Maybe she had realized, once we'd reconnected, that we'd both changed too much. That she didn't actually want to be with me anymore.

None of that should matter, when it came to doing the right thing. I hadn't left the Navy for Moira; I'd left it because I knew it was wrong. It should be easy to leave it again. But the voyage here had been so uneventful, and my crewmates so pleasant, that the whole thing had gotten to me. Made me feel like an officer again. Made me love the Empire again, which I knew I shouldn't do.

Marcus watched me pass through layers of distress before finally interrupting, "Let's not get ahead of ourselves. There might be a way to do it. I need to talk with the team that's organizing the forum, let them know there's a third party that wants in. I won't tell them who. First they gotta agree to it in the first place. And if they do, maybe we can find a way to get your words out without putting your face up there in front of everyone."

It wouldn't be the same, though. If the prince and Knauss made their impassioned speeches in person, and I turned in a written argument to be read aloud, there could be no comparison. I'd heard both speak. The prince was charismatic, inspiring. Knauss could sell waste air to a pirate. Even in person, I wasn't sure I could compete with either of them.

"All right," I said. "Do what you can. I appreciate this."

"I'd be the hypocrite Moira thinks I am if I didn't," Marcus said, pushing away from the railing. "I'll be in touch."

I stopped at the plaza on the way back and made it back to our rooms just before the diplomatic staff did. They were in a sour mood.

"A bait and switch, is what I call it," stormed Liu. "Why didn't they tell us there would be Earthers here? We would have brought a bigger guard."

"They specifically restricted the number we could bring," Blackwell pointed out.

"I'm worried about the forum." The prince sat down and let Sagan replace his shoes with slippers. "I expected to be sitting down with a few influential people. If we're instead campaigning to a crowd, I wonder if we should have sent one of our more political leaders. The prime minister, even, instead of me."

"You're an excellent public speaker," soothed Liu. "That part, I don't think we need to worry about."

I stayed in the kitchenette, preparing lunch with the items I'd bought. There was some kind of purple taro paste, crispy sweet potato rounds, bananas, and a tofu curry. I wasn't sure what any of it would taste like, but the vendor had assured me these items would go over well.

"I think I was wrong about them being open to an alliance," said the prince. "I had assumed if they asked us here, it was because they were thinking about it, but with Earth here too? I can't imagine what they're playing at."

"They seemed nervous to me," said Blackwell. "I wonder if Earth has been making threats. We tend to see Venus as comfortably sitting out the war, but they may be worried it will reach them. They have no ships of their own. Their only bargaining chip is the carbon-fiber plant on Aphrodite."

"That's a pretty big chip," Liu pointed out. "Everyone that sails needs it, and nobody else in the system makes it, or has the endless supply of carbon it would *take* to make it. Even if Earth took the station, Venus could simply stop sending up the carbon. Nobody else has the knowledge to navigate the atmosphere here."

"That's been the case as long as I've been alive," said Blackwell. "But something has changed, or they wouldn't have us out here. I can't help but think that if they could continue excluding all outsiders, they would be."

I brought out the tray and they moved on to opinions about the strange food. But I kept turning over in my mind what Blackwell had said. What was different now? What did Venus have to gain by bringing us out here? What did they have to lose if they didn't? I had to learn the answers to these questions if I had any chance of bringing them around to an alliance with Liberty.

After they were in bed, I lay on the settee, eyes hunting the darkness for answers. Not about Venus and the diplomatic situation. About Moira.

I had been so sure I knew her like no one else. Because I'd known her from back when we were children. That had to count for something—for everything.

If it didn't, then I had nothing going for me. We had nothing else in common besides where we came from. Not class, not education, and certainly not personality. We'd had so little time to reconnect. I knew hardly anything about the person she was now. I had assumed that knowing the person she used to be was enough. This was the first time I'd been forced to notice the difference.

She was out of my star, that was for certain. Confident, beautiful, sharp-witted. Not for her, my months of angsting. She knew what she wanted and went for it. If I'd met her today, I'd have been tongue-tied. Only her obvious interest had given me the confidence to think myself worthy.

But maybe I wasn't, never had been. Maybe I had been her adolescent crush that she'd briefly, stupidly wanted to win. Just to prove she could. And then once she had me, she hadn't known what to do with me. She'd gotten rid of me.

That was a lot to pull out of a single piece of her history. But it wasn't just that. She'd barely written to me since we'd been apart. I'd written her every week I'd been at home, and she had written only twice since she'd arrived on Mars. What was she doing with her time? What did she dream for our future? Instead it was mostly vague flirtation, things she could have said about anyone.

Like Marcus, for instance.

I switched on the light and got my notebook to draft a note. Surely writing to her would make me feel better. I thought of my words winging their way across the system in radio pulses, reaching her in a matter of minutes. Or at least, reaching the planet she was on. That would have to pass for closeness.

Dear Moira, I was surprised to discover

You might have told me

I don't know if I know you anymore.

None of it was any good. I couldn't have this conversation by radio, the letters hidden in meaningless drivel. It took me half an hour to write a paragraph, and I had so much more than that to say.

At last I wrote,

Have connected with your contact. Not sure yet what to do for the forum. Lucy.

21

MOIRA

E ighty people went to prison, for what? To shut down the sew-ing machines for six hours?"

I was in Khan's underground hideout, pacing his tiny room.

"As part of a larger strategy of rolling strikes—"

"How does that help anything? Every time you do one of these, you have fewer people to do them with!"

"And they have fewer people to run their mills and work-shops," Khan pointed out.

I paused in my tirade, thinking for a moment. "Aren't the prisons overflowing with all of this?"

Khan shook his head. "They rent out the convict labor. The Founders were taught early on in school that it's unthinkable to own a person. But to *rent* a person, that doesn't trouble their sleep."

I threw myself into the one chair in the room, which threat-ened to collapse under me. "You can't just leave Harrington and the others on a chain gang!"

Khan rubbed his chin thoughtfully. "If only I had someone who could lead a mission like that ... someone with military experience … someone who's actually carried out a prison break before …"

I glared at him. "Oh no you don't. I told you there was nothing I could do."

"Which was a lie, of course. What you meant was that there was nothing you *wanted* to do. You have nothing but time till your ship comes back to orbit, but you *choose* to spend it serving coffee."

"I quit that job," I muttered. "And I've been trying to find your bombers, too, for what that's worth."

"So you don't mind helping me." He wheeled a little closer to my chair. "I'm not asking you to dedicate your life to the cause. But *if* you could run a mission releasing some of our imprisoned workers, it would make a great difference to us."

"I just don't see a difference," I said, disconsolate. "So I free eighty workers, or whatever. And they come straight back and do another strike and get thrown back again. And the Empire continues to *not care* just like it never cares."

"Things are changing, slowly," said Khan. "We're putting in front of people's eyes, all the time, that we don't consent to this treatment. We're not allowing them to pretend it isn't happening, like past generations did. The young Founders of today think differently than their parents, and they vote. In time—"

"Things are changing at a glacier's pace," I said. "I thought things were about to change when I was a teenager, and now they're worse than ever. People are dying, waiting for things to change."

"I'm an old man," said Khan. "Older than I should be, because of my time in Deimos Prison. One way or another, I'm going to die at some point. The only thing that comforts me is the thought that someday, the people of Mars might be truly free. Even if I don't live to see it."

I looked at the floor. "I just want to live to see Lucy again," I whispered.

"Where was that fear when you broke me out of Deimos?"

"I had nothing to live for then," I said. "I have everything now. My happiness feels so—fragile. I'm afraid to move."

"That's what they want," said Khan harshly. "They want you to fear. To despair. Isn't that what that show of force was at your friend's workshop? Every time they fire into a crowd? They want you to believe there is no point, so that you'll stay home."

"How do you know they're not right? We have so much more to lose than they do."

"And yet they're frightened too. If they weren't frightened they wouldn't have to clamp down as hard as they are."

I tried to imagine fear behind those policemen's hard faces. Under the helmets of the Imperial Guard. I could hardly believe that. "If their fear is making them come down this hard, maybe we should back off." I wondered what it would take to turn down the temperature in this city.

"Not an option," he said. "You know it's never taken provocation for them to hurt us. They'll always be afraid, because they know they're hurting us, and there are more of us than there are of them."

He was right on that count. Things had been so much calmer five years ago, but that hadn't stopped the injustice. Hadn't stopped good sailors from being thrown out airlocks, men like my father thrown on his ear after a life of service.

"Just promise me this is the only thing you'll expect," I said at last. "Just let me rescue my friend. Don't try to frog-boil me into your revolution."

He gave a careful nod. "Just this one mission. I won't ask anything else."

This was the truth, as he perceived it. He wasn't a liar. But I had a sneaking suspicion that as scenarios shifted, he'd try to rope me in again. Or, with or without his effort, I'd end up involved. A revolution didn't seem the type of thing you could let in, just the tip.

The Sea of Clouds

revolution didn't seem the type of thing you could let in, just the tip.

22

LUCY

The next day was spent on meetings. The prince met with work team leads, trade managers, and community leaders, trying to win their support ahead of the forum. Almost as important, he probed for their motivations.

I attended most of these meetings, now that he knew the Earthers were on the station. He wanted some muscle along with him, and I was the closest thing available. I wasn't convinced I could actually fight an Earther if I needed to, not with them comfortable at this gravity and me still constantly exhausted. But I did have a folding knife concealed in my coat, despite our assurances before coming down that we wouldn't bring any weapons. If discovered, I'd simply claim it was a normal part of Navy kit. Got to … splice those ropes, or something.

Mostly I sat and listened. On the third day we met with a woman whose job was setting quotas for trade—or, perhaps, heading a committee that set them?—and communicating those quotas to Aphrodite. It was hard to say. Venusians had the habit of saying "we" for everything, regardless of whether or not anyone else was actually involved.

"We never export much hydrogen," the woman was saying. Jemma, I thought her name was. Her hair was a flaming, artificial red and her dark skin was freckled with gold. "We have enough, but really just enough for what we'll ultimately want. We have many times the oxygen we need, however, and are happy to trade it."

"It seems to me," said the prince, "that you have an excellent deal going on. You would benefit just from *giving* it away, and carbon too. But because other people want it, you can price it as high as Earth does."

"Just because we don't have capitalism in the stats doesn't mean we don't understand it, Elliott." The Venusians, after observing the prince's obvious discomfort when they used his first name, had settled on his last. "If Earth sets the price at forty Earth dollars per ton, it would be foolish for us to ask for much less. After all, we can only bottle it so fast no matter how high the demand is. Best to get the highest price we can for the goods we provide."

"Even knowing everyone but Earth is barely surviving because of the high prices? My government isn't your only customer. You sell to independent shippers as well, and they are constantly going out of business because of oxygen prices, among other expenses."

Jemma sat back in her chair. "You're pleading on behalf of independent shippers? We could cut them a special deal and it still wouldn't leave Mars any better off."

"True," he said. "I just wonder how you square your foreign policy with your radical unselfishness at home."

Jemma was quiet a moment, playing with her pen. "Do you have children, Elliott?"

A hard-to-read expression flitted across the prince's face. "No."

"Well, imagine someone else, then. A shopkeeper, with children. She'll cut a hard bargain with her customers, but if her children ask her for breakfast, she just gives it away." She laid down her pen across her notebook. "We're a family here. We aren't in business to get rich. We're in business to provide a high standard of living in the stats, and to terraform the surface for eventual habitation. But both are massive jobs, especially the latter. At our current rate of change, it will take almost a millennium before the pressure is low enough to live on the surface. That isn't fast enough."

The prince tried another tack. "We provide more of the minerals you need to capture carbon than Earth does, don't we?"

She picked up her pen again. "Well. Yes, naturally we do more business with you, because you need our product more. Earth's atmosphere is self-sustaining, while Mars always needs to be fed. Oxygen and nitrogen are our main exports to you, with carbon fiber a distant third. Earth only buys carbon fiber, and the minerals they send us are negligible."

"Then why do you need to deal with them at all? You turn out a limited quantity of carbon fiber every year. You could sell all of that to us."

"You can't pay us what Earth does. You give us minerals, and yes, that's important in the long term, but Earth provides biological materials that only exist there. Mars's ecosystem is limited and temperate zone only. Earth has almost infinite biodiversity. We're constantly buying new seeds from them, animals that can be farmed on a small scale, and so on. We have to keep the trade routes with them open, or they'll permanently limit our agricultural diversity."

The prince stared down at the table. It was true, there was no way we could compete with Earth in that market. Finally he said, "If the status quo is working for you, what is this all about? Why bring everyone out here?"

Jemma sat up straight and put her pen down. Up to this moment, it had been a relaxed chat about trade. Now her face was closed as tight as a Martian who'd been asked about their sex life. "That's not what this meeting is about."

"What *is* it about?" Frustration seeped into the prince's voice. "What are we even doing here if we don't know what deal is on the table or what the stakes are?"

Jemma sighed. "This is the part where we share what we're looking for, what our respective situations are. The forum will deal with the actual decisions to be made."

"Can you promise me that, Jemma? That we will be told the entire story of what this is all about at the forum?"

She was silent for a long moment. Then, "I think we've covered everything we can hope to in this meeting." She picked up her pen and notebook and got to her feet. "Can you find your own way back to your rooms?"

"*That* didn't go well," he said, out in the hallway. "Are they ever going to tell us what this forum is about?"

"If you ask me, my prince," I ventured, "they have some special deal in mind, and they're trying to decide who deserves it more. But they specifically don't want the loser to find out what it is. They'll hear us out, vote, and then the winner gets to find out what they won."

"A popularity contest for mystery prizes. That did sound like what she was driving at. I'm tempted to pitch a fit and refuse to participate without full disclosure. But I can't afford to, not knowing what I risk losing."

We took a flight of stairs upward, toward the plaza level. "Very clever of them, really," I said. "If we were alone and negotiating with them, we could put stipulations on the negotiations, refuse to play if they aren't more forthcoming. With the Earthers here, they can play us against each other. What we won't give them, Earth will."

"That's their entire foreign policy strategy. Play the two powers off against each other. If there were only one, they wouldn't have much leverage."

"Which is why they won't give a monopoly to either of us." The stairwell opened up into the plaza, and I stepped out half a pace behind the prince.

"Blackwell said as much. It was worth bringing up, because I wasn't sure they saw it that way. But." He shrugged. "It confirms everything we assumed about them."

A crowd was gathering at the far end of the arcade, near the radio desk. There was some commotion, and someone was running away from the knot of people. The prince started forward, and I hurried to keep up.

Only to stop dead once I saw who was in the middle of the crowd. On one side, Blackwell and Liu. On the other, Knauss and two others in black suits. I quickly ducked behind someone so Knauss wouldn't see me.

The prince still seemed set on plunging into the middle of the whole thing. "My prince, please," I urged, plucking at his sleeve. "It's a security risk having you anywhere near the Earth delegation."

"Don't worry, Prescott, it's not as if they're fighting. This is a neutral field. Nobody has any weapons."

Nobody was *supposed* to have any. My knife felt heavy in my coat. Who knew what the Earthers had. A single gun could throw the Empire in disarray.

But he was right after all. All they were doing, in the middle of the anxious crowd, was talking. Ms. Knauss had realized, sooner than Blackwell it seemed, that her real audience was the crowd, not us. "Don't you feel a little out of place here, Martian?" she was saying. "Must be strange to be treated as an equal by commoners."

Liu had a handful of Blackwell's sleeve in her fist, and seemed to be urging him to keep his temper.

He kept it, at least as well as Knauss was. "Oh really? I would think an Earther would feel out of place anywhere they aren't allowed to buy."

The prince finished elbowing through the crowd. I hung back, ashamed. I should have been right beside him. It was a failure on my part. Though perhaps I was due for it. "Why, Miss Knauss," the prince said graciously, with a slight bow. "I haven't seen you since before the war. How is Earth, these days?"

"I wouldn't know," said Knauss, not mollified. "I haven't been home since before the war."

"That's a shame," he said sincerely. "I am sure both of us feel the same in wanting this terrible war to be over soon."

"You ought to control your foreign minister," said Knauss. "He was very rude to me. If this war is ever to end, it will require better diplomacy than that."

"Indeed it will, madam," he said with another bow. "Toward that end, let's bid farewell for the moment. There will be much to talk about at the forum soon. No need to spoil it by getting ahead of ourselves." He took Blackwell by the arm and led him away.

Once we were out of the plaza, Blackwell began to defend himself. "I really am sorry for the scene, Your Highness. Though I would like it to be known that I didn't begin it."

"Of course you didn't," the prince soothed. "You've been keeping your temper with Earthers since before I was born."

"With *that* Earther in particular," Blackwell said. "But this time I was put a little off-balance by the news."

He held out a sheet of paper, holding a radio message from the ambassador on Aphrodite. She was in the habit of sending down the news from Mars when she got it, and it beat having to read the same stories in the Venusian paper.

The prince stopped walking to read it. "More unrest?"

"Keep going, sir."

"A bombing. In Utopia? That's *your* province."

"Yes, sir. Of course no more specific news has reached us. I assume it was in the city, perhaps at a factory or public building, like most of these bombings are. But I don't know it. My wife or children or grandchildren might have been hurt. And I have no way of knowing. It … robbed me of my equanimity for a moment, sir."

The prince nodded and handed the paper back. "You deserve more than a moment to deal with this, Blackwell. Take the rest of the afternoon off. Prescott will go radio the ambassador and see if any further updates have come through."

It was hard, between shadowing the prince and nagging the ambassador by radio, to find much time to speak with Marcus. I met him again late that evening at a table in the plaza. He was eating an enormous sandwich. "Don't mind me," he said. "I just got off shift and need to refuel."

I joined him with the drink I'd just purchased. One of the shopkeepers had said it was the closest thing to tea he could offer me, made from herbs. I took a sip. No. Not very much like tea at all.

"Did you make any progress?"

"Yeah, I talked to StatOps."

"By StatOps, you mean Talia."

He chuckled through a bite of his sandwich. "You got me."

Here in the bright light of the plaza, it was easier to examine his broad, tattooed face, which settled by default into a friendly expression. He was as unaffected as an Earther and more relaxed, perfectly willing to either help or banter, whatever was required. In another life, I would have liked him. But I couldn't stop picturing him with Moira. Was this what she liked, really? It made more sense than her with me. Much more.

I pulled my mind back to the conversation. "You all talk a good game about equality," I said. "But I'm definitely noticing the same people show up in influential roles over and over. We haven't had to meet with entire committees most of the time, just one person, and it turns out that one person has a handle on everything that's going on."

He shrugged. "Not sure how anybody could avoid it. Some people don't like leadership. I know I don't. And some people work so hard that sooner or later they're the team lead whether they want to be or not."

"So equality is just a myth. You still have leaders."

"No. It's not the same."

"How is it different? How is Talia different from our prince?"

"The fact that if we don't like the job she's doing, we vote her out," he said promptly. "Every important position is elected. Sure, we always elect the same people to some things, because they're good at it. But they know we don't have to. That's the difference. If your Emprex screws things up, who's going to vote them out? They stay in there forever."

"Parliament is elected," I said. "It doesn't seem to help much."

"I didn't know you had a parliament. Does everyone get to vote?"

I opened my mouth, shut it, and took a sip of hot non-tea. "Well. I'm not going to try to defend Mars to you. If I were, I wouldn't be—" I took a quick, guilty look around. No one was in earshot, and no one was paying much attention. Nothing wrong with one of the Martian delegation sitting and exchanging ideas with the Man on the Street. "I wouldn't be here on behalf of Liberty," I finished, more quietly. "What did Talia say?"

"She's willing to have you speak at the forum, but she can't make that decision on her own. The forum committee is going to have to vote."

I leaned my forehead on my fingertips. "Nothing can be straightforward with you people, can it?"

"The price we pay. Talia had quite a few questions for you—or for 'my contact,' I didn't say who you were."

I inclined my head. "I appreciate that. The fewer people who know, the better."

"The first one is, what do you even have to offer us? Liberty produces gases for Mars. We don't need gases, we need minerals."

"We can produce minerals just as well," I said. "There's plenty of most everything in the asteroid belt; we can pick rocks rich in whatever we're looking for. Liberty produces a little iron and silica on a small scale already."

"What we need is calcium and magnesium."

"That's possible too. It would take time to convert the refining equipment, but if we were regularly doing business with you, it would pay off."

"And what do *you* get out of it?"

"Carbon fiber, like everyone needs. Can't sail without it. And we could also import organics, food especially. Liberty isn't big enough to produce much, either in quantity or variety."

Marcus nodded, brushing the last sandwich crumbs off his fingers. "Fair enough. But you're small. You'd never be the size market Mars or Earth are."

"True. And I suppose you're worried about us running past any blockade the others might set up."

"Not especially," he said, looking somewhat vague. "That is, I'm sure you're competent enough to find a way."

There was something shifty about his attitude. "The prince can't for the life of him worm out of anyone what this forum is *about*," I ventured.

"It's about building a closer relationship with one or another of the forces in this system." Marcus widened his eyes innocently.

"I doubt any of your guests are that stupid. There's something specific you want to give one of us, and you won't say what it is until you've picked your winner."

"Sure you're not reading into it too much? They do say Martians are paranoid."

I gave him a flat look. "You need to work on your poker face, if you want to be that brazen. I suppose you know what it is and won't tell me either?"

He grinned, the red swirls on his cheeks buckling into a new pattern. "I do, and I won't. I did tell Moira I wasn't going to compromise Venus."

"Everyone on the stat knows," I said, narrowing my eyes. "They say three people can keep a secret if two of them are dead. I find it implausible that out of almost ten thousand inhabitants, none of them is going to tell us."

"It'll take you longer than a week to look among ten thousand people to find one who will tell you," he said with a wink. "Don't waste your time. It'll all come out eventually."

23

MOIRA

Harrington was being kept, with a large number of others, at an Olympus mine near Armstrong City. We headed north by train—we meaning me, Soares, and some other revolutionaries I didn't know well.

It was just this one job, I had told Khan. I still couldn't see a way that Liberty could actually be any help to the revolution, and I wasn't here representing Liberty anyway. Coelho seemed to want to run it like his private fiefdom and at this point, I was fine with it. At least there would be a place for me to go when the *Mariposa* came back.

But I'd brought Harrington down here, and that meant I had a responsibility. I'd pegged her for just quiet, but really, she was fragile. Months as rented convict labor in a mine wasn't going to do her any good. I needed to get her out and get her back to the *Mariposa* where she could work through her shit in peace.

We took different routes and gathered in a forest outside the mining camp. This was Chin-Hawking land, belonging to one of Mars's richest families. Mining here on Mars was strictly regulated by environmental laws; the one thing no one wanted was to ruin a second planet the way Earth had been. After all that work of terraforming it, the biosphere remained brittle; it wouldn't take much to dysregulate it.

The upshot of that was that you couldn't mine just anywhere, and the families whose land was placed conveniently had prospered. The slopes of Olympus Mons were ideal, because the old volcano was riddled with lava tubes. No disturbing the thin blanket of fertile soil with digging; you could simply go in and take out what you needed. The outer slopes were covered with pines, the estate's woodlot.

Soares had the guns, carefully shipped inside a wooden case, and passed them out. "What happens now?"

"We can't come in the front, because it's swarming with police. But we have an alternate route, thanks to Tayag." I nodded at the old man, a former convict miner himself. "We'll climb the scarp at the edge of the slope and head upward about a mile. About that point is a window where the tube is caved in. We'll climb down on ropes and approach the mining area from the rear."

"Sounds like a lot of climbing," said one of the men skeptically.

"Quit your bitching, it's not like it's Earth," said Soares. Mars's gravity would make the climb easier, and falls less dangerous. Though, at the height of the cliff circling the mountain's base, a fall from the top would still kill us.

We moved through the forest, our footsteps crunching on pine needles and releasing a pleasant scent. There was no birdsong—Mars has few birds. From out of sight came the hoot of a steam whistle from camp—probably the start of the shift. Khan had said it didn't matter if there were multiple shifts, because whichever shift we rescued would be of use to his cause. But, of course, it mattered to *me*. I was here for Harrington.

The sun rose in the sky as we climbed. The cliff face wasn't sheer; rockfalls here and there made it possible to scramble up. At last we stood on the towering ridge, sweat turning to ice as the chilly wind touched it. Here on Olympus Mons, it was the mild northern winter. Mars's atmosphere was thin even at this altitude. At the top of the mountain, it couldn't sustain life.

But we had no interest in going that high. We hiked through patchy woods, jumping over streams of glacier melt lined with jagged red rocks. The revolver felt heavy in my belt. I'd have felt more confident with a cutlass.

At last we reached the "window" in the lava tube, a dark hole in the ground the size of a small pond.

"You sure this leads into the mine?" asked Soares.

"You can see the light coming in from inside the mine," said Tayag. "It's just too high for everyone to escape that way."

"Will they see us coming down?"

"Shouldn't. There's a curve in the tube between here and the main diggings. You only see a little glow coming around the corner."

We secured the ropes and started climbing down. Inside it was almost completely dark, till our eyes adjusted and we could pick out the red-orange stone within, gilded with algae and lichen. The sunlight made a great irregular splotch on the tumbled rock of the cave-in.

We crept around the corner and paused to take in the scene. The tunnel was broad and high as a cathedral, lit with fiberoptic lights lining the walls like little stars. A mine-cart track ran down the center, with carts half full of crushed rock. On either side, the dim silhouettes of prisoners were shoveling rock into the carts.

I stole along the tunnel wall, trying to stay out of the light. The noise of scraping shovels and rattling rock covered my footsteps. As I passed the last mine cart, coming near the row of diggers, the nearest figure stopped and peered at me.

"What is Mars?" I hissed, the easiest password. Should, at

least, weed out random unrelated convicts. Not that I cared if, in the end, we happened to release some of those as well. I just couldn't be sure they wouldn't shout out.

"Mars is the planet and people," returned a husky voice, and I stepped close to grip their arm and whisper in their ear. The prisoner handed me their shovel and made off quietly into the dark. I moved to the next prisoner in line.

On the other side of the tunnel, I saw flitting shadows as the other revolutionaries did the same. Prisoners were fading into the darkness, toward the faint glow of the hole we'd come in. I had passed the word to over a dozen when I heard the shout. "Shovels down!"

A guard had seen or heard something, wanted silence to make it out. The prisoners, true to their habit of noncompliance, kept shoveling. The guard grabbed a bullseye lantern and jumped on top of a full mine cart, training the light toward the end of the track.

A single report echoed down the tunnel, and the guard collapsed. Soares's voice rang out. "This way, prisoners, go go go!"

The sound of shoveling stopped and shadowy figures pushed by me in the dark. I kept moving along the wall, hoping to guard their retreat. With the sound of Soares's gun to alert the guards, we didn't have much time.

I had my gun in my hand, but it did no good. I couldn't tell who was who in the darkness. Twenty guards could have run right by me and I wouldn't have known. I couldn't see the rest of my team, only crowds of running shadows.

When I did see the guards, I heaved a sigh of relief. They had chosen the obvious approach, coming at us with lanterns and rifles. The light dazzled my eyes, and I hit the ground. Picked out by their bright lights, I'd never pass for a prisoner.

I rolled behind a rockfall and peered out. The guards brought their rifles forward. I aimed carefully and squeezed the trigger.

The bang, in this enclosed space, was deafening. I had missed, but a moment later a bang from the other side of the tunnel brought down one.

I ducked behind my rock pile while a volley from the guards rang out. I heard cries—not any of us, I thought. They were shooting indiscriminately, and were hitting the prisoners.

I ducked and shot and ducked and shot again, and finally got one. In that time the rest had already fallen.

"More will be coming," I called to the others. "Do we have all the prisoners?"

"Everyone in this section," Soares called back. "But we have to cover their escape."

I clambered between the mining carts and came over beside her. "Their escape is covered. No more guards in sight. We need to fall back."

"What about the guards back in camp? They'll loop around the way we came and catch the prisoners on top of the mountain."

"They can't climb the cliff that fast," I argued. "This was all in the plan."

"We need to get back to the mining camp and take that," she insisted.

It was madness. We were only a dozen people and I had no idea how many guards were back at camp. "We're falling back; that's an order."

There was a moment's sullen silence, and I wondered what I'd do if she refused to listen. My crew had never refused to follow orders, but I didn't have that kind of relationship with Soares.

At last she said, "All right," and we started moving back toward the exit.

Beneath the window was a chaos of prisoners in drab, dusty uniforms scrambling up the ropes. It isn't hard to drag fifty to seventy pounds of weight up a rope, which is what a person's body amounts to on Mars. But some of the prisoners had blistered hands, some had gunshot wounds, and no one was moving very fast. We had at least fifty prisoners to get out, and only three ropes.

Leaving the men helping the prisoners to their work, I brought a few along with me back to the curve of the tunnel to guard our exit. I shielded my eyes from the light to preserve my night vision and hunkered down.

But to my surprise, no more guards came. I started to worry. Perhaps Soares was right and they would try to circle around and get us on the upper slopes. If they had a helicopter, the whole plan was done for. They could simply rise over the cliff and shoot us like clay pigeons.

When the last prisoners had made their way up the ropes, our team scrambled up. I blinked my watering eyes against the light and shaded them to look at the horizon. No aircraft in sight. It was half a mile from the mining camp to here, including the cliff. By the time anyone got up the cliff, we'd be long gone.

Harrington was not among the group we'd rescued. We had about fifty people, but nobody had any idea where she was. All they could tell me was that they had been divided into groups and only one group had been sent to the Chin-Hawking mine. The rest could be anywhere. I bit down on my frustration. At least Khan would be happy. I wasn't.

Our route from here led us west, across the slope of the mountain through patchy trees, to a spot Tayag remembered. A deep ravine where another lava tube had collapsed would lead us down from the mountain. The train tracks passed close, and we should be able to grab the freight trains full of crushed rock as they passed by.

We had just come out of the trees when I heard a telltale drone. "Get back!" I screamed, and the group fled back under cover. I peered out from under a tall pine. Yes, a chopper—a rare sight, here. Almost certainly looking for us.

But it didn't circle the area or mess around at all. Instead it buzzed directly across the sky till it dropped below the edge of the ravine.

"That wasn't a police helicopter," said Soares. "Those are blue."

"If it's not looking for us, then something's in the ravine." I looked at Tayag.

"Don't look at me," he said. "Last time I was here there was nothing there but rocks and brush. The entrance to the lava tube is at one end. It opens up to the valley at the other, beside the train tracks."

I crept from under the trees and lay down on my belly by the edge of the ravine, sheltered by a clump of blackberry brambles. Down below, the empty ravine we had counted on was gone. Instead there was a tiny village of yellow pine shacks and a line of rails leading from the cave mouth to where the ravine opened out into the valley.

It was a second mining camp. The Chin-Hawkings had been busy, with all this bonus convict labor. The helicopter had touched down in the middle of the camp, and the prisoners were drawn up in neat rows between the helipad and the mine entrance.

I wished I had my spyglass with me. Harrington must be down there. But there was no way to get to her, not with all the prisoners out here in plain daylight. We didn't have a map of this lava tube either.

The rotors slowly stopped turning and there was a sudden cheer from the guards. Whoever was inside had stepped out, though I couldn't see them from this angle. When they came around the chopper, flanked by russet-coated Imperial Guard, I discarded the idea that it was a mine inspector, or even Chin-Hawking himself. This was someone more important. Trailing a deep blue gown, they passed between the rows of prisoners to the mine entrance and cut a red ribbon.

They turned and I recognized who it was—not from her face,

but from the sparkle on her brow. It was the princess, the heir to the throne, Maria Sophia. Of course, the Emprex needed to curry favor with the wealthy Chin-Hawkings to fund the war. What easier way than to send their daughter a short helicopter flight away to cut a ribbon?

She walked back to the middle of the camp to shake the hand of a gentleman and begin a speech, which I couldn't hear more of than a few echoing vowels. It didn't matter. I was already creeping backward to the others.

"It's a no go," I muttered. "The only thing I can think of is to try to loop over the lava tube and keep heading west till we're far away from this mess." The princess would have brought imperial guards, the police would be out in force—most likely the reason they hadn't pursued us at the first mine—and the trains might not even be running. We could not have had worse luck.

Suddenly the ground shook and the air thumped with a massive boom. I darted back to the edge of the ravine. Princess, helicopter, and half the mining camp were hidden in a cloud of white smoke. The hydrogen tanks must have gone, whether on purpose or by accident there was no way to know.

The prisoners, terrified, were running into the mine. I waved to our own group. We'd never get a better diversion, if we wanted to rescue this group of prisoners as well. We ran down the steep side of the ravine, my original team with their guns out, the rescued prisoners wielding whatever walking sticks they'd happened to collect.

The steam cloud was already beginning to disperse by the time we reached the bottom, revealing a gruesome scene: dead bodies laid flat like fallen trees, scattered shrapnel from the exploded tank. The princess and her imperial guards were definitely all dead. So was the gentleman who had shaken her hand. I wondered if it was Lord Chin-Hawking himself, or someone else.

The mine guards and the police were in chaos, some rushing

into the blast zone, others following the prisoners, shouting at them to stop running. We shot as many as we could. The shock of being set upon by an armed opposition for once made the rest fall back, and we rushed into the mine.

Most of these lava tubes did open up eventually, I told myself as the light from outside dimmed and went dark. I followed the mine-cart tracks by feel; those would have to be clear for the carts to run. I couldn't see my own feet. In front of and behind me, the footsteps of the prisoners echoed off the walls.

"Stop," I called at last, striking a match. "Get close to me. I'm not letting anyone any further till we account for who we have."

The prisoners clustered around the light. Soares handed me a candle stub from her pocket, and I lit the wick and shook out the match. I waited until all sounds of footsteps had stopped before going around with the candle looking into everyone's faces. There were all the prisoners who had come from the first mine with us. Those from this mine wore the same drab uniforms, but theirs were cleaner. At last I spotted Harrington.

"You're welcome," I said, a little sourly. "Anyone in your batch you don't know?"

She shook her head. "Is the man in plain clothes with you?"

I moved forward along the track till I spotted him, a short dark-haired man in brown. I switched the candle to my left hand and put my right on the butt of my gun. "Care to explain?"

He looked up at me nervously. In his hand was a lantern, unlit. "Am I among friends?"

"Depends," I said. "What kind of friends were you hoping for?"

"Friends of the people," he said. "Are you Khan's Brotherhood?"

I gave a sharp nod. "And you're the one who just murdered the princess, yeah?" Only reason I could think of someone who wasn't a prisoner would come with us. Especially bringing a lantern already, as if he had meant to come this way beforehand.

He burst out, "That wasn't the plan! That is, it was always the plan to blow the mine entrance. Before anybody was in it, so nobody would be hurt. But then when the princess stepped out, I thought, isn't that better? I mean, if we want to strike a blow at the Empire."

He was gabbling. He was very young, I realized, twenty at most. Not the mastermind of this plan, I didn't think. I took his lantern from him and lit it with my candle. The arching ceiling of the tube came into view overhead, lit by the dancing flame.

"I guess I have you to thank for cutting the lights." I raised my voice to address the others. "Some of you in the back will want to keep an eye out for anyone trying to come after. They'll likely come with lanterns if they do."

"More likely they'll try to wait us out," the bomber volunteered. "This tube isn't supposed to have an egress."

"I assume you ran into it because you know it actually does?"

He nodded. "I can show you."

We followed the bomber, whose name was Perez, past the end of the cart tracks and through the curving tunnel. With only about one candle stub per ten people, it was slow going over the rocky ground. At least it wasn't also scattered with broken-up rock and tools as the other had been.

"I don't know how friendly we want to be with this guy," said Soares, low, as she came up to walk alongside me. "Bombings like this are exactly what Khan wants to stop."

"It's the first lead I've had on those bombings since Khan asked me to look into it," I answered. "I'm going to be as friendly with him as I have to, to find out who he's with."

We made our way out of the tunnel through a narrow crack about two feet wide. Perez had left a rope hanging ready, and we slowly made our way out one at a time. We trekked further through the forest till we were well away from the lava tube, and then began separating into groups. We were far too many to be able to keep a low profile together.

I claimed Perez for my group. "I have my own way home," he said stiffly.

"Is it hopping a freight train?"

He frowned. "I don't know if I want any of you coming with me."

"There's only one city near here," I said. "We're all going to the same place to get lost there."

He consented in the end, and I found myself hanging on the outside of a freight car beside him. It wasn't a comfortable way to travel, but it wasn't my first time. If you're poor, it's the best way to get around, and the engineers can't be bothered to stop you.

As the train slowed to cross the river, we leapt off and tumbled onto the grassy bank, a few at a time so we could scatter. I watched Perez and jumped when he did.

"I admit, I'm impressed with the job you did today," I said, climbing to my feet and dusting off my pants. "I wonder if we in the Brotherhood could be doing more."

"You could be doing *so much* more," he agreed. "Peaceful methods have been tried. It's time to put the pressure on the Emprex. Make them know the people won't be kept down any longer."

"So I can join your group?"

He hesitated. He probably was supposed to ask them first before bringing a new person along. But at last he said, "All right. I'm sure they'll like to see the person who rescued a hundred prisoners."

24

LUCY

The ambassador finally radioed that evening with the infor-mation that Blackwell's manor was untouched. The bomb had taken out a government building in Vivero, killing twelve, including a judge.

In the morning, as our delegation was keeping time, we passed back into daylight. Venus does not rotate, or barely, but the winds whip around the planet in four days. It had been day when we landed, but soon after, the stat had traveled onto the nightside, blown by the hurricane-force wind.

Now it was dawn again, and the upper level—the farm, as the Venusians called it—was awash in golden light. We rode higher in the clouds than before, so only trailing wisps of yellow mare's tails came between us and the sun. Beside and below the stat were towering oceans of vapor, big cauliflowers the color of mustard, whipped and swirled on the tops by the different speeds of wind.

I had no real business up there; I was only taking the scenic route to get to the radio office. That had suddenly become my job, to check in there several times a day for further news from Mars.

The prince, who hadn't made any remark before over the unrest at home before, was suddenly concerned by it now that a bomb had struck close to Blackwell. The few hours' uncertainty about Blackwell's family had changed it, in his mind, from a distant concern to a present danger.

But perhaps that was unfair. Maybe it was just being this far from home that did it. Even I was upset, and theoretically I should have been on the side of the bombers. Whoever they were, they were upset with the status quo, as I was. But I knew it couldn't be Khan's people. He had been so adamant that violence wasn't the way. Was he losing control of his organization?

I arrived at the radio office, and the woman behind the counter gave me a familiar smile. "No new messages," she said. "Your friend picked them up already."

That earned a frown. I had volunteered to get the messages, in part, so I'd have an excuse to be at the office often to stay in touch with Moira. It would be too easy for a well-meaning clerk to hand Miss Liu my private messages to take to me, and then there would be questions about who I was writing to so often and why I felt the need to send them under a false identity.

"You didn't give her my personal messages, did you?" I gave my identifier.

She shook her head. "Nothing for you today, sorry."

"That's all right," I said. "I just always want to pick up my private messages myself."

She winked. "Never fear. The rules are very strict."

The door behind her swung open, letting out a rattle of sound from the telegraph machine. A man came out with a broadsheet, which he pinned to the wall behind the counter.

Normally, I wouldn't have stopped to read it. Any really urgent news for us was sent by the Aphrodite ambassador, usually ahead of its public release here. Anything more mundane, I'd as soon catch in the evening paper, complete with Venusian editorializing. This time, I stopped dead at the headline.

ASSASSINATION ON MARS! it screamed on the masthead. Then, below,

> *Escalating violence on Mars has claimed the life of one of the royal family. Sophia Maria Elliott, the daughter of the reigning Emprex and heir apparent to the position, was touring a new mine near Armstrong City when a bomb went off beside a hydrogen tank nearby. It is unclear whether she was specifically targeted or simply unlucky. Ms. Elliott was killed instantly, along with fourteen other people. Many others were injured.*

The blood drained from my face. Princess Sophia, the elder child of the Emprex. The one too precious to send to Venus. The one who stood between my prince and the throne.

I turned away from the counter and set off at a run. The prince could not, *must* not hear about this from anyone else. Had Liu picked up a telegram that gave advance warning? If so, she'd have told the prince already. If not… I pushed myself to run faster, despite the constant drag of gravity.

It seemed Liu had arrived back at our rooms only moments before. She stood just inside the doorway, while Blackwell and the prince drank coffee on the couch. Sagan was nowhere to be seen; probably out getting something for breakfast.

"Your Highness," Liu was saying, "there's been word from home."

He got to his feet and reached for the telegram in her hand. "Let's have a look."

She pulled it closer to her chest. "Perhaps you ought to take a moment to prepare yourself."

"Nonsense." He snatched it from her hand and flipped it open. His dark eyes flicked side to side a moment, and then his breath huffed out. He closed his eyes and took a slow breath in and out.

"I pray you all excuse me," he said, opening his eyes. Their charismatic sparkle was gone. "I need—I need a moment—" Handing the paper to me, he bolted from the room.

Blackwell's eyes fixed on Liu. "Well? What news is so terrible?" he demanded. I could well imagine his thoughts. An attack by Earth, an uprising of the commoners…

"His sister is dead," I said shortly.

The room was silent. Of course we were all sad for the prince's loss, but their minds would be going where mine had. With the princess dead, our prince was next in line for the throne. We had the heir to the Empire, here, on foreign turf, with our enemies housed in the same city.

"If we had known the stakes would be like this, I'd have insisted on bringing a company of marines," Blackwell said, getting up and starting to pace.

"He can't be out alone," said Liu, thinking faster than I was. "I'll go after him."

"I'll come too," I offered.

She shook her head. "No, Lieutenant. I want you here." Before I could protest, she was gone.

I hated being under the command of civilians. Properly we should all stay with him until we had him in secure quarters again. But of course Liu had no notion of imperial security, less than I had, and I wasn't even in the Guard.

They were gone several hours. Blackwell sat at the table, composing and encoding a message home, asking if we should call off the negotiations and come home. Sagan returned, bearing hot rolls. I told them the news, and they sat down heavily in a chair. For a good minute the valet only stared blankly at the table, in far greater shock than I would have imagined. Surprised to be facing a future as valet to the Emperor?

At last Sagan looked up. "Where is the prince?"

"He went out. I suppose he wanted to be alone. Liu went with him though."

Sagan's face was troubled. "I ought to see if I can find him."

"It's fine," I said. "Liu can provide anything he needs. And we'll never find them, not knowing where they went. All we'd do is make the Earthers suspicious, running all over looking." Sagan gave a reluctant nod.

By noon, however, I had come around to Sagan's view. Blackwell was already out delivering his message.

"I'm going out," I said. "With the Earthers around, I'd feel better if we all knew where he was at all times." It was a defiance of orders, and it would draw attention, but he had been out of contact far too long.

"I'm coming with you," Sagan declared, struggling to their feet.

Just then, Liu came back in. Alone.

"Where is the prince?" I demanded, none too respectfully.

"He wanted to be alone," she said.

"Not on this station, at this moment!" I cried. "The Earthers know everything we know by now, and it would take so little—"

"Calm down," Liu said. "He isn't *alone*, exactly. He's at a private establishment, in good company. Far be it from me to judge how he deals with his grief. If he wants to cry on some Venusian's purple breast, it's his lookout. He went in and he did *not* want me to join him, so I came back."

"You think he's in a *brothel*, ma'am?" Sagan choked out.

Liu curled her lip. "There's no need to be vulgar. Still less to be shocked. Your position involves being discreet about this sort of thing. This can't be the first time."

Sagan's dark eyes were hollows of emotion; what emotion that was, they successfully concealed. "It isn't his habit, ma'am, is all I meant."

"Well, when in Rome, I suppose." Liu flopped down onto the settee and took a cold roll from the tray. "Has Blackwell radioed home?"

"That's what he went out to do," I said. "He's probably there waiting for an answer."

The answer, when it came, was to carry on as best we could. This forum was the best hope Mars had for an ally, and we couldn't let Earth deal with Venus without us. Besides, a Martian ship would arrive at Aphrodite in three more weeks, and it could escort us back when the negotiations were over.

"Mars doesn't have a ship in the fleet that can escort the *Adamant*," I pointed out. "We'd outdistance them in a day."

"Can't you just let out half the sails and go slower?" Liu asked.

"We could, but we'd be less safe than going on alone. The speed she makes is enough to outdistance any fighting ship." I wondered who had made that decision. A civilian, probably. Or one of the old crusts at the Admiralty who only knew about the way things had always been done.

Still the prince did not return. At two o'clock I set out to find him. The hospitality district—as the Venusians called it—was on our level, near the main square. It was a wide, well-lit hallway of the ubiquitous white plastic, lined with archways on either side. These had names, at least: one was labeled Dance Club, and the one across was Discreet Encounters.

I hesitated before reluctantly pushing open the door to Discreet Encounters. It was dim inside, with purple mood lighting. A comfortable sofa and a few armchairs filled most of the small room. Two women and two men were sitting in the chairs, playing cards.

They all looked up. One of the women, who was wearing a corset, garters, and thigh-high fishnets, put down her cards. "A patron!" she hissed at the others, and then, "What kind of experience are you looking for?"

A man in a silk robe put in, "These Martians will never tell you straight. Let's get her a brochure."

My face warmed. "I—I'm actually not here for the, ah, services. I am looking for someone. You've had another Martian here today?"

They all shook their heads. "We've had nobody for hours," said the first woman. "Two in the afternoon isn't a busy time."

"And we've never served any Martians," the man put in. "Not here. On Aphrodite, though…" He let out a whistle. "Those poor creatures have *years* of frustration to work out. And they *do*, believe me."

I swallowed. I didn't want to think about any of that, because it only made me think of Moira. How many years of stifled longings *she'd* had to deal with, when she had finally cracked my shell. And how much more I had to get out of my system, if I could only see her again.

"It's very important," I said. "If one came to this district, where do you think he'd go?"

He frowned. "Don't suppose you know his kinks."

"Of course I don't!"

"Bet he'd like Madame's. Martian nobles love to be dommed."

He was not at Madame's, which turned out to be some sort of fetish dungeon. Nor at Talk 'n' Tatas, which boasted therapeutic conversations in the nude. It was startling just how many different bawdy houses a city of this size could support; but then, it seemed many of the workers only did it part-time.

A few of the places admitted that the prince might have been there earlier; that they didn't really keep track of who came in, and several people had gone off duty at noon. But he certainly wasn't there now.

I went back to our rooms, hoping he'd returned, but he hadn't. Liu and Blackwell were there alone. "Sagan went out looking for him too," Liu volunteered.

"He wasn't anywhere in the hospitality district," I said, trying and failing not to sound accusatory. "You should have waited around for him."

"He explicitly told me not to!" she protested.

"Security is more important even than his orders. Especially now. I should never have left his safety to a civilian."

Liu turned red and opened her mouth. Blackwell lifted a hand. "Well, then. As an officer. What do you suggest we do now?"

I sighed. He was humoring me, to make the peace, but he was right that we should look to the future instead of laying blame. "We need to sweep the whole stat, as best we can. He probably went off alone, so we'll want to check the farm, observation decks, anywhere isolated. Liu, you stay here till Sagan gets back, and then have them wait here while you check the farm. Blackwell, you search the main square and then the observation decks on this level. Ask anyone you meet if they've seen him, but tell them not to spread it around that we're looking. We don't want the Earthers to learn he's alone."

"And what are you going to do?"

"The lower levels," I said. "It's a warren down there, but I know my way a little."

Hours of heavy trudging later, we reunited over a cold dinner. I had walked miles, crashed parties in the observation decks, interrupted couples on the bottom-level catwalks, and seen no one who'd noticed a solitary Martian man.

"I thought for sure he would have been back by now," sighed Liu, picking at the noodle dish.

"Sagan," I said. The valet looked up, as if startled out of a long train of thought. "Is this like him? Does he go off alone for a long time when he's upset?"

"It's nothing like him," Sagan said firmly. "He always wants to be around people. He'll unburden himself to a complete stranger if there's no one else around."

"It's possible he's doing just that," suggested Blackwell. "Met someone friendly, went home with them, and is staying for dinner. It might be easier to talk to someone outside of it all than one of our little group."

"He wouldn't wander off without telling anyone where he was going," Sagan insisted. "He certainly never did on Mars."

"I don't think we can afford to be optimistic," I said. "Not with the Earthers around. I think we should tell Talia we suspect the prince has been kidnapped."

25

MOIRA

Perez's group hung out in an abandoned warehouse two blocks from the river. From here, you could only just hear the thump and clatter of the factories nearby. Sunlight streamed through dirty windows onto heaps of old crates.

I say group, but it was really just two other people: one blond woman with her hair tied severely back, and one beefy man who didn't say much. I followed Perez tentatively, worried they'd be annoyed at him bringing a stranger.

Instead, they barely noticed me in their annoyance at Perez. "We said to shut down the mine," said the woman. "Not try an assassination without checking it with us!"

Perez looked deflated. "I mean—you can't honestly expect me to pass up a chance like that!"

"The Emprex has another child, but that mine was vital to their war effort," snapped the woman. "They sell the minerals to Venus for carbon fiber."

"Are we trying to stop the war effort, or to take down the government?" asked Perez.

"Maybe you should leave the strategizing to us and do what you were told! Some revolutionary army we are, if nobody can follow basic orders."

He sighed. "I'm sorry. Next time—"

"There isn't going to be a next time," the woman said. "We have to assume people saw your face. You'll be the most wanted person in the Empire. We have a place for you to lie low for the time being."

Perez nodded sadly. His type was obvious: upper commoner, probably training to be a clerk. He'd picked up the revolutionary vibe and decided on a radical approach, like the students in the café. Unlike them, he'd actually taken action. But this wasn't the ticker tape parade he'd imagined.

"What about your friend?" asked the woman, turning to me at last. "Do we trust her?"

"She helped me get away clean from the bombing," said Perez, somewhat generously considering he'd planned his escape fine without us. "She's one of Khan's."

"We don't get along with Khan," said the woman. "He refuses to have anything to do with us."

A lie. Interesting. Khan had never been asked. "His pacifist approach isn't really working," I said. "Some of us are getting tired of picking at the Empire when decisive action could make a much bigger difference. I could probably get a dozen—"

"We don't need a dozen people," the woman interrupted. "The fewer people in a cell, the more secure it is. But we might have a job for you. I'll have to find out from my own contact. Can we meet here tomorrow?"

I nodded. I trusted her as far as I could throw her, but I couldn't miss a chance to find out more.

I stayed in a disturbingly seedy hostel that night with a few of the escaped prisoners. In the morning, I cleaned up as best as I could and went to the Armstrong City library. It was a small affair, mainly for the education of clerks and merchants, but it did have a fat volume almost every Founder had on their shelf. *Who's Who.*

I had no idea who the blond woman was, but I couldn't shake the impression I'd gotten from her accent. Founders can't help pronouncing every syllable of every word, the g's on the ends of -ng words and the t in often. I knew from Lucy they got a slap on the hand with a ruler from a very young age if they picked up commoner slang or slurred their consonants. By the time they were grown, that linguistic perfection was pretty much fixed.

The blond woman had been trying not to sound like that, but it had come out. She was a Founder. And if she was, she'd be in this book. Unfortunately, I had only her face to go on, and many Founder families look alike, being descended as they are from the same thousand families. It took me all morning, squinting at black-and-white photos, to make a good guess at who she was.

Natalia Kelly-Wang, of Hesperia. Second child of a reasonably wealthy family. Her mother was a member of Parliament for the Blues. Odd, the Blues were always pro-mining. Why would she want to destroy mines? Rebellion against her family?

Almost everything she had said in the warehouse, I was pretty sure was a lie. Destroying one mine was nothing. There were plenty of other mines. And this one would be put out of commission a good while thanks to the destruction of the hydrogen tanks anyway.

There was also the comment about being part of a cell and needing to consult with her contact. I didn't believe that. If this had been a cell, it would have had more than three people. And if a high-ranking Founder was part of a terrorist organization, I doubted they'd make her a middleman. There was too much she could be doing directly, if she actually cared.

And of course the lie about having tried to partner with Khan and getting turned down. She'd had no way to predict I knew otherwise.

I had to think about this differently. What would be the immediate effects of destroying a mine, that wouldn't be served by killing a princess? Might be a financial hit to Chin-Hawking, though the man was rich as Midas and wouldn't be hurt much. He'd be mad, I supposed.

There. That would explain it. I got up and fetched a political paper. Vasily Chin-Hawking was Tribune, not that anybody expected him to do his job and advocate for commoners' rights. My dads had voted for him; they thought a rich man like him would care less about political interests. I was skeptical on that point. After all, he hadn't hesitated to use convict labor. But there was an election in a few days. Perhaps he'd been trying to cater to his base.

I stopped when I found his last speech. Sure enough, he'd just announced his support for a number of labor demands, like an eight-hour workday and a ban on child labor. He was going to propose a law in Parliament tomorrow, which was his right as Tribune. He couldn't vote on it, but he could force the rest of Parliament to consider it. Naturally neither party would like it, especially not the industrialist Blues.

I leaned back in my chair and sighed. Was that it, then? Bombings specifically to influence politicians? That would explain the geographic spread. This way, there would be one bombing in every district, and every member of parliament would *feel* at risk— while none of them would actually be killed.

For a moment I wanted to laugh. Poor Miss Kelly, when she discovered a bombing she'd planned had taken out the Princess. She must be having a conniption.

I took out my list of dates and places. Sure enough, as I

flipped through the political papers, the bombings all seemed close to some influential politician. A few days ago, one had hit a courthouse across the street from the Utopia residence of Terence Blackwell-Alexendrovich, Member for the Greens. It had shaken him enough he'd missed the next session of Parliament, where the new labor policies had been discussed.

I stayed so long I missed lunch, trying to trace the effects of these bombings. One member of Parliament had abandoned the Russets and become a Gray after a train bombing near her home. Another Russet had mysteriously died of a heart attack at 52. Not a bombing, but I had no reason to think these people would stick to bombings.

I got an old edition and found the election results for the year I'd left Mars. There were twenty Russets then. Now there were only five. Most of the remainder had died—by unspecified illness or accident. Their places had been taken by partisans of other parties.

The only question, I wondered as I put the papers away, was what to do about it. Presumably the conspiracy was made up of Founders; Lucy could have done more about that than I could. A word in her ear would have sent her haring off to hunt them in their own habitats, where she could go and I couldn't.

But she was on Venus now, knocking the socks off the Venusians I assumed, and I only had two choices. Show up tonight and offer to take a bombing job, or not. I wasn't sure offering to do a bombing would help anything. Clearly Miss Kelly-Wang wasn't going to tell me anything other than where to bomb and when.

Then again, there was a third and very simple option. I couldn't take down the whole counter-revolutionary conspiracy, but I could do something about the two I'd met.

But when I arrived at the warehouse a few hours later, Miss Kelly and her henchman weren't there. I waited for an hour, the gun like a hot rock against my ribs and the creaks of the empty building making me jump. But they never showed.

Probably they had had second thoughts about allowing a new person they hadn't personally chosen. Or else Kelly really did have a higher-up in her organization who had nixed the idea. Or rubbed out Kelly herself, for her failure.

I only hoped the secret hideout they had promised Perez was real, and not a grave.

26

LUCY

Isn't it a bit early for you all to be panicking?" Talia leaned both elbows on her desk. It had taken some searching to find her; she'd been off shift and someone had had to pull her away from her dinner to come back to her office.

"You don't understand," said Blackwell, his voice strained. "He's our *crown prince* now."

"We aren't panicking, per se," I said. "But it's very strict protocol never to leave him alone, and he knows that as well as we do. We're concerned and want him back in our rooms where we can know he's safe."

Her face remained incredulous. "His sister just died. Don't you think a person's due some time alone to deal with that?"

"In other circumstances, he certainly would be," I said. "But with the Earthers here—"

"You think they're going to hurt him?"

"I have no idea what their orders might be. We were not even warned ahead of time that they would *be* here. It simply isn't appropriate for a prince, in foreign territory and among enemies, to be anywhere without an armed guard!"

Talia frowned. "We have no weapons allowed on this stat," she said firmly. "Nor on Aphrodite. We host Earthers and Martians from time to time, with little incident."

"Please," said Blackwell. "Can you humor us and help us look?"

That worked a lot better than anything I'd said. She stood up easily, despite her size and the crushing gravity, and said, "I'll do what I can."

"If you would," Blackwell added, "please take care that the delegation from Earth doesn't learn he's missing."

By whatever system they used to muster manpower, the Venusians had made their own careful pass of the stat's corridors. "And we did check the Earthers' rooms, too," added Talia, leaning on our doorframe the next morning. "Told them we were concerned about CO_2 levels in their rooms, and got a look in each one. There wasn't an extra person in any of them, nor anything big enough to hold one."

That told me nothing for certain. If I had been the Earth delegation and interested in kidnap or murder, I would have come up with a different hiding place than their rooms. But it was something.

"Do you agree, then, that he isn't just staying out late?" Blackwell prompted.

She gave a slow nod. "Yes, it's very strange. Either he's had some kind of accident or ..." She trailed off. "The committee met last night, and we have decided to open an investigation. It'll be managed by one of you, since you have an interest in it."

Liu and Blackwell exchanged a look. "Lieutenant Prescott, of course," said Blackwell. "She's here as our military escort."

"You mind coming with me, Prescott? I want to make plans."

I cast a wistful eye behind me. Sagan had spent the night worry-baking, and had ruined several souffles in Venus' higher gravity before finally perfecting one. It was a beautiful pillowy creation, rising out of the dish like one of the clouds all around us. Clearly intended to astound the prince when he returned, but instead it seemed Liu and Blackwell would have to eat it by themselves.

"Of course," I said. Finding the prince was the most important thing, and I was glad to finally have the locals' cooperation. "Perhaps over coffee?"

"*Naturally* over coffee," she said, shutting the door behind us. "I was up half the night shift."

There was coffee *and* a plate of chocolate donuts in Talia's office. "Here's the thing," she said, settling herself behind her desk and taking a donut. "We like our privacy and we did not want anyone in your delegation wandering into restricted areas. But, since we've somehow failed to keep one of you safe, I think we owe you total openness." She laid on the desk in front of me a printed card that read, *Please cooperate with the bearer on a mission vital to the stat. For more information, contact Talia.*

I stared at it. "Is this…the keys to the city, so to speak?"

"Remember, we're a full democracy and virtually anarchist in most respects, except for the stuff we're absolutely totalitarian about, like atmosphere safety." She dunked a piece of donut in her coffee. "There are a lot of different ideas on this station and I can't make anyone cooperate with you. But this'll get you most everyone. If they don't like it, they can come to me and I'll explain it. Everyone's pretty anxious to have this forum go off okay. A missing person is the opposite of that. They'll help you out."

I reached toward the card, but she put down two fingers on it, holding it still a moment. "I want you to understand this is a huge show of trust for us. And we'll want that respected."

A catch. Of course. "What do you mean?"

"We like our privacy," she said. "There will be things you turn up that are no one's business but ours. Can you promise to keep private everything you learn that doesn't have to do with your missing prince?"

"On my honor as a gentlewoman," I said. *What honor?* If I'd been her, I never would have trusted me. Doubly so if she knew how many times I'd forsworn myself.

She took her fingers off the card. "I hope this demonstration of our trust in you proves we had nothing to do with Elliot's disappearance."

Now that was a thought. I'd stayed focused on the Earthers, but in a place as chaotic as Venus, who knew what goals some factions might be working toward? "I have no doubt of that," I said, pocketing the card.

"Now, we need to think about who can work with you. I'm happy to assign someone, or a couple someones, to you for the length of the investigation, and pay them for their time."

"I assumed your police," I said, blinking.

She gave an embarrassed laugh. "We don't exactly *have* police," she said. "With no hoarding of resources, there are very few things that would be remotely worth stealing. And with no weapons, there isn't much violence either. The occasional crime of passion, which our mediators deal with. But nobody who works full time at it. There just isn't enough trouble in a city of under ten thousand to make up a full-time job."

Clifton, the closest city to my home, had a population that size and at least forty full-time police. But I supposed it took more police to enforce a rigid class system than it took to keep order among happy equals.

"I've put together a list," she was saying. "People with some amount of relevant experience. Some were security on Aphrodite, others do some mediation or social work."

I scanned the paper she gave me. Just a collection of names, as far as I was concerned. Then my eye caught something, and I read back over.

"Marcus Van," I said. "Is that the one who works in the chemical plant?"

"You know him?"

"Had lunch with him once. Is he good at finding things?"

She chuckled. "He's good at wandering from job to job, at least," she said. "He's done some mediation and some social work, but I mainly put him down because he's done so many jobs in the stat that I figured he'd have a good handle on everything that goes on around here. He gets bored easily."

"Why me?"

I had found Marcus leaving a coffee shop, with a cup the size of my forearm. "You were on a list of Talia's."

"I'm sure there are more qualified people on it."

"I'm not. Seems like none of you have the faintest idea what to do with a crime."

He stopped walking long enough to take a noisy slurp. "It's true. We don't."

"And you were the name I knew. Besides, it saves a lot of trouble that you already know what I'm up against."

He narrowed his eyes at me. "Do you *want* to find the prince?"

"Yes!" I sputtered a moment. "You think I'd torpedo the investigation?"

He started walking again. "How am I supposed to know what

you would or wouldn't do? You're the one secretly double-dipping your loyalties."

That stung. "Liberty has nothing to gain from a disputed succession on Mars," I said, a little snippily. "Mars may not like us, but we're trade partners."

"So you'll do this just as part of your cover?"

"I'm doing it because…" I walked in silence a moment, down a flight of stairs. "Really, because I like him. The prince is a decent person. Mars can only benefit from having him around. And after all this time together, I consider him … well, a friend."

Marcus took a long drink before grinning at me. "There we are, then. A good reason for me to put my job on hold to help you."

"You wouldn't otherwise? Talia said you were easily bored. The chemical plant doesn't sound exciting."

"More exciting than knocking on doors to find a missing person who's not even important for any reason beyond classist bullshit." We were at the chemical plant now. He handed me his cup. "Let me run in and give notice."

⤫

We ended up at Marcus's apartment, a one-room affair with no kitchen and an unmade bed. It did, at least, have a table and two chairs. "Sorry about the mess," he said, moving a pile of clothing off one of the chairs.

I searched for a way to ask why he lived in such a dump. Was this standard, and our rooms were something extra fancy to make Venus look better? "Is this," I ventured, with a gesture taking in the room, "standard, for the stat?"

"What, the room?" He paused, mid-rifle through a drawer. "No, not really. It's the free room you get if you're single and don't want to pay any rent. And since I don't usually spend any time

here, I don't see the point in spending hours for something nicer."
He turned back to the drawer and finally unearthed a pen and paper. "Let's make a list of everywhere he could be. You've checked
where he went missing?"

"In the hospitality district," I said. "Miss Liu left him at the
entrance, so either he went in and left again before I came looking,
or he waited till she was gone and then went somewhere else. It's
possible he was only trying to shake her off. By the time I came,
nobody could say for sure if he'd been there or not, because some
people had gone off shift."

"So, we'll need to find out who else was there at the time and
interview them," he said. "I can do that."

I repressed a loud sigh of relief. I did *not* want to go back there.
Then I remembered he had slept with Moira, and felt annoyed
again. Venusians and their loose ways. Of course he wouldn't
mind. "The other possibility is a private home. I don't think we
have the manpower to knock on every single door in the city, not
with only two of us."

"We can just make a radio announcement. Talia will put it in
for you, I'm sure."

"A radio announcement?" I repeated, puzzled. "I'm talking
about private homes."

He looked blank for a moment. "Oh! You don't have radios
in your homes on Mars, because of your prejudice against electricity."

"It's not a prejudice," I said testily. "Artificial intelligence
actually killed billions on Earth and Mars. We're trying to avoid
a repeat performance. I can't fathom why Venus doesn't bother."

"We couldn't. We need power here to heat and cool the stat
and to run the chemical plants. We'd soon run out of air if we
didn't have electricity."

"You don't *need* to have radios in your homes," I said. "Or
electric lights, or clocks, or elevators."

"It would be a lot to give up, just because we were afraid of what might happen."

"What did happen!" I cried. "And might again!"

"Not from electric lights," he said, rolling his eyes. "You know why you people find it so easy to give up electricity? Because it's easy for you to replace it with manpower. Because human life is cheap to you."

I let out a huff of incredulity. He was really too much. The fact that he wasn't wrong in the least only made it worse. I took a deep breath and forced my shoulders down. "Anyway. An announcement. That would tip Earth off that he was missing."

"I don't know how we can avoid that," he said, twirling his pen around in his fingers. "We have to check every place on the stat. Soon everyone will know a search is on. And they're bound to mention it to the Earth delegation eventually."

I picked at my lip. I didn't much like letting Earth know anything, especially not that. What if they weren't responsible for his disappearance, and found him before I did?

But no. Odds were a million to one they were the ones responsible. Who else had any reason to go after him? "Let me check with the foreign minister and get back to you."

He made a note. "All right, hospitality district or private home. Where else? Where's the most likely place for him to be?"

"Dead," I said shortly.

"What?!"

"It's hard to hide a living body in a place this size," I pointed out. "And we've looked fairly thoroughly already. A dead body is a great deal easier to conceal."

Marcus looked sick. "We haven't had a murder here in years. And that was a heat-of-the-moment thing. Nobody tried to hide a body."

"You have to admit the possibility," I said. "Obviously it's not what I want, but I assure you, the Earthers wouldn't think twice."

"But why? What do they get out of killing the prince?"

I rested my chin on my hand. I had just assumed they had done it, because, after all, they hated us. "Well, he's the Emprex's heir now."

"Yeah, and? Is he a particularly *good* heir? Is he more hostile to Earth than the next runner up?"

"Next in line is Duchess Alexandra Elliot-Hawking. His cousin. She's supposed to be something of a wastrel. Certainly wouldn't be good for the war effort if she were on the throne, but on the other hand, the Emprex is still alive and not that old. I would hope the war would be over before either one of them would actually succeed."

"So. Not much immediate help to Earth to murder him."

"Unless they just want him out of the forum next week," I pointed out. "He was sent for a reason; he's both a symbol of how much the Emprex cares about these talks *and* a fairly good speaker himself. Half the planet's in love with him."

"In that case they might as well leave him alive as not. Once the forum's over, they could return him."

"Again. *Much* easier to kill a man than to hide one. And if they dropped a body outside, we'd never find it."

He folded up his paper, stood up, and stuck it in his pocket. "You're wrong about that, and I'll show you."

It was a long walk from his room upstairs to the airlock, and my feet ached. I wondered if feet ever adapted to higher gravity, and how long it took.

"The airlocks aren't secured," he explained, handing me a mask and a coverall. "People go in and out all the time."

"Easy to sneak him out, then."

"Easy to walk out. Not so easy to bring a struggling captive, or a corpse." The airlock opened and a couple men came in. Marcus gave them a nod.

"I can think of a lot of ways to do it. In a barrel, maybe."

"God, you're morbid." He preceded me into the airlock. "They murder people a lot on Mars?"

"A decent amount. Most are never solved." Everything I told these people about Mars made me more disturbed. So many police, so many unsolved murders. Then what were the police for? Keeping order, of course. Riot shields and gas. Beating little boys for selling candy on the corner.

But who was I to get prissy about it? I'd killed far too many people myself to ever fit in here. First for the Empire, and then against it. I was a criminal by any perspective you took.

Briefly I imagined telling that to Marcus. Telling him about my part in airlocking Maxwell, a man I had liked and admired. About accidentally decompressing the *Valiant* and watching the bodies scatter out into space, dying before my eyes. Or the combat deaths, at close quarters, one hand keeping hold while the other slashed, blood crawling over my hand by capillary action.

Behind my mask I could feel my cheeks paling, my hands sweating inside my gloves. I didn't know why I was thinking about it now. I shook my head to dismiss my morbid thoughts. Today, at least, I was on the side of life. The outer door opened, and we walked outside.

This airlock wasn't the one I'd come in through, five days ago. We had come around, by a walkway under the landing platform, to the right-hand balloon. Here, mechanics were servicing one airplane, and a group was pushing another into a tentlike hangar.

Marcus walked over to the edge, hooking his gloved hand into the safety netting. "Do you think you could drag a dead weight your size up this thing?"

I stared up at the netting, which was about twenty feet high.

"*I* couldn't," I said. "I can barely lift my own body here. Could you?"

He shook his head. "I could get myself over. Not a body. Even if the weight weren't a problem, how would you climb with at least one arm taken up holding it?"

I touched the netting, which was plastic like everything here. It was crusted with yellow sulfur deposits that crumbled off under my glove. "They could cut it, though."

"Let's check, then."

We walked the entire length of the netting, and then hiked to the rear of the platform and checked the netting there. Nothing was cut or even disturbed.

"You see it isn't possible," he said. "The one place we never lose anything is over the edge. If something's lost, it's lost here on the stat. Doesn't mean we'll ever find it, but it hasn't left."

"What about by plane?"

Marcus agreed it was a good question, so we went into the hangar and asked the workers what flights had left since midday yesterday.

"None," said the leader, his mask hanging loose around his neck. "We had nothing since yesterday morning, and Talia grounded everything today."

I had to admit Marcus was right: wherever the prince was, he hadn't left. I thought of this place as almost a space station, but it was childishly simple to get rid of things on a space station. Here, it would be much more difficult.

Still. I didn't dare hope he was alive just yet. There were plenty of places to hide a body. Luckily, most of those might hold a living person just as well.

We checked the sulfuric acid tanks, dredging the bottom to check for fragments, before going inside to search the farm.

"Look for disturbed earth," I said. "Any new plantings. It would be a perfect place to hide a body."

"We don't even use earth, per se," said Marcus, digging up a handful to show me. The stuff was fine and black, but smelled ashy instead of earthen. "It's a combo of plastic crumbs, organic waste, and inorganic carbon foam. It makes a good matrix for the roots, but it's not very nutritious. We have to add in everything the plants need."

"Imported?"

"Mostly. We do have a couple mining stations to get minerals, but it's honestly easier to bring stuff down from orbit than to dig it out of the ground. Space, at least, isn't crushing you down with the weight of ninety atmospheres."

I knelt down and pushed a finger into the artificial soil. It was fine and loamy, easy to dig in. "Let's split up," I said. "Examine any place big enough to bury anything."

The farm was designed for enjoyment as well as food production. Meandering paths, dotted with occasional stairways down, led through groves of coconut palms and trellises of tomatoes and beans. There was even a corn maze. I found my way through it and to a little aquaculture garden. An artificial river flowed through a rice paddy and into a pond dotted with lotus. Under the water were the darting shapes of carp.

I wanted to enjoy the beauty, but all my eyes could appreciate at the moment was the excellent spot this would be for hiding a body. Weight it down with—hm. Did they use metal or stone for anything here? Could one steal some without it being noticed?

"Lieutenant Prescott," a voice called, and I looked up. The sound of my name, my proper name, in a proper Martian accent, brought a faint smile to my lips.

"Miss Liu," I replied, spotting her on a low, red-painted bridge and making my way over.

She sat by the water, legs folded daintily beneath her, trailing her fingers in the water. She wore a light seersucker suit in white, with a red silk scarf tucked around her neck. Her hair fell loose, except for a section at the front that was caught up in a knot at the crown of her head. "You must be run off your feet, looking for our prince," she said, as I sat down beside her.

"Yes." I wondered what else I could say. I didn't want to sound short with her, but she hadn't left me with many openings.

She didn't seem offended by my brusqueness. "It's beautiful here. I suppose I imagined they would have all the crops in straight lines, trying to get every calorie per square foot they could."

"The Venusians seem to know all about blending form with function."

"It's something we have in common with them," she agreed. "My brother's farm is very scenic also. He divides all the pastures with hand-fitted stone walls. It's really an art, getting the regolith to stay up without mortar."

"I've seen the style," I said. My family's farms had had nothing of the kind, and they were owned by First Landing Bank now.

"Perhaps I should mention it in the negotiations," she said. "I want them to realize they have more in common with us than with Earth. Both planets try to do things in a human way. A way that supports both body and soul. The opportunity you get when you start a whole new society from scratch."

And Mars bollixed ours, I thought. "They've certainly been very friendly. I hope that's a promising sign."

"Have they let you look in the Earthers' rooms?"

"Talia had them searched."

"She should have let you look yourself. There could be clues she missed." She edged a little closer and lightly rested her hand on my knee. "Miss Prescott. I want to apologize for being so distant on the way over. The prince is—" She sighed. "He has a way to him, doesn't he? He gives you his full attention, and that makes you want to give yours back. But he doesn't really mean anything by it, does he?"

I looked up from her hand to her face. She looked earnest

enough. "I don't think so," I said gently. "It's just his way with everyone."

"I feel I've acted the fool," she said. "Not that I was interested in his position—that's far more than I could ever be comfortable with. But he just seemed so attentive, I thought it meant something, and that turned my head a little."

"No shame in that," I said. She sounded like she was apologizing, but I didn't understand what for. That she had looked like an adventuress? Insofar as I'd judged her that way, I'd kept it to myself.

"With him missing, I feel…more clarity, I think, about what I want. About *who* I want." Her fingers tightened slightly on my knee, and I glanced down at them in dismay. What could I say to gently hint I wasn't interested? I'd been let down easy any number of times, but somehow I couldn't call any of those delicate words to mind.

I looked back up, flushing and trying to stammer out something, but Miss Liu was gracefully rising to her feet. "Best of luck on the investigation," she said. "I feel certain you will find him." Then she moved away, silk scarf fluttering behind her.

For several minutes, I sat stunned by the water. This was a complication I hadn't expected—a distraction I didn't need. She was everything a person of my class ought to want: beautiful, elegant, well-connected. Everything, perhaps, I would have wanted, if it weren't for Moira.

Was I kidding myself, thinking I could have anything else? My class gave me privileges, but it was also a prison. There was a path my life was supposed to take; I'd tried to escape it, yet here I was again, treated like a gentlewoman, doing an officer's job. It felt like fate was trying to push me back to my old life, the old expectations.

I wanted to resist it—I had to. But if Moira weren't there waiting for me, I wasn't sure I could hold out. There was too much pressure to be what the Empire wanted. It would be so easy to slip into a courtship with Liu, just to improve my connections, just to please my family, and find myself stuck fast.

For a moment I was caught up in the idea. What a relief it would be, to be with someone who understood me, who would only ask for the things I knew how to give. Someone of my own class. With Moira, I cared too much, and thus everything hurt far too much. A woman like Liu wouldn't expect to be loved like that.

What I needed, at this moment, was a letter from Moira, one that really made her feel close. One where she understood, without my having to tell her, what I needed. But she hadn't even replied to my last.

27

MOIRA

When I got back to Landing, the whole city was in mourning. Even people I knew were revolutionaries wore crepe on their hats. Nobody wanted to be the only one without one.

And it wasn't like the princess herself had deserved to die, not really. She was a symbol of the Empire, but I couldn't have told you what she thought or what sort of ruler she might have been. Without changing the system, we could keep killing the royal family one by one, and the unjust rule would just pass to the next of them. It was typical of the Founders to have the line mapped out to a hundred degrees removed. Lucy was probably in that line somewhere, eventually.

I stopped at my room at the Spacer's Rest to freshen up before going to see Khan. Harrington was there. "Can I come with you?"

I turned, still buttoning my shirt. "Why?"

"Why not?" she asked reasonably. "I'm clearly as revolutionary as you are, by now."

"A great deal more, I'd say. But I only need to give him back his gun and tell him I'm leaving soon. You don't need to be there for that."

"I just...I would like to meet him." She turned her big blue eyes on me. "He's always been a hero of mine."

I'd been given a password of my own when I'd taken the mission for Khan, so I didn't have to wait for a guide. I took Harrington down with me and through the dim tunnels of the undercity. "Down *here*," she breathed, as I cracked a chemical light to make to glow. "It never occurred to me. No wonder the police haven't found him."

"They still could, if you can't keep a secret."

She was offended. "Of course I can."

Khan shook her hand politely when we were ushered into his room. Harrington blushed and smiled and had nothing much to say, so Khan signed a copy of a pamphlet for her and sent her out again. By his attitude, this sort of thing happened all the time. I felt a little bad I'd brought her here if she was only going to fangirl at him.

Once she was gone he turned to me. I saw he had the morning paper in his lap. "Twenty-six guards and police killed," he said. "The princess killed. The Tribune injured. That wasn't how I hoped this mission would go."

"We had nothing to do with the bombing," I said quickly. "That was someone else."

"I didn't think it was you. Unhappy coincidence. But I have my regrets about sending you out there. The papers are all calling for my head. They think I did it."

"I know who did it." I explained what I'd learned. "They've been tamping down any progressive movement for *years*," I finished.

Khan nodded. "It explains some things. I've been watching the anger of commoners grow and grow, while the Founders never budge an inch. I have awakened the people, but it isn't enough. It's worse than nothing, if none of the Founders care."

"Some do." I thought of Timothy, and of Lucy. Decent people, unhurt by the Empire, choosing to care when they could have looked the other way.

"Not enough. I don't understand how it isn't everyone. How anyone can live next door to oppression and ignore it." He fidgeted with his newspaper, folding the corners and smoothing them out again. As long as I'd known him, he'd been calm, conjuring up an emotional appeal at will, but never personally out of control. For the first time, I was seeing cracks in his serenity. "Since I came back, I've felt this urgency. This pressure to make a change now, before it's too late."

"Too late?"

"Before violence breaks out," he explained. "Think. We're sitting atop a volcano right now. The magma inside is pressing up, and the crust won't yield. Somehow there has to be a release of pressure. Chin-Hawking understood that; he was trying, in his self-serving way, to help. Now he has resigned. Parliament has recessed for two weeks to mourn the princess, and the tension in the city is higher than ever. There was another riot while you were gone, not one of our own protests. The people are getting impatient with me. They want change now, not when Parliament gets around to it."

"They're never getting around to it," I said. "I was right, wasn't I? This conspiracy is shutting down any chance of that."

He folded the newspaper, turned it, and folded it again. "Perhaps you're right. But you're also wrong. Putting our heads down and bearing it isn't going to work anymore. The harvests were bad this summer; the price of bread is skyrocketing. The war taxes are squeezing the people dry. The Navy keeps impressing sailors, and the sailors keep dying. I'm telling you in all earnestness, Moira. If we do nothing, violence will break out all the same. There will be blood in the streets."

I imagined that, fighting from street to street throughout Landing. The commoners armed with crowbars and broomsticks. The Imperial Guard armed with bayonets. It wasn't hard to guess whose blood would fill the gutters.

"The tribune election is announced tomorrow," I ventured. "Do you suppose—"

"The challenger will win by default, with Chin out of the race," Khan said. "And of the two, Chin was a little better. He at least understood the market can't flourish without us. I don't know much about this other man, Anderson."

"You know they're writing you in," I said.

"A stunt. And I'm concerned. If most of the votes are for me and they call it for Anderson, the people will riot again. Every riot costs lives. But I don't know what else anyone was supposed to do. I can't very well stop them from writing me in if they want to."

I nodded. "If things get ugly, I'll have a ride for you or anybody else soon. The *Mariposa* is supposed to be back in orbit today or tomorrow."

"I can't leave my people," he said. "But I have a few who are ready to go. Are you sure you want to leave, Moira? This is your home. You can stay here as long as you want. Down here, if the streets are too dangerous for you."

I shook my head. "No, it isn't really my home. Not anymore. I've changed, it's changed. I've got my dads settled here in the city and I'll be happy to set sail again. Liberty isn't perfect, but it's a place I can be for the time being."

"Say hello to Lucy for me."

"I will if she ever bothers to write." I forced a light smile. I hadn't heard from her since I'd set her up with Marcus. Could she be angry that we'd dated? I hadn't pegged her for the jealous type, but what did I know after so many years?

"Be well, Moira," he said at last. "I believe that everywhere Martians go, we bring Mars with us. It's how I felt on Deimos. I hope you feel us with you on your travels."

I gave a quick nod, cleared my throat, and left. Harrington was nowhere to be found, so I told one of Khan's men to let her know I'd left if she came looking for me and went up to daylight again.

28

LUCY

The next day there was a reception for both delegations with guests from every sector and workgroup of the stat. It was held in an observation lounge looking out at the clouds, with colored lights strung everywhere and soft music playing from a record player.

But Venusians didn't grasp the basic point of a high-class party, which is exclusion. A ball at the Imperial Palace was full of carefully-constructed rituals, costumes, and customs which, by intent, not just anyone could master. The point of an event like that is the pride in being invited at all while others aren't. Enjoyment is secondary, if it's present at all.

This party was nothing like one of those. Liu stood bewildered in a red silk gown, next to Blackwell in a white evening jacket, while people in increasingly wild costumes were introduced. Some wore almost nothing, while others were bedecked with flowing nylon streamers. They drank a strong liquor made from pineapples; they told funny stories and laughed loudly; they danced like they were making it up as they went along.

I positioned myself, in my gold-trimmed navy dress jacket, behind a large potted plant and watched the fun. Moira would have liked to be here. I wondered how she would have danced, in her tight low-slung trousers and her cropped shirt. She would have been the star of the party.

I was tempted to join in, but Knauss was here. I didn't dare bring any attention to myself. If she did recognize me, I couldn't be sure if she'd denounce me to Blackwell or blackmail me on her own, but she was sure to turn it to her advantage somehow.

Marcus came up with a plastic cup of pineapple liquor. "Why are you hiding in the corner?" he asked. "The Martian stick too far up your butt?"

"It isn't that," I said, taking the cup without drinking. "Tell me. Is all of the Earth delegation here? Every person they brought with them?"

He scanned the crowd, lips moving as he counted. "I think so. I'm pretty sure each delegation was only allowed five."

I set my cup down on the edge of the refreshments table. "Want to duck out early?"

"I don't, in fact," he said, but he was already following me out into the hallway. "What trouble are you up to?"

"Talia checked their rooms," I said, as we moved away from the sound of music. "So she was able to say for sure the prince wasn't there. But she didn't check for clues. Seems like my chance, while they're not at home."

"You could have just asked Talia to look again."

"How is she supposed to convince the Earthers she needs to search their rooms a second time?" We reached the Earthers' rooms, which were just opposite the main square from ours. I would have preferred to be further away, but on a stat this size we'd never be far enough away for me to be comfortable.

I inspected the door. If it was marked in any way, it was too subtle for me to see. It was possible they would know someone had been here, but that didn't matter. If they had taken the prince, they would expect it.

I carefully turned the knob and pushed the door open. No booby traps so far. I flicked on the light. The front room looked like ours, with a settee, a table, and a kitchenette. On the table was a plastic binder, which I carefully flipped through without picking it up.

"I don't see how that's relevant to your search," said Marcus. "I shouldn't be letting you do that."

"And yet you are," I said coolly, glancing at the pages. This had nothing useful, just schedules and jobs for each person. When their meetings with different workgroups were and who would get dinner made. I had hoped for a radio code list, but naturally they weren't dumb enough to leave that out in an unlocked room.

"Do you have some kind of beef with me?" he asked, as I moved on to look in their cupboards. Just coffee grounds and cups. Though what would they have if they'd kidnapped the prince? If he was kept somewhere else, whatever food he needed would be with him.

I closed the cabinet. "I'm sorry, have I been rude?"

"Martians are great at showing they hate you without being rude." He still stood in the middle of the room, arms folded, not participating in my search.

"You haven't done anything wrong," I called as I moved into the bedrooms. These were even less revelatory than the living room. Clearly they had left their rooms ready for inspection. A gambit, perhaps? Choosing to leave their rooms open to see what we'd do?

"Then why are you ... like this?"

I checked under the beds. Nothing. "I'm not a personable person, Marcus," I said at last. Which was true. I managed all the lying I did by being as wooden when I wasn't lying as when I was. I had imagined I could hide my discomfort with him behind my usual formality, but apparently not. "And if you've been flirting I missed it."

He took offense. "I haven't been—I'm not saying you were supposed to—"

I came out of the bedroom. "What *have* I been doing that bothers you? Focusing on the job at hand? I have a lot on my mind."

"It's mainly the death glare you give me whenever I talk to you."

I blinked. So much for concealing my feelings. Usually I was better at it than this.

"I thought you just hated Venusians," he said, "but you're nice enough to Talia."

I knelt down to look under the couch. "I admit it," I said, "there is—what's this?" I put my head down to see better. "Can you come look and confirm I didn't put this here?"

Marcus came over and knelt down. There, under the couch, was a tiny gold object. "What's that?"

I reached under and took it out. It was a gold cufflink, engraved with the House of Elliott's rocket symbol. I held it in my palm for Marcus to see.

"The prince's?" he asked.

"The very same. So if they had him here, and there was a struggle..."

"If so, they cleaned up well after."

I inspected the carpet. No scuffs, no stains. And it was beige; if they had gotten blood out of beige, it would have shown.

Just then I heard voices in the hallway outside. "We should go."

We slipped out and I shut the door carefully behind me. The voices were coming from the left side, so I dodged right. Marcus followed close on my heels, while I picked turnings at random.

That led us to a dead end and an elevator. I punched the button, while Marcus said, "You know, I could have led the way. I know my way around."

The voices came closer. "It looked like they were leaving our rooms," said an Earth accent. "They went this way."

The elevator still hadn't arrived. I pried the door open and peered down the shaft. The car was down below, not moving. The operator was probably at the party. For all their work ethic, Venusians didn't care to keep regular hours.

"What are you doing?" hissed Marcus, as I carefully grabbed hold of the ladder lining the inside of the shaft.

I swung the rest of my body inside. Damn, this sort of acrobatics wasn't easy in the punishing gravity. "Come on or don't," I said.

With an incredulous look, he climbed into the shaft after me. I pushed the door shut and started climbing. "I knew Martians were a little uncivilized, but this is just *beyond*," he said. "Or perhaps it's a double-agent thing?"

I paused and cocked my head. "I think it compounds."

We reached the next floor, which was the farm level, and I reached to open the door. "Wait," said Marcus. "You were going to tell me why you hate me."

"It isn't personal," I said, yanking the door open. I stepped out. "I just don't like people who sleep with my girlfriend."

He scrambled after me. "I didn't—Moira's your girlfriend?"

We were in a shady walkway of coconut palms. "Yes," I said. "Which means I ought to appreciate you for trying to help her. Instead I'm jealous of you. Since we have to work together, it's best if we put that detail behind us."

He shook his head ruefully. "What was Moira thinking?"

"I imagine she trusts you better than anyone else she knows here. And if she does, I do. I just also don't like you. I'll get over it."

I slipped the cufflink into my pocket and walked away.

Once I'd brushed the grime from the elevator shaft off my coat, I returned to the party. The Earth delegation had left, as I'd thought. I joined a group of people clustered around Liu just as she pronounced, "It's obvious Earth is trying to sabotage the forum. That's why they kidnapped our prince."

I gave her a significant look, and she extricated herself, saying, "Tell everyone. Maybe we can still find him. He's got to be somewhere on the stat."

The group broke up, and Liu turned to me. "That should help your efforts."

"Are you joking?" I demanded. "Here we've been carefully trying to avoid spreading the news around, in case the Earth delegation finds out."

She rolled her eyes. "The Earthers know, because the Earthers did it. It's pretty obvious. Who else would have?"

"Wouldn't it make sense to let me complete my investigation before you make up your mind?" The cufflink was a clue, for sure, but she didn't know about that.

"Your investigation will go better with more people looking," Liu said, unruffled by my criticism. "Besides, the forum is in two days. Don't you think it helps our cause for them to know the games the Earthers are playing?"

I blinked. It was true, it did make us sound like sympathetic victims. That might play well here. But it sounded a little Machiavellian to use a tragedy like that. "*If* they did it," I said.

"We need whatever help we can get, without the prince here," she pointed out. "I don't think Blackwell has the same charm."

She wasn't wrong. But I felt strange about it all the same. Somehow, despite all the evidence that Mars wasn't, as I had once believed, the planet of impeccable honesty, I still expected a certain gentlemanly straight dealing.

I spent the rest of the day trawling quiet parts of the stat, while Marcus talked to the hospitality workers. I finally trudged back to our rooms well after dinnertime. The others looked up hopefully when I came in, only to look away in disappointment a moment later. My face must have said it all.

Sagan left off cleaning the kitchenette and came over to ask me quietly, "Have you eaten, Lieutenant?"

"Yes. Don't worry about me. I may be out most of the day tomorrow also, and I'll handle my own meals."

They walked away heavily, leg braces jingling slightly. I sat on the couch, feet throbbing, and watched them work. Sagan had been so sure the prince would never visit a brothel. Was it just an unusual change of habit, or did Sagan know something the rest of us didn't? If he'd had any secrets, his valet would be the one most likely to know.

I forced myself back to my feet. "Sagan, may I have a private word?"

Their brown eyes were startled. "Of course."

The prince's room was as I'd seen it before: tidy, everything in place. Both beds were immaculately made; I couldn't tell which Sagan had slept in the night before, and which the prince had failed to. The dresser between the two beds held fresh flowers.

There was one large chair in the room, commandeered from the living room, and Sagan directed me to sit. I dropped into it gratefully. "Please," I said, as they continued to stand, "this is in-formal. Don't make yourself uncomfortable on my account."

Sagan hesitated. Perhaps, despite their discomfort with the gravity, they would prefer to stand. But they sank onto the nearer bed with a soft sigh.

"Yesterday morning," I said. "When Miss Liu said the prince was in the hospitality district. You seemed surprised."

Sagan nodded and was silent. Of course. Keeping their master's secrets was a huge portion of their job; they would know better than to volunteer information. Even a corrupt servant would expect to be paid to gossip.

"If there's anything at all that might shed any light on what happened there, I need to know. Everything in this investigation is being kept as an imperial secret. Nothing gets out about this, before or after the prince is found. Not even," I added on a sudden impulse, "to the prince himself."

Sagan nodded and folded their arms. "I am not sure anything I know would be helpful," they said slowly. "I am convinced the prince didn't go to a brothel. Perhaps he pretended to, to shake off Liu. She was probably trying to be…" They trailed off. "You know how she's been, with him."

"I had gotten an impression, yes." So I wasn't the only one who had noticed her interest in him. "You think he dislikes the attention?"

"I know he does," Sagan answered. "He's charming with everyone; that's his job. That doesn't mean he wants any of the people who swarm around him looking for the same thing."

Strange. No interest in casual sex; no interest in his marriage prospects either. And his marriage prospects included almost everyone. He was almost thirty; surely in all that time he'd met at least a few people who weren't purely mercenary. He certainly had enough charm to coax sincere attraction out of people. Unless he rejected everyone preemptively for fear they were only after his connections.

"He isn't asexual, is he?" I said suddenly. He'd declared himself indifferent, but that didn't mean anything, not for a man at his level of society. The Emprex could have demanded it, while he secretly avoided any connections. That certainly would explain why Sagan knew he wasn't at a brothel.

They fixed me with a strange look. Or perhaps the only thing strange about it was the direct, steady eye contact, something they usually avoided out of deference. It changed their whole face from unprepossessing to something very sharp and alert. "Lieutenant Prescott, can I trust you?"

"Of course," I said. "I told you—"

"You said an *imperial* secret. An imperial secret may be told to the Emprex. Must be, in some cases. I want this to die with you. I don't know you well enough to know whether you're safe with it. But I don't have the access you have to find him myself, so it seems I have little choice but to trust you."

"It dies with me," I said firmly, leaning forward in the chair. "Nothing is more important than finding the prince. Certainly nothing you can have to say."

Sagan drew in a deep breath. "The prince is my husband," they said quietly. "In everything but name."

I let myself fall back against the cushions. Shocked? Yes. But mostly shocked at myself, for not noticing. I'd picked up on the prince's strange obsession for keeping his valet close, and somehow missed the most obvious explanation. Classism, was all I could put it down to. It hadn't occurred to me to think of the prince and his valet as peers in any way. Which was rich, coming from me. What would Moira say?

"I see," I managed.

"He can't have gone off looking for a brothel," they continued. "I'm convinced he was looking for me. He would want to tell me the news immediately. He'd have left Liu in the hospitality district in the hopes of getting to talk to me alone."

I nodded. That broadened, immensely, the area where he could have gone missing. "Where were you?"

"Picking up ingredients for lunch, in the main square."

"Did he know that?"

Sagan chewed their lip. "I'm not sure. I might have said. Or I might have only said going out. But he'd look for me there first, don't you think?"

"It's the most obvious place," I agreed. The square would be harder to kidnap someone from than the hospitality district would. There were always people there. But in the halls and stairs between the two of them, there were empty stretches. Could the prince have vanished along the way?

"How do you think he'd react to his sister's death?" I asked. "Were they close?"

Sagan shook their head. "Not at all. They each grew up with their own band of nannies and handpicked friends, years apart. But they did have a deal, between them. That when the Emprex died, she would give him permission to marry."

"Did the Emprex know about the two of you?"

"No. We didn't bother asking. Their feelings on morganatic marriages were obvious. The Emprex thought it diluted the pure blood of the Founders." Their dark eyes flashed. There was a lot of anger stored up behind the valet persona. "So we settled on this. Keep it secret, so the Emprex wouldn't separate us. And when they died, then the princess would ascend and Kostya and I could retire somewhere quietly—or as quietly as we could. She promised to allow it."

"But with her gone—"

"The Emprex would insist he marry as soon as possible. One heir is too risky."

I thought back to the prince, white as a sheet, stumbling out of the room. No, he wouldn't have been rushing off looking for a stranger to console himself with. His entire life, his dreams, had just evaporated before his eyes. Of course he'd seek out his partner to commiserate.

Unless, of course, Sagan was lying through their teeth. I

couldn't rule that out. I had no way to confirm anything they told me without the prince here. It was entirely possible that the valet had murdered the prince themself, with all of this tangle of a secret relationship only a distraction. But it seemed needlessly complicated. Sagan could have murdered the prince at any moment in the past several years, if they'd had a mind to.

"Thank you for trusting me with all this," I said. "I wish I had more hope to offer in return."

"Just find him for me," Sagan said, with quiet intensity. "Find him for all of us."

29

LUCY

There were two possible routes between the hospitality district and the main square, neither one more isolated than the other. Both appeared to be residential; quiet hallways, but not empty. It was certainly plausible that the prince might have found himself alone in one of these, or alone except for his attackers. But it didn't seem likely. The brief period when the prince was unguarded couldn't have been predicted. The Earthers couldn't have planned to wait for him in the hallway, because they wouldn't have known he would be passing by.

A crime of opportunity, then. They had passed by him unexpectedly, made the split-second decision to kidnap or kill him, and set upon him then and there. It didn't seem likely. Unless they'd been looking for an opportunity since we had arrived.

And then once they had him, what would they do with him? There was no subtle way to drag either a resisting prisoner or a corpse out of those halls. They could either take the stairs up to the main square, or go back toward the hospitality district, where there was more foot traffic.

I slowly traversed the routes again. I was alone this morning: Marcus was busy going over the hospitality district with a group from StatOps. The hallways, like the halls everywhere, were full of doors. If I had just captured an enemy and needed a place to stow him, that would be the automatic answer.

I began knocking on doors, one at a time. The first door opened on an elderly couple. "Oh," said the man at the door, "it's one of them Martian diplomats."

I held out the card Talia had given me, and the old man inspected it. "Help you?" he asked. "You need help?"

"I'm looking for my friend," I said, projecting my voice in case he was a little deaf. "A young man with long, dark hair. Have you seen him?"

He turned to his husband. "We haven't seen anyone like that, have we?"

"Haven't had any visitors but our granddaughter since we came onto the dayside," the other old man replied, from a recliner where he sat tucked in with a brown-and-orange afghan.

"Your granddaughter?" I asked.

"That's me," said a voice from behind. I turned to see a violet woman striding down the hall. "You're not bothering my grandpas, are you?"

"Oh, never," said the man at the door.

It took me a moment to remember her name. "Alix!" I said at last. I'd spoken with her the first day here. She'd bought me a pineapple ice. "Do you live in this hall?"

"Right next door. That's why I heard you. I like to keep an eye on my grandpas."

"Of course." I turned my authorization card over in my hands. What would really be helpful was a picture of the prince. "Have you seen a young man—Martian—with long black—"

"I've seen all of you around," she said. "You mean the handsome one. The team lead."

"Prince George Konstantin," I said. "He's very important on Mars."

"When did you last see him?"

"Yesterday," I said. "He was last seen here in this hallway, near the hospitality district."

She shook her head. "No, sorry."

"Can you help me knock on the rest of the doors?"

"Our Alix will help you," said the old man at the door. "She's an angel in disguise, I tell you. An angel in disguise."

Alix gave the old man a kiss on the cheek before shutting the door. "You think he might be in one of these apartments?"

"Are they all apartments, along this hallway?"

"Most of them." She accompanied me as we knocked on door after door. No one had seen the prince. Or heard a scuffle the day before.

Some of the doors we knocked on, no one answered. I took a notebook out of my pocket at the first one of these. "I'll have to come back later."

"It's fine," said Alix, opening the door and peeking inside. "It's not like we're snooping. Yo, George! You in here?"

I shifted from foot to foot, feeling anxious. At least she was the one trespassing on people's homes, not me.

"Don't worry," she said, pulling her head out again and shutting the door. "I know everyone on my hall. I'll have them give their place a better search when they get home."

Together we trawled the entire hallway, as well as the alternate route, with no luck. People were cheerful and happy to help, for the most part. Some were working on art or small crafts; others just sat and listened to the radio. I had a pang of homesickness. It had been so long since I'd had a cozy day indoors with my own family. Better yet, a cozy day with Moira, in a little house that was ours. We'd never had that. I wasn't sure how we ever would.

But I couldn't feel too sorry for myself, thinking of the prince.

Sagan would be worried sick; they tucked their emotions down deep to avoid detection, but inside they must be suffering. And the prince, too, if he was alive. Even if he did get found, how could they ever get the quiet retirement they both wanted?

"Sorry I wasn't more help," said Alix, as we reached the end of the second hallway. "Should I ask around?"

"You may as well."

I met Marcus for lunch, to go over his findings with the hospitality district workers. "Nobody served the prince," he said, taking out his notebook. "Nobody saw him at all."

I nodded. "That's the impression I got from his valet. They said he never frequents those places."

Marcus chuckled. "Martians always say they don't."

"Sagan was in a position to actually know the prince's habits." I didn't want to say more than that. "My current theory is that he left Miss Liu at the entrance to the hospitality district, after implying to her that he was going in. Then he went looking for Sagan, probably in the main square."

He frowned, doodling on his paper. "You're saying we have to interview all the people who might have been in the square the day before yesterday?"

"No." I sighed. "We'll have to make that announcement, like you wanted. Asking for anyone at all who's seen him after noon that day. And ask people also to check any out-of-the-way spaces in their homes and workplaces."

We spent some time drafting a message that worked. He folded up the final draft and put it in his pocket. "The Earthers will hear this too, of course. If they're using the radio in their apartment."

"They'll find out soon enough," I said. "We've had to talk to a lot of people already, and the rest of my delegation is telling people, too."

"You still think Earth is responsible?"

I leaned my forehead on my hands. "I don't know what to think. Earth has no plausible means. Venus has no possible motive."

"There are a lot of Venusians," he said earnestly. "We don't all think the same. In all of those people, maybe there's someone who really hates Martians. Or the prince in particular."

"I can't imagine who could hate the prince." I sank into silence, absently arranging and rearranging my empty dishes. My napkin got spread out, folded, spread out again, tucked into the paper cup. "It doesn't even look like hate. Hate leaves tracks. Isn't that what you said? Or Talia did. That crimes here are usually crimes of passion and thus don't need a detective because they weren't planned out ahead of time or hidden afterward."

Marcus rescued the cup from my fidgeting hands and tossed it into a nearby recycle bin. "It's true. If it was pure anti-Martian terrorism, they'd kill him and leave the body lying as a warning to everyone. This isn't that."

No. It had to be toward some goal, a goal that wasn't served by simply letting him lie. "What sorts of different views *do* Venusians have?" I ventured at last.

"There's ten thousand of us in this stat alone," said Marcus. "And you know the joke, if you've got two Venusians in a room, you've got eight points of view."

"*Eight?*" I chuckled. "No, I hadn't heard that one."

He started drawing a chart. "Okay, so take one axis of opinions. Opinions on foreign policy. That's what you care about most, yeah?" He wrote *foreign policy* on the first column of the top row and started filling out the rest of the row. "We've got people who think we should cut ties with Mars over your human-rights record and ally more closely with Earth. We've got people who think we should cut ties with Earth because of their economic imperialism. They say sooner or later Earth will try to take us over."

"They would," I said darkly. "Once they were done with Mars. The corps don't like limits on where they do business."

"They don't like *anything* existing they don't own," he agreed. "Okay, then you've got the majority view, which believes in keeping the balance in the system if we can, so we can continue to play both of you off each other. It's worked so far."

"But it only continues to work as long as Mars remains independent," I said. "If Mars loses the war, there's no longer a division of powers within the system."

Marcus got that cagey look on his face again. "That's … a very real concern," he said at last.

I leaned forward. "Marcus. Is there another column here I should know about?"

"There are so many different—"

"I think I need to know this," I said.

He leaned back. Sighed. "Let's put it this way. In our last vote, we decided to consider this danger and try to broker power within the system. This forum is to decide which side we're going to support."

That, we had already guessed. What else could it be for? "But some people didn't agree with this, obviously. Would someone try to stop the forum, after failing to get the idea voted down?"

Marcus's eyebrow shot up, while the rest of his face relaxed. I had clearly moved away from his big secret. "If they're trying to stop the forum, they'd go after the Earth delegation next."

I nodded. "So if they make a move, we'll know." I didn't suggest warning the Earthers. If Ms. Knauss were kidnapped or murdered, I wouldn't shed a single tear over it. She'd backed Moira into a corner and put her life in danger twice with her ridiculous contracts. The solar system would be better off without her.

But the Earthers weren't stupid; if they didn't know about the prince's disappearance, they would soon. And if they hadn't done it, they'd suspect they were next, and take any precautions they could. If they weren't already.

I stared off to the side, at the people passing by. I had come close to Marcus's big secret, and then lost the trail. It was something about brokering power in the system. The prince had also noticed the stonewalling in that direction. He had known the Venusians wanted some kind of new deal, or had one to offer as a prize to the side that made out best in the forum.

What if he had stumbled upon the truth? Would the Venusians have arrested him, to hold him till after the forum, so that he couldn't tip their hand? It would be rich of Talia, to appear so open while knowing the whole time where the prince was.

But then, she'd reminded me that she wasn't in control of everything that happened on Venus. Was that a hint, that I would have to look among her own people for the answer? They had no police to hold a person, but they also might not stop someone who chose to do it themselves.

"Marcus," I said, turning back to him, "where are we *not* allowed to go?"

30

LUCY

Marcus was still grumbling when we got down to the next-to-lowest level. "You can't honestly expect me to specify the exact place we'd least like you to find and then lead you to it."

"Of course not," I said. "But Talia was vague about exactly where we should or shouldn't go, when we first arrived. She only said some of the lower levels might be dangerous and we should get someone to guide us. What if the prince blundered into somewhere because he didn't know he wasn't supposed to be there, and it ended up being dangerous?"

"The factories, then?" We were standing in a wide, low-ceilinged hallway. Electric lights burned yellow and artificial, but it still seemed a little darker down here than up above.

"I suppose. I thought I'd just wander around aimlessly and see if anyone appears to tell me I can't be here."

He shifted nervously from one foot to the other. "I feel ridiculous," he said. I searched his face. Awkward, or concerned I'd find something? I couldn't be sure.

Wandering vaguely took me straight to the chemical plant

where Marcus worked. The main hall led right to it. "We should look here," I said, when he halted at the entrance.

"Why would he have gone in here?"

"Because he was curious? Because he wasn't paying attention? Because the hall leads straight here? I don't need a reason; I'm checking every single thing I can."

The plant was a hot, crowded warren of boilers and pipes. Of metal, for once. Funnels on top of the boilers led to long pipes running into refrigerators. It was like nothing so much as a giant whiskey still, because it had basically the same function: taking the atmosphere and the condensate from the clouds, and using distillation and freezing to separate them into their component parts.

"What do you make in here?" I asked, over the noise of the machines.

"Everything," he said. "Oxygen. Nitrogen. Water. Hydrocarbons. Shit-tons of raw graphite to send up to the carbon-fiber plant on Aphrodite. Some amount of sulfur, but we throw most of it away. Nobody could ever use the amount of sulfur we get."

"Plastic?"

"That's a different plant. We make raw materials in here, make them into other things in different factories."

"Could someone get in here, stuff a body in one of those boilers?"

He gave me a disgusted look. "What? No! At least—well, no. People are always in here. Each boiler has to be watched all the time, so that when it reaches the right temperature, we can draw off and condense the gasses. Same with the condensers and freezers."

It was true, the place was busy, and every boiler had someone watching it. Marcus still called a foreman over to explain. "If you see anything weird, anything at all," he finished, "tell me or Talia."

We went on to a plastics factory, a textile factory (more plastics), a food processing plant, and a lab where mold grew in vats to make penicillin. No one had seen the prince. No one had seen any sign of a corpse, or a part of one.

Across from the lab was a small, closed door. Unmarked, like all the doors, but this one was closed. A woman sat on a stool beside the door, reading a book. "What's in there?" I asked.

"Nothing," said Marcus, at the same moment as the woman said, "Recycling."

"That's what I meant," Marcus added. "Nothing helpful. Just trash. It isn't a big room."

"I have to look in *all* the rooms," I said.

"Talia would have checked this one herself," he argued. "You said she looked around the first night."

"He could have been moved around in the past couple days." I did not say, *who says I can trust Talia?*

I looked the woman by the door up and down. She was lean, well-muscled. Despite her relaxed pose, I could have sworn she was a guard. Was this Venus's secret? Marcus's resistance made me suspect so. I pulled Talia's card from inside my coat and handed it to the woman.

"I need to see inside this room, please," I ventured. "We're looking for a missing person."

She barely glanced at it. "Talia told me you might come here. Our secret will have to be your secret. Can I trust you to keep it from the rest of your delegation?"

Marcus spluttered. "So I could have told her all this time? I've been trying so hard not to—"

"It clearly didn't work," interrupted the guard, getting up and putting her book down on the stool. "Talia's right, we owe it to the Martians to be open, considering their guy was lost on our watch." She took out a key and unlocked the door.

The room beyond was large for a door that small, as large as the factory floors on this level. But there were no machines, only piles upon piles of round bundles, as big as . . . Well. There was only one thing I knew three feet long and maybe a foot around. Something I knew intimately.

"These are torpedoes," I whispered, as if the room itself could explode if I spoke too loud. "I thought you people were pacifists!"

"Only if the rest of you let us be," he answered at the same volume. "Even on Aphrodite, we have to play tough with you and the Earthers because we can't trust you to behave. And now the whole system is a war zone. We have to pick a side."

I stared at the torpedoes. There were hundreds of them, enough to supply dozens of ships. It could outfit most of the Martian fleet. But... "You have no ships," I said. "You're not planning on entering the war."

"We can't," he agreed. "We don't have the resources to build up a military at this point. No, the idea was to make weapons, offer those in exchange for trade and protection. Give up our neutrality, but hopefully stay safe with one of your fleets looking out for us."

"You can't pick them. Earth devours everything, you know they won't leave you alone once they've gotten rid of us."

"They will if we get on their good side before they're done devouring you," he pointed out. "Whereas if we come in on your side, they may still win and then they'll want to get even with anyone who helped you."

My stomach sank. Of course, tactically speaking, they had to pick the winner, and that was almost certainly Earth. We had barely been able to hold them off with all our strength, while Earth played its games of conquest more or less in their free time. The people on Earth itself barely knew or cared what happened in space.

And that didn't bode well for Liberty Station either. The Venusians might want to support Moira and her pirates, but it was a long shot at best. The inward-looking Venusians would see it as a risk, far too great a risk no matter how much they sympathized.

"Do you really think these weapons will make that much difference?" I asked at last. "Earth, at least, has no trouble outfitting its ships. Do they even care for your support?"

"They have nothing like these," he said, laying a hand proudly on one of the gleaming cylinders. "They're auto targeted. Little electric gizmo inside helps them seek out your enemy. All charged up and battery operated; you won't need to get your hands dirty handling any of the electric parts. And they're more powerful than anything you've got now. They can pierce right through the radiation plating, if they get a good hit."

I shuddered. I'd been in ships bombarded with heavy fire: concussions so strong they would fling a man across the sail deck and break his skull like an egg. But I'd also seen a hull breached: men spilled out into the hard black vacuum with their air freezing into crystal fog. I knew which death I'd pick.

Marcus was watching me, my arms wrapped around myself as if to protect my tender underbelly. "You see why we didn't want either of you to know."

That brought me back to myself. I had days before the forum to think about the consequences of these weapons. Right now my mission was still to find the prince, before the forum if at all possible. And this was a clue, a great screaming clue I needed to decode in a hurry.

"Are you *sure* the Earthers don't know about this?" I asked. "If all of you know, all it would take is one person to tip them off."

"Nobody tipped *you* people off."

"Nobody likes us." I smiled bitterly. "Some people might like Earth. They seem very much your style, at least until they've got you to mortgage your soul to them."

He frowned. "Earth *is* polling ahead, last I heard. But so what? If Earth does know, what exactly would they do differently? They can't steal the weapons, not while they're down here in the atmosphere. Earth doesn't have any shuttles to come down here, or any pilots that know how. All they can do is put on their best showing at the forum, same as you."

"Or take our best speaker, to give themselves an edge." I turned to leave the room. I had seen enough. "If you don't think they'd do it, you don't know them at all."

I came back to our rooms in the late afternoon, frustrated with my lack of progress. I was finding out clue after clue, but nothing that pointed in the direction of anyone particular. I knew where the prince had vanished from, and I had found out one giant motive for anyone, but none of that even narrowed down the suspects. Galileo stat had ten thousand Venusians, and by Marcus's math, that meant forty thousand opinions. At any rate, far too many suspects and possible interests to investigate them all before the forum the day after tomorrow.

Sagan was at the kitchenette alone, boiling coffee in a little two-chambered pot. "The others are out campaigning, Lieutenant."

I joined them at the hot plate. "A clever little pot," I said. "I suppose the hot water is forced up through the grounds as it boils?"

"Thinking of a better method for space?"

I considered it. "Ah, it would never work. Steam doesn't go up at all in space; it goes everywhere."

Sagan got two cups and saucers out of a cabinet.

"None for me, thank you, it's too late in the day," I said.

"Just a splash with milk, ma'am? They have no cows here, but the coconut milk is acceptable."

I nodded, and the valet started foaming the milk. When the coffee was ready, they poured it through the foamed milk in a pretty swirl. "That's how the Venusians do it, ma'am."

They put the coffee pot down without pouring the second cup. "Please," I said. "I didn't mean to interrupt your own cup."

Sagan gave me a sharp look. "So now that you know my secret, you care to treat me like an equal?"

My stomach sank. I liked Sagan, had liked them from the beginning, but I knew no way to prove to them I wasn't a classist. I wasn't even sure I wasn't one. I sighed. "It just seems silly to stand on ceremony when there's only two of us here," I said, carrying my cup to the table. "Join me or not, whatever makes you more comfortable."

It must have satisfied Sagan, for they poured a cup and sat down across from me. "Since we're sharing secrets," they said, taking a careful sip, "perhaps you could tell me how the investigation is going."

I frowned. "Not well. I've been searching for days and don't seem to be any closer. Virtually anyone on the stat could have done it. And I don't know the Venusians and their politics well enough to know if any of them might have, or which ones."

"You don't think it was the Earthers then?"

"Certainly they're the obvious possibility," I said. "But there are only five of them, and I don't know how they could have kidnapped the prince so quickly or without any traces. Whereas Venusians, at least, might have a larger number in their conspiracy, and be able to pass unnoticed in more places."

Sagan took another drink. Their movements were as graceful as any Founder's—more so, because they had to be. One can't be a prince's valet and look like a village yokel. "Which Venusians have you been talking to?" they said. "Just the leaders?"

"And random individuals," I said. "I can't parse their divisions. No one seems to want to talk about them, and yet they all acknowledge they have strong political differences. Just nothing they want to share with me."

"You're asking in the wrong places, then." Sagan set down

their empty cup. "Do you have anything to wear besides that uniform?"

"A few things." I finished my coffee. "Why?"

"I'm taking you out," Sagan said firmly, standing up and taking both cups. "Get dressed."

Half an hour later, we were walking through a residential hallway on the mid-levels. I wore buff trousers, a white shirt, and a crimson vest. A tailcoat would be more appropriate on Mars, but here on Venus, I felt the need to be less formal.

"Where are we going?" I asked.

"A place I found the other day," Sagan replied. We reached a nondescript white door, between a violet painting and a rainbow tapestry. Sagan gave an odd knock, three taps and then three more, and the door opened.

Inside was small and dim, with tables shoved into the corners. Music played softly from a record player, something with a throbbing beat and a voice in a language I didn't know.

At the tables, people were sitting and drinking. It reminded me, more than anything, of the low-class bars in Landing, below the elevator, where spacers liked to gather. Of course there was no class here. Yet something about it felt the same: the dimness, the griminess of the walls. Strange, in a place so ubiquitously white and clean.

The drinkers looked up and spotted Sagan. "Sagan!" they called cheerfully, shoving onto the tiny couches to leave two chairs open for us.

We sat down. I eyed Sagan curiously. What sort of place was this, and how had they found it? The host, a burly man with a beard, hefted himself out of a chair in the corner and served up two mismatched glasses of clear liquid. "I don't have anything to trade this time," said Sagan.

The man waved dismissively. "What you brought last time pays your way. Who's your friend?"

"Lucy," said Sagan. "You could call her the hired muscle of the delegation."

Everyone at the table laughed. I felt my face warm. I might not be made of muscle, but I knew my way around both sword and pistol. Not that I had either one on me.

I carefully sipped my drink. It was as strong as Navy rum, with an unpleasant acetone aroma. My eyes went back to Sagan with an unspoken question. All the time I'd been here, no one had asked for money. My credit chit was adequate for anything.

"This is a private club," they explained. "Not on the jobs distribution system."

Meaning, I supposed, illegal. With no real police force, and a motive to evade the law, I should have assumed capitalism would spring up. The hours system was like a finely manicured lawn; without constant tending it would quickly produce weedy patches. I caught the host's eye and raised my glass.

The host responded with a nod. To Sagan he said, "Can your friend keep her mouth shut as well as you can?"

"Like an iron trap," Sagan replied.

"The public bars all have to admit everyone," the host explained. "It's not about the money. Here I can choose my clientele."

The hum of conversation had resumed, over the low music. Had to keep the volume down, I supposed, to avoid complaints from the neighbors.

Sagan beckoned the host a little closer. "Lucy here is trying to find our missing Martian," they said. "Don't suppose you've heard anything."

He shook his head. "Not more than I heard on the radio. Can't imagine why anyone would mess with the delegations."

"Maybe someone who didn't want the forum to happen," I suggested. "Or someone who wanted Earth to come out looking better."

"If there were someone with an idea like that, I'd have heard it," he answered. "I know about every illegal racket on the stat, which I assume is why Sagan brought you here."

"It would take only a few people to pull it off," I said. "One or two to overpower him, and someone to hide him. I've checked every public place on the stat, but he could be in anyone's home."

The host shrugged. "Of course it's possible. But much more likely it's one of you than one of us."

I blinked. "Us?"

"You foreigners," he clarified. "Earth and Mars are both hotbeds of crime. That's why Aphrodite's such a mess but down here where you're not allowed, *this*," his gesture took in his tiny speakeasy, "is what passes for criminal activity."

I sat in silence for a moment. His careless word choice had set something turning in my mind, something I needed to finish thinking through before I said anything.

"If one of you did try this," Sagan said, "who would it be? Who's most down for mischief, of anyone you know?"

The host leaned back on his heels and stared at the ceiling. "The Xenos, if I had to guess," he said. "On this stat that's dozens of people though. But they're the type that would want to."

31

✴

LUCY

We stayed till our drinks were gone, making conversation with the clientele, before heading back to the upper levels.

"I suppose the Xenos thing is a lead," Sagan said, "but so far as I know that's an entire political party here. It doesn't narrow it down much."

"Xeno for xenophobe?" I asked.

"Yes. People who want to shut down Aphrodite and never terraform, just keep Venus completely self-sufficient. It can't be that common a view, but I have heard of them before."

"I see we've been going about our diplomacy the wrong way," I said. "The prince, Blackwell, and Liu should have been spending their time hanging around in bars. Then at least we'd have learned about the actual divisions here, instead of the show of unity they put up in public."

"I'm sorry we didn't pick up more that was helpful to your investigation."

"I did learn one useful thing. The radio notice has gone out. That means I need to talk to Talia. If he's been holed up in someone's apartment this whole time, someone will be coming forward now."

I parted from Sagan at the main piazza, so they could pick up something for the others. It was almost dinnertime by now, and I was ever-so-slightly intoxicated from the speakeasy's home-brewed hooch. No time to sober up, but I got fruit juice and a paper packet of fried mushrooms. That would at least soak up some of the alcohol.

Talia was still in her office, tidying up her desk in preparation for leaving. "Ah, Lucy. Your radio notice went out."

"So I heard. Has anyone come in to give information?"

"I got a few notes." She handed them over. "Nothing especially helpful."

I leafed through the slips of paper. Someone had heard a clamor in the hallway a little before noon and thought it might be a kidnapping, but it was in the other balloon, clear on the far side of the stat. Someone thought Earth might have done it, "because we all know they hate the Martians, don't we?" True but unhelpful. Someone suggested "one of the Martian proletariat" must have done it, because of their natural class resentment. I couldn't rule out that Sagan had done it, but it didn't seem likely, even if their whole story to me was a lie. They were far too frail, in the high gravity, to overpower much of anyone.

"Thanks anyway," I said, and returned to our rooms.

After Liu, Blackwell, and Sagan were asleep for the night, I sat up on the divan, wondering. It seemed almost impossible that the prince had gone missing Tuesday afternoon, between the hospitality district and the main square. No one had seen him in the hospitality district, no one would have known to look for him in the halls, and if he had reached the square, someone surely would have seen him.

But my focus on that window of time relied entirely on one person: Liu. That was the thought the bartender had planted in my mind when he said "one of you." Everyone ought to be a suspect. Only Blackwell was entirely in the clear, since he'd been in the room with me the entire time. Sagan, theoretically, could have found him wandering the stat and somehow hidden him away. But that relied on no fewer unlikely chances than my theory of Earthers setting on him in the hallway.

Liu, however, had been with him the entire time. If her story was in any way inaccurate—if, perhaps, she'd separated from him sooner than she reported, or in a different place—that opened up the entire stat as a possibility, and a larger window of time. We'd asked the entire stat if they'd seen the prince at any time after noon. I should have asked if they'd seen him any time after nine o'clock. Perhaps I could have gotten a very different answer.

Not that it really mattered. Marcus and I had checked everywhere except private homes, and if he was in one of them, someone would have come forward. Unless the person who lived there was hiding him on purpose, in which case we had no lead. Perhaps we could try to follow the bartender's Xenos suggestion—see if we could find out who was a part of this group and knock on *their* doors. It didn't seem like the kind of group that would publish membership lists, but maybe Marcus would have some guesses.

I rested my elbows on my knees, discouraged. I felt like we'd checked everywhere in the whole stat. It was as if the prince had vanished. Perhaps his body had simply been broken down into component parts. There was plenty of sulfuric acid available. I imagined his lifeless body in some Venusian bathtub, drowned in yellow liquid, fizzing. I rubbed my eyes. Marcus was right, my mind was a little twisted. But didn't it have to be, to find someone twisted enough to kidnap the prince?

With a jerk I leapt to my feet. We had checked the entire stat. And we had confirmed that no one had left the stat since noon Tuesday. But what if the timing was off, and someone had left at eleven?

For a moment I hesitated. I could wake Liu and question her again. Ask if she was certain about the time she had parted from the prince. Had she picked up a coffee or taken a walk between then and coming back here?

But I didn't much want to go in her room, see her in her nightgown with her hair across the pillow. Moira was the only person I ever wanted to see in that state. And anyway, Liu would be cross at being awakened.

And really, it came down to her having lied or not. If she had, she wouldn't tell me. Surely she'd been aware her omission would interfere with my investigation. She didn't seem to care about it. She'd already made up her mind the Earthers were to blame.

I threw on my coat and went out. The lights were still on in the halls, since the night shift was still awake and busy. No point in waking up Marcus either. I knew my way to the airlock.

I stepped into a vinyl coverall and fastened the tabs. My coat made an awkward bulge in the hindquarters; I wished I'd left it off. Then the oxygen mask, with the hood pulled tight around the edges to cover all my skin. I could be anybody in this thing. And so, I assumed, might the prince have looked, if he'd somehow been lured out here.

Outside, it was night. Day didn't break again till sometime tomorrow—or rather, we didn't break into daylight till then. Floodlights stabbed through the dim fog, which left each light haloed and vague.

I stalked across to the largest hangar, where the front gate stood open. Two anonymous figures in the same baggy blue coveralls were pushing a plane out. I pulled out my pass from Talia, which I'd moved to the coverall pocket, and approached them.

"Excuse me," I said. "I'm Lucy Prescott, with the Martian delegation."

They stopped pushing the plane. One leaned on the wing while the other came to talk to me. "Oh yeah, you were here Wednesday."

In that get-up, I couldn't have known my own mother. "So you know I'm looking for our missing prince."

"Got nothing new to tell you," he said. "None of us at the hangars have seen him."

"You wouldn't know him if you saw him," I pointed out. "Have any planes come or gone lately?"

"Nothing since Wednesday," he answered. "Talia asked us to ground flights till we found the prince. Which is really going to screw with the forum; we've got hundreds of people here for it, and as soon as it's over, people are going to want to go home. And we can't just go any time. We have to go when we're near the stats they're going to. These planes don't have unlimited range."

"What are you doing, taking this one out?" I asked.

"Just finished painting it. Gotta get it out of the hangar and make room for another one. Always easier to paint inside, where we can unsuit."

I nodded. "When was the last time a flight did go out?"

He fiddled with his glove, pulling it tighter. "I wouldn't know. Let me go look."

He went into the hangar and beckoned me to follow. I hesitated. I felt like I was causing these people no end of trouble, and probably for nothing. But I had no other lead. I might as well try.

"The roster's inside," he said, opening an airlock inside the hangar. I followed him, after a moment of billowing air, into a small office beyond. In one corner, stairs led down. Convenient. There was a skybridge under the runway, so why not put stairs and an extra airlock here in the hangar? But it bothered me that no one had shown me this before. If someone had wanted to smuggle a prisoner out to the airstrip, this would make a perfect pathway.

The man pulled off his helmet, revealing green hair and sharp blue eyes. "Here's the roster," he said. I bent over to look. This page had only the names of planes serviced—naturally, since no flights had gone out. I reached to flick the leaf backward and see Tuesday's flights.

I was interrupted by a sudden movement out of the tail of my eye. I might be in unfamiliar circumstances, but Navy training dies hard. I ducked and spun around.

A spanner whipped through the air over my head. The green-haired man had meant to brain me from behind. His eyes registered surprise, and he moved to make another blow.

Not for nothing had I trained to fight at this gravity. I stayed low and aimed a punch at his gut. It connected, but his only reaction was a whuff of breath. Not enough.

I glanced around for a weapon. This was Venus: no swords to be found. I grabbed a long-handled scrub brush in the corner and held it out in front of me. Its weight dragged at my arm like my weighted sword at home.

"I seem to have struck a nerve," I panted. "Don't want me to find the prince?"

"Down with all classist overlords," he said. "And Earth's capitalist scum too. Venus doesn't need you." He swung again with the wrench, clumsily.

I parried. Robbed of the element of surprise, he wasn't very good at this. Which was lucky, because he was about three times as strong as I was, having grown up here. "Where is he? Who took him?"

He didn't answer, but his eyes went to the roster. Of course. If the prince had left on a plane, the answer would be in that book. I tried to move closer to it.

He blocked me, legs in a wide stance and wrench held high.

He might not be able to hurt me, but he could stop me from getting at the roster. More importantly, he could stop me from getting to the stairs beyond the desk. The airlock was behind me, but I had left my oxygen mask on the desk. No good.

I feinted toward the desk, waiting for him to move rightward to block me. Then I did a shoulder roll to the left, passing by his leg. He lumbered after me, swinging the wrench. With a flick of my brush handle, I knocked it out of his hand.

"Fucking hell," he muttered, shaking his fingers.

A quick stab with the end of the handle to his solar plexus doubled him over long enough for me to grab the entire roster and dash for the stairs.

The skybridge was abandoned at the moment, so I kept running. Until I hit a crowd of people, I couldn't feel certain the green-haired man wouldn't pursue me. My feet hurt and my lungs burned. It was like running in my weighted vest, except I couldn't decide I'd done enough and could stop.

At last I reached the end of the skybridge, which opened out on an observation lounge. From here, broad windows looked out at the underside of the runway and down on the clouds below. A few people were here, drinking coffee or reading the paper. A quieter spot to gather than the noisy plaza.

I collapsed into a chair and dropped the roster onto the table in front of me. This was the information that had brought a Venusian to violence. It had to be important.

I flipped through the pages until I found the record for Tuesday. There had been one arrival, at 10 am. Before that, a single departure, at 9:30 am. The scrawl in the *pilot* blank read "Franz." Or "Frank"? The plane was named "The Fridge," an odd name for an airplane. It had returned at 11:30.

Not enough information to tell me much of anything. No last name on Franz/k. No destination written. No passengers listed. But it fit within the window Liu and the prince had been gone.

Most importantly, the green-haired man hadn't wanted me to have it.

Who had been aboard that plane? Where could it have gone? It couldn't be somewhere far, since it had only been gone two hours, but the stat was always on the move. What was nearby changed constantly.

The Venusians couldn't even keep track of that information on their own. They read stat forecasts in the paper, showing the stat's position, stats passing nearby, estimated times of dawn and dusk as it crossed onto and off of the dayside.

In the corner of the observation lounge was a newspaper rack. On one side were today's papers, neatly stacked. People didn't usually keep a copy; they took one, read it, and put it back for the next person. On the other side were discarded papers from previous days, ready to be recycled. I dug through the pile. How often did they clear this rack out?

It went back as far as Sunday. I dug out a Tuesday paper and brought it back to my table. On the back page were maps with arrows showing direction and velocity. Galileo was rocketing westward behind a large arrow, as always. The closest stat was hundreds of miles away. I frowned. I had simply assumed that the prince had been moved to another stat, but at that distance, I couldn't see how he could possibly have been transported that distance in two hours.

There was one small square near the double oval symbolizing Galileo, just west of the terminator dividing day from night. I hunted for it in the map key. *Mining station*, it read.

I straightened and stared out the window into darkness. The plane had gone down through the atmosphere, into the punishing heat and pressure, to visit a mining station. The innocent explanation was that they normally went down there, to service the station. The sinister explanation was that they'd thrown him out of the plane, to be pressure-cooked alive.

Only one way to find out. If the mining station was near the terminator, we should be close to it by now. It had been night on the stat since yesterday. I went back to the newspaper rack and got today's paper. There was the forecast, looking so much like Tuesday's: the terminator, the little square for the mining station, the double oval of Galileo coming up on both fast. Below the text read, *Dawn, 8 am.*

I took out my watch. It was three in the morning. Nobody I needed to talk to would be awake. But with us coming upon the mining station that fast, I couldn't afford to wait. I folded both papers, tucked them inside the hangar roster, and set off to find Marcus.

The Venusian distaste for locks on doors came in handy. I flicked on Marcus's light and picked my way through piles of dirty laundry to his bed. "I beg your pardon," I said, shaking his shoulder.

"Gah—wha—" His arm flailed up from the bed and flung over his eyes. "You barbarian, you monster, you *Martian*, and you people call *us* uncivilized!" He rolled onto his face.

"You're terribly eloquent for someone who's pretending to still be asleep," I said. "Get up, it's a real emergency or I wouldn't be waking you."

A few minutes later, he was wide awake. "You should have gotten me sooner," he said, grabbing the roster and the newspapers to have a look for himself.

"I got you the moment I found out," I protested.

"I mean before stopping to look at this. You were attacked. You should have told somebody."

"Who? You don't have police."

"Anybody! Any random person would have helped you!"

"I don't know that! It was a random person who attacked me. I've been wandering around this stat for a week assuming I was among friendly people, but apparently not!"

He took a breath as if to argue, then let it out. "We have to scramble, is all. We have," he squinted at his clock, which read four a.m., "four hours to get down there and back. And the Fridge isn't prepped."

"And we don't have a pilot."

He gave a little grimace. "You have a pilot. Didn't Talia tell you, I do a little of everything? Go get one of your Martian friends, if you want. I'm going to the airstrip with backup to get our ride prepped."

32

LUCY

I battled with myself the whole way back to our rooms. Should I wake Liu and ask her what had really happened? A confrontation might save us a trip, if I could get an honest answer out of her about where she'd really been when she had claimed she was with the prince. But on the other hand, if she had lied before, she could do it just as well now. And I was beginning to suspect she was in this much deeper than a false alibi.

Instead I crept quietly through the apartment and into Sagan's room. Sagan was struggling to their feet by the time I got the door open. I suspected that, if it weren't for the high gravity, I'd have a knife at my throat. Valet, lover, bodyguard—Sagan wore many hats.

"I might know where the prince is," I whispered. "Will you come?"

They had their braces on in a moment, threw a jacket over their plain clothes, and followed me out into the hall. On the way, I explained what I had found.

"So it was a Venusian plot all along," Sagan said, as we finished suiting up and got into the airlock. I carefully put my knife in my outside pocket this time.

"It can't have been only them," I said. "For them to know when their opportunity was, one of us would have had to tell them. And for us to think he had gone missing at noon when he had really disappeared in the middle of the morning required one person to lie."

"Liu."

"Yes." The door opened on foggy darkness, pierced with shafts of light from the floodlights all around. In front of us was a slender figure in an environment suit.

"I thought you'd come this way," came a voice, muffled by an oxygen mask. It was Liu.

In a flash I realized my mistake. If she'd worked with the green-haired man, obviously when he couldn't stop me, his first impulse would be to go get her.

"So it was you," I said. "You kidnapped the prince?"

"Hardly kidnapped. Relocated him. Temporarily."

I started forward, only to stop when I saw what she was holding in her hand. Silly me, thinking I was such a rulebreaker to smuggle a knife onto the stat. Sodium lights glinted on the muzzle of a pistol.

"You're not getting on that plane," she said. "We have your Venusian friend already. Just go back to bed. I promise I'll deliver the prince in due time."

My mind raced. Here, with Sagan and me standing side by side, Liu could cover us both easily with her pistol. Sagan couldn't move at any decent pace, so it was up to me.

I lunged sideways, rolling on the ground, and regained my feet two yards away to continue running sideways. It was risky— moving like this, I might escape her first shot, but if she fired a few she was sure to get lucky.

But she held her fire, and after a moment I realized why. I

was between her and the soft, plastic side of the balloon. If she fired, carbon dioxide and sulfuric acid would start leaking into the stat.

I wasn't sure if it was her altruism that kept her from doing it, or if she was just worried about getting caught, but it was enough. I ran along the side of the balloon, and she dashed after me.

I may be stronger than I look and better at fighting, but there's nothing I can do about my short legs. Liu gained on me fast. Soon she'd be too close to worry about missing. I lunged toward the balloon and grabbed hold. The plastic was covered in a wide nylon netting for workers to hold onto when doing repairs. I hoisted myself up and started to climb.

I heard Liu curse, but she didn't give up. Before I was twenty feet up, she was climbing after me. I kept moving, to keep as much distance between us as I could. Dragging my massive weight after me made my arms burn. My breath huffed loudly in my mask.

This couldn't last. Too soon, I ran out of balloon to climb. The netting curved upward toward the top, and I stood shakily on the broad surface.

It was so large as to seem almost flat, and so tightly filled with air my feet made no indentation. Just a wide plastic field, slightly dewy with sulfuric acid, through which I could see the soft lighting along the walkways below. I had a sudden wave of vertigo. I wasn't just high above the farm level below, I was miles above the planet's surface. If I somehow slid off the balloon, I would fall and fall until heat and pressure killed me.

But Liu hauled herself up over the curve of the balloon, and my fear of heights was replaced by more present danger.

I didn't have the balloon behind me anymore. If she was inclined to shoot, there was nothing to stop her.

I decided to stall. "Why did you do it?" I called as she came closer.

She stopped, twenty feet away. Close enough to shoot me whenever she wanted. "Why did you find out about it?"

"Process of elimination."

"Not how. *Why?* I got you onto this mission because of how badly you flubbed Liberty. You didn't seem the type to actually pound the pavement trying to do your job. I wasn't sure if you were stupid, lazy, or disloyal, but it had to have been one of those! And now you've surprised me. I didn't give you enough credit."

It was so absurd, being complimented by a woman with a gun trained on me, that I gave a slight bow. "Thank you."

Wisps of her dark hair had worked loose from her hood. "I'm tempted to offer you a job."

That woke me up. I hadn't thought who she might work for, what might be her motive. Had we been working at cross purposes the whole time? I couldn't see how kidnapping the prince helped the revolution, but perhaps there was a method in it. "What, a job doing treason?" I put disdain into my voice, but privately I was intrigued. There were kinds of treason I could get behind.

"Never," she said, taking a few steps forward. I stepped the same distance back. "I'm as loyal to the Empire as you. But some things the Empire has to do in secret. The left hand can't know what the right hand is doing."

"Meaning the Emprex can't know?"

"Parliament knows," she said, stepping forward again. I stepped back again. "A group of leaders in Parliament set up my organization, so the Emprex can keep their hands clean of some of the dirtier things we have to do."

My heart sank. She wasn't like me at all. "And what *do* you do?"

Her gun was down at her side now. She thought she was convincing me. She moved forward again, and I moved back. "We manage threats to the Empire."

"Like the prince?"

She laughed, continuing to creep forward. I took a careful step back, reaching in my pocket for my knife. If she did get close enough without shooting, I might stand a chance. "The prince is no threat. But we can't afford to lose Venus as an ally. I've studied democracies. The way to sway elections isn't with great rhetoric. It's with dirt on the opposition. You were *supposed* to point the finger at Earth—it would have been so easy. We've gotten so much sympathy from the Venusians the past few days."

I shook my head. "Not from your green-haired friend."

She chuckled, a hollow sound through her mask. "No. I told the Venusians a different story." She stepped forward. I stepped back. "I don't know if you have it in you to do this kind of work. It takes intelligence to keep the stories straight, and good acting skills. But you've done well enough on this for me to give you a shot at it. Go inside, tell them you found out what happened. Tell them the Earthers kidnapped the prince, that you saw the proof. If you can do that convincingly, I'll have more jobs for you. My organization needs good people. People who want to keep the Empire how we remember it."

I felt around with my feet before stepping back. The surface of the balloon was curving under my feet. I was on the outboard side now; behind me was nothing but empty sky.

"How *do* we remember it?" I asked. I couldn't see a way I could survive this, but I had gotten used to that feeling. On the off chance I found a way out of this, I wanted to find out everything about Liu's organization I could. These had to be the people I was looking for. The people who had kidnapped Khan.

"Orderly," she said. "Stable. These Venusians don't understand what we are. Nobody could ever understand who wasn't one of us. But you understand, don't you? You went to school, you're in the Navy, you've been shaped like I have. Shaped for a purpose. If it isn't to rule, what do we even exist for?"

Her words were hitting home. I couldn't help that. I'd felt

like an outsider everywhere but with my fellow nobles. If I wasn't shaped for a purpose, I was broken for no reason.

"Ah," I said, taking a careful step down the curve of the balloon. I didn't dare look down, but I could feel it getting steeper. "You're trying to preserve the neofeudal system."

"Exactly," she said. "If it weren't for us, the Russets would be taking away everything that makes Mars what it is. When a radical movement comes up, we take it down. We've been at it longer than you or I have been alive. Khan's the example you might remember. But there have been others you never even had to learn, because we took care of it." She stepped forward again, her gun lowered but still ready. "You have us to thank, that you grew up in peace and privilege."

Suddenly I went hot all over, hotter than the warm atmosphere had managed to make me. *Thank* her? For keeping this horrific oppression going? For the privilege that was the one thing standing between me and Moira all along?

No, Moira didn't understand me. Liu was right, nobody did. But I wanted to be misunderstood by Moira more than I wanted Liu's sympathy.

I took a deep breath through my mask. My first loyalty, I'd been swayed from. But I'd be damned if that meant I was easy to sway. It only meant I'd had to find the right cause before I could truly commit. Not, ultimately, because of Moira. Because it was the right thing to do.

I took my hand out of my pocket. "I believe in your mission," I said, taking another slow step backward. "But—"

I slipped. I let my foot slide off the smooth plastic and skip past several strands of netting. If I judged this wrong, I'd plummet to a crushing death. But at the last second, I caught at the netting. I gasped for breath, kicking one foot and one arm free of the netting, like I couldn't get a hold with either.

Liu carefully picked her way closer. "Why shouldn't I just walk away?"

"I'll do it," I gasped, trying to sound panicky. Given the fifty kilometers of crushing acid clouds below me, it wasn't hard. "I'll tell them it was Earth. I'll show them the evidence you planted."

"Your word on it?"

"My word as a gentlewoman. Just give me your hand!"

She stuck her pistol in her waistband. Crouching down and grabbing the netting with one hand, she extended the other.

I reached up one hand and grabbed hers. My feet braced themselves in the netting, wrapping the nylon cord around my ankles. A trick any sailor can do without looking; in space, feet aren't for walking, they're for bracing.

She hauled on my arm, but I didn't budge. "I don't know—if I can get you up—with this gravity," she panted. "Can't you help me out here?"

I groped with my other hand down by my waist. "I think I've got a grip," I said, my fingers closing on my knife. "Right—here." I dragged hard on her arm, stabbing upward at her with my left hand.

I buried the blade in her shoulder. Her fingers lost their grip and she slid down past me. I had to drop the knife and grab the netting again to avoid being dragged after her. For a moment she clung to my hand, left arm hanging limp. If she would only get her toes into the netting, let go of me and grab on, she might save herself.

Instead she whispered, "Why?"

"I'm loyal to Mars," I said firmly. "Mars, the planet and people." I released my fingers and pulled my hand out of hers.

I turned away, grabbing the netting with both hands in case she got hold of me again. But she didn't. I heard a long, fading scream, and then nothing.

For a moment I hung there, wishing things could have gone

differently. Wishing I could serve my homeland in a way that wasn't killing, in a way that didn't leave me feeling like a monster.

It had been a long time of peace for me, on Venus and on the *Adamant*, without having to take part in any violence. But of course it was no better than a temporary reprieve.

I added Liu to the tally in the back of my head; thirty-seven if I had the numbers right. Every time it got easier. I had never wanted it to.

Then, laboriously, I dragged myself back up.

I made my way over the balloon and back to the airstrip. The Fridge wasn't hard to find: a fat, stubby, almost shapeless plane, made not of painted aluminum but of acid-etched steel. My knife was gone, but I hoped at least Sagan would be there. Perhaps two of us, working together, might overpower whatever accomplices Liu had left here.

I ducked into the open hangar behind the plane and looked around. No sign of Sagan. I picked up a heavy crowbar and crept back over to the Fridge. The outer airlock was closed, but a stubby lever stuck out. No complicated opening mechanisms in a place where pressure deformed metal.

Taking a deep breath, I pulled the lever and stepped inside. When the door shut, an electric pump started running loudly. No way to sneak attack in this place. I hefted my tire iron and stood ready. The airlock door here was opaque steel: no glass windows on a thing like this. I was going to have to go in blind.

The inner door opened on an unfortunate scene: two men, my old green-haired opponent and a similar-looking man with brown hair, each aiming a weapon at me. Or a tool—it looked like those were nail guns of some kind. Of course; just like me, they'd grabbed what they could for weapons. It just happened they'd found something better than I had.

I lowered the tire iron and pulled the oxygen mask off my face. "What are you doing?" I asked. "Liu played you for fools. She's not trying to stop the forum, she's trying to throw it to Mars by making Earth look bad."

They exchanged a glance. "I don't care what Liu thinks," said the brown-haired one. "We used her to get what we wanted. Even if the forum goes forward, we've made our point."

In the cockpit of the plane, Marcus sat, strapped in and his hands tied. "Sorry, Lucy," he said. "I didn't even make it to StatOps."

"It's all right," I said soothingly. There was still one asset left, and I didn't know where they were. Had Sagan gone to get reinforcements instead of heading out here? That would have been the smart thing to do.

We were interrupted by a loud clang from the rear of the plane. Then two quick zipping sounds. I was still looking for the source when both brawny men collapsed onto the floor.

A panel of sheet metal still wobbled on the floor, exposing a gap into the inner workings of the plane. Inside that compartment was a masked figure.

They took off their mask and held up a tiny, slender gunlike object. "Flechette," Sagan said, as if that explained everything.

I hurried to help them out of the hole in the wall. "If you had a weapon this whole time, why didn't you use it on Liu?"

"It doesn't have the range," Sagan said. "And instead of letting her get closer, you went running around like a maniac. Next time follow *my* lead. I was trained for this."

I threw back my head and laughed, half admiring, half only relieved. "Sagan, you're a treasure. No wonder the prince likes you."

As we dragged the two men out by the airlock, Sagan explained what they'd done. Since the airlock had been too obvious of an approach, they'd disassembled the underside of the plane, climbed through a repair access, and made their way through the innards of the ship to the crew compartment.

"I'm not going to judge you for taking the obvious route, though," Sagan said, as we repaired the damage they'd made to the plane getting in. I was dismayed to see they'd simply taken off an outer panel and covered the gap with a tarp and some duct tape. Not an expedient that would have worked in space at all. For that matter, I wasn't entirely sure it was safe here. "After all, you provided me with a diversion."

Marcus had the plane powered up by the time we were done. "It doesn't look like you broke anything inside the engine," he told Sagan. "Though I really can't recommend monkeying about with electronics when your planet's in the dark ages. You don't know how any of it works."

"I know not to break the wires," Sagan said. "It isn't rocket science."

"You could probably do rocket science too, if you wanted to," I said. I was in a mood to give Sagan all the credit for everything. "It's not hard. Consistent thrust! It's like sailing with training wheels."

Marcus taxied us toward the runway. "Get buckled in," he said. "This isn't like coming down on the shuttle. There's actual bouncing."

I grimaced. "I found the shuttle bad enough."

"Should be pills in there."

He wasn't joking. The wind screamed and buffeted the tank-like plane as if it were a child's toy. To make it worse, there were no windows, only a series of radar screens. Marcus hunched over his controls, back tense. This wasn't a pleasant routine for him; it was taking all his attention.

After several minutes of sickening descent, where my weight fluctuated with every bump, the wind's buffeting started to fade.

"We're out of the wind belt," Marcus said. His radar panels showed topography below us—strange cliffs and valleys, etched in green lines.

The steel plating of the plane's body started to groan. The pressure would keep increasing the lower we went—more like descending into an ocean trench than landing a plane. The sound of the propellers changed, like they were driving through soup.

"You sure it can handle the pressure?" I asked, purely to vent my nervousness.

Marcus squinted at the displays and didn't answer. I exchanged a worried glance with Sagan. Finally he said, "Hold on," and flipped some switches.

The sound of the propellers cut out with a lurch. We were weightless for a moment. I wanted to ask what was the matter, but Marcus was clearly too focused on what he was doing to answer. We glided down for at least a minute, while my breath caught in my throat. Were we just falling out of the sky?

At last Marcus turned the propellers back on and the plane steadied out. "One of the engines was overheating," he said. "Had to turn off both for a reset."

"Are they cool now?" asked Sagan.

"As cool as I can get them without plummeting to our deaths," said Marcus. "It's *hot* outside. This plane is supposed to be able to handle it, but clearly something's up with the coolant system."

"Can we fix it once we're on the ground?"

"We can't go outside at all down there," he said, as if Sagan had said something profoundly stupid. "And we can't afford to take our time. The whole time we're down here, the stat is still moving on the wind. The longer we take, the harder it'll be to catch up."

Suddenly he cut off and got very busy on the controls. The

altimeter read fifty meters. The straps dug into my shoulders as the plane slowed.

And then, all at once, the wheels were dragging on the ground with a smooth roar. Somehow, despite flying blind through thick acid soup, Marcus had stuck the landing.

The entrance of the mining base fastened directly to the plane airlock, closed by a twelve-inch thick notched wheel that took two of us to roll aside. Inside, pallid electric lights revealed a drab, industrial hallway.

"There's not much here," said Marcus. "This way are the openings for the drills, and that way is machinery that extracts carbon from the atmosphere and injects it into the ground."

"Where would you hide a prince, if you had one?" I asked.

But he must have heard our voices, because he came running up the latter hallway—coat rumpled, long hair tangled, but, to my considerable relief, alive. Sagan flew at him, digging their hands into his hair and bringing his face close for a kiss. I pulled my gaze away after a second. One didn't want to be rude.

Marcus caught me grinning. "You knew about this?"

"It's been my job these past days to know everything."

There was a loud slap and I looked back at Sagan. "That's for being an idiot," they said, a scolding finger just shy of the prince's nose. "You know better than to go to a second location with *anyone* without a fuss."

He didn't seem offended that Sagan had just committed assault against his imperial person. "It was only Liu," he said in a small voice, and kissed them a second time.

When we lifted off, the propellers labored worse than before. The brief stay at surface heat had clearly done them no good. "There's a line of coolant inside each wing," said Marcus. "Anyone want to take a look?"

The stubby wings were hollow, and Sagan was game to climb

inside one. The prince turned to me. "It was Liu that brought me down there, you know that?"

"Yes. I shouldn't have trusted her as long as I did."

"I don't understand it, though. She told me it was for the good of the Empire, and I'd understand in the end."

"She had the idea that the forum would go better if you had disappeared, and the Earthers got blamed."

He frowned. "If I haven't lost count, sitting in a windowless room with a box of ration bars, the forum is today."

"Yes."

"So why isn't she here with you? If it was all a scam, seems it's about time to pick me up."

I opened my mouth. He was asking too many questions, thinking a little too hard. It was a relief when Sagan shouted from inside the wing, "The coolant tube has a knot in it."

"Like, deliberately put in there?" Marcus called back.

"Yes. And I can't untie it without taking it off the engine for a moment."

I was already on my feet, opening up the panel to reach the other wing. Sure enough, this one was tied too.

"Is any coolant getting through at all?" Marcus asked.

"A trickle."

"Hold on," he said. "I'm going to shut off the engines. If they're this hot with a little coolant, they'll break down on us if you cut them off. As soon as the engines are off, you both fix the tubes."

"While plummeting to the ground?" I asked.

"I'll keep us in the air as best I can. Birds fly without engines; we can do a bit too."

"Birds can flap their wings," I muttered to the roaring engine beside me in the dim interior of the wing.

The engine cut out, and my guts leaped for the ceiling. But I was braced tight inside the tiny compartment, so I didn't knock my head. Quickly I slipped the tube off the nipple on the engine, untied the knot, and put it back. "Done!" I shouted.

"Done!" came Sagan's voice.

The engine sputtered back to life, sounding a little better now. I crawled out, inspecting my blue environment suit. It had grease and coolant in several places. Better on this than on my normal clothes.

I hadn't finished belting myself back in when the prince said, "So where *is* Liu?"

"She wouldn't let us come and get you, my prince. She promised to deliver you in due time, but—well, as you point out, now *is* the right time. So I am not sure she intended to do it at all."

Sagan was watching me intently. "You never said what you talked about, up there. Did she explain herself any?"

I took a deep breath. "She claimed to be part of an organization authorized by Parliament, with the goal of keeping Mars stable. A conservative, anti-Russet faction of some kind. She claimed credit for imprisoning Alexei Khan. She said it was for the good of the Empire for me to give up trying to find you, and go tell the Venusians the Earthers had taken you."

The prince frowned, taking all this in. "I don't understand," he said. "You refused?"

"Of course I did! I thought she might let you die down there!"

"I appreciate the loyalty," he said with a slight nod of his head. "But technically, as an officer, you answer to the Admiralty, which answers to Parliament. I suspect she was telling the truth about her organization. We've been following the Privy Ministry for years; they're no friend to my family, unless they find us useful. Those Greens and Blues in Parliament would do anything to take the Russets down, including subtract me from the equation, if they thought it expedient. I'm far too revolutionary to be allowed near the throne. And if she was, doesn't she outrank you? Wouldn't your duty be to do as she says? I know you're no Russet yourself;

you've made yourself known as both apolitical and scrupulously loyal."

His eyes turned on me like dark spotlights; I felt exposed. "I find it expedient to appear so, my prince," I said at last. "In reality, I'm ... I would not want to live on a Mars where all populist impulses were secretly put down. That's not what I believe in. Mars is the planet and people."

I had spoken from the heart, but the prince had read Khan. He'd catch the reference. His eyes widened. I braced myself for him to question me further, but instead he only said, "I think we're entering the windy altitudes."

The turbulence was starting to jounce us around again. Marcus said, "I'm going to have to stay here longer than before. We've fallen behind the stat, and to catch up we'll need to spend some time in a faster belt than they're in."

The "faster belt" was moving 180 miles an hour, and new currents slammed into us every few seconds, like a giant cat batting at some fascinating toy. The prince clasped Sagan tightly, trying to keep them from being shaken against the side of the plane.

When we finally burst out of the lower cloud deck and in view of the stat, the western horizon was all a rosy glow. The sun was almost visible as a deep red smear on the air, shading to orange and yellow higher up. From there it was easy flying; Marcus landed us without a bump.

When we tumbled out onto the airstrip, Talia already stood waiting with a group of others. She shook Marcus's hand first.

"You've done Venus proud," she said. "And you, Elliott. I can't tell you how relieved I am to find you well."

We hurried inside to prepare for the forum. We had only an hour, and the prince in particular was a mess. Though I also hadn't slept, and had gotten dressed in the dark. Only now that I had finished my mission did I remember about Venus's weapons.

The forum could turn the entire course of the war, and I'd given my word not to tell the prince.

I'd keep my promise, if only because it didn't matter now. He would do his best, regardless of what the stakes were. Nothing I could tell him could motivate him any more.

33

MOIRA

The tribune election was always announced, by tradition, from the steps of the House of Parliament. If you cared to, you could go and watch from the street below, so long as you stayed on the outside of the wrought-iron fence at the bottom of the stairs. Usually, though, nobody came but reporters and a few of each candidate's supporters.

Today was different. People were packed into Government Square and spilling out down Opportunity Street. It was a restless, muttering crowd. No one really expected a good result, but they wanted to know. What would they do if Khan had won the majority of write-in votes? There wasn't any plan that I heard. They had done it "just to see," and now they were about to see.

I half hoped the write-in campaign had fizzled out. Surely if he had only gotten a few votes, the city would calm down some. Then again, would the people even believe a result like that? I wouldn't. It seemed likely the government would alter the numbers.

I elbowed my way through the crowd till I was against the

fence, near the side. It wasn't so much that I wanted to see as that I didn't like being surrounded on all sides. I'm not a city person and don't like to be jostled. Besides, if the crowd did get rowdy, I wanted to be near the edge. From here I could turn and dart along the fence and down a side street if I needed to.

The doors of Parliament opened and a magistrate came out, bewigged and robed in black. Along with several clerks, he made his way to the edge of the steps.

"We are pleased to announce the results of the election for Tribune of the People," he called out, reading from his ceremonial scroll. "Due to the highly unusual nature of this election, the court was forced to convene to decide how the votes should be interpreted."

The crowd stirred and muttered. Somebody said, "Bullshit." But I was puzzled. They shouldn't need to convene a court to figure out that Khan wasn't qualified.

"Usually, of course, the office of Tribune is reserved for full citizens," the magistrate went on, his voice cracking with the effort of projecting over the crowd. "But, as no citizen received a plurality of the vote, the court ruled that an exception could be made. We announce the new Tribune for Imperial Year 500 shall be Alexei Khan, contingent on his acceptance of the election."

The crowd was dead silent for a moment. I don't think any of us had the slightest idea how to react. Someone started cheering so we went with that. I clapped my hands together as if in a dream.

Why? Why would they turn around and give us what we wanted?

It only took me a second to figure it out. They were as afraid as I was. They knew the whole city would erupt in violence if they didn't. They had weighed the available choices, remembered the Tribune had almost no power anyway, and decided to handle this thorn in their side the most obvious way: pull him out of hiding, make him a figurehead, and let the rest of the revolution flounder wondering if we'd won or not.

The news would reach Khan soon, if the government hadn't reached out to him already. I wondered what he would do with it. I had a bad feeling about this whole thing. Somebody in the government was killing people left and right and had wanted to get their hands back on him since he'd escaped from prison. He shouldn't go.

But it would be like him to do it. He was a firm believer both in the democratic process and in self-sacrifice. He'd do it because he knew, as well as I did, that things couldn't go on the way they were. And perhaps he'd be able to make some small changes from that position. He would have the right to attend Parliament, demand they at least discuss the rights they were depriving us of.

The news spread through the city as a sound of crashing pans. I heard cheering from streets away, spoons banging on pots, even firecrackers. Bad idea, firecrackers. In a city this tense, they'd be taken for something else. People in the square were dancing, singing, kissing each other.

The crowd grew over the next hour. By hooking one foot in the iron fence, I could hoist myself up and see more people coming down Opportunity Street. I wondered what the lawmakers inside the House of Parliament were thinking, watching the people converge on them. Were they imagining what would have happened if they'd made a different choice?

Far away, the mass of people started parting. A low brown car was edging through the crowd, barely idling to leave the people room to move. A government vehicle? It had to be. None of us had cars.

Parliament's doors opened and released a troop of magistrates and a dozen Imperial Guards. The guards descended the steps, waiting till the car had hissed to a halt before opening the gate.

Khan climbed out of the car, without his chair for once. He

walked slowly and gingerly, as if each step hurt him, but he was walking, leaning on—now that was odd. Beside him was Harrington, carefully supporting him on one side while Soares was on the other.

Harrington must have hung around after I left and found a way to make herself useful. Or perhaps she had been the one to deliver him the news. Either way, there was no reason to resent her, as she made her way up the stone steps beside him. Somebody had to do it, given the weakness of his muscles and the fragility of his bones, and it certainly couldn't be me, not where the police could see.

Slowly, slowly, he approached the magistrates at the top. The crowd grew hushed, watching him climb. We wanted a speech, but more than that, everyone wanted to see him in the flesh, be truly convinced that he was still alive, that he would be our Tribune.

My mind kept turning over the puzzle of Harrington. Why she'd left her ship to come over to the *Mariposa*, why she'd attached herself so thoroughly to me, why she'd gotten herself imprisoned when the outcome was so obvious. She'd explained all that, but none of it really made sense to me. That wasn't how I would have acted in her shoes.

And she'd been so eager to meet Khan. Resentful that I hadn't taken her along, and then, as if in a fit of pique, proving her revolutionary credentials. Then the second I'd taken her to see Khan, that had been the last I'd seen of her. So much for her need to stick to me like glue. I'd assumed she'd found a new emotional crutch, but maybe it wasn't that at all.

Khan was nearing the top of the stairs when I finally put it all together. I stuck my foot in the rail of the fence and vaulted over. "Khan, watch out!" I shouted, taking the steps two at a time. I didn't need to touch Harrington. All I needed was to get behind Khan.

I was ten steps behind him when she pulled away. Just side-stepped, gracefully, as she had almost reached the top. If I had been any further away, I would have thought it was an accident. That he'd lost his hold on her, missed a step.

He lurched sideways and plummeted down, crashing full-length on the stone steps. I raced up seconds too slow, catching up his head in my hands to pillow it off the hard stone.

His face was crumpled with pain. Several of his brittle bones must have broken. "Are you all right?" I asked, like an idiot. I could feel blood seeping through his hair.

He smiled up at me, teeth white in his dark face. "I am all right," he said. "You must make sure Mars is all right."

I looked vaguely around me. "Mars is fine, Khan." My lips twitched, but I forced them straight. I had to keep it together for him.

"Who is Mars, Moira?"

He was trying to teach me something. Even then. That was when I burst into tears, not polite ones. Mouth contorting, voice a choked mess. "Mars is the planet and people," I sobbed. "You know that."

He did not answer, and I could see in his eyes that he was already gone. I looked up at Harrington, tears and snot still smeared across my face. "Why'd you do it?" I demanded hoarsely.

"To preserve Mars," she said coldly. "That's what it's always been about."

I suddenly remembered the crowd at my back, the stairs that exposed us like a stage. The magistrates looked shocked. This hadn't been their plan, but with Harrington's admission, they couldn't believe it was an accident.

I carefully laid Khan's head back on the steps and stood up, facing the people. Raising my bloodstained fist, I shouted, "They killed Khan!"

The crowd rushed forward, breaking the gate and vaulting

the fence. The Imperial Guards tried to stop them, but they were overwhelmed.

I stood, panting, on the stairs, while the crowd surged around and past me. They wanted Harrington, they wanted the magistrates, and for the moment they feared nothing. If I turned, I might see whether the magistrates had escaped inside or the crowd had gotten them. But I was too paralyzed to move.

This was it, I realized: the volcano. I had wanted to leave it alone, cool it down somehow. Khan had wanted to offer it some kind of vent. Parliament had tried to placate it, and Harrington had meant to make it despair. But now it was erupting, and nobody had any chance of stopping it.

That meant the choices were now completely different. Not push it forward or hold it back, because it was surging forward regardless. But help it win or let it be crushed. It was obvious which one I had to do, which one Khan would have wanted.

I looked up at the sky where, beyond the blue of our manufactured atmosphere, the *Mariposa* would be hitting orbit about now.

Oh yes. I knew what I could do.

34

LUCY

The forum was held in the main plaza, which had been filled with plastic chairs of every conceivable design. I realized after a moment that these were simply the chairs of the citizens, brought from their homes for the occasion.

Our delegation was seated on a row of purple chairs at the front, with the Earth delegation across the aisle. Blackwell and Knauss stared daggers at one another, until the prince noticed and patted Blackwell's knee. I felt a sudden warmth at having him back again. I had thought myself divested of monarchist impulses, but this was a man I didn't mind following. Though the fact that he was born a prince had little to do with it.

Knauss spoke first, with a great deal said about Earth's economic dominance in the system and how thoroughly Venus and even Mars relied on it. She pointed out trade numbers showing they dwarfed Mars in imports from and exports to Aphrodite. And then she started in with a diatribe on Mars's human rights record, its current ongoing unrest, the well-known problem of Martian sailors deserting at ports and begging to be taken in by anyone else.

I listened with a crushing sense of discouragement. Who would choose anyone but Earth, when, regardless of how Venusians might feel about it, Earth supplied so much trade? The Venusians I'd spoken to had hinted as much this entire time. I wasn't sure I'd spoken with anyone who planned to vote in Mars's favor. Let alone anyone who could ever consider voting for Liberty.

At that thought, dread suddenly set into my mind. I hadn't written anything out for Talia to read. I hadn't, in fact, planned what to do at this forum at all. I had been so distracted by the events of the night before that I had somehow imagined walking in, sitting down, and watching everything get decided without me.

But I couldn't do that, not after everything I'd gone through. Especially not after all Liu had said. With the Privy Ministry dedicated to wiping out any hope of reform, Liberty was more needed than ever. With those weapons, Moira's band of pirates could face off both Earth and Mars indefinitely. Nobody would dare to oppose them.

The prince was speaking now, and I listened with half an ear. He, clearly, hadn't forgotten to prepare. It was a beautiful speech, charismatically delivered as always.

"At heart," he was saying, "Venus and Mars are the same. Places built of hope, of a place away from the domination of corporatism and greed. Places we built with our own ideals, out of nothing. And now that we've built them, Earth wants a piece of it. You know as well as we do that they hate your independence as much as they hate ours. If we fall, their attention will turn on you next—with all the resources they've stripped from us, to spend on subjugating you."

I stared down at my lap with an increasing sense of panic. It was like that nightmare of being called upon to recite at school when you had somehow missed the lesson. And to make things worse, when I stepped off the little plastic dais, I'd no longer be an officer of the Imperial Navy. I'd be a traitor, subject to execution, if I went home with my crew, and I had no other way off Aphrodite once the Venusians inevitably returned me there.

It wouldn't take long for the news to flash back home, at which point my pay would be confiscated from my parents' bank. The house by the shore would be sold. My parents would take William and try to find somewhere else where they could live in poverty.

But it didn't matter. This wasn't a choice, like I had made before, when Moira sent me back to Mars. That hadn't hurt anyone, except me and (maybe) Moira. This had serious consequences for the entire system—almost certainly, the consequence of Earth getting hold of game-changing weapons and conquering Mars for good. And if I thought for a second they would leave Liberty alone after that, I'd be kidding myself.

The prince finished his speech and returned to his seat. "And now," said Talia, "we're due a third speaker, on behalf of Liberty Station, though I don't know who they are or if they'll appear. I was told they might submit something in writing, but since I haven't received anything, I assume they'll be speaking in person if at all."

I leaned forward in my seat, about to stand up. A hand on my knee interrupted the motion. Sagan heaved themself to their feet and carefully made their way up to the dais.

I fell back in my seat, dumbstruck. They had no business giving my speech. They had no connection to Liberty. How had they even guessed the third speaker was me? I sat like a stone. Sagan could, if they cared to, speak against Liberty and destroy my cause. Yet somehow I trusted them. I would have avoided trouble more than once if I had trusted them before. So I kept my seat and watched Sagan mount the dais.

They made a sober figure, in their neat black suit and close-cropped hair. The room, packed with Venusians, was almost silent. Somewhere in the back, a baby made a small squawk. Someone coughed.

Sagan began, their quiet voice magnified by an electric device on the podium. "For as long as I've lived, for generations, for centuries, it's been the same. Before we even left Earth the first time. Some oppressing others. The corps, the kings, it didn't matter, only that some were on the ground and others were standing on our necks. You could try for a reshuffle, but that only changed the style of boot. It never changed which necks were there to stand on."

Their voice strengthened, warming to the theme. "But all along there's been a dream. A dream to actually change the way things were, to make it good not for a few but for everyone. The Martian founders dreamed it, for a little while. Till they realized that it was a better bet to try to climb on top than to topple the whole thing. Which is what destroys the dream every time. Easier to get behind the wheel of the machine than to break it.

"It's been four hundred years the Martian poor have been dreaming this same damn dream. It pops up here and there and the Founders try to pick apart what they did wrong, how did they let the power of the people break out? Did they say something, did they do something that made us need to rise up? No." Their voice sharpened. "No! We have always needed this. Every minute since we're born, we're only waiting for our chance."

I stole a sidelong glance at the prince. I feared that, despite his democratic sensibilities, this would be a bridge too far. After all, he had just gotten up himself, saying the opposite. But his eyes were fixed on his partner, while his hands kept flitting up to wipe his cheeks.

Sagan kept speaking. "And you, you've been dreaming it with me all along. Haven't you? Isn't that why you set yourselves up in a place no one else could live, in a place where the corps and the kings couldn't follow? You knew, if we could just get a little time, we could build something better than has ever been before. And you're spending every single hour that isn't keeping you alive, trying to build a place for the rest of us to come to. That's a beautiful thing, but we don't have time to wait.

"You can't tell a poor man of Mars who has never owned a square of land that was his own, that a thousand years from now his descendants will walk out in the air and have a place to stand. That means nothing to him as he grinds his soul to pieces in the factories.

"And I feel, right now, the stirring of a faint little wind, the one that tells you the weather's about to turn. I've been waiting my whole life quietly for a chance to make a change. Hoping that someday the big one would come, the revolution that changes it all.

"It's happening. And it's suddenly happening very fast, everywhere at once. It's happening on Mars, and the Founders are looking scared. It's happening here, because you've made up your minds to do something other than huddle down and hope you get left alone. And it's happening on Liberty. They're building an ideal that could mean the world to the revolution on Mars, to limiting the power of the corps, to keeping the solar system safe for your trade.

"If you ever believed the dream is real, you can't vote for corps or princes. You have to use your vote for the people, because while kings and corps divide, the people everywhere are one." There was a brief pause, as Sagan seemed to have run out of words, not knowing whether or not they were finished. Then they ducked their head, murmured, "Thank you," and trudged back to their seat.

For a moment the silence remained unbroken, and I held my breath. Then there was an instantaneous outpouring of sound. The Venusians leapt to their feet, a few at first and then more and more. I glanced backward at the crowd. If there was anyone still sitting, I didn't see them.

Sagan reached the prince and looked nervously into his eyes. He smiled back, and Sagan broke into a grin. They didn't touch—they couldn't, not with Blackwell still here and watching—but the look that had passed between them said volumes.

"Should we stand too, sir?" Blackwell asked the prince, over the thunderous applause. "It wouldn't do to seem ungracious."

I glanced sideways to see what the Earth delegation was doing. If they were standing, we certainly could get away with it too.

But the seats across the aisle from us were empty. I racked my brain to think when I'd last seen them sitting there. Certainly they had sat stonily through the prince's speech.

"My prince," I said, rising to my feet as he did, "I need to go see something."

He nodded, and I hurried away, Sagan behind me. "The Earthers left just as I came down from the dais," they said. "They can't have gone far."

"They can't have left the stat in any event," I said. "Nobody but the Venusian pilots know how to fly those shuttles."

The crowd started to quiet down and resume their seats. It was only because of the decrease in noise that I heard it: two quick sharp pops, coming from the other end of the plaza.

I broke into a run. It sounded like it had come from the radio office. When I came panting up, a crowd had already gathered. Ms. Knauss stood just in front of the counter with another Earther, both holding guns.

A call from inside said, "Done!" and the two Earthers in front of the counter laid their guns on the floor and raised their hands.

"Go ahead and arrest us," said Knauss smugly. "It's too late to stop what's happening."

Talia and another StatOps woman pushed through the crowd and laid hands on the two Earthers.

"There's another inside," I said, rounding the counter with my knife out. Behind the counter, a body sprawled on the floor, blood pooling from underneath.

The door behind the counter opened and the third Earther emerged, unarmed. I grabbed his shoulder. "What did you do?"

He didn't answer, but let himself be piloted over to Talia. I left him with her and ducked back behind the counter and into the radio office.

Inside the tiny office was another body, toppled onto the floor beside the radio desk. I sat down and put my finger on the telegraph key, thinking a moment. Then I tapped out, GALILEO STAT TO APHRODITE STATION. DID A MESSAGE JUST COME OUT FROM US?

After a moment they tapped back. YES BUT IN CODE. NO ADDRESSEE.

I frowned. Why shoot two people to send a message to Aphrodite, without directing it to anyone? Or was there anywhere else this message could go?

"What is this all about?" asked Talia, looming in the doorway. She didn't ask me why I had pushed forward and taken over. I suppose we'd been through enough that I'd earned her trust.

"Is there anywhere else this radio can reach besides Aphrodite?"

"Any of the stats on Venus," she said. "We have repeater satellites all over orbit, so we don't lose contact with Aphrodite when it's on the wrong side from us, and so we can bounce stuff to any stat. Or rather, all the stats at once."

I stared unseeing at the radio receiver. With repeater satellites in the picture, that would make a strong radio signal in all directions. If there were Earth ships in the area—

The radio suddenly began beeping wildly. THREE EARTH SHIPS APPROACHING AND NOT ANSWERING HAILS. FRIENDLY SHIPS IN AREA, THIS IS A DISTRESS—

The beeping stopped. Talia gave me a horrified look. "Earth is attacking?"

I turned around in the chair, resting my forehead on the high back. "Of course. They could see from the cheering how the vote was going to go. I assume they also knew about the weapons, by the way. So they're attacking your gateway to the rest of the system. Without Aphrodite, you can't get the weapons to Liberty or anywhere else."

"But it's madness," she said. "They can't come down here, and if we don't shuttle the raw carbon up there, the fiber refinery can't run. They need the fiber."

"They don't need it as much as they need to win the war," I said. "I imagine they've been saving a stockpile since they found out about this forum. Always count on Earth to have the upper hand in any economic battle."

"I don't suppose Sagan has a ship," she said.

For a moment I blanked. Then it connected. "Sagan wasn't the Liberty contact," I said. "They're just a better speaker than me."

"You? No wonder I didn't get a written message, then. You've been far too busy." She grinned wryly. "*You* don't have a ship?"

"No." I gave it a second's thought. "I'll have to steal one."

She goggled at me. "Is that how you Martians do things?"

"It's how Liberty does things," I said. "We *are* pirates."

35

MOIRA

It took me over an hour, struggling against the crowd, to make my way back to the elevator district. Several times, helicopters stuttered overhead. The first time, the crowd cleared the street, darting into the shelter of buildings, but it didn't pause or trouble us. I realized they weren't there to police us, but to evacuate Founders. I saw one family standing on the roof of their five-story home, three children peering over the ledge into the street till their mother yanked them away.

I felt like I had stepped into another world, a strange parallel dimension where the monsters turn and are terrified of *you*. What did those people, towering so high above the street, have to fear from us? But perhaps they were right. There were so many of us.

The streets were chaos. Some people just smashed windows and took what they could. Some people broke things for no purpose at all. I saw a bus suddenly *whuff* into a fireball. On Constitution Street, a large group of police charged toward the mob, only to be taken down by cobblestones and sticks. Something had shifted in the past few days. People had stopped being frightened and gotten angry. I turned my head away.

The telegraph office was abandoned, unsurprisingly. I smashed the glass and went in. The radio was frantically beeping with queries from Phobos, which I ignored in favor of manning the transmitter. From here, I shouldn't need to get Phobos to repeat the signal to reach the *Mariposa*—at least, not if it was where it was supposed to be.

MARIPOSA, YOU THERE? I tapped out, in spacers' code. It took a few tries to get through. Marron should have kept his radio cranked up whenever he was in range, but somebody was slacking.

After ten horrible minutes, during which the sounds of the riot outside only strengthened, his reply beeped through the receiver. DEPENDS WHO'S ASKING.

I explained the situation and what I wanted him to do. He was all too eager to please. I signed off and left the telegraph office. I needed people—it didn't much matter who.

It took breaking into two buildings to find one with stairs leading down into the undercity. In one of the central crossings, I found Soares and some others, gathering weapons. "Good, you're here," she said when she saw me. "We're trying to bring some order to the chaos. The crowds broke into Parliament, but there was no one there. Not sure it's going to do any good to hold the building if the members just decide to meet somewhere else."

"It's not," I said shortly.

Soares's face was pale and drawn. Nobody had chosen her to be leader of anything, but she was one of Khan's deputies who hadn't lost their heads and she was actually on the spot. She was feeling the responsibility hard. "What if we split into teams and try to take all the police departments and guardhouses?"

I looked around at the score or so of people she had with her. "I have a better idea."

The next step was to go and see my dads. I suspected that Bill would have gone straight home to Ramesh when the rioting had broken out, and I was right. I made Soares and the half-dozen she'd brought with her wait outside while I talked to him.

"Dad," I asked urgently, "who controls the elevator? Is it directed from the top or the bottom?"

Ramesh interrupted me. "Moira, are you getting involved with this nonsense? You've got to learn to keep your head down."

"I tried, Papa, but it's a little late for that. Everybody's going to get swept up in this whether I get involved or not."

"She's got to do what she thinks is right," said Bill. He turned to me. "It has to be coordinated. They have to send one up from here just as one is entering the gravity well from up there. So it's controlled from both sides."

"But who makes the decision? If things are chaotic down here, does the elevator just shut down?"

"The schedule is very strict," said Bill. "If they drop the car and we don't send ours up, or the other way around, it could mess up the system. So there's people still at the bottom now. One goes up at five, empty or full."

That didn't leave us much time. The bright side was, there would be no way for them to stop us from up there.

Bill came with us to the elevator, though he refused the offer of a gun. "I'll just talk to the others for you. I'm not into violence."

That was a bit of a lie; he'd been a tavern brawler back in the day. But those days were long behind him. All my life he'd raised me to look for the peaceful option, for all the good that had done.

The road leading to the elevator was blocked at the end with a makeshift barricade: crates, barrels, a table, a broken wagon. We scrambled over and reached the large open area around the elevator pad.

It was almost empty of people. Crates and boxes were stacked up and no one was loading anything. Bill knocked on the door of the little control house beside the pad. "No admittance!" someone shouted from inside.

"It's Bill Singh! You need help in there?"

"What we mainly need is security," she called. "I've got the door locked, but if the rioters come in here, I don't know what I'll do. We could lose the whole elevator if they interfere."

We exchanged glances. "I'll see what I can do," Bill said. "Meanwhile, uh, my daughter wants to know if you're still selling tickets."

"Are you crazy? At a time like this?"

"Never a better time to get off this planet."

"Now there's a thought. Panicky Founders charging in demanding a trip to Phobos to wait out the riot. God help us."

Soares got tired of the back and forth and hammered on the door herself. "How about this. You give us a ride on that elevator, and we make sure you can get it off the ground."

"Who are you?"

She kicked in the door. Inside, a very nervous woman sat at a row of dials, with a radio beside her.

"I have a gun!" the woman cried.

"No, you don't," said Soares. "If you did, you wouldn't be sitting with both your hands in sight, telling me you had a gun."

"You can't interfere with the workings of the elevator!"

"Lady, I just finished telling you, I don't want to stop the elevator from going up. I want to go up *on* the elevator."

The woman gave a nervous glance at the clock, which read ten minutes to five. "It's not even hooked up yet."

A window inside the control building looked out at the elevator pad, where the massive cable emerged from the ground and disappeared into the sky. A skeleton crew with a steam crane was maneuvering the car into place.

I turned away from the open door of the control building and looked down the street. Beyond the barricade, a cluster of people was approaching. I went down the wooden steps and up to the barricade.

"Stop!" I shouted, showing my gun.

They came to a raggedy halt. I recognized the leader—the red-headed kid from the café, the one in love with violence and the sound of his own voice.

"Who are you?" he shouted. "Still kissing the boot even when it's not there?"

I felt like I deserved a medal for not shooting him right there. "I'm with the revolution," I said. "We need this elevator."

"Why? That's the machine that sells away our minerals, takes our boys away to fight in their wars. We'll be better off without it."

I rolled my eyes, though he was probably too far away to see it. "Do you want to just hurt the Emprex, or do you want to actually build something better?"

He clearly hadn't thought that far ahead. But he'd remembered the few dozen men at his back, and he didn't see anyone else at the barricade but me. So he started walking again, gun held ready.

I ducked my head down and checked behind me for the others. Soares and Bill were still arguing with the elevator operator, but the others had gathered at the barricade with me. I gave a nod, and in unison we jumped upright and opened fire on the red-haired kid's faction.

I dropped the red-haired kid on the first volley, but there were more of them than us, and they broke into a run. We had made a good dent in their ranks by the time they hit the barricade, but once they were upon us, it was a mess of grappling and stabbing and shooting. I had a gun in one hand and a knife in the other, and sometimes I got mixed up and hit people with the gun.

It hardly mattered. We got them all before they reached the elevator pad, that was the important thing. One of Soares's men was dead, and another too badly hurt to be much help. I dragged her into the gap between two crates and plugged the gunshot wound in her shoulder with the torn-off sleeve of my coat.

Bill came out of the control building. "Well, that didn't go well," he said. "I thought she'd be happy you defended the elevator, but instead she's hung up on you being revolutionaries."

"Doesn't matter," I said, my eyes on the elevator car. It was hooked up now; nothing to do but start the engine. "She's going to hit that switch whether we're on it or not. They all will. They don't want us on it, but they can't cancel the launch without endangering the elevator. We're getting on, and they can try to stop us if they want."

But I hadn't taken five steps toward the car when I heard the tramp, tramp, tramp of Imperial troops.

"Didn't take them long to get their shit together," Soares commented, squinting at them from the top step of the control building.

"We can't take them all on," I said. "Quick, get in the car!"

Bill put a hand on my arm before I could move. "Give me your gun," he said. "You can't use it up there."

"I thought you were a pacifist now."

"Good thing about being a pacifist, when I ask for a gun, you know I'm serious." He put his big hand over mine and took the gun. "Go. I'll do what I can."

I ran for the car, last of our squad. The team getting it hooked up shouted at us to stop, but we ignored them and piled inside the wide-open elevator door. I slid the door shut and sealed it.

Above the door, a clock ticked down to five. The second hand was sweeping the last quarter. Would they risk screwing up their launch to get us out?

They did not. The clamps released, they pulled a cord, and the engine roared to life. The elevator started to rise, ticking along the cable.

I peered out the window as we passed the level of the barricade. Bill's head came into view as he rose to shoot and vanished as he ducked again. Still alive. But there were at least a hundred soldiers approaching. I hoped he had the sense to get out of there, now that it was too late for the troops to stop us.

We continued to pick up speed, and Bill dwindled away to a speck. Then the elevator pad was a gray square in a toy city, and then the city itself shrank to a brick-red patch amid the green of farms.

I collapsed to the elevator floor, too exhausted yet to climb the ladder through the car and find myself a seat. We had made it, and with ten people out of the twelve we'd started with.

But we hadn't come up clean. Phobos would know we were coming. There were hundreds of people up there, and we were only ten.

Well. Time enough to worry about that when we got there.

36

Lucy

The vote was tallied within hours; the Venusians voted so often they had it down to a science. Before the results were half in, it was obvious there would be no real contest.

A team started going over the shuttle that would take me to orbit. Marcus insisted on coming along, as well as the pilot who had flown us down to the stat the first time. The prince wanted to come too.

"Respectfully, my prince, isn't this treason?" I said, as we both stood inside the hangar, watching the suited figures crawling over the shuttle outside the window.

"Respectfully, my lieutenant, Sagan told me about you," he replied. "You're no one to talk."

"I'm ready to face the consequences," I said. "Are you?"

"As the heir to the throne, I'd have to try pretty hard to get disowned," he said. "If the Emprex won't pardon me, I'll regretfully exile myself." A grin broke out on his face. He looked happier than he had since the death of his sister.

"Don't get too excited about that prospect," I warned. "You'd make a better emperor than we've had in generations. I'd hate for you to jeopardize that."

"I can only do what's right in the moment," he said. "And now that the Venusians have voted, carrying out their wishes is only our duty."

The shuttle was loaded with a small fraction of the torpedoes available; neither the shuttle nor a single ship could carry the whole load at once. But even that small sample would be enough to make a definitive point against Earth or Mars.

The prince, Sagan, and I boarded last. As the shuttle shot off the end of the runway and began to climb, the already excessive gravity of Venus redoubled. Sagan was gasping.

"All right, my love?" asked the prince.

"Once we get—out of this—god damn gravity well—I will be," they panted.

Within a few minutes, the massive engine behind us cut out and Sagan got their wish. "Orbit achieved," said the pilot. "Aphrodite's still a thousand klicks away."

"Close enough to see what's happening?" I asked.

"Come try the telescope."

Aphrodite was a fat disk, bulging in the center where the zero-g carbon fiber manufactory was. A few ships hung nearby, winking like stars in the light of the sun, but none of them was firing. Too far to see if any of them was the *Adamant*.

"Well, they haven't destroyed the station," I said. "I assume their transmission cut out because the radio dish was hit."

We slowly drew nearer. When we were definitely close enough to notice, but too far yet to shoot at, the pilot switched on the radio. "New Brasilia shuttle, requesting permission to dock."

After a moment it crackled, "Shuttle, you are *not* cleared to dock at the station." I glanced at the prince. It was an Earth accent speaking. "Please return to New Brasilia."

"I blew up a fuckton of fuel to get up here, Aphrodite," the pilot responded. "Big load of raw carbon for you to process. If I gotta bring it back down again, I don't know when I can make another trip."

There was a pause. If this didn't work, we had to go to plan B, which involved spacesuits. Neither the prince nor Sagan had any EVA training. I didn't relish that idea.

But apparently the bait was tempting enough. "Very well, New Brasilia shuttle. Please dock at the hub."

The hub of Aphrodite Station did not spin; the carbon fiber had to be made in zero-g. That made it an easier place to dock—the only one where the massive shuttle could. The shuttle gradually adjusted orbits until we were close.

Sagan unzipped a valise and started handing out weapons. Flechette pistols for Marcus and the prince; a collapsible poniard for me. They kept two short knives, one hooked and the other straight.

"Good lord," I said. "The ambassador told us to take no weapons!"

Sagan did not smile. "The ambassador sent *you* to protect us. I didn't feel entirely confident that would be enough."

I grimaced. "I'm not completely useless."

"Of course not. In fact, given your experience in zero-g combat, I hope you'll lead the way."

I tucked the poniard in my belt. I wasn't sure if I was being flattered or sacrificed. Perhaps both.

We piled into the airlock and braced our feet against the inner hatch. When the outer hatch opened, we'd be ready to explode outward.

There was a gentle *clunk* as the magnetic ring around the airlock latched onto the shuttle. Marcus cranked the outer door open, and the station's hatch behind that.

The space around the airlock was disappointingly empty. The hub was a wide cylinder, maybe half a kilometer deep and sixty meters in diameter. Bubbles near the middle housed the carbon-fiber factory, and slender ladders snaked outward toward the edges. It was hard to get my bearings; was I floating in a tall tower or a tube lying on its side?

A cluster of Earthers came handing themselves up the ladder—real Earth Force, in their light blue uniforms, not subcontractors for once. "Sorry for the delay," panted the leader of the batch. "It's very chaotic here today."

I almost laughed. Chaotic? They had just attacked a neutral nation and were occupying a station that had been the one peaceful territory the entire war. Did they think we didn't know what an Earth uniform looked like?

Then they were close enough to see our weapons, and I pushed toward them to engage, trailing one foot on the outside edge of the ladder so I could control my trajectory. Behind me, I heard the hisses of the prince and Marcus firing their flechettes. One went home, piercing one of the Earthers in the throat and leaving him flailing and showering red drops.

Then I was hand-to-hand with another one, and I could pay no attention to anyone else. She had a long knife like a machete, which outreached mine, but I blocked with my poniard and hooked my leg around hers. Bracing the other on the ladder, I flung her away from me. Out in the empty space, she had no handhold; she hung in the air angrily shouting.

When I turned, the other Earthers had all been dispatched, either killed or stranded. Marcus looked ill. Sagan's two knives were hanging in the air before them, while they reached in their pocket for a handkerchief to clean the blood off them.

I raised an eyebrow. "Who taught you to fight in space?"

"The Imperial Marines," said Sagan placidly. "It was a two-week course at Phobos."

I thought of my months of training aboard the *Mariposa* and sighed. Sagan was too much.

The ladder ended at the junction between the motionless hub and the spinning station. It was an unnerving transition: just a narrow, circular gap to pass through, but everything on the other side was sliding sideways. The prince and Sagan eyed it skeptically.

"If we jump down there, do we start falling?" asked the prince. "How fast does the artificial gravity catch on?"

"It doesn't catch on till you're spinning, which means you have to be holding onto something," I said. I knew in my head how the whole thing worked, but it was a different thing to put into practice. Like stepping onto an escalator, which I'd done for the first time on this very station: if you half ignore what you're doing, it works; but if you stand there staring at your feet, hoping for the right moment, it never comes.

I pushed off the ladder and through the gap. For a moment I hung in air while the wall beside me slid past. Then I reached out and grabbed the netting lining the wall. With a jerk I felt down to my shoulder socket, it yanked me up to speed. The rotation spun the blood out of my head and back to my feet, making me feel normal again, if a little swollen in the ankles.

I looked up through the gap, but I had already moved away from the others. Then I spotted them on the netting behind me.

"That was terrifying," said the prince.

"Worse than being left in an empty mining station for four days?" asked Marcus.

"No."

We jumped down to the floor a few feet below. We were still far hubward of the main concourse, making the gravity weak and vertigo-inducing. Marcus walked over to the nearest elevator and punched the button.

Sagan glared at him. "That isn't going to make a very good tactical entry."

Marcus saw the wisdom of this. "The stairs are every fifty meters."

By now we had been off the shuttle for ten minutes. If the pilot had stuck to the plan, she had left as soon as we had disembarked and would try to reach a new orbit over the horizon from Aphrodite. Either we would catch up to her in whatever vehicle we managed to abscond with...or we wouldn't.

We hurried down what seemed like endless stairs. No wonder Marcus had wanted the elevator. I couldn't imagine anybody using these stairs outside of an emergency. At last they opened out onto the mezzanine level of the concourse.

Aphrodite wasn't a simple wheel in space like Liberty. It was big enough to seem like a small city, with one main street and buildings on either side. Only the street curved upward slowly, confusing the eye.

But I'd never seen the place quiet before. All the shops were closed, and nobody milled about in the streets as usual. The neon lights were still on, blinking out BATHS and DANCING and VACANCY. One casino still played a peppy tune from tinny speakers.

I crept close to the railing and peered over. In the street below, a number of Earth Force troops patrolled in little squads of four. Sabers on their hips showed they weren't there to play.

I retreated back against the upper storey of shops. "They must have a curfew of some kind in effect," I said. "Those men patrolling the street aren't looking for anybody in particular. Just keeping everyone inside, I think."

"Where should we go from here?" asked Marcus.

"That depends, where are we now? I don't know this area."

"This is the purple quadrant. Martians usually stick to the green quadrant."

"Then that's where we need to go," I said. "Last we were

here, the *Adamant*'s launch was still docked at the airlock nearest the Martian Embassy."

We started moving spinward, staying close to the buildings for cover. At first, we saw no one. The soldiers stayed in the street below, and we were too far from the railing to be seen from down there. But, before we'd reached the end of the purple sector, we spotted another squad approaching from the opposite direction.

I flattened myself against the wall of the restaurant beside us. "Don't suppose there's any alley near here we can dodge down," I hissed to Marcus.

"No, all the shops here are flush to each other," he whispered back.

Sagan pulled out their straight knife and started trying to jimmy the door open. Before they could make any progress, the door swung open. "Get in here," a voice hissed.

We all ducked inside. It was dim inside the restaurant; in the light filtering through the blinds I could make out chairs turned upside-down atop tables.

"Who are you people?" asked the owner of the voice, a stout man in his forties.

"One from Galileo, and this lot is from Mars," said Marcus. "What's been happening here?"

"Lord knows. Earth troops docked and started manhandling everyone. There was even some shooting! They should know better than to fire guns on a space station."

"I'm not sure they care what happens to us. Did you catch the forum?"

"Oh yes. Was heading to my polling place when the violence broke out. I'd been going to vote for an Earth alliance, but obviously I'm not going to do that now."

"It seems they figured out they were losing, and this is them kicking over the board and saying they won't play," said Marcus. "I'd lay hours they knew what the stakes were, too."

"Liberty's going to win it, aren't they?" said the man. "That speech was something."

"By a huge margin. Galileo authorized us to carry out the will of the people."

"You're bringing the…" He raised his eyebrows significantly.

"Trying to get a ship so we can."

"Here," said the man, stepping among the tables to a door set into the back of the room. A narrow flight of stairs led upward. "All the attics on this side of the street connect. You go up there, you can get a long way before you have to go back out on the street. Anybody bothers you, tell them Paul sent you."

We hurried up the stairs, not looking back. The attic was a maze of broken chairs and tables, lit by a bare bulb. The prince had to duck his head to avoid hitting it.

"Just keep moving spinward," said Marcus.

We picked our way through dozens of attics before the end: attics full of boxes of old jewelry and trinkets; attics full of phonograph records; attics full of dildoes and bondage gear. I wondered what the owners of the various shops would make of our footsteps overhead.

At last we reached a blank wall. "Here's our way down, and let's hope the people below are friendly," said Marcus.

But when we tiptoed down the staircase, no one was home. It was an empty barber shop, with rows of chairs, mirrors, and sinks. We peered out through the blinds.

"I don't see anyone," said the prince. "We'll have to be out there to see further."

"I know where we are," said Marcus. "This is the edge of the green quadrant. The shops end here because there are a couple of airlocks."

"The ones we want?" I asked.

"I think so. The Martian embassy is just a few buildings down, on the lower level."

I closed my eyes and tried to remember disembarking at Aphrodite just over a week ago. Had there been a barber shop on the corner? I remembered a glittering display just across the street, some theater or other. Opening my eyes, I looked at the view. I could just see the top of the display across the street, on the main level.

"Yes," I said. "This is the place, but we want the lower level airlocks."

There was nothing more we could do to check for soldiers outside, so in the end we made a break for it. At the end of the row of shops, an escalator led down to the main level. We sprinted down it and reached the street.

This area was like a very short cross street: to our left, it crossed the main concourse and led to a set of airlocks, one on the main level and one above. To our right, there was a small security area and then the airlock I remembered coming through when we'd arrived. A large window beside the airlock showed nothing but empty space.

"Keep moving," I muttered to the others and dashed across the street, weapon in my hand. There was no way to keep our movements hidden now.

In the distance, just this side of the curve that cut off the view, a squad of soldiers came down the concourse. They saw us only a moment after I saw them. One gave a shout, and they all broke into a run.

The prince passed me, long legs flying, and Sagan on his heels, much faster now at Aphrodite's half gravity. Only Marcus, puffing a bit, kept pace with me. I pressed on more speed, and he kept up. I was the slowest of us all.

As my breath was beginning to grow ragged, the somber façade of the embassy finally came into view: no neon lights, only a row of fake plastic pillars. We reached the doors while the Earth soldiers were still a stone's throw away. If they had guns in reserve, this was all over.

The prince pounded on the door with his fist. "Open in the name of the Emprex!" he cried. There was a sound of sliding locks, then the door opened inward and we all fell inside.

37

MOIRA

I woke, mouth sticky and eyes full of grit, when the last of my weight was gone. That meant we were almost to Phobos, which hung on the balance point between the downward tug of gravity and the upward tug of centrifugal force.

Around me the others were yawning and stretching. "What's the plan?" Soares asked me.

"The plan," I said. "Yes. A plan. I definitely have one of those."

"You don't have a plan?!"

"I have a general idea," I said, a little defensively. "If we can just get onto the station—"

"They won't let us out of the elevator," she pointed out.

I considered the layout of the elevator dock—not a thing I'd given much thought to before, but I'd been on it any number of times. The elevator cable actually burrowed straight through the moon and out the other side, where it swung a counterbalance weight that made the whole thing possible. So the elevator dock was below the surface; it didn't open out to vacuum.

I got out of my seat and went searching the elevator car. It was a large one, the size of two train cars put together, half cargo and half passenger seating.

"They have to load the cargo through a different hatch than we came in," I pointed out. "They load it when it's lying flat on the dock, and then set it upright against the cable when it's time to launch."

"I'm sure they'll be watching the cargo hatch as well," Soares said skeptically.

"The hatch the cargo comes *out* by," I said. "But that's not the hatch the cargo goes *in* by, is it? What we want is a hatch that's not hooked up to anything, so we can get out into the tunnel."

I slid open a panel and crawled into the cargo hold, which was half full of random items. Just whatever had been lying around, I supposed, to make up the expected weight. I felt all around the bulkheads, looking for a hatch. Unfortunately, it seemed the loading hatch was simply the whole side of the cargo hold, the same side that held the smaller hatch. That was no good. It wouldn't open while the elevator was docked.

I didn't have time to get discouraged. I started opening boxes and peering inside. Soares poked her head in and looked around at the floating food containers, mineral crates, and random tools. "What are you doing?"

"Just looking for anything helpful," I said, around a mouthful of fruit leather I'd poached from a crate. "Feel free to pitch in."

Soon everyone was rifling crates. Tayag was the one who found the jackpot: a crate holding two EVA suits. Nice ones, too, brand new. I inspected the tiny, careful stitches and the brass fittings.

"This is perfect," I said. "We can get out before we reach the dock."

"But there aren't any batteries, or oxygen tanks," Soares protested. "That's not safe."

I waved a dismissive hand. "We'll be in them for five minutes, tops," I said. "What do you say? You and me? The rest are lubbers, no offense."

"What do we do, then?" asked Tayag.

"Wait in the cargo compartment," I said. "Fight your way out if you can. Surrender if you can't." I already had one leg in a suit. We had no time to waste if we were to get suited up *before* the elevator docked.

The knobbled surface of Phobos was looming close by the time we were both ready. We shut the others in the cargo compartment, to leave the passenger compartment as our airlock.

Soares touched her helmet to mine to speak, since we had no radio without batteries. "Can't go too soon or we won't reach the surface at all," she said.

I knew it. Phobos's gravity is weak, so weak you barely feel it. I watched the surface approaching till I could see the craters, the airlocks, and the shiny dome of the observation lounge. "Now," I said aloud, and blew the hatch.

The air rushing out shoved us far from the elevator. We kept moving toward the surface, because we kept the elevator's momentum, and landed on the surface with a mild jolt.

Beside me, Soares stumbled. She had landed closer to the tunnel than I had, and was starting to fall. If she fell in the tunnel, she would drift slowly till she reached the core of the moon, where there was nothing but the walls and the cable. It would be a long climb back up. I grabbed and steadied her.

She tapped the bottom of her helmet to sign *thank you*. I pointed up ahead, to the lumpy extrusions of the station where it rose above the surface to emit a few maintenance airlocks, and we started to walk.

It took two steps to realize that was impossible. There just wasn't enough gravity to keep us to the ground, even with our heavy suits on. Any attempt to walk turned into a giant, terrifying leap. From here, you could jump and end up drifting in space. Inside the station, it was easy enough to push off walls, but here there were no walls.

In the end we lay on our faces and crawled, the way you might at the bottom of a pool, using tiny craters as handholds. My breath came back to me stale and hot. Space has a reputation for being cold, but that's a lie. Or, at least, it doesn't much matter how cold it is without a breeze to carry your sweat away. In a suit, you steam like a potato in tinfoil.

I reached the airlock and felt for the emergency lever. My head was already beginning to ache, and sweat was running down my back and soaking into the cloth lining of the suit. Soares struggled to her feet beside me.

I found the lever, but it wouldn't budge. Soares gave me an impatient look, and I touched my helmet to hers. "Meteor must've got it."

"Bastards should have fixed it." Her face was red and streaming with sweat. I wondered if I looked the same.

Carefully I bent down, picked up a bit of regolith, and bashed the lever until it came loose. Then I was able to grab it with sausage fingers and pull upward. We staggered into the airlock, shut the door, and moved to open the inner hatch. Here on Phobos, they didn't bother to lock them from inside. A security flaw, I supposed, but they didn't expect Earthers to ever make it this far. Not with several ships in orbit nearby.

The inner hatch opened and the air rushed in, blowing us backward. I unlatched my helmet and gulped air. "Remind me never to do that again."

Soares dropped her helmet, where it drifted slowly to the floor and bounced once. "I already *did* remind you."

We were in an empty hallway, made only to access this one airlock. Once we found a locker to pack the suits in, we left them and started moving. We had a whole station to take over and nothing but a knife apiece.

38

Lucy

We were surrounded by nervous embassy staff, one of whom darted behind us to shoot the bolts home again. In front of us, the ambassador bowed deeply. "Your Highness. I can't tell you what a relief it is to have you back with us at this difficult time."

I glanced at the door behind us. "Are we safe here?"

"So far they've left us alone," said the ambassador. "But I can't guarantee they'd respect diplomatic territory when they didn't respect a neutral nation."

"I doubt they'll target us," said the prince. "Their grievance is with Venus at the moment."

The ambassador waited for further details. Receiving none, she ventured, "Where are Blackwell and Liu, Your Highness?"

"We didn't bring either of them with us," he answered. Technically true, but leaving much out. I wondered how he would ever explain his misadventure over the past four days. If Liu was working with the knowledge of Parliament, the mere fact that he still lived would require explanation. On the other hand, perhaps the Emprex would protect him from having to explain himself.

"I didn't see the *Adamant*'s launch at the airlock where we disembarked," he went on. "Is it gone?"

"No, it's on the other side now, Your Highness. Not that it matters. Given the heavy Earth presence in the area, it would be inadvisable to attempt to leave Venus orbit yet."

The prince gave me a sidelong glance. I wasn't entirely sure how to read it, but I suspected he didn't care for the ambassador's advice. "Is Captain Vasiliev here, ma'am?" I asked. "I need to report."

Vasiliev was in a small back room, along with Alves. She leapt to her feet to salute when the prince and I entered. "Your Highness!"

The prince carefully shut the door behind us. "I need to leave the station as soon as possible," he said. "Are you willing to command the ship under my orders?"

She looked startled. "Your Highness, my orders come from the Admiralty."

"In theory, yes, but you are the top-ranking officer we have access to, with the radios down."

"What does the ambassador say, sir?"

The prince took a slow breath in and out. "She was concerned about the safety of such a move. I'm not at liberty to disclose the reason for such urgency, but I truly believe my safety is best served by breaking orbit immediately."

Vasiliev's face was distressed. "Sir, I—certainly my duty to the Emprex—my orders were explicit on one count—"

"That I was to be a passenger, not a commander," he finished soothingly. "I do understand that, Captain. But my diplomatic mission resulted in a new commitment I've promised the Venusian people. I must take the *Adamant* to fulfill what I've promised."

"To Mars, sir?" she asked skeptically.

"Not exactly to Mars."

Her chin jutted forward the slightest bit, and I knew she'd

made up her mind. It was the right choice, legally speaking. The choice I, as a Navy officer, should also have made when it came to obeying legal orders or protecting the prince.

"I beg your leave to report to the ambassador, sir," said Vasiliev stiffly.

"By all means, let us both go discuss it with her," said the prince, allowing her to precede him.

That left me alone with Alves. He looked the same as ever: bald head, heavy black brows, nervous energy. He was sitting at a small radio desk in the corner, tapping his fingers without touching the lever.

"Is that separate from the main antenna? Does it still work?"

He looked up. "No. I try once in a while, but get nothing. It's possible it can transmit even if it's not receiving."

"I don't think so. Aphrodite was transmitting to us when it suddenly went dead."

He sighed and turned toward me in his chair, leaning back against the wall. "What's the prince want to get on the ship now for, anyway?"

"I can't tell you that," I said. "I'll tell you this, though. Earth took this station to keep us from doing it. They are that set on stopping us."

His head perked up. "It hurts them if you succeed?"

"Terribly," I said. "But it doesn't help Mars particularly, so I don't expect the ambassador to agree to it."

He rubbed one finger on the crease between his chin and his bottom lip. "If we—well, even if we could get them to agree, how would we get to the ship? They're not likely to get a launch from here to there."

"How far out is the ship?"

"Thousand meters. Nothing, really, but that's open space between here and there. One shot from an Earth ship could take the launch out, and even if we got to the ship, they'd all start targeting her and she's basically undefended."

I frowned. That was a problem. I had no real intent to convince the ambassador; I suspected the prince was currently having no luck on that point. I might suborn Alves, but I needed a plan better than this.

"Do you suppose," I said, inspecting my nails, "someone with an EVA suit might do it?"

"A thousand meters? With no tether? They'd have to be suicidal. And a dab hand on the jets. Nobody uses those much, it's always hand over hand."

"You're pretty smooth, handling yourself in an EVA," I said. "And the concept of the jets is no different from piloting with thrusters."

"You're talking about doing it in orbit," he said. "Where none of the directions work the way they do in open space."

"Haven't you ever piloted a launch in orbit? It shouldn't be that different."

His eyes were sparkling at the prospect. Then he frowned. "It doesn't matter," he said. "We don't have suits."

"This is a space station. *Someone* has suits."

At that moment there was a commotion in the room outside. I stepped out. Someone was hammering on the door. "Earth Force! Open up!"

"We have diplomatic immunity!" the ambassador called through the door. "This building is legally Martian soil!"

"I don't fucking care what's Martian soil," said the Earther outside. "I'm gonna say this one time. Open the door and I take you all into protective custody. Or we break it down and you take your chances on getting hurt."

That meant, most likely, that they'd found the squad we'd left floating in the hub. And put two and two together with the people they'd chased into the embassy. Not good at all.

The embassy guards formed a half-circle around the door, hands on their swords. I grabbed Marcus's shoulder and pulled him backward. The prince, seeing me, caught Sagan's eye. We all slipped back into the back room with Alves.

"Marcus," I said quickly, "I think we could do this if we had EVA suits. Do you know where some are?"

"There are some in lockers by every airlock," he said. "But—"

I held up a hand. This was no time to be arguing. "And can you think of a way out of this embassy besides the way we came in?"

"I can do that," said Sagan. "The ambassador was just telling me. She wants me to get the prince out the back way and find a safe place to hide while she surrenders to the Earthers."

Sagan led us to a back room, jumped up, and pulled down on a ceiling panel that unfolded into a rickety set of stairs. I went up first, to check if it was safe.

I found myself in a tiny tattoo parlor. Or a shop that looked like one. The windows were lit with neon advertisements of the place's safety and painlessness, but the "open" sign was turned off. And there was no sign of any actual tattoo equipment here.

"Clear," I said, and the others trooped up.

"Always good to have a back way," Sagan said, coming up in the rear. The stairs pulled neatly back up, hidden behind a counter.

"All right," I said to Marcus. "We need an airlock, and we need one that's not being watched. It'll take time to suit up, and if the Earthers see us leaving, there's no point to any of this."

Alves spun to look at me. "Us?"

"You and me," I explained. "You don't have to, if you'd rather not, but two of us increases the chances one of us will make it. And I don't think anyone else here is capable of it."

Alves hesitated briefly, then gave a nod.

We took another stairway into another connected row of attics. "I know where to take you," whispered Marcus as we picked our way through more accumulated junk. "The airlocks we use the least are halfway between here and the hub. Basically useless for transit, because they aren't near anything, but we use them for repairs."

A dozen shops down, we descended again. Marcus wasn't sure of his direction in these windowless attics, but he thought we were close to another stairway to the hub.

This shop was a clothing store, and it was occupied by an older woman and two young men. Clearly everyone had sheltered in place when the Earthers had arrived; some at home, others at work. Perhaps some while out shopping. The nearer young man saw us first, letting out a stifled shout.

"It's all right," said Marcus. He explained a little of what we were doing.

"The Earthers passed by not two minutes ago," said the woman. "Should be a little bit before they come by again."

Marcus moved toward the door. "Wait," I said. "We don't all need to go up to the airlock."

"You're right," said Sagan, with a firm look at the prince. "I was told to find you somewhere safe to stop. This is better than anywhere they'll be going."

The prince nodded and turned his courtly charm on the shop-keepers. They were happy to let him stay "though, if the Earthers come in here, there isn't going to be much we can do about it."

Sagan said grimly, "That's all right, I'll handle them."

Marcus, Alves, and I slipped out into the street. As promised, there were no Earthers in sight. The stairway lay in a gap between buildings a few doors down.

My legs ached by the time we reached the airlock. Beside the airlock was an elevator door. "I'm beginning to see why you Venusians love those things," I said.

Marcus was red in the face himself, even though the gravity here was only half what he was used to. "Keep your voice down," he said. "Voices echo up and down these stairwells. You can shout clear to the hub from the bottom."

I helped Alves suit up, and then Marcus helped me. Putting on the EVA suits was a tedious process, impossible to do in a hurry. The entire time I tried to listen for approaching footsteps. Every move we made sounded, in the echoing stairwell, like someone coming.

Marcus handed me my helmet. "Be careful," he said, as if that were necessary.

A voice echoed through the stairwell—whether from above or below, I couldn't tell. "Take the elevator, check every floor."

Earthers.

"Worry about yourself," I said. "They'll catch up to you."

"I know my way around."

I clapped the helmet onto my head. I really ought to thank him, somehow, after all he'd done. I'd long since forgiven him for sleeping with Moira. "You've done the Martian people a great service," I said at last, my voice hollow inside the helmet.

He shrugged. "I try." But there was a sly grin pulling at the side of his mouth, and he clapped my shoulder warmly before stepping back to let Alves and me shuffle into the airlock.

As soon as we stepped out of the inner lock, the spin of the station flung us outward—fortunately less than at the rim, but still a wild tumble that took us several moments to correct.

"You steady?" asked Alves over the radio. He had recovered himself more quickly, cruising ahead of me toward the horizon.

I touched my tiny thruster again, till my speed was closer to what I wanted. "Steady," I said.

"You see her?"

I scanned along the arc of Venus, flaming gold in the sunlight. There were many ships in the area, most Earth ships or private ships belonging to Earthers. A few Martian merchants had been in port. No Martian warships, which now struck me as a terrifying oversight. Aphrodite had always seemed safe before.

From here, all the stubby cigar-shapes looked the same. You could tell Earth ships, usually, from the circular shape of their sails, but in orbit no one's were out. A few ships were close enough I could see rows of lights from the tiny windows beside the gun-ports.

At last I spotted the slenderest little cylinder of the flock, glinting in the sun against the stars behind. "I see her."

"Nice and easy," he said. "She's a bit above us."

I touched the controls and my rear thruster fired. To move to a higher orbit, you don't actually steer upward. You only speed up a little, and that carries you away from the gravity well. Like a ball thrown harder goes further before it curves back to the ground.

Thinking of a ball made me remember that I was falling. That's all orbit is, a fall that never ends. The planet below looked like a ball of fire, waiting to receive me if I ever slowed down.

"Talk to me, lieutenant," said Alves, tension in his voice. "You don't talk to me, I don't know if you're holding up."

"I'm..." It was an effort to pull my eyes off the glowing clouds below and back to the *Adamant*. She was too low in my vision; I hadn't burned the thruster long enough. I tapped the control again, gently. "I'm all right," I said at last. "It's strange to be out here without a tether."

"Fucks with your head," agreed Alves. "We're more than halfway there."

He was better at judging distance than I was. A little mirror in my helmet let me see the station shrinking behind me, but I couldn't say how far it was now, not without a sextant. "Should we be decelerating?"

"Not till we've crossed her orbit," he said. "Once we've done that, we'll want to shift into it so we stay even with her."

I touched the thruster controls again. I still was coming in too low; I'd pass beneath the *Adamant* at this rate. Had it been a mistake to come with Alves? He could have handled the transit without me. But I wasn't sure he could take command of the *Adamant* without an officer along.

"Coming along her orbit now," said Alves. A puff of frost from his thruster pack showed he was beginning to decelerate.

I eyed him and the *Adamant* ahead. The ship looked large now, bigger than Alves from where I was, but the two weren't in line as they should be. Alves looked above the ship, which meant I was below both of them. Still. I put on a little more thrust. It didn't seem like enough, so I added a little more.

"What the fuck are you doing, Prescott?" Alves shouted in my ear. He must be watching me in his mirror. "Give it a second to see if you've got it right. You're overcorrecting!"

A moment later I could see he was right. Alves passed across and below my view of the ship, too fast. I pushed the control the other way. I had to decelerate fast or I would rocket past the ship, just above her.

"Don't overcorrect now," he warned. "Just wait a second to see how it takes."

I watched the ship, Alves, and Venus swerve in my view. "It wasn't enough."

"Okay now, give it more. Just the slightest touch. We're close now."

I touched the controls again, but nothing happened. No wisp of frost alongside me.

"Look at your trajectory now. Do you need more?"

I pressed the control again, but I already knew it would have no effect. I'd blown through my fuel in my nervous overcorrection. Now, when I finally had good reason to panic, I felt oddly calm. After all, there was nothing now I was expected to do. I would either overshoot the ship or I wouldn't, and I could simply watch it happen. "I don't think so," I said neutrally. "Do we have worked out what we're going to say when we get inside?"

"Figured I'd let you do the talking."

I watched the ship looming closer and closer. If I missed it, it would be by a few meters at most. "We need to tell them to meet the Venus shuttle on the far side of the planet," I said quickly. "The prince wants us to bring the cargo on that ship to the location Venus has selected."

Ahead of me, Alves gently bumped the side of the ship and grabbed hold, mere feet from the airlock. A masterful piece of EVA work; he could be a specialist if he weren't already vital as a bosun. He turned to watch me. "Fuck, Prescott, you're coming in far too high!"

"I am aware," I said quietly. "I'm out of thruster fuel."

He scrambled up the side of the *Adamant*, berating me as he went. "The first rule of EVA isn't hand over hand along the rails, *lieutenant*," he spat. "The first rule is you communicate with your partner constantly."

I was fifty meters away now, and coming in fast. I could see now I wasn't going to make it. "Didn't see much point," I said quietly. "There's nothing you can do."

He had reached the starboard rail and was picking at the bundle of furled sails that lay against the side. "There fucking *is*," he said breathlessly, "and you didn't leave me any fucking time to get to it!"

He hauled on the mainmast, which swung upward across my path. Inside, on the sail deck, the lever would have slammed to the floor, shocking the crew. But it was enough. I reached out and grabbed the folded bundle of sails, praying my speed wasn't great enough to snap the delicate mast.

It held.

I hung, gasping, clinging to the mast for a moment. "My God,

Alves," I said shakily, "if I weren't going to be tried for mutiny for what I'm about to do, I'd recommend you for a commendation."

I carefully handed myself down the mast to the side of the ship, and we made our way to the airlock. Alves rapped on it with his fist.

The poor crew, to be startled like that, at a moment Earth ships were occupying the station. They probably wondered if they were under attack. But when the spacer at the airlock peered through our visors, her face lit up, and she started shouting soundlessly to someone inside.

We got unsuited while Shen watched from the quarterdeck. "Permission to come aboard, sir," I said, once the helmet was off.

"It seems," said Shen, with an amused smile, "that you already have."

39

MOIRA

Soares and I split up. She had the idea of taking over the solar panels that powered the launching laser, the station's only use of electricity. I had somebody I wanted to find.

My EVA jumpsuit was a common enough outfit for a stationer. No one challenged me as I made my way to the center concourse. I approached the radio desk. "Hey," I said to the woman at the counter, "is Trey around?"

She narrowed her eyes at me. "You clearly haven't been here long."

"What?"

"Trey got airlocked a few days ago. They caught him passing messages."

No wonder I hadn't heard from Lucy. My first reaction was sadness. Trey had been a good guy. My second, shameful emotion was relief—Lucy hadn't snubbed me, she couldn't get through. Then that was supplanted by terror. Had they traced the messages back to her?

"Passing messages?" I asked, having no difficulty sounding shocked. "For who?"

She shrugged. "Earthers, I guess. Or pirates. The Navy didn't bother to tell me before they arrested him."

"Well. Thanks anyway. Can you put this message in the queue?" I sailed a folded paper across the desk.

She frowned. "I think the radio office in Landing is still closed. Is it interplanet?"

"Just local," I said.

"Wait," she said, after she'd tucked it into the local slot. "Why don't I know you? We were told the elevator would be running empty for a while because Landing is full of riots."

"I came up yesterday," I said.

She nodded, and I hurried away before she could ask anything else. My hope had been to enlist the stationers in some kind of uprising of their own, but without Trey's help, I wasn't sure how to start. Why should they trust a stranger coming in, talking treason? I might be a judas for all they knew.

I headed down to the cargo level, where uniformed stationers sorted packages and dragged gas canisters from one airlock to another. Moving as if I had somewhere to be, I checked the place out, while carefully not looking directly at anyone. A good chunk of what went on here was smuggling, and I didn't want to be taken for an inspector.

But I did keep my eyes open. There were no Founders down here at present, at least none I could see. It seemed to be business as usual. The last they had heard on the radio was that there was unrest in the city, and that in itself was nothing new. They didn't know how serious it was.

The reality few on the streets wanted to admit was that it wasn't *serious*, not yet. It was one thing to riot in the street for a few days, terrifying the nobles and making the police hide in their precincts. It would be another to keep any of it going. Sooner or later, people would need to get back to their usual affairs, and if we didn't have some kind of revolutionary government running the city by then, the imperial troops would come right back. And they'd be very careful to crack down even harder than before, in their fear we'd do the same thing again.

But if we held Phobos? That couldn't be so easily undone.

All at once, the lights went out. A smattering of shrieks came from the baggage handlers. The bustle of work stopped. It was so black I could open and shut my eyes and see no difference. I groped blindly around myself till I touched the floor. At least I thought it was the floor.

"Did someone hit the fiberoptic line?" a male voice asked.

"Anyone remember where the chemical lightsticks are?"

This was what my message had told Marron to do, a way of buying myself some time. During Landing's day, Phobos was in shadow, and it got its light from a number of orbiting crystals that bounced sunlight down to fiberoptic lines on the surface. Marron had taken out the one currently in use.

"Wait!" I cried. I had no idea how long the blackout would last, and I'd better use the time.

"Who's that?"

I hesitated a moment. Was Khan right, that I'd given people hope? "Moira," I said at last, "of the *Mariposa*."

"The one from the song? That mutinied and took Liberty Station?" Without a look at their face, it was hard to judge what the intensity in their voice meant. Eagerness, or anger?

"That's the one," I said. "I want to talk for a second, in the dark where nobody can take down names."

"Okay then," said the male voice that had spoken first, a few yards to my right. "What do you have to say?"

I swallowed. "The revolution is starting downstairs," I said. "The Founders made Alexei Khan tribune, and then they killed him. The people have risen up. The Emprex has escaped to the country."

Someone gasped. Someone else hissed, "We'll end up paying for it in the end."

A familiar feeling. We'd been here so many times before. I couldn't count the number of revolts that had been put down in history, not least because we never studied them in school.

"I guess you've learned what I did. Hope is poison. Resistance only gets you hurt. And you're not wrong, it's really nothing more than a riot at the moment. If we let that be all that happens, it won't be remembered even as a riot. The Founders will come back to the city and all the revolutionaries will be punished. They'll make for damn sure this can't happen again."

There was a mutter of agreement.

"When I was on the *Mariposa*, while it still belonged to the Navy, we made that mistake. Planned a mutiny and didn't follow through. We couldn't get enough people on board. We couldn't agree on our moment. Of course the brass cracked down hard. We lost two good people because of it, and then things were even harder on the rest of us."

They were silent at this. They knew I had the credentials here. "But what if the problem was, we waited too long? The people aren't asleep, we're waiting. We're waiting till enough of us want a change, till we have enough strength, till we can make it stick for real. Aren't we? Or did some of you forget? Did you think 'not till we can make it work' meant never?"

"You'd have to prove you could make it work," said the male voice, the work gang leader I assumed.

"It's wartime," I said. "Most of the military is in space right now. Navy on the ships, marines here and on Deimos. If we took the elevator, that's half our opposition right there cut off. And they'd have to make terms if they wanted to bring anyone or anything up or down. And suddenly they can't blame *us* for hurting the war effort if we don't do what they say. We'll run the war effort, and they can help us or get out of the way. Mars for the Martians, for the people."

"That's treasonous talk," said a voice to my left.

"Treason's about to be meaningless, if we decide it's going to be," I said.

There was a moment of silence. And no wonder. Everyone already knew where they stood on the revolution, and the vast majority of people chose to stay out of it. They didn't have to decide if it was right, because they couldn't risk it anyway. Now all the figures had changed, and they would have to recalculate.

"Hope," I said, "is only a poison in small doses. If we're going to have it, let's drink deep. I broke Khan out of Deimos prison. My crew took Liberty Station. I can take Phobos, if you're with me."

My heart pounded. If hope wasn't a poison, it was certainly a drug. I'd been riding the high since yesterday, a buzz that was equal parts terror and determination. I didn't know what I'd do if I failed. Die, probably, like any number of failed revolutionaries before me. At this moment, I couldn't take the possibility seriously. I'd lived my whole life under the Empire's boot, and now I finally had the power to strike a blow that counted.

"I'm with you," said the male voice to my right.

There was a small movement to my left, someone moving away from me. Didn't want to get caught in the middle?

A few more voices chimed in. "Let's do it. We'll never get a chance like this."

"I will if you will."

There was more movement. People getting away from where they'd been standing. Scared of having their voice matched to their face.

"I'm not doing it," said someone. "I just can't risk if it doesn't work."

"Come on," said a person next to them. "None of us can risk

it not working, so we'll make it work. There's a lot of us right here in this room. More than there are marines."

The voices in the room slowly hashed out the issues. Minutes were ticking by. As Mars turned and we swung round in our stationary orbit, we'd soon land back in the light path of another crystal. I wasn't sure if we could wait for everyone to make up their minds.

"All right," I started to say, when a green light flashed in the darkness. After a moment of blinking, I saw a woman hanging by the wall, holding a green chemical lantern. She swept it from side to side, inspecting everyone's faces.

"It's a bunch of traitors in here," she said. "I'm reporting the lot of you."

I launched myself toward her, feeling inside my jumpsuit for my knife. But someone else got to her first, wrenching her arms behind her back and tying them with package twine. "Sorry 'bout that," the man said quietly. "I could have guessed she'd be the one to go telling tales."

"Anyone else we need to worry about?" I asked, snagging the lantern out of the air. "Everyone willing to follow my lead?"

There was a shuffle throughout the packing room, as some drew close to make a plan and others subtly hung back, hoping to sit the whole thing out. It was frustrating, but I understood. Maybe that was how Khan had felt about me, the last time I had spoken with him.

It took only a few minutes to hash out a plan. These people knew the station inside and out; they knew better than I did where the weak points were. But none of them had raided a space station before, while I'd done it twice.

We took a few minutes to hunt by lantern light for box knives and crowbars. The marines themselves wouldn't have much better, here where a gun could ricochet and kill the person who fired it. Then we split up into teams.

The ceiling of the baggage level was riddled with holes leading up to the passenger level, so people could toss baggage up and down as needed. That meant it was easy to move to the upper level from multiple points. I joined the team coming up by the largest concourse, where marines were always stationed to watch the customs lines.

The concourse was a chaotic mess of green lightsticks and shadowy bodies. Instead of jumping in with a shout and attacking the marines, we mixed with the crowd until we got close to a cluster of soldiers.

They hung in the air, back to back, holding lightsticks and eyeing the crowd. The lieutenant was shouting, "Please remain calm. Light will be restored in a moment. Please stay close to the ground so emergency personnel can pass overhead."

We came upon them like shadows and killed the lieutenant and two others before they even got their swords out. The rest started shouting, and the crowd began to push away and scream. Some of the bystanders seemed to want to help us, others to stop us, and that was when they didn't actually know who we were. I decided to clear things up by grabbing one of the surviving soldiers and holding him in front of me with my knife across his throat.

"You lot better settle down real fucking quick," I shouted. "We're taking this station for the Revolution and you can help or get out of the damn way."

The marine twisted in my arms, trying to get around to see my face, but only succeeding in making us both spin in midair. "Please, sir, I don't want to die," he said, in a broad Mariner accent. An enlisted man. "Let me go and I'll stay well out of the way."

"Would you have let me go, if I didn't have you by the neck?"

"I do my job, sir."

"When your job is enforcing the Empire's will, I don't have much sympathy," I said. But I took a piece of cord from one of the baggage handlers and tied his wrists. "Luckily I have a use for you."

By this time much of the station was subdued. People were pressing themselves against the walls to stay out of the way, and my new allies appeared in the different tunnels to report their areas clear of marines.

I dragged my captive to the radio desk. The nice lady who had taken my message took one look at my knife and tucked herself politely under the counter. I kicked in the inner door, picked out the desk with the placard LOCAL, and dragged the operator out of his chair before he could reach for the handset.

"Sorry," I said to the other operators. "We've taken the station and if you have any sense you'll make yourself scarce."

They looked at me, at my trussed marine, and at one another and dived for the door.

"Alone at last," I said to my marine. "I need you to send a message."

∽

Half an hour later, we had as many captains and lieutenants as we could gather. By now the lights were back on, the marines were stuffed in Phobos's tiny brig, and the civilians were confined to a single concourse to keep them out of the way.

"What's the meaning of this?" demanded a captain with muttonchops and very red cheeks. "Where's the station commandant?"

Unfortunately for us, the station commandant was currently the center of a cloud of floating blood globs. Apparently some of the baggage handlers *really* hadn't approved of the job he was doing, and hadn't followed my instructions to take him alive.

"My apologies," I said to the assembled crowd of officers. "I had to tell you there was an important meeting with the commandant to get you to come. But I wasn't lying. I'm the new commandant, and the agenda for this meeting is your surrender."

The man scoffed. "Surrender? When we have twelve ships in the area?"

I looked at Soares, who looked at the woman manning the radio desk. She held up seven fingers. I turned back to the captain.

"I'm afraid your numbers are being reduced at the moment," I said. "Several have, on receiving a message from us, chosen to mutiny. At this point, your answer doesn't affect whether you win or lose. It only determines whether you go downstairs on the next elevator, or out the airlock to find your own way home."

The officers surrendered. I watched the last of the battle through the observation dome: launches flying between the loyal and newly revolutionary ships, as the *Mariposa* laid down covering fire.

When it was all over, I announced our victory on all the radio channels and reunited with Soares and the rest of our team from Landing. It turned out the baggage handlers, accustomed to dealing with a certain amount of contraband, had turned a blind eye to Tayag and the others. They had joined in our insurrection in a different part of the station.

"I suppose I should get back downstairs," said Soares when I came out of the radio office. "You've got a handle on things here."

I blew out my cheeks. "I wasn't planning on staying," I said. "I only took over the station because it was the only easy way off-planet."

She gave me a look. "Easy?"

"Well, compared to the alternatives. I need to get back to

Liberty. Right now, it's run by an Earther who couldn't give two shits about the revolution. I need to take it back. With Liberty's ships, and the ones we've captured, we should be able to take on any Imperial opposition."

Soares nodded. "Even holding Landing and Phobos, there's no guarantee we'll keep them. Much less overthrow the Emprex."

"One thing at a time," I said. "Right now, all I want is for my girlfriend to call me back."

40

✴

LUCY

I have new orders from Captain Vasiliev," I told Shen, when I arrived on the quarterdeck. "We are to rendezvous on the far side of Venus with a shuttle from the surface and pick up a cargo there."

"How are we supposed to do that without emergency fuel?" Shen demanded. "If we raise sails in sight of the Earth ships, they'll put a hole in them immediately."

I frowned. "We have thrusters still, don't we? We could adjust to a lower orbit, catch up with them that way. The Earth ships would barely notice us edging away."

His lips moved for a moment, calculating out the math. "Very well. Alves! Stand by to thrusters!"

We shifted only a small amount lower, into a slightly faster orbit, and crept away from Aphrodite at a snail's pace. I watched the station almost imperceptibly shrink. Hopefully our departure was as difficult for them to notice. After all, they were busy dragging the station for mystery intruders. I hoped they hadn't found Marcus. Or the prince.

It took over an hour for Aphrodite to disappear over the horizon, and the shuttle finally appeared up ahead. I cranked up the radio. "*Adamant* to Venus shuttle. This is Lieutenant Prescott. Do you have fuel to shift to a lower orbit? We'd like to meet you, but we don't have much delta-v left."

The radio crackled with the pilot's voice. "I've got the wiggle room. I'll meet you."

Shen had been anxiously pushing back and forth across the sail deck, but stopped when I hung up the receiver. "What *is* the cargo?" he asked.

The moment of truth. Once the weapons were on board, he'd never allow them to be brought to Liberty. Passing materiel for war to an enemy was treasonous by any definition; no Navy officer would have ordered such a thing.

"May I speak to you in private, sir?"

Shen went below into the captain's mess. I followed him. "You see, sir," I said, when the door had been shut. "The Venusians particularly wanted us to carry that cargo to a specific destination."

"I understand that," he started to say, turning to the sideboard to offer me a drink.

It was the opening I needed. I pushed hard off the wall and in a moment had my arm around his neck and my poniard just grazing his side. "The Imperial Navy doesn't get that cargo," I hissed in his ear. "I'm taking command."

He made a small squeak. In a fair fight, he could have taken me, but traitors always have an advantage. I should have felt worse about that than I did. Shen was, after all, not a bad sort. But instead I felt a kind of pride. I had finally struck a blow for the revolution. Until it came to it, I'd never been quite sure I'd be able to do it. Not after so long practicing the habit of obedience, of respecting the chain of command.

I fought back an irresistible urge to monologue, tell Shen

exactly why I was doing this and how it was justified. But the less he knew, the better. "I'll keep you safe here for a while," I said, pulling a white napkin from the sideboard and gagging him with it. Another served to tie him to one of the bracing straps on the wall. "I mean you no harm." He stared at me, eyes wide, as though I'd grown a second head. Surely I was the last person he had expected to mutiny.

I took his tricorn hat, so the men would know I was on duty. We always wore them on the quarterdeck, but mine was still in my luggage, back on the shuttle.

Alves was waiting outside the captain's mess. "Do *I* get to know what we're doing?"

"It's weapons," I said shortly. "The Venusians are selling them to Liberty Station."

"To the pirates?" he asked. "Why?"

"Because there are only two forces in the system that reject both corps and kings," I answered. "Venus is one, and Liberty's the other. Natural allies. Hopefully, the weapons will be used against Earth. But I can't let Mars take them, or they'll use them on Liberty and take the station back."

He gave me a skeptical look. "So your solution is to bring them onto a Martian ship?"

I shrugged. "It was the only ship I was in a position to steal."

"You bastard," he said, without rancor. "You've been double-dealing for the pirates this whole time?"

"All I need to know is whether you're with me or not." The poniard was ready under my coat, but I thought I knew the answer.

"I'll do anything that hurts Earth," he said. "But I can't promise anything of the crew."

"We'll worry about that later." I went out onto the sail deck and vaulted the quarterdeck railing. "Mr. Zhang, report!"

"The Venusian shuttle has matched our orbit, sir!"

I went over in a launch to claim the weapons. The spacers I took with me eyed the missiles greedily.

"Don't get too excited," I said. "This isn't a fighting ship. These are cargo."

The pilot came close to whisper in my ear. "Are you sure these will get to Liberty?"

"I'll find a way," I said. "Is it all right if I use a couple on your current difficulty?"

She grinned. "I was hoping you would. Going to make it hard to get the rest to you if you don't."

We tucked the torpedoes wherever we could inside the ship: in gaps in the food storage, in the passenger staterooms, and in place of the old ordnance, which we jettisoned.

"These had better actually work," muttered Alves, as the crew carefully strapped each one into place. Who knew how ticklish their ignition switches might be.

"If the Venusians say they do, I believe it," I said. "Their tech is much more advanced than anything Earth or Mars has."

I returned to the quarterdeck, heart pounding. I'd never actually commanded a ship before, let alone in battle. I'd always been able to call upon the real captain if anything interesting happened. But I had been through enough to know what to do. I took a deep breath.

"Mr. Alves, beat to quarters!"

The men leapt into action, beaming with pride. The hours since Earth had taken Aphrodite would have been a nervous, frustrating time. Of course Shen wouldn't have tried to engage the Earth ships, not with the *Adamant*'s limited armament. But the men would have wanted to. Nothing a Martian sailor hated like passing up a chance for battle.

"We will be loading the Venusian ordnance," I told the gunner. "I am told we can handle it the same as the old torpedoes, but it's important not to fire it anywhere near the station. There is a chance it could target the station itself and damage it."

His eyes were wide with respect. Normally we thought of stations as invulnerable, with their huge mass and thick radiation plating. "Aye, aye, sir."

I went up the sail deck to the forecastle to see the station approaching. "They'll have noticed we went away by now," I told the midshipman stationed there. "Probably assumed we were fleeing. When they see us coming back, they'll be on the alert."

"Can we take so many ships, sir?" Zhang asked anxiously.

I eyed the glinting specks hovering around the wheel of the station. There were a dozen, though by my best guess, only eight were Earth warships. "All we need is to make the station too costly to keep," I said, with a confidence I didn't entirely feel. "These ships have offloaded most of their men onto the station as an occupying force. My hope is that, when they see us attacking, the Venusians on the station fight back against the Earth Force on board."

I returned to the quarterdeck, making sure all was secure. There was a single chair there, for the captain. My chair. Everyone else was expected to brace for impact on their own, but the captain was valuable enough, and idle enough, to be belted in.

"Mr. Alves, we will be passing below the station and the other ships. Roll the ship to present our starboard broadside. Mr. Hendricks, we will load and man only the starboard guns."

There were only five guns on each side, but that would take most of the men we had. Half the crew was on Aphrodite for shore leave. They had presumably been taking it in shifts.

"*Adamant* is oriented and ready, sir," reported Alves.

"Man the bowchaser, Mr. Alves," I said. "A lucky shot like you had a few weeks ago wouldn't go amiss."

He grinned. "I don't believe that was luck. Sir."

I cranked the radio up to see if the Earth ships were bothering to radio. They weren't. Either we would attack or we wouldn't, and they felt secure in any case.

"Mr. Zhang!" I called up the sail deck. "Inform Mr. Alves he may fire when ready!"

Nothing left for me to do but take my seat and belt in. It felt strange. Stranger still knowing the rightful commander was tied up under my feet.

It was a long time before Alves took his shot. We heard the faint *shunk* as the torpedo passed through the gun port. I bit my lip, frustrated that I couldn't see. I had to rely on Zhang's reports, shouted from the forecastle. "Torpedo is away, sir! Looks dead on for the ship in front, sir!"

There was a long, anxious wait, during which I got out of my seat again and joined Midshipman Ivanov at the wide stern window, to see if the target was in view yet. We were creeping slowly up on the station; I could see a wedge of it starting to come into the window.

"Torpedo has hit, sir!" Zhang cried, excitement in his voice. "It looked like it wasn't going to but it swerved and hit it dead amidships! Looks like the hull is breached, sir!"

I watched the other ships carefully. They knew we weren't just passing by now. They slowly started to roll, presenting their broadsides. We were close enough now to see the double row of gunports on each. It would take them a few moments to man the guns and be ready to fire.

"Mr. Hendricks, have your men fire at will!" I cried. "Target the Earth warships."

There was a disorganized series of shots, and then at last I could see the torpedoes streaking toward the enemy. Three slammed into one ship almost at once. To my shock, the hull didn't only breach. The torpedo had gone far enough into the hull to hit the fuel tank. The ship split in an enormous ball of fire, silent and quickly extinguished when the air was gone. The remaining pieces of the ship rocketed in separate directions, pushed by the force of the explosion.

For a second I was mesmerized. Then I realized what was happening and darted for my chair. "All hands, brace for impact!" I shouted, belting myself in.

There was a loud slam, a jolt, and a hideous grating sound, and then it stopped. Hartnell, perched on the grating beside the starboard gun deck hatch, looked up at me inquisitively.

"Piece of hull got us," I explained. "We'll have to do an EVA later to see what damage it did."

A scuffle came up from the gundeck as the men hurried to reload. "Hold your fire," I ordered. "Ivanov, crank up the radio."

The sound crackled across the sail deck. "—age, we repeat, please disengage. We are ready to discuss terms."

I got up and took the handset from Ivanov. "We are not interested in terms," I said. "Please leave the system immediately."

"Who *are* you?" the Earther voice asked.

I stood a moment, handset resting lightly against my chest. It was important that Earth know it wasn't Mars who had beaten them.

"The people," I said at last.

There was a pause, as the Earther digested that. Was it Venus who had the weapons still, or had they been delivered to a Liberty agent? He must have decided it didn't matter. "We need some time to collect our men from the station."

I was tempted to let them, to save Aphrodite the trouble. But if the Earth ships regained their troops, what was to stop them from pulling the same trick the second we were out of sight?

"No," I said. "But I suspect if they lay down arms immediately, the Venusians will be reasonable."

I hung up the receiver and took a deep, shaky breath. It was too soon to be certain if the Earth ships would really withdraw.

Outside the window, they were rolling to present their upper decks to the sun again. That was something.

But Ivanov was staring at me. "The people, sir?"

Hartnell looked over the rail. "Where is Lieutenant Shen?"

I swallowed. Here it was. Alves (I hoped) and I against three loyal midshipmen and twelve spacers whose loyalty I couldn't predict. I knew better than to assume all spacers were potential mutineers; Hendricks, at least, had turned down a chance at the weapons locker when he'd had one.

"Mr. Zhang," I called up to the bow, "pray ask Mr. Alves to come aft."

Zhang didn't need to say anything; Alves was already scrambling up from the gun deck. As he handed his way along the sail levers, I deliberately unclipped my tricorn hat.

The men were coming up through the starboard hatch, confused. I left my hat hanging in the air beside me and started unbuttoning my coat. They watched in puzzlement.

Once the dark coat with its gold braid and epaulets was resting against the quarterdeck railing, I began to speak. "Thank you all for your assistance just now. You've struck a blow against Earth dominance in the system, which, whatever else happens, is invaluable to everyone else who lives here.

"If you haven't already noticed, this is a mutiny," I continued. "I intend to steal this ship and deliver the weapons from Venus to Liberty Station, which the Venusians tasked me to do. I do it not because I am disloyal to Mars, the planet and people, but because I reject the domination of the Empire."

I paused and looked at them. The three midshipmen were shocked and upset. The men had the same unreadable look they always had when they felt threatened: they didn't dare bat an eyelash lest it signal some kind of intent.

"I understand not all of you will want to participate in this act, which will undoubtedly have consequences with the Empire."

Consequences. I didn't want to think of those. It was a little too late to change my mind. "Anyone who wishes may board the launch now. You will be returned to Aphrodite with Lieutenant Shen."

I hoped, by speaking this way, I would present the whole thing as a fait accompli. They were used to following orders, and here I was standing over them at the quarterdeck, handing them down.

Hendricks, though, bolted sideways. He had put two and two together when I'd said Shen would be returned to the station and realized he must be locked in the captain's mess.

Alves pushed off from the ground and slammed him against the grating that fronted the quarterdeck. "Don't do it," he said. "Don't you see this is our chance?"

Hendricks struggled against him but couldn't get free. "Am I the only bloody person on this ship who wasn't waiting for a chance to turn traitor?"

"That's one for the launch, then," I said, with all the calm I could. "I assume the midshipmen will want to as well. This isn't your fight."

Ivanov and Zhang nodded, but Hartnell shook his head. "Maybe it is my fight," he said slowly. "Maybe it should be everyone's fight."

It startled me, though in retrospect it shouldn't have. He had been perpetually angry the entire time he'd been aboard. I had assumed it was because he was spoiled and didn't like to work, but perhaps the voyage had disillusioned him with the Empire as my first posting had done to me.

Hartnell shook the others' hands, and they moved toward the launch, still looking shocked. Alves brought Hendricks, no longer fighting back. He seemed resigned.

I stared out at the rest of the men. "Anyone else?"

They glanced at one another. Planning out how to rush me? Waiting to see if the others would go?

Eventually Bergeron spoke up. "I'd like to stay with the ship, sir. Given what's happening back home, it seems it's best if we all choose our side. Most of us aren't from any kind of family to speak of. Our side is always going to wind up being the people's side when we can get away with it, if you know what I mean."

I nodded slowly. "Can you please get Lieutenant Shen from the captain's mess and escort him to the launch?"

The launch departed with those few on board, as well as two men to pilot the launch and hopefully return with it, and I was left staring at my hands, confused. Why had they given in so easily?

Of course I knew the crew, being common, had less reason to be loyal to the Empire than the officers. But there were still the consequences to think of. The Empire did like to keep up with its paperwork. They'd be marked deserters and under penalty of death if they were ever caught back on Mars. Had none of the men families or homes they wanted to return to?

I leaned over the rail and called to Bergeron. "You said what's 'happening back home.' Imagine I've been otherwise occupied for a day or so. What did I miss?"

"Oh," she said, turning to face the rail, "they say the revolution has begun, sir."

Epilogue

Lucy

I stepped out of the airlock at Liberty Station half a pace behind the prince, on his right hand. On his left was Sagan, sober as ever in their black suit, any weapons invisible beneath it.

Moira stood waiting for me, as I knew she would be. It was simply implausible that a woman of her caliber would remain second place on the station for very long. Once she returned to Liberty, she'd surely take command over from Coelho—and so she had.

"Welcome to Liberty Station," Moira said, with a polite nod. The proper revolutionary greeting for a prince, I supposed. She was wearing a berry-red coat, tight brown trousers that tucked neatly into her knee-length boots, and a crisp white shirt, unbuttoned several buttons so the dusky shade of her skin peeped through.

I wanted to tear it all off and take her right on the concourse. Instead I said, "Thank you. Prince George Konstantin of Mars accepts your hospitality."

The prince cut me a swift sideways look. He knew, by now, about Moira. He must wonder why I was putting on the stranger act.

I wondered that myself. It had just seemed a lot more natural than the alternative. When had I ever run openly into her arms, like Sagan had done with him?

Or I was just scared. That possibility couldn't be overlooked.

Moira gestured spinward, toward the food court. "Your passengers can avail themselves of Liberty's hospitality. We don't have many kinds of food, but at least it's fresh. You, I need to speak with privately about the cargo you said you were carrying."

My heart sank. Of course that was the next part of the play, the one where one of us came up with some excuse to go off alone. Why didn't I want to do that?

"There's nothing to tell," I said. "We've fulfilled our duty to Venus by bringing it here. What you do with it after that is your concern."

Her dark eyes flickered. I realized I'd hurt her, which surprised me. Somehow I'd assumed she felt the same hesitation I did. It had been such a long time. "I suppose we should speak about where to offload it," I said quickly, stepping forward.

I had to almost scamper to keep up with the pace of her long legs, as she strode anti-spinward toward the gardens. She was angry with me, and I deserved it.

"I never got your last message, if you sent one," she said after a moment. "My last was putting you in contact with Marcus. Did you get it?"

"Yes," I said. It took me a moment to remember my brief, surly response. "Never mind what I wrote back, it doesn't matter." Suddenly I wanted to brush everything under the rug, lie, say anything that brought us back to where we'd left off.

She slowed down among the bean trellises. Stopped and scuffed her foot. "We took Phobos."

"So they told me. That message got through before Aphrodite lost communications. I suppose you've heard their story by now? They've fixed their dish?"

"I got their point of view, anyway."

I took too long to say anything, till the silence had set in. It felt far too thick to break. Sunlight streamed through the huge window and turned the bean leaves translucent, heavy with green light.

"Why did—" I began, at the same moment she asked "Is your—"

We both stopped. She glared at me. "You first."

"No, y—"

She grabbed my wrist. The first time she'd touched me in a year. Her fingers were like fire. "You. First. I'm not having you hide things from me again."

I stared up at her, at that lock of dark hair brushing her cheek, and felt my lips reluctantly coming unglued. "You never told me you liked men."

She blinked, then snorted. "What, Marcus? You're mad about that?"

"How could I not be mad about that?! You might have at least warned me."

"I didn't know he'd bring it up."

"So you just meant to hide it from me forever?"

"I didn't mean to mention it because it wasn't a big deal! He and I were never serious. Just one of a lot of people I slept with because I didn't have you. I suppose you were celibate all those years?"

"Of course I was," I snapped at a cluster of bean pods. I couldn't face her right now. "I couldn't feel anything for anyone. I guess I'd assumed all those years you were hurting like I was."

"Not everybody deals with pain in the same way."

"You deal with it by sleeping around?"

She rolled her eyes, pushing her hair out of her face in a frustrated gesture I remembered. "You're just hung up because you didn't know I was bi."

"You weren't when we were younger."

"People change. Find out things about themselves. Try things. It doesn't mean I wasn't honest with you."

I picked a bunch of green pods and started snapping off the stems. "My *problem* is that people change. I don't know you. You don't know me. We know who we were as children. It doesn't mean we still work as a couple now."

She turned so quiet that eventually I had to look up. Her face was cold and flat. "So that's it," she said. "You're breaking up with me."

I swallowed hard, turning back to the bean pod. One thumbnail slit it open, and I picked out the tiny embryonic beans. "I don't know how I'm supposed to know," I said. "You'll always *say* you want me. You have to, having committed this far. But do you even understand how much we've both changed?"

"Oh, I know we've *changed*," she said, low and poisonous. "You changed so much you joined the fucking Navy. And then when you got your head out of your ass about that you went straight to pretending to be a spy."

"Pretending?" I repeated. "I did everything I set out to do. I got you those weapons."

"A lot of different people's hard work got us those weapons," she said. "But it's like you to think of yourself as the hero of the common man. A thing no one ever asked you to be."

"So, what, you'd prefer I *not* care?"

She shook her head in frustration. "I didn't come here to argue politics with you. I followed you here because I have been waiting for you all this time, and now that you're here the first thing you do is pick a fight about whether or not I even want to be with you. Because you need constant assurance I want you, or else you assume I don't."

I focused hard on the beans, picking out one at a time, smashing it between my fingers, and dropping it on the ground. It was a terrible waste, but I needed something to do that wasn't looking at her face. If I looked at her face I would cry. She was more beautiful than I remembered, and I wanted her more than I had wanted anything in my life.

"I don't know if you *do* want me," I said softly. "The me that I am now, today, not just what you remember from when we were kids."

"That's rich," she spat, "coming from a person who could have stayed with me and *chose* to go back to Mars."

"You told me to go!"

"I gave you *permission* to go," she said. "You're the one who leaped on it. You're trying so hard to get away from me, and you're trying to make it my fault."

"No!" I cried. "That's not what I'm doing."

"I believe that's not what you think you're doing," she said. "You're always the last one to know why you do the shit you do. But I'm getting better at reading between the lines."

"You don't know me," I said, low and intense, ripping a bean pod lengthwise into tiny strips. "And if you keep making assumptions like that you're never going to."

I flicked my eyes over her, like catching a glimpse of the sun. If I didn't linger, I wouldn't get burned. Her dark eyes were hot as coals on mine.

I tried to look away, but she grabbed my face with both hands, forcing it towards hers. I felt the last of my doubt and anger melt and dribble away. I was so tired of being alone, of forcing myself to make decisions and deal with the consequences. I wanted her to just decide for me, tell me my misgivings were nonsense, make me forget the time we'd been apart.

She kissed me, sudden and hard, her hands on my face keeping me upright when I might have fallen. It was like a drink of water in a desert. My hands flailed behind her, having dropped the shreds of green fiber. I was about to bring them to her, hold her close to me, when she pulled away.

"I'm tired of guessing," she said. "I haven't left you in any doubt of how I feel about you. I'm tired of chasing you down and convincing you. Maybe it's your turn to convince me."

She turned abruptly and walked away. I watched her go, stricken. She was right. I'd made her chase me since we'd been reunited, and I'd never spared a thought for what that did to her.

I wanted to run after her, but I knew, like I knew myself, that this wasn't something I could patch up with a lot of words. She wanted proof, not protestations.

Instead I knelt down and cleaned up all the shredded vegetable bits. It was obvious now how I should have played it: presented the weapons to her like a gift, praised her for what she'd done on Phobos, told her the revolution would make a new Mars where she and I could be together without having to be pulled in half.

Because I believed all that. If the revolution succeeded, both she and I could return to Mars, technically traitors though we both were. Class would be abolished and nobody could stop us from being together. Maybe, with the removal of one obstacle in our relationship, my mind had invented a new one.

But the old one wasn't really gone. Phobos and Landing in the hands of the revolution still left most of Mars in Imperial control. More work would have to be done, and I realized all at once whose job that was.

She wanted proof? I would give it to her. I would give her a free Mars. It was the only gift big enough to mean anything.

The story continues in

UNDER

FALSE COLORS

In the conclusion of the trilogy, the Martian people must secure their rights once and for all—at the risk of destroying everything Mars has built over centuries.

Lucy runs from her feelings to Earth, where she tries to gather new allies for the Martian people. Shattered but stubborn, Moira navigates the criminal underworld of Halfpoint Station. But to unearth a plot that threatens the nascent revolution, they will have to swallow their pride and reach out to one another.

Separated from their beloved by the tides of war, Sagan takes up a rifle and marches with the People's Army. This is their chance to win their rights at last—or is it a betrayal of the man they love?

GLOSSARY

Adamant: a fast courier vessel of the Martian Navy

Alexei Khan: a revolutionary writer and organizer who was thought dead but was then rescued from Deimos Prison

Alves: bosun aboard the *Adamant* and a defector from Earth

Aphrodite Station: an orbital station around Venus

Ares Station: the former name of Liberty Station when it was under Martian control

bearing: a ship's position, speed, and direction, as calculated from the stars

beat to quarters: summon the crew to battle stations

Bergeron: bosun's mate aboard the Adamant

Bill Singh: Ramesh's husband and Moira's father

Blackwell: foreign minister of Mars

bosun (also bo's'n or boatswain): the spacer in charge of the sails

bow chasers: small guns facing forward

broadside: cannon fire from all the cannon along one side of the ship

Brotherhood of Able Spacers: the spacers' union

Catherine Vasiliev-Scott: lieutenant who commands the *Adamant*

Coelho: pirate leader of Liberty Station

Deimos: Mars's smaller moon, home of a prison

downstream: the direction all the planets orbit

Earth Force: the corporation which provides military defense to Earth interests in space

Emprex Julien Elliott: titular head of the Martian government, though the main power rests with Parliament

EVA: extravehicular activity, a spacewalk

forecastle (also fo'c'sle): a bubble-shaped window at the bow of the ship

Founder: a member of Mars's nobility, descended from the first settlers

Galileo: the largest stat on Venus

hammock: a sack for zero-g sleeping, clipped to the wall

Harrington: an EVA specialist, formerly of Phobos, later on the *Mariposa*

Hartnell: second midshipman aboard the *Adamant*

Hendricks: arms master's mate aboard the *Adamant*

Imperial Guard: ground army under the Emprex's command

impress: to force a spacer into service for the Navy

Ivanov: senior midshipman aboard the *Adamant*

judas: someone who encourages rebellion only to expose those who participate

Landing: the capital city of Mars, at the foot of the space elevator

leeward: the direction away from the sun

Liberty Station: a space station in the asteroid belt, formerly owned by Mars, now run by pirates

lieutenant commander: a lieutenant by rank who commands a ship temporarily, called captain only ceremonially on the ship

Maggie Borisov-Harcourt: youngest crew member on the *Mariposa*, formerly a Navy midshipman

Marcus Van: an old friend of Moira's, who lives on Galileo

Mariposa: a former Navy vessel now under Moira's command

Marron: a pirate serving as bosun on the *Mariposa*

Michael Shen-Armstrong: first mate aboard the *Adamant*

midshipman: an officer in training, usually a teenager

Moira Singh: pirate captain of the *Mariposa*

Ms. Knauss: a high-ranking Earth Force agent

Nguyen: able spacer aboard the *Mariposa*

parole: an officer's word of honor to obey the terms of their captivity

Phobos Station: the station at the top of Mars's space elevator, located on Mars's larger moon

port: left on a ship

Prince George Konstantin (Kostya) Elliott: second child of the Emprex

Princess Sofia Maria Elliott: older daughter and heir to the Emprex

prize money: the share of money each crew member receives after taking an enemy vessel

quarterdeck: a raised platform at the stern of the ship, allowed only to officers

Ramesh Singh: Moira's father, who trains horses for a noble household

Russet Brotherhood: Alexei Khan's followers

Sagan: valet to Prince George Konstantin

Singularity: a disaster in Mars and Earth history in which artificial intelligence caused the deaths of millions

Soares: a member of the Spacers' Union and an associate of Alexei Khan

space-bound: unable to return to a planet because of atrophied muscles and bones due to long periods in space

spacer: an enlisted sailor of the Martian Navy, not an officer

starboard: right on a ship

stat: a floating city in Venus's atmosphere

stern chasers: small guns facing aft

sunward: the direction toward the sun

Talia: head of StatOps on Galileo—the closest thing they have to a leader

Tayag: a member of Khan's Brotherhood

Timothy Popov-Johnson: a Martian noble with revolutionary sympathies

Trey: a radio office clerk who passes messages for the revolution

upstream: the direction opposite the planets' orbits

Vasily Chin-Hawking: one of the richest men on Mars and the People's Tribune in the Martian Parliament

Yao: a teenage girl serving on the *Mariposa*

Yekaterina Liu-Johnson: the deputy foreign minister of Mars

Zhang: youngest midshipman aboard the *Adamant*

Author's Note

This book was written in the summer of 2021, when protests (yet again) rocked my country over injustices we can never let ourselves get used to. I began this series without any thought of it being particularly relevant or timely, and yet the news keeps confirming the things I write in all the worst ways.

Meanwhile the Venus facts are as real as I could make them given our current level of knowledge. While a hell planet at ground level—hot, acidic, with pressures to rival the bottom of the sea— it's quite balmy in the cloud deck, and oxygen balloons would float easily in the carbon-dioxide atmosphere. Some scientists believe life could exist within the clouds there.

Do not try the stunts in this book at home. Always fasten your tether while spacewalking, never expose yourself to the raw atmosphere of Venus, and do not talk to cops.

For more on my books, my favorite science, and occasional Star Trek rants, visit sheilajenne.com.